THE FIFTEENTH MINUTE

The Ivy Years #5

SARINA BOWEN

Rennie Road Books

PRAISE FOR THE FIFTEENTH MINUTE

Sarina Bowen's Ivy Years is my favorite New Adult series of all-time! — **Elle Kennedy, New York Times bestselling author of *The Deal***

"Sarina Bowen is a fantastically gifted storyteller. I'm a huge fan and she's at the top of my auto-buy list. Everyone should be reading her books!" — **Lorelei James, NY Times Bestselling author**

A love story brimming with emotion and tenderness. Read it and fall in love like I did. — **Kristen Callihan, USA Today bestselling author of *The Hook Up***

For Keyanna, who knows that a sense of humor is everything.

Chapter One

MY OWN PERSONAL DARTH VADER

Come what come may,
  Time and the hour runs through the roughest day.
  —Shakespeare's *Macbeth*

Lianne

I *promised* myself that I wouldn't spend my second semester of college huddled in my room playing DragonFire. So even though I have just broken into the Dark Portal with fifty golden life credits and a new set of magical nunchucks, I reluctantly freeze my avatar and put my controller down.

Naturally, my screen erupts with messages from other players. *Hey, Vindikator? Where are you going?* And, *Don't leave now, we're close to the diamond palace!*

My reply is brief but truthful. *Gotta go to class!* Grabbing my trusty baseball cap, I pull it down low over my eyes. Then I put on my coat, lift my bag and run out of my dorm room.

Over the holidays I considered quitting DragonFire cold turkey. But that seems too harsh, because gaming is how I relax.

Instead I'll restrict myself to no more than ninety minutes a day. That leaves me almost an hour tonight to feed my dragons and explore a few of the corridors I found this morning.

It will have to do.

Trotting down the stairs and out into the pretty stone courtyard, I start to wonder if ninety minutes is enough. If my cyber pals send me a bunch of messages, responding will eat into my gaming time...

The semester is only a couple of hours old, and I'm already rationalizing.

Running late now, I dash across College Street and then take a shortcut through the English Literature building. The brick theater department is just in the distance. I love the old architecture of this place—the gargoyles and the gothic archways. But I didn't choose Harkness College because it looks like a well-styled movie set. I chose it because I wanted to be a real college student. I wanted the whole package—stodgy professors, thick books, parties and hanging out with friends in the dorm.

I hadn't meant to spend the first semester hiding in my room, but fitting in here is a lot harder than I expected it to be.

Before Christmas, though, things started looking up. I have two good friends now, even if I'm kind of their third wheel. And I've made a pact with myself to spend even more time with people rather than screens.

Though screens are pretty awesome. And I like my other identity—Vindikator. On the Internet, nobody knows you're an actress who made millions wielding a magic wand. I can go all day without hearing a single Princess Vindi joke.

I've almost reached my destination when my phone begins ringing like a broken doorbell, each new chime a text from my manager. I pull it out and skim the messages. *Lianne, answer my calls. Where are you? Call me back ASAP.*

When I'd decided to go to college at age nineteen like a normal girl, I'd tried to lay down the law with my manager. When school is in session, I want him to at least try to respect my schedule.

He doesn't.

Now my phone begins to play the "Imperial March" from *Star Wars*. I would happily ignore my own personal Darth Vader, except I'm heading into class, and I don't want to have to shut my phone down to avoid his impatient updates.

"Bob?" I answer, stopping on the slate pathway. "I'm heading to *class*. What's the big deal?"

"I sent you a script. You should have it this afternoon."

No lie, I get a little tingle just hearing those words. Even though the next two years of my life are already spoken for, everyone wants to be wanted. My heart flutters like a butterfly. "What is it?"

"Your next Princess Vindi part."

Crunch. The butterfly hits the pavement. "And that's news?" I ask, my tone becoming less polite. That's the trajectory of a call with Bob—I start out promising myself I'll be nice. Thirty seconds later, I'm yelling. "We're not shooting until *May*. Why do I need to read it in January?" Besides, I'm doing that film whether I like it or not. I'm under contract.

Luckily, this will be the very last Sorceress film. After this summer, I never have to be Princess Vindi again. I never have to wrinkle my nose and turn anyone into a frog or wave my scepter to fight off the devil.

"You need to read it because there's a clause we need to renegotiate. You need a nudity clause, babe. The Princess is supposed to get it on with Valdor in this film."

"What?" I yelp. "That's not in the book."

"But their relationship is implied. So the screenwriters put it in."

My stomach turns over. "A sex scene? Seriously?"

"It won't be too spicy because they need a PG-13 rating. Read the script, and then we'll negotiate what you're willing to do. We'll try to get them to pay you more."

Shit! I can hear in Bob's voice how much he likes this idea. The man would sell me into slavery if it meant more cash for him.

"I have to take a call with Sony now," he says. "Look for my FedEx."

"Wait!" I yelp. "What about the Scottish play? Have you heard from the director?"

"We'll talk later."

"Bob!" I shout. "I know it's against policy for you to listen when I talk. But that part is *everything* to me. You said you'd—"

"Gotta jump," he says, and the line goes dead.

Damn. It. All!

Not only am I now unsettled, but I'm late for my class. Shoving my phone into my bag, I jog up the steps and into the building, then down the hallway toward the room where my seminar on twentieth-century theater will be held.

I prefer to get to my classes early and sit in the front row. It's not because I'm a nerd. It's just that I don't like making an entrance. But today I'll have no choice. When I finally arrive, it's exactly one minute past eleven. And the door to room 201 squeaks.

Of course it does.

At least a dozen heads turn in my direction as I slip into the room. The professor—he would be the skinny man holding a sheaf of hand-outs and speaking to the group—pauses mid-sentence to witness my arrival.

That's when I hear the first snicker and see the first pair of eyebrows arch in amusement. From somewhere in the room comes a hissed whisper. "Princess Vindi!" It's followed by a chuckle.

I don't look around for the source of the laughter, because it's better not to know which asshole is already poking fun at me. And anyway, I'm scanning for a seat.

It's just my luck that this room features a giant conference table instead of rows of chairs. Feeling panicky, I realize there aren't any more empty seats at the table. The rest of the heavy wooden armchairs are pushed back against the wall. I grab one and wrestle it toward the table. The quicker I can sit down, the quicker those eyes will go back to the professor. But the chair squeals in protest on the wood floor, and if I'm going to sit at the table, two students are going to have to scoot apart to accommodate me.

There is a terrible pause while I wait for someone to catch on and make a space.

Kill me already.

The professor sighs and pulls his own chair aside. The student next to him clues in and makes a bit more space. So now I'm dragging a beast of a chair past three other students to finally fit myself into the only available slot.

Eight years later I'm finally seated, and the table nearly reaches my chin. Did I mention that I'm quite vertically challenged? Tease me and die.

"Where were we?" the professor says. "Ah, yes. On your syllabus, please make a note of the due dates listed on page two. There is no web page for this course. I like to do things old-school."

The reading list is lengthy, but I don't mind. This is why I came to Harkness—to swim in the deep end of academia. To get out of Hollywood and to be a normal college student. I picked Harkness for its rigor, not for the benefit of my social life.

Good thing, because I don't have a social life.

It's not that I expected to find fangirls at a place like Harkness. Students here are too busy taking over the world to care about me. But I didn't count on being *mocked* for my strange little career. On the first day I asked an upperclassman where to find the bookstore. His answer: "You just ride your broom over there, right?"

The howl of laughter he got for that little joke echoed through me for days.

It's not something I'd say out loud, but it's *weird* to find myself in a place where I'm utterly uncool. Take me a few miles from here, walk me down the hallways of the local middle school—it would be a mob scene. I'd be asked to sign so many autographs that the Sharpies I carry in my bag would run dry.

Here? I'm a pariah. I'm the girl who got into Harkness by being famous, instead of by slaving away on the math team or the debate squad in high school. I get it, I really do. I'm a poster child for privilege. Before he died, my father was Hollywood royalty. And my mother is a known diva and playgirl. The first time I rode a yacht to the Cannes film festival I was four.

Though I've been earning my *own* wad of cash on the big screen since I was seven, nobody cares. At Harkness, it's all held against me—something I hadn't anticipated. I hadn't known that, by choosing such an elite college, I'd found the one place on earth where I was least likely to be respected. The epicenter of my own uncoolness.

Live and learn.

Good thing I didn't come here to be popular. I came here to earn a degree so when I finally reach the limits of my patience with Hollywood's bullshit, I won't be too old to go to college.

"Now let's begin by introducing ourselves," the professor says. "Just give us your name, your year, and which of the plays you're most excited to read this semester."

Easy enough. I skim the syllabus to pick out my answer. There are a lot of plays by dead white men here, but I guess that's to be expected.

The student beside the professor is Bill, a junior. And he tells us how excited he is to read *Mother Courage and Her Children*, by Bertolt Brecht.

Ugh. Well I guess Bill and I will never be friends. I hate Brecht.

Weirdly, five out of the next eight students also pick that play. And then the skinny dude in the beret sitting next to me practically orgasms while telling us how much he loves Brecht. "His treatment of corruption is seminal," Mr. Beret says. "The twentieth century would not have been the same without his character Arturo Ui. That play is transcendent."

Really, dude?

Now it's my turn, and I remember I promised myself I'd speak up more often this semester. "I'll play devil's advocate," I offer when everyone's eyes fall to me. "Brecht is clever, but he isn't subtle. Sometimes I'd rather lose myself in a story and let the play make its points in a way that isn't so brutal. So I'm looking forward to reading Wendy Wasserstein with all of you."

There is a deep and terrible silence, which makes me feel panicky. Was that too pushy? Really?

Mr. Beret snorts audibly. "Brecht's genius is not always accessible."

The second after he says it, my neck begins to burn. I'm not used to having my intelligence insulted to my face. It takes a great deal of effort not to argue with him. I mean, I first saw Pacino perform Arturo Ui when I was six years old! I've probably seen more onstage genius than anyone in this room. Times ten!

Instead of defending myself, I just sit there grinding my teeth.

"You didn't tell us your name or your class," the nerdy professor says quietly.

And that's when I want to sink into the floor and die, because he's right. I was so busy speaking up I forgot to follow the instructions. Even worse, it's *such* a Hollywood asshole thing to do —to assume everyone already knows your name. "Sorry," I say quickly. "I'm Lianne and I'm a freshman."

The death silence lingers a moment longer before the girl on my right speaks up. "I'm Hosanna, a sophomore, and I like that the syllabus has a mix of serious and less serious plays. I'm looking forward to reading the Neil Simon."

Beret boy groans, and I'm grateful to my neighbor for thumbing her nose at what is clearly a room full of hardcore intellectual snobs.

The professor starts speaking again, inviting us to dive right into the first play on our list, which is *Private Lives* by Noël Coward. Nobody is staring at me anymore, but I still have that sweaty, uncomfortable feeling of having put myself too far out there. I just want to go back to my dorm room and play another round of DragonFire. Is that so wrong?

I write my name on the top of my syllabus, and then read the second page. There's one big paper due in place of a midterm, and then a final exam. Fine. But class participation counts as thirty percent of our grade. Oh, joy.

But it's what I read at the bottom of the page that really horrifies me. The Professor's bio. *Dr. Harlon Overstein has most recently published in* American Arts and Letters *and is the foremost American expert on the plays of Bertolt Brecht.*

Well, slap my ass and call me Sally. I've just insulted our professor's taste in twentieth-century theater and his entire career.

Kill me already.

Somehow I make it through the ninety-minute class without embarrassing myself again. When I finally emerge, blinking in the January sunlight, it's past noon. Last semester I would have bought a take-out salad to eat alone in my room. But since I've promised to turn over more new leaves than a hurricane in the rain forest, I head over to the Beaumont dining hall instead.

This bit of bravery is rewarded when I spot my neighbor (and one of my only friends) Bella at a table just inside the door. She's sitting with Bridger, one of her ridiculously attractive hockey player pals. "Hey munchkin," Bella says. "How's the first day back?"

I let the short joke slide, because Bella has never once asked me where I keep my magic wand, or asked me to cast a spell to clean up the bathroom we share. "Pretty painful. Can I sit?"

"Of course."

I drop my bag over the back of the chair. And after I grab a cup of soup and a salad, I collapse into the seat. "I've had a stupid morning. You?"

"Fricking scary. Back-to-back science classes are going to kick my ass." She tips her head to the side to acknowledge the redheaded guy sitting beside her. "But these are the classes that Bridger takes for fun."

"I'm available for tutoring," he says over the rim of his coffee cup. "But I don't accept money. You have to pay in babysitting. An hour for an hour." Bridger has custody of his ten-year-old sister.

"I see," Bella says. "So you and Scarlet could go out alone some night?"

"Exactly."

Bella winks. "Okay. It's a deal. How is Lucy, anyway? I haven't seen her in a while."

Bridger sets down his mug. "She's having a rough time. We just passed the one-year anniversary of mom's death. So that kind of sucked. And then Lucy's best friend moved away, so she's down in the dumps."

"Poor baby," Bella sympathizes.

"We've had better months."

Now I feel like a jerk, because I've just spent the last half hour fuming about berets and overzealous ass-kissers. But I don't really have it so bad.

"I feel a night at Capri's coming on," Bella says. "Bridge, you could feed Lucy pizza for dinner tonight."

"We might make it over there if she doesn't have much home-work," he says.

"You're coming too, Lianne."

"Is that so?" My voice may not show it, but the idea of a night out with the hockey team gives me a little thrill.

"You know you want to." Bella's smile turns sly. "DJ will probably be there."

I've been an actress all my life. So I don't blush or go all shifty-eyed when Bella mentions DJ. But she isn't wrong. Before Christmas break, I'd met him once at Capri's Pizza when Bella and her hockey team friends dragged me there. That was a month ago. But ever since then I'd found myself scanning the campus walkways for the hottie I'd met that night beside the jukebox.

Do I want to see him again? *Heck yes.*

"Huh," I say casually. "I *am* trying to get out more. But I'm not going to drink so much this time."

"Good call," Bella agrees. "I wasn't going to mention it. But it *is* easier to get a guy's phone number if you can still focus your eyes at the end of the night."

I groan, because Bella is never going to let me live that night down. "Thanks for the tip."

"You're welcome. Be ready at seven."

———

After lunch I have a History of Art lecture. But once that's done, I'm free to go back to my room and obsess about seeing DJ again.

The weird thing about being me is that I never have to wonder, "Will he remember my name?" Everyone under the age of thirty knows my name. It's not vain of me to say that—it's just a fact. And not because I'm amazing. It's because the Sentry Sorcerer films are so popular. The first one came out ten years ago when I was nine. The script that arrived this afternoon from Bob's office is for the fifth one.

I haven't opened it yet, because I'm afraid to read the spicy scene. Getting naked on a sound stage in front of forty crew members sounds terrifying. In the meantime, it would be awesome to have actual sex with a person who isn't getting paid to touch me.

That sounds simple enough. But in my life, nothing ever is.

For tonight's adventures at the pizza place, I do my face in a style I'll call "Monday Casual." Brown mascara, but no eyeliner at all. A whisper of gold eyeshadow. I want to look good, but I don't want to appear too eager.

When Bella sticks her head in from the door to the little bathroom that connects our rooms, I'm just finishing my lips— a lip stain by Stila and my favorite drugstore brand gloss over it. The gloss tastes like cherries, but it's been two years since I got close enough to a guy to share it with him.

Sad but true.

"Let's go," she says.

My stomach does a dip, and I grab my trusty baseball cap and follow her out the door.

It's a Monday night, so Capri's isn't crowded. Bella sets us up at the hockey team's favorite table. "You're eating pizza with me," she announces.

"Great. I'll have a slice."

"*Wow*. Who are you and what have you done with Lianne?"

I flip her my middle finger on the way to picking up the beer she's poured me.

Last semester I'd followed the rules set out for me by my asshole manager—no carbs or beer (because of carbs). But my New Year's resolution is to stop listening to all the assholes in my life who want to control me. If I gain a couple of pounds, my career won't end. Right?

I hope so, anyway.

Bella wanders off to order pizza. "Where's Rafe tonight?" I ask when she reappears.

"He took a catering gig at the dean's office. They pay time-and-a-half for wearing a shirt and tie. He might turn up later."

The hockey team begins to arrive two or three guys at a time. "Hey, Bella!" they greet my friend, plunking their big bodies into chairs around our table. Trevi, the team captain, ends up beside me. He shrugs off his team jacket and gives me a friendly smile. Then he tosses his wallet on the table and announces that he'll buy the next round.

"Hi, Lianne," Bella's friend Orsen greets me. (It's a huge help to me that the team wears their names on their jackets. I never get anyone's name wrong.) "Can I sit here?"

"Sure," I say a little too brightly. I'm trying not to watch the door for DJ. Since I spent my Christmas vacation at Bella's house in New York City, I've socked away quite a bit of intelligence about the hockey team. So I know DJ is Trevi's younger brother. And I know DJ lives in an off-campus house with Orsen, the goalie.

But Trevi and Orsen are here already, and I'm starting to worry that DJ isn't going to show.

More people trickle in, and I scan their faces hopefully. There's Bridger and his cute little sister, who slides into a booth against the wall. And Bridger's girlfriend Scarlet who plays goalie for the women's team.

I'm oddly jittery, waiting for DJ to appear, which is crazy. The room is full of attractive guys, but none of them affect me the way DJ did that night in December. It was partly those dimples and the way his big, dark eyes crinkle in the corners when he grins. But it wasn't just his looks. His smile makes me feel warm inside. While we talked, he looked at me the way a boy looks at a girl he's trying to get to know—not like a fan or a dude who thinks I'm an amusing celeb sighting. And DJ knows a lot about music, which means that we had plenty to talk about. The night I met him, we nerded out about the rise of EDM during the last decade.

Distracted by this geeky memory, I accidentally knock over

my beer in its plastic cup. "Damn it," I swear, standing up so it won't run off the table's edge and onto my jeans. *Smooth, Lianne. Real smooth.*

Trevi moves fast, tossing a small wad of pizza napkins onto the spill. "Let me get some more," he says.

"I'll grab them," I insist, darting away before he can do it.

When I return, there's another girl sitting in my seat. She's very attractive. I'd almost say stunning, except there's something hard in the smile she gives me.

"Hi?" I toss the napkins onto what's left of the spill and brace myself for a Princess Vindi joke.

The interloper smirks. "Can't you, like, wave your wand to clean it up?"

Yep. There it is. A Princess Vindi dig, *and* she's taken my spot.

"Amy, seriously?" Bella snaps from my elbow. "You're in her seat."

The girl puts a hand on Trevi's arm. "I need to see my man. You don't mind, right?" She grabs the dampening wad of napkins and chases the last of the liquid across the wooden surface.

From across the table, Orsen winks at me. Then he moves over one seat, making space on the other side of Bella.

So I move, because it's the path of least resistance. Besides— Amy's portion of the table will be sticky, and now that's her problem. Though I still want to punch her. Sitting in my ex-chair, she's angling her body toward Trevi, showing me her back.

I've noticed that some people at Harkness are determined to ignore me. Like they've decided I've had more than my share of attention, and it's their job to even things out.

The hockey team has been mostly nice to me, though. Maybe it's because these are the *real* celebrities of Harkness College. Their team made it to the Frozen Four last year, and with most of the team still intact, they're expected to do well this year, too.

Trevi refills my beer and then pours one for his evil girlfriend.

He's missed Amy's bitchy exchange because he's busy arguing with another hockey player about the Winnipeg Jets.

I'm just about to ask, *aren't the Jets in New York?* But then I remember those Jets are a football team and save myself the embarrassment. My sports ignorance knows no bounds. I'm bored by their conversation, but I wish I weren't. It's nobody's fault I grew up among people who bet on the outcome of the Tony Awards instead of the Stanley Cup.

I want to fit in—it's just that I don't speak the language.

Even as I'm rounding out this depressing thought, another male body appears in the doorway.

I don't have to turn my head to be sure it's DJ. I've been waiting so long to see him again that I just *know*. He's there in the periphery, hands stuck in his jacket pockets, leaning against the door frame talking to one of the players. The muscular breadth of his shoulders is exactly how I remember it. His confident stance draws me in.

All at once, my pulse quickens and I feel a little dizzy. As if I'd walked out onto the edge of a diving board, and felt it wobble beneath my feet. Am I going to talk to him again tonight? Could it possibly be as much fun as last time? And what will I find to say?

The sad truth is that I'm better when I'm holding a script.

For several minutes I sit still, as if enthralled by the complexities of the Jets-who-don't-play-football. DJ stays where he is, and so do I. There aren't any seats open near me, though. So if I want to talk to him, I'm going to have to make my own luck.

Rising, I dig a couple of quarters out of my pocket. I don't head over to DJ, because I'm not that brave. Instead I make a beeline for the jukebox in the corner. I put in my quarters and then I check out the selection. The last time someone updated this puppy looks to be during the 1990s. And it's a problem, because I need to play something that reflects the girl I wish I was—easygoing, casual, a little bit hip.

Hard to do that when I'm staring down at choices like Madonna's "Vogue" (a perfectly good song, but not exactly cutting edge) or "Achy Breaky Heart."

Then *my* heart kicks into a higher gear, because I feel him approaching. I'm desperate to turn and look, but I make myself pick a song instead. I'm proud to say I don't spare him a glance until I've tapped in the code for the track of my choice.

Only then do I stand tall and turn to him. And, whoa—my memory hasn't even done him justice. I'd remembered the thick brown hair and the dimple that's darkened by his five o'clock shadow. But his eyelashes are darker and more devastating than I remember, and was his mouth always so full and sinful-looking?

And now I'm staring, damn it!

"Hey there," he says, parking one hip against the scarred wooden paneling. "Remember me?"

"DJ, right?" It comes out as a croak. Because I'm cool like that.

God help me—his smile is slow and sexy. "That's right. I'm surprised you remember, though."

I clear my throat and try again. "Are you saying that because we only met once? Or because I got senior-prom drunk that night?" I never went to a prom, but I heard another actress say that once and it sounded cute.

He rewards me with an even bigger smile. "You said it, not me." His eyes drop to the jukebox. "Pick out something good?"

"It wasn't easy."

"Right? I love this old thing, though." He rubs the gleaming surface of the jukebox, and I am suddenly fixated on his wide, masculine hand. I wish I could pick it up and compare the size of it with mine. I want to know if his skin is rough or smooth...

That's when I notice the abomination coming from the jukebox. An electro-beat that I'd never choose, and some ridiculously high male voices...

"Interesting pick," DJ says, and the corners of his mouth are twitching.

"Hell!" I bend over the box, peering at the song codes again. "How is this possible? I was trying to play MC Hammer's 'Can't Touch This.'"

DJ chuckles. "And instead you got..."

The chorus from the long-forgotten Color Me Badd kicks in, singing "I Wanna Sex You Up."

Nooooo! Either my subconscious has betrayed me or the machine is miscoded. It's probably fruitless, but I have to at least try to distance myself from this error. "You should know that I would never willingly play a song by somebody who can't spell 'bad.'"

"Really?" He grins. "Yet you went for some Hammertime. And that dude spells 'mother' with a 'u' and an 'a.'"

Argh. If my daggers from the DragonFire game were real, I might turn one on myself. "DJ, your grasp of nineties hits is..."

"Impressive?" His smile is cocky, and I have to restrain myself from reaching up to measure it with my fingertips.

"I was going to say *thorough*, if useless."

He puts one of those strapping hands on his chest. "Woman, bite your tongue. I get paid cash money for knowing my nineties hits. It's the best job ever."

"Oh. The hockey rink gig, right? That's why they call you DJ." It's coming back to me now. For the hundredth time I curse myself for getting sloshed the night I met DJ. But I'd been so immediately attracted to him that it made me nervous. Kind of like I was feeling now.

He smiles again, and I'm staring. Who knew I was a sucker for dimples? "That's right," he says, and I try to remember what we were talking about. "There are some nineties hits that would never see airtime if it weren't for hockey games."

"Really? Name one."

"'Ice Ice Baby,' by—"

"Vanilla Ice," I finish. "Yeah, okay. I can see that."

"'Cold as Ice,' by Foreigner," he adds.

"That's not a nineties tune," I argue. "It's 1977."

DJ tips his head back and laughs. "Your knowledge of seventies hits is—"

"Impressive." I finish. "'Cold as Ice' was B-sided originally before it was released as its own single."

His eyes widen. "Marry me," he says after a beat.

I giggle like a schoolgirl. (Footnote: I was never a schoolgirl. But if Hollywood scripts are to be believed, they giggle plenty.)

"Are you, like, a Foreigner fan girl?" he asks. "Or do you have encyclopedic knowledge of all seventies music?"

With a shrug, I just shake my head. The truth is that my father was friends with Lou Gramm. In fact—one of the reasons I know so much about music is that my father loved to talk about it. He's gone now. But when I listen to my iPod, I feel closer to him.

I don't mention any of this to DJ for two reasons. It's name dropping, which I loathe. But also—so many Harkness students assume I'm stupid. I don't mind at all if DJ thinks I'm smart. It's a nice change.

"What other songs are kept alive by hockey?"

He starts talking again, and I do my best to listen. But I'm distracted by the way his full lips move when he talks and by the five o'clock shadow roughening his jaw. He's wearing a flannel shirt that looks soft to the touch. And there's a V of skin exposed at his chest that teases me. I get just a glimpse of a dusting of dark hair against olive skin.

I have to work hard not to stare, wondering what he'd look like without that shirt on.

So this is what people mean by *attraction*. He is the magnet, and I feel the pull. It tingles in my belly. It resonates in my chest whenever he laughs. Hopefully I'm nodding and agreeing at all the right junctures in this conversation. Because whenever he smiles I experience a loss of executive function. Last time beer was the culprit. Tonight it's just him.

The loudspeaker crackles to life. "Pie thirty-seven! Thirty-eight! Forty!"

DJ cocks a thumb over his shoulder. "I gotta get that. Be right back."

When he walks away, I return my attention to the jukebox. My heart is pounding and my palms are sweaty. Talking to him is exhilarating and terrifying.

If there's another nineteen-year-old in the world with less game than I have, I pity her.

Chapter Two

PIZZA IS LIKE A '90S HIT

DJ

Lianne Challice is chatting me up.

As I fetch the pizza I ordered from the window, I try to decide whether or not I'm going insane. Maybe all the stress in my life has finally cracked me.

But no. When I deposit the pie on a table, her big eyes cut from the jukebox over to me, before darting away again. She is so freaking cute and so feminine that it's making me crazy. Her mouth is like a little red candy that I'm dying to taste. And who has teeth that straight? She intimidates the fuck out of me, to be honest.

I make another trip to the pizza counter for paper plates and napkins. Usually we just grab slices off the tray like animals. But tonight I'm trying to be classy. The idea makes me snicker to myself. *As if.* Impressing Lianne Challice isn't something I'm capable of. But I'm having fun trying. And there hasn't been a whole lot of fun in this year for me. So that's something.

Years from now I'll look back on this night and laugh. *Guys, did I ever tell you about the time I chatted up a movie star?* I mean, my father is still telling people about the time he sat one table over from Tina Fey at Nobu.

Lianne sneaks another glance in my direction and I beckon to her. "Have a slice?" If she wants one, now is the time. In a minute my brother and his teammates will fall on the pizza like seagulls.

"Thank you. I guess I should. I didn't make it to the dining hall tonight."

"Your enthusiasm for Capri's pizza overwhelms me," I tease. "Aren't you a fan?"

She slides a slice onto a paper plate, considering the question. "Pizza is like a nineties hit. Pretty good, especially if that's all there is and you're hungry."

My own slice stops halfway to my mouth and I laugh. "Seriously?"

"What?"

"I don't know if we can be friends," I say before taking a bite.

"Because I don't love *pizza?*"

I shake my head. "Who doesn't love pizza? It's, like, a basic human desire." I cram a bite into my mouth to prove my point. Smooth, right?

She bites her bottom lip, and I realize I'd rather have that for dinner. "It's okay. But it's mostly just something you eat when you're in a hurry or need to feed a crowd on the cheap."

"Ah, I see," I say when I can speak again. "The problem is that you haven't had any *great* pizza. You're a freshman, right? You don't know all the glory that is Harkness pizza. Have you been to Gino's Apizza?"

Lianne shakes her head. "I don't think so."

"She doesn't think so," I scoff. "Baby, if you'd had great pizza, you'd remember." And now I sound like a real perv, but Lianne Challice is smiling at me, watching me with her big doe eyes, and I feel it like a drug. "They make everything from scratch. Even the sausage. We'll go together, so I can prove my point."

Annnd I think I just asked a movie star out on a date. Here comes the crash and burn.

First her eyes widen just a smidge. Then two pink spots appear on her face, one on either cheekbone. "Well, it would be a shame to live in this town and never know its true pizza greatness."

I replay that sentence in my head and realize that she didn't turn me down. "True," I agree. "Do you think Thursday would be a night to experience pizza Nirvana?" I'm overselling the hell out of Gino's now, but it's working for me.

She gives me a serious frown, and I'm hoping she's not busy on Thursday. Because I have back-to-back hockey games to DJ on Friday and Saturday. "Thursday it is. I shall prepare to be amazed."

Now I'm just standing here giving her a big cheesy grin, but I don't know how to stop. Luckily, Orsen pops me on the shoulder. "Can I have a slice, dude?"

"Go for it." The guy can have anything of mine he wants. I owe him big for renting me a room in the house his parents bought last year as an investment. The other guys living there are all seniors. But this summer I was suddenly in need of a new place to live. So my brother called Orsen and space was made. I've got a tiny room they didn't consider big enough to rent out, but it works for me. I was clinging to my Harkness enrollment by my fingernails, and Orsen threw a net under me.

He did it as a favor to my brother, the team captain. But I appreciate it nonetheless.

"Orsen is a good guy," Lianne says, as if she's read my mind.

"True."

"Your brother, too. But I'm not so sure about his taste in women."

I laugh so suddenly that I almost choke on a bit of cheese. "You noticed that, huh?" I ask when I can speak again.

"It's pretty hard to miss."

"Yes it is." Finishing my slice, I wipe my hands on a napkin. Then I park my ass against the wall beside Lianne and survey the room. It's the usual scene—hockey players refueling after practice and the puck bunnies who swarm Capri's to get close to them. Amy is stapled to my brother's side because she knows there are other sharks circling. Though my brother has shown no signs of wanting to trade Amy in for a newer model, even if I wish he would. "Let me tell you a little story," I hear myself say.

"Sure?"

"My brother had a high school girlfriend—Georgia. She was captain of the tennis team, and he was captain of the hockey team..."

"They were the golden couple," she says, and I nod. "Was she nicer than Amy?"

"*So* much nicer. I was sixteen when they were seniors, and I had the biggest crush on Georgia. I used to tell her so all the time." The memory makes me smile. "Leo hated that. But it was our little joke. She was awesome. They were together for years, and I thought they might stay a couple even though they were headed for different colleges."

"But they didn't?"

I shake my head. "Over winter break, she went to a tennis training camp in Florida. One night she was walking back from hanging out in someone else's dormitory." And now I realize too late that this story is just too scary for a night of pizza and jukebox music. "She, uh, was attacked."

"Oh my God." Lianne has a terrified look on her face now. "Was she okay?"

I am clearly an idiot for telling her something so dark. But it's been a long time since anyone listened to me quite like Lianne does. Clearly I've forgotten how casual conversation works. "Yeah, she was okay eventually. I mean—she was trauma-tized and missed a bunch of school. But my brother was awesome. For months he went over to her house every day after school to watch movies with her. He read homework assignments to her. He brought her cupcakes. He made funny videos to cheer her up. He never stopped, even though she was really a mess."

"Wow." Her eyes dart over to Leo and then back again. "What happened?"

"Georgia got some counseling and eventually went back to school. And then he held her hand on the way into the building and out, and he drove her everywhere until graduation, so she'd feel safe."

"Damn."

"Yeah. He loved Georgia. A lot. But the day after graduation, she broke up with him. She said she wanted to wipe the slate clean."

"Ouch!" Lianne's eyes are still round. "That's not how I hoped this story ended."

"Me neither." My whole family was stunned when she cut him loose. "Anyway, Amy is the latest in a string of bitchy girlfriends. I think he picks the ones that are made of Kevlar. Maybe he doesn't really love them, but he can't really get hurt, either."

"That's depressing."

Yep. Good going, DJ. "I know. I'm sorry. I was just trying to explain why my brother does what he does. Even when I feel like taping Amy's mouth shut, part of me gets it."

Jesus, Leo *cried* when Georgia left him. I don't think he'd cried since the third grade before that.

"What happened to Georgia?" Lianne asked. "Do you know?"

I wish I did. "She went to college, and friends have told us that she's doing really well. But I've been thinking about her a lot lately. I wonder how she's doing." And now it's time to change the subject, for everyone's sake. Lianne is finishing her slice in dainty bites, so I offer her another.

"No thanks," she says. "I should go, anyway. I've got some work to do."

"You know it's the first day of the semester, right?" I really don't want her to leave.

She picks up her beer glass and drains it. "Yeah, but I have..." She cuts herself off with a frown.

"What?"

"To, um, read something for work." Then she starts speaking really fast. "No big thing. I-better-go-it's-getting-late." She grabs her purse off the table and tucks the strap over her shoulder. Lianne is making a getaway but I don't even have her number yet.

She tries to slip past me but I catch her hand in mine. "One sec. There's one thing you forgot."

Those long eyelashes lift, and she's staring up into my eyes. Looking...nervous. That can't be it. Nobody gets nervous about flirting with me. "I did?" she asks.

"Yeah. If I'm meeting you for dinner Thursday, then I need some way to contact you."

"Oh," she breathes. "Okay. Hang on." She digs into her bag, hopefully to find her phone.

"Hey, Deej?" My brother Leo—or *Trevi* to everyone in this room, as if he's the only one with rights to our last name—is suddenly at my elbow.

"Take the pizza," I hiss. *And then fuck off.* His timing could not be worse.

"Dad needs you to phone him tonight," Leo says. "He says you're not taking his calls."

"Fine," I say, my eyes on Lianne. Her phone is clutched in her small hands, and she's tapping her passcode into the screen with shiny pink fingernails that remind me of candies.

Can my brother not take a hint?

"Okay, ready?" Lianne looks up and smiles at me.

With an open hand, I lay my palm across my brother's face and nudge him away until he melts back into the Capri's crowd. Then I pull my phone out of my pocket. "Okay, shoot." She rattles off the number and I test it to make sure I've got it right.

When I'm done, my phone notifies me that I've missed another call from my dad. Big surprise.

"I'm heading home," Lianne says.

"Let me walk you out," I say.

Lianne makes a sound that I can't quite interpret. A squeak, almost. But she waits for me. So I cup her elbow in one hand and lead her to the side door.

"I didn't know there was a door here," she babbles.

We step outside. The side street is quiet, as always. Her eyes are wide in the glow of the streetlight, and I smile for no reason at all.

"Um, thanks for the pizza," she says.

I shrug. "Don't thank me yet, smalls. Thank me after I introduce you to Gino's."

Her eyes narrow. "Really? We're doing short jokes now?"

"Hey!" I lift both hands in surrender. "I thought that was something we had in common."

She cocks her head to the side. "Why?"

Seriously? "I don't exactly tower over people, either." Though it's kind of her not to notice.

Lianne lifts her chin and looks into my eyes. "Everyone towers over me."

This is surprisingly true. I actually have to look down to see her properly. And when I do, I see that her expression has shifted to something dreamy. There's a stirring in my chest I haven't felt in a long time. And it's not because the girl looking up at me is famous. Right now I don't see Lianne Challice, star of stage and screen. I'm looking at a girl who's ambivalent about pizza but awesome with rock music trivia.

And she wants a kiss.

For the first time in months, my mind goes quiet. I hope the moment lasts, because the stillness is as beautiful as the hopeful eyes of the girl in front of me. My hand extends to catch her cheek in my palm. The air around us is cold, but her face is warm to the touch. "I'll see you on Thursday," I whisper.

Her nod is almost imperceptible. She's quiet. *Waiting*. The moment yawns open. We both know what's supposed to happen next, but I hesitate. After all that's occurred, I still know the steps but I no longer trust the dance.

I sweep the pad of my thumb across her perfect cheekbone. Then she leans into my hand. It's slight—almost imperceptible. But it's there. A sign.

It's a short journey to her mouth, but I say a little prayer along the way. *Please*.

On the first pass I'm still cautious. I take just a brush of her soft lips, landing on her jaw. She smells of berries, I think. Something sweet. I pause there, pressing a kiss to her skin, and she shivers. Then instinct kicks in. I slip my fingers to the nape of her neck and pull her closer to me. The warmth of her small body finds mine, and I *have* to kiss her. I turn my head a few degrees and find her soft mouth with my hungry one.

The noise she makes is a whimper. I kiss it away. Her lips taste as sweet as they look. I angle my head, deepening the kiss just slightly. Maybe because I haven't done this in a long time, or maybe because it's Lianne Challice I'm kissing—but all my senses are dialed up to eleven. I feel every inch of her body where it touches mine, and the sweet scent of her hair is making me crazy. I'm a loose wire sizzling through the air, humming and electrified.

But still wary. That's probably never going away.

Her lips part, and I take only a little taste, my tongue finding hers for a split second before retreating. She groans, and leans into me. It's one of those moments where we're either going to stop, or things are going to rapidly escalate.

And I know what I need to do.

I kiss her one more perfect time, and then ease back. She releases me reluctantly, her chin dropping, her teeth on her lower lip.

Catching her chin in one hand, I tilt her face up to mine. She looks...embarrassed. But I don't see why that should be. I kiss her perfect forehead, her sweet scent enveloping me once again. "Sure glad I came out for pizza tonight," I whisper.

"Me too," she breathes. "Um..." She gives herself a little shake. "I should go."

"You going to be okay from here?" My voice comes out husky. There's no reason to worry for her, though. We're right on campus, and a half a block away students are spilling out of the concert hall, where a performance has just ended.

"Yeah," she whispers. "Goodnight."

She gives me a shy smile before she walks off down the sidewalk.

I watch her go, feeling like a heel for not walking her home. But I don't want to explain that I've been asked by the dean of students not to set foot inside student housing this year. The trouble I'm in is both terrifying and completely embarrassing.

Speaking of trouble.

Even though I'd rather focus on Lianne and that amazing kiss, I pull out my phone and redial my dad. If I avoid him any longer he's going to get mad, which will only make things worse for all of us. "Sorry," I say when he picks up. "It's been a really busy day." That's sort of true, anyway.

"Daniel," he says, his voice serious. "Son, I need you to call the new lawyer back tomorrow. He wants to get to work clearing your name, but he can't help you until he hears from you."

"Okay," I promise. The trouble is I've already made this promise and then broken it. And Dad isn't going to put up with that anymore.

"*Tomorrow*, Daniel. This guy is the very best. He's a specialist, and he's on your side. I can't understand why you don't just call."

How is it so hard to explain? It's like being sent to an oncologist. *Hey, the cancer doctor is on your side. Why aren't you looking forward to the appointment?* In this case, the specialist isn't trying to keep me out of an early grave. He's trying to keep me at Harkness.

"I will call him after my first class," I promise again. I'm going to do it, too. I'll get this off my back so I can enjoy my date with Lianne. My first date in months.

"You do that," he says. "I need you to keep the faith."

"I will." But it's an empty promise, because keeping the faith requires having some in the first place.

We hang up, and I lean against Capri's brick wall and wonder for the hundredth time whether my father even believes I'm innocent. He says he does. But my father is all about damage control. He's an accountant and a devout Catholic. He married my mother when they were both twenty-one. My brother came along a year later and began breaking records right out of the womb. Star athlete. Super scholar. Most likely to break every heart on the North Shore of Long Island.

Then there's me. The other brother. The difficult one. Even when they don't say it, I can hear my parents thinking: *why can't you be more like your brother?* And that was *before* the college accused me of a heinous crime.

It's getting late now, and it's really freaking cold out here. So I go back inside Capri's to grab my coat and say goodnight.

At least one thing went right today. While I walk home by myself, I'm humming "Cold as Ice" by Foreigner and remembering the shape of Lianne's smile.

Chapter Three

A SIX-SECOND CROSSFADE

Lianne

I wake up slowly on Tuesday morning before my alarm. But that's because another kind of alarm is going off on the other side of my wall.

Separating my room from Bella's are two wooden doors and a small bathroom. That may sound like a decent divide, but acoustics are strange. Our bathroom seems to amplify the sound of my two best friends getting it on.

I have no idea what a "normal" amount of sex in a relationship is. I've never had a relationship, and I've barely had sex. But wherever the mean lies, I'm fairly sure Rafe and Bella are several standard deviations past it. Most nights I fall asleep to one of the playlists I've compiled to drown out the sounds of their passion. (A six-second crossfade is sufficient to cancel out the grunts and dirty talk that make it hard to look them in the eye over brunch the next morning.)

Mornings are trickier. I'm half asleep right now, my limbs heavy. But I become slowly aware of furtive little gasps and a low moan coming from the next room. My phone and earbuds aren't on the bedside table where I sometimes leave them, either.

My heavy eyelids fall closed again, and I drift for a moment. Maybe it's the porn soundtrack next door, or maybe it's inevitable. But my sleepy brain picks that moment to remember a wonderful thing.

DJ kissed me last night.

Rolling onto my side, I smile into the pillow. He was so, so cute. And even sexier than I'd remembered. Every time he grinned that boyish grin, I became a little stupider. By the time we got outside, I was practically in a nervous coma.

But it was so worth it. When he'd pulled me against his hard body, I'd wanted to scale him like a tree.

I still want to.

The noises from next door have picked up the pace. My breathing accelerates just imagining what it would be like to have a man like DJ want me so badly he was breathing hard and making those low, eager grunts. Because I'm polite, I put my palm over my exposed ear to muffle the sound of the grand finale. But now I can hear my own heartbeat glugging along, wishing for someone who's not here. I squeeze my eyes shut and think of DJ again, his moist lips, the hint of beer on his tongue. His fingers in my hair...

When I lift my palm off my ear a minute later, it's quiet. I could get up and go out for coffee. But I don't have class until ten today. So I lean out of bed just far enough to grab the FedEx envelope that arrived yesterday afternoon. When I tear it open, a fat script tumbles onto the quilt.

Nightfall. Screenplay by Roland Sebring. Based on the novel by Helen Botts.

I wonder what Helen Botts will think about Princess Vindi showing some skin. I've met Helen Botts, and she's a lovely silver-haired librarian type who now drives a Bentley. I suppose if Helen

Botts doesn't like the movie, she can weep into her royalty statement.

Lifting the cover, I flip to the first page. Let the skimming commence. They've opened the film at the castle gates. Lucifer has found a way to appear like a storm cloud over the city, terrifying the children.

Yada yada yada.

Princess Vindi's first line is on page eleven. "I am not interested in your excuses, Lord Shelter. The time for excuses has passed."

Sigh. It could be worse. In fact, I'm sure it *gets* worse. I keep flipping.

The sex scene is on page 132.

They grope, caress, moan and fondle. Vindi's robe slides off her velvet breast. Valdor ducks his head to catch the pink teat carefully in his fangs. The camera pans downward to reveal clothing falling to the floor. With a heated rush of sexual urgency, Vindi mounts Valdor. The soundtrack rises with the keening writhings of intercourse. Valdor's shouts are increasingly loud. The camera pans Vindi's milky white, heaving bosom as she screams in consummation. Cut to Vindi's shuddering face. Valdor moans deliciously, pulling Vindi softly into his embrace.

I let out a shriek.

A few seconds later Bella comes tearing through the door, mouth gaping. Her eyes skate around the room until she finds me in my bed. "What is it? A spider?" She's wearing a Harkness Soccer T-shirt and nothing else except the flush of someone who was recently...

Gah.

I fall back onto my pillow. "There's no spider, Bella. I wish that was the problem."

"What is it then? Hang on..." She darts into the bathroom and reappears a second later wearing her bathrobe.

Words can't do the problem justice, so I hand the script over.

Her eyes scan the page, and I know exactly when she's found the object of my horror. Because she bursts out laughing.

"Stop," I whine. "It wouldn't be funny if it was you."

"Oh, honey," she giggles. "I'm sorry. Do you really have a velvet breast?"

I throw my stuffed bear at her. "You mock my pain. I can't shoot a sex scene. And I really can't shoot a sex scene with Kevin Mung."

She cocks an eyebrow. "Why doesn't that boy take a screen name? He's pretty to look at. But I always think of mung beans."

"Stay on topic." I grab the script from Bella. "This is ten times worse than I thought it could be." I feel sick just imagining a roomful of leering cameramen and me with no clothes.

And *Kevin*. Shoot me.

"Let's break down the problem." Bella sits on the bed. "Is it the boob shot? Is it the scream upon consummation? Is it the *mounting?* Is it the awful, awful writing?"

"It's...all of the above. And..." I shudder. "Kevin. He happens to be, um, the only one I ever..." I can't finish the sentence. I just look up into Bella's blue eyes and pray she'll understand.

Her mouth falls open. "You've tasted the mung bean?"

There's a snort from the bathroom where Rafe is brushing his teeth, and I want to *die*.

Bella flicks my door shut and frowns at me. "So, not only do you have to shoot this awful scene. But it's with a guy you've doodled? Was this *recently?* I thought he was dating that singer."

I protest with a violent shake of my head. "We were fifteen. We did it because..." I bite my lip and realize that I really don't know why. "Because on a movie shoot, there's a lot of doodling. And I was young and socially inept." *Still am.* "And I thought it would make me cool. Instead, it just made people talk about us behind our backs."

Bella cringes. "That sucks, honey. Is it awkward with him now?"

"No, actually. We're good friends—good friends who never *ever* talk about that night. But this would *make* it awkward."

"So put your foot down," Bella suggested, wrapping her arms around her knees. "I've seen you in action. You're like a very small lion tamer. Just crack that whip and tell them you won't do the scene."

"I'm going to have to."

"Wait..." Bella frowned at me. "Did you say the *only* guy you'd ever...?"

Ugh. "Unfortunately. I don't meet a lot of guys. Or—I meet them, but it's always on a set, where everyone knows everyone else's business. I learned that lesson the hard way. Or I thought I did. Last year I kissed a model at an Oscars after-party. And he sold the story to a British tabloid."

Bella's face was all shock. "Seriously? I mean, don't take this the wrong way. But why did they give him cash? I mean, I'm not *paying* DJ to find out what happened when you ducked out the back door of Capri's last night. I'm curious. But it's not worth money..." She waits.

I say nothing.

"Okay," Bella tries. "It's not worth *much* money. Perhaps a small bribe. And I'll beg if necessary. Or you could just spill already. Did you or didn't you fool around with DJ?"

My room door opens a crack to reveal Rafe's face. "Wait. Lianne hooked up with DJ?" His smile is about a mile wide.

"I didn't," I say quickly. Protecting myself is a reflex. These are my friends, though, who only want me to be happy. "But there might have been kissing."

Bella lets out a whoop. "I *knew* you had your eye on him! Did you give him your number?"

"He asked me out for Thursday. Well, sort of. It's just pizza."

But Bella's face is lit with victory. "This is *so* exciting. Something to look forward to. Now call that manager you're always yelling at and tell him where he can shove his heaving bosoms."

It's only six a.m. in L.A., so it will have to wait a few hours. "I'll do it," I vow.

I catch my arrogant manager after my first class of the day, and the call goes about as well as could be expected.

"Bob, I'm not doing that scene as written."

He sighs. "I know that, babe. But you know this script will be rewritten by fifty different people before it makes it onto the set. So it's a waste of time objecting to this or that word. Instead, we'll just lay out what they're *allowed* to do. Maybe we'll say that side boob is okay, but no nips. Or yes to ass cheek and no to full frontal."

I experience a shudder from my "nips" to my ass cheeks. "How about no scene at all. A kiss and fade to black." I could survive a kiss with Kevin.

Again with the sigh. "I can't sell that."

You mean you don't want to. "How about this—you get me some progress on the Scottish play, and I'll give you side boob." I can't believe I just formed that sentence. It sounds as if we're describing a cut of meat at a butcher shop.

He's as noncommittal as always. "I'll see what I can do."

Unsatisfied, I shove my phone in a pocket. Now there's nothing left to do but survive a few more days of classes before I can go on a date with DJ. At least I have that to look forward to.

Chapter Four

THE DAY THE MUSIC DIED

DJ

I do as I'm asked. Finally. When everyone is out of the house except me.

The whole debacle is deeply embarrassing. And even though I'll bet everyone who lives in Orsen's house has heard about the accusation against me, I never talk about the case. Never.

Part of me is hoping that the lawyer can't take my call. He must be a busy guy, right?

No such luck.

"Daniel," he says, his voice booming and confident. "It's a pleasure to get you on the phone. I've read your file, and I think I can help."

"Um, thank you, sir." But I feel no relief, because I just don't trust him. "I, um, know you don't know me. But before we begin, I just need to tell you that I did not...do what they're accusing me of." I can't even bring myself to say the word, because I don't want it on my tongue. "So there's no compromise I'm willing to make."

"Whoa there, son. Let's slow down just a little bit. I'm not going to ask you to compromise yourself in any way. What's interesting to me about your case is how ridiculously the college has handled it. They haven't given you a *chance* to say, 'I didn't do this.' And that's not right."

Even though that's all true, my heart is already pounding against my ribcage. I have never known real stress until this year.

"My first job will be to get the college to give us a private hearing."

"They, um, haven't been willing to do that, sir. The first lawyer my father spoke to couldn't get anywhere with them."

"I know. But you can't defend yourself if they won't hear you out. So my first job is to demonstrate all the ways that they've mishandled you. To defend you, I first have to go on the attack. We have to accuse the college of violating your rights."

Now I'm starting to sweat, because *attacking* is the last thing I want to do. I just want the whole issue to fade away. "But if they drop their, um, claim, I'm hoping to stay here."

"Of course you are. But unless we can make them own up to their failures, they're going to just decide this thing behind closed doors and send you a letter with their decision. We have to make it clear that you didn't get to tell your side of the story, and that you're being mistreated. By the time this is over, I'm going to make sure everyone knows how poorly they've behaved."

He waits for me to say something, but I've got nothing.

"At some point you and I are going to have to spend a couple of hours discussing the details of the night in question—last April eleventh. But today we're not going to do that."

"Okay," I say quickly. I'm not looking forward to telling him the intimate details of my sex life.

"But today I want to ask you about August twentieth. The day the dean called your home in Huntington."

"All right." That's another painful story, but at least there's no nudity involved.

"Your file indicates that the phone call on August twentieth was the first communication you had from the college. Are you absolutely sure they didn't reach out before then?"

"Yes sir."

"So the phone rings out of the blue. And who's on the other end of the line? Tell me exactly what happened."

I think of this moment as The Day the Music Died. Just remembering it, my heart does a drum solo, because my father and I have gone over this a million times. If I'd handled everything more carefully on that summer day, everything might be different. "The caller was a secretary for the assistant dean of student services. I didn't catch the secretary's name. She said if I had thirty minutes to spare, the dean would like to speak to me. So I said that was fine."

"You didn't ask, 'What is this about?'"

"No. I wish I had. But I don't get calls from the dean's office..."

"You were intimidated."

"Hell yes." I remember standing there in our kitchen, feeling worried. But I had an hour before my shift at the seafood restaurant where I wait tables in the summertime, so I just said I'd take the call. "The dean came on the line—"

"Assistant Dean Maria Lagos."

"Right. She said she wanted to ask me some questions about the night of April eleventh." I *should* have gotten off that phone and asked for a proper meeting. I should have told my parents there might be some kind of problem. But I didn't do that. "I told her I didn't know off the top of my head what night that was. She said it was the night of a party, and also a young woman had asked to stay in my room, and I said, 'You mean Annie Stevens?' And she said yes."

"Let me stop you right there," the lawyer said. "Did the dean ask your permission to tape the call?"

"No. She didn't mention anything like that. And I don't think she taped it, because there were times when she stopped asking me questions and said, 'Just a moment,' like she was trying to catch up with her notes."

"Did she tell you she was taking notes?"

"I could hear the keyboard clicking." I remember thinking she was a fast typist.

"Okay. What happened next?"

"She asked me about the early part of that night. The party was in the next entryway, where a lot of freshmen were serving drinks to other freshmen, so I was freaking out. There's a rule against hard alcohol on Frosh Court, but nobody follows it."

"What did you tell her?"

"The truth. I went to the party, and Annie was there. The dean asked if I drank alcohol and I said yes I drank some but not very much."

"Did she ask you to quantify exactly how much? Did she talk about ounces, or ask you to count up the number of drinks?"

"No. She asked if I was drunk, and I told her I wasn't."

The lawyer asks me a couple more questions. He's focused on procedure—what questions I was asked, and how precise they were. I get it—he's trying to show the college that they didn't gather enough information to figure out what happened that night.

But I just don't see how this is going to help. The college isn't trying to send me to jail. They're only trying to decide if I can stay at Harkness. There are thousands of guys who'd like nothing more than to take my spot. The college can do whatever it wishes.

My father and I went over this, too.

"Daniel, at what point did you figure out that Annie Stevens had accused you of sexual misconduct?"

Maybe I'm slow, but it had taken a while before I'd figured out where the questions were leading. "Well, I was worried about the underaged drinking until the dean's questions shifted to my dorm room. When she started asking me about Annie sleeping in my room, I didn't know why she wanted to go there. Staying in someone else's room isn't against the rules." I sighed. "I am the biggest idiot alive."

The lawyer actually laughed. "No you're not, son. You just don't think like a criminal."

I didn't *used* to. But after someone accuses you of being one, it changes your entire outlook.

"Daniel, please tell me exactly how personal the dean's questions became."

My head begins to ache. "She made me give, uh, the play-by-play of our entire encounter. Who kissed who, which hands removed which clothes. I told her all this, but I was really nervous. It's not an easy conversation with anyone, and of course I'd just caught on to the fact that someone had a problem with it. My first thought was that maybe Annie wasn't eighteen or something. But that would be weird. It was second semester..."

"I'll run a background check on her and we'll rule that out. But what else did the dean ask?"

"After everything I described, she'd stop and say, 'And how did she give consent for that? Was it verbal?' And I had really good answers for almost all of those." Because the whole encounter had been Annie's idea.

"All right. And did you get the sense that the dean took careful notice of your responses?"

"I guess so. But I can't be sure."

"I see. So after this detailed conversation last August, what happened?"

I had the world's most uncomfortable conversation with my parents. And I began to worry, and never stopped. "I got a letter five or six days later telling me I was on social probation."

"Right. I have to tell you that I've read and re-read this letter, and it's a pretty interesting document."

"What do you mean?"

"It's *incredibly* specific about the probation they imposed on you—where you can and can't go, and exactly how you should avoid contact with Miss Stevens. But on the subject of what it is that you're supposed to have done, there's nothing. I've never seen anything like it. Either it was written by someone who has no experience investigating sexual assault, or they're being vague on purpose, because they're not feeling confident about the accusation. And now they've let five months pass without deciding your case."

Like I don't know that.

"It's possible that they think the case against you sucks, but they're trying to be sure they give it adequate attention anyway. There's a law called Title Nine. Most people think it's about school sports, but it's broader than that. Sexual discrimination and harassment."

"Okay."

"These past few years colleges have been threatened with losing certain sources of federal funding if they don't demonstrate that they're fighting harassment and also sexual assault. And that's a fine idea, right? But colleges—even well-funded ones like Harkness—keep proving that they have *no clue* how to investigate sexual violence. And when they get it wrong, it hurts *everyone*. Think about it. There are girls who are raped, but the college bungles the investigation. On the other hand, there are guys like you who are at the wrong end of bungled investigations."

"Federal funding," I repeat slowly.

"That's right. Just like everything in life. Money is the driver."

My head gives a fresh stab of pain, and I wonder if it's even possible to get out of this mess unscathed. When I first learned that Harkness College might throw me out for something I didn't do, I still didn't quite realize the seriousness of the situation. But then my father explained that my Harkness transcript would show that I'd been suspended for disciplinary reasons.

In other words, if Harkness kicks me out, I'll be untouchable.

"Well, Daniel, we're going to have to leave it here for now, because I have a lunch meeting. It was a pleasure speaking to you.

If I have any more questions for you before I press the college for a hearing date, can I reach you at this number?"

"Sure," I say. "Anytime." I'd promise anything right now if it meant getting off this call.

He tells me he'll let me know if he gets anywhere, and then I thank him and hang up.

I spread out on my bed and stare at the ceiling. This lawyer number two—Jack—he sounded more knowledgeable than the family lawyer who'd first tried to help sort me out. But it might not even matter. The last guy explained to me that I was just another customer, and Harkness was free to decide at their whim that they didn't want me anymore.

Last summer, even as my parents were freaking out, I kept thinking that it was really just a big misunderstanding. I honestly believed the college would call me back and say, "Never mind. You weren't the guy we were looking for."

But that never happened. Two lawyers later, my panic had shifted into something heavier, like dread.

It's lunchtime, but I can't enter most of the dining halls on campus, because they're inside the twelve residence houses. And my "agreement" with the college states that I can't enter the houses until my case is decided. So I eat a lot of sandwiches from the deli.

I'm not hungry right now anyway.

Chapter Five

AREN'T YOU FUNNY

Lianne

The next two days crawl by.

There are classes to occupy my time. On Wednesday I pass another ninety painful minutes in the company of the foremost expert on Bertolt Brecht and his legion of ass-kissing minions. I learn that Beret Guy has at least two of those hats because he wears a purple one to our second class.

Thank God nobody can read minds. Because I use all my extra time re-living DJ's kiss. Even as I watch the professor's face move, I'm standing beside Capri's brick wall again, and DJ's dark eyes are coming closer. Then his beautiful full mouth teases mine, tickling the oversensitive skin at the corner of my mouth. I hold my breath, and he kisses me for real...

Gah. It's all I can think about.

When I get a text on Wednesday afternoon, I yank my phone off my desk, hoping it's him. But instead it's Kevin Mung, by co-star. We're close in the way people are when they've been to the wars together. I know all his tics and he knows all of mine. But if it weren't for years of filmmaking together, there's no way we'd ever be friends. We are nothing alike.

Hey babe, his text reads, because he calls everyone babe. Even his mother. *Did you read our scene? Nearly pissed myself laughing.*

Of course he did. Kevin never takes anything seriously. Usually I find it annoying, but in this case I'm glad of it. At least somebody will be relaxed and carefree when the awful scene is finally shot. If it's shot. There was still a ray of hope that someone would see the light and cut it.

I told Bob that it has to be fade to black. Can you please say the same? I need a little help here. Kevin and I have the same manager, which makes us sort of like siblings at a moment like this. Sometimes we gang up on Bob if we need something done.

Except...if Kevin and I are siblings, that means...ew. Okay. We are *so* not siblings.

A moment later my phone rings, and it's him. "Hi," I answer, realizing that it's probably the first time I've spoken to Kevin in two months. On the set of our films we never went five minutes without talking. But when we're not shooting, he forgets I exist.

"Hey," he says, his voice breathy. "You okay, babe? Is the scene seriously bugging you out?"

Why yes, it is. I'm bugging out so hard I'm like that deadly alien in Men In Black. But cuter. "I'm not thrilled about the scene."

"Don't panic yet. You know the shit in the script isn't what ends up on the screen."

"True. But I can't afford to be ridiculous. And I don't know how, um..." I can't finish the sentence. Shooting a sex scene terrifies me. There's no intimacy in my life. And none of this is anything I can really discuss with him.

Kevin's chuckle is warm in my ear. At least today I've got sober, compassionate Kevin. He doesn't make many appearances. "Maybe you should go find someone to rehearse with you," he suggests. "You've always been the kind of girl who takes the extra rehearsal."

"Aren't you funny," I grumble.

"Stop worrying, Li. Even if they shoot something awful, you know how it goes. The whole thing will get edited down to a two-second kiss."

He has a point. Except that I'd still have to take off my clothes in front of the cameras. And the time lag between the shoot and the edited copy was months of waiting. "Or we could just skip it entirely."

"Put your foot down, then," he suggests. "What are they going to do? Fire you? That's not happening."

"I might." But then Bob will freak out and I'll have to listen to him badger and threaten. That might even be worse.

"Hang in there, princess. Hey—are you coming to my premier next month?"

I'd forgotten about it. Kevin wasn't in college like me. While I'd started classes, he'd done a voice-over part for a Pixar animated feature, and the premier was in New York in a few weeks. "I'm not sure yet," I hedge. "Can I bring a date?" That would make it more bearable. I don't know who I would ask to go with me. A girl can dream, though.

"Sure, babe. Be fun to see you. I'll have my publicist call you."

"Cool. I'd better do some homework now."

"Homework is for suckers."

I didn't agree, but there was no point in arguing. Kevin rode the success of the Sentry Sorcerer movies hard, becoming the kind of Hollywood party boy that he'd always wanted to be. "Thanks for calling," I say instead. "See you soon."

"Later, babe!"

I spend the next ninety minutes checking up on my video game dragons and waiting for DJ to call. Like the loser I am.

When he finally texts me to work out the details, I make myself wait exactly ten minutes before replying. And then I spend the next two hours wondering if a fifteen-minute lag wouldn't have been better.

There ought to be a manual for this.

We make plans to meet at Gino's, and then I move on to worrying about what to wear.

When Thursday finally drags its ass my way, I'm kind of a wreck.

Doing my face is easy—some mascara and just a hint of silver eyeshadow to reflect the light. And a lip stain that can withstand a pizza dinner. But dressing for my date turns me into a character in a bad sitcom. I ransack my closet, wondering which of my clothes will make me look more confident and sexier than I really feel.

For starters, I put on skinny jeans, because even I know to wear jeans to a pizza joint. Anything else would look like I was trying too hard. But the rest of the outfit is more trouble. I pull on a black turtleneck, but when I look in the mirror, *meh*. Too Princess Vindi.

Pretty soon half my clothes are on the bed, and I hate all of them.

I settle on a button-down shirt cut from a drapey T-shirt material. It's a little big on me, but I like the silky feel of the fabric.

Then I stare into the full-length mirror on the back of my closet door for way too long. "Bella!" I yell. "Are you decent?" I'd heard Rafe's voice over there, too. And now there is silence, which means they've either left or are making out.

After a beat, my door opens. "What's up? Want a mini Snickers?" She extends her hand, offering me candy. "And the calories don't count, because they're fun-sized."

I wave off the chocolate. "Does this outfit say, 'Splitting a pizza on a random Thursday?'"

She squints at me. "I guess? I mean—I wear hockey T-shirts every day. I'm not the one you should turn to for fashion advice."

"You're my only female friend, so can you just try to phone it in?"

"In this case, your only female friend is not your best call. Rafe?" Bella hollers over her shoulder.

"Yeah, *belleza?*"

"Lianne needs a consult."

Now I'm embarrassed. "It's just pizza," I say, wishing I'd handled this problem by myself.

Bella's exquisite boyfriend pokes his head into the room. "It's never just pizza," he says.

"It isn't?" And is that a quaver in my voice?

He shakes his head. "This is a date, *pequeña*. Did you steal that shirt from someone twice your size? It's like you're hiding in there."

"You say that like it's a bad thing."

Rafe comes into my room and stands in front of the open closet. He flicks the hangers aside one after another. Then he pulls out a sweater that I haven't worn in a year, holding it up to my body. "This is good."

"It's pink," I argue.

"Yeah, but it's *small*. Just try it."

"All right," I grumble. "Turn around, Rafe."

He spins to face the bathroom and I whip off my too-big shirt and slide the sweater over my head. "Okay. What do we think?"

After he turns around, Rafe whistles. "Yeah, baby. That sweater says, '*Hola, señor.*'"

I'm not sure I agree. There's a hint of cleavage, which is good, I guess. But the sweater just highlights the fact that I'm shrimpy *everywhere*. "Small clothes just make me look small."

Rafe grins at me in the mirror. "Not *small*. You're fun-sized."

Bella pops another candy into her mouth. "Don't know if you noticed this, chickie, but DJ isn't exactly King Kong."

"What do you mean?" Rafe and Bella exchange an amused glance while I adjust my so-called boobs. "Wait—what is DJ's name, anyway?"

"Um, is that a trick question?"

"DJ is his *nickname*," I point out. "What's his *real* name."

"Well, it's Trevi. *Duh*. But of course we call his brother that. So he needs his nickname."

Sigh. The hockey crowd is big on last names and nicknames. I lean over my keyboard and begin typing like mad into the web browser. I find him on Facebook, and learn that his real name is Daniel Trevi. So at least I have that going for me—a single bit of data proving he's a real person and not some figment of my imagination.

"Thanks for all your help," I tell Bella. "You two can go back to pawing each other. I'm good."

Bella crosses her arms so I know she's about to deliver some kind of advice. "We're not done here. What are you wearing over that?"

"My coat? Is *that* a trick question?"

She rolls her eyes. "Tonight you leave your baseball cap at home, missy."

"What?" I'd feel naked without my hat. It's bad enough that I can't wear dark glasses, too, because the sun is already down.

"She's right," Rafe argues. "No hat tonight."

I'm so used to concealing myself that I pull open a drawer and hunt around for something sexier than a baseball cap. "I need at least a scarf, then."

Bella leans forward and pulls one out of the drawer. "This is pretty. It sparkles."

I consider the piece she's holding. It *is* pretty—sort of see-through, with tiny sequins that catch the light. It's whimsical and feminine. But I never wear it. "That one itches," I complain.

"Sometimes we must suffer for beauty," she says, tossing it around my neck.

Right. "Says the girl in sweatpants."

"When is DJ getting here, anyway?"

"He's not." I grab my coat. "He had a study group go late, so he asked me to meet him at the restaurant."

Bella raised an eyebrow. "That's odd. Gino's is on kind of a dark corner..."

I wave off her concern. "It's a five-minute walk, Bella. Thanks for the consult."

She turns to follow Rafe into her own room, but then pauses in the doorway, a teasing smile on her face. "Don't worry. If I hear you guys through the door, I'll turn on some music."

My stomach bottoms out. I want more of DJ's kisses, and then some. But the thought of hooking up with him is nerve-wracking, because I don't know what the hell I'm doing. I've never asked a guy to come home with me. It's hard to imagine those words coming out of my mouth.

Bella winks at me. Then she gives Rafe a little slap on the ass and they shut the door. But I can still hear them talking. "You never help me pick out my T-shirts," Bella teases her boyfriend.

"Eh," he says. "I would just toss them on the floor. I like how your clothes look when I throw them on the floor."

"Do you now?" Bella asked. "Show me."

Check please. I don't have to start up a playlist, though. Not tonight. I grab my purse and go for the door. For once I don't need to sit alone in my room while they get frisky.

I stand on the landing for a second, another wave of nerves shimmying through my stomach. But I want this, even if it's scary. So I button my wool coat over my carefully selected outfit and I trot down the stairs and out into the night.

Chapter Six

IT'S COMPLICATED

DJ

My phone rings about half an hour before I'm supposed to meet Lianne. The caller is my little sister, Violet. She's a senior in high school, and we've always been pretty close. "Hi shrimp," I answer, even though Vi is almost as tall as I am now. "What's up with you?"

"Danny! They scheduled my Harkness interview for February third! Dad said I could spend the night before and take the train home afterward. So can I stay with you?"

I glance around my tiny room. She could have the bed, and I'll sleep on the couch. "Any time. But if you stay with Leo, you can see the dorms. Isn't that the point of a Harkness visit?"

"Eh," she says. "I've been seeing the dorms since the first time we dropped Leo off when I was fourteen. It's you I never see."

This is true. I've been ducking her lately because of all the weirdness in my life.

"Danny, why is Dad so grumpy this week? When he talks to you, it's in his den with the door shut. What the hell did you do?"

Nothing. "Ugh, it's complicated. Dad is just riding me about school stuff." It's hard for me to talk to Vi lately, because lying to her isn't something I want to do. But my sister doesn't know about Annie or the case against me. When the ugly call came at the end of the summer, Vi was away at the Girl Scout camp where she's a counselor. And when she came home, my parents chose not to tell her about any of it. "She'll worry," is all my mother said. But all I heard was, *hopefully this all blows over before lots of people hear about it.* Vi isn't known for keeping secrets.

So now I'm stuck dodging my sister's questions. It's awkward, like everything else in my life.

"Do you need me to kick Dad's ass?" Vi offers.

I chuckle. "Maybe. I'll let you know. What else is going on?"

"Since you asked," she says. "I have a new boyfriend. Remember Caleb? The lacrosse player?"

"Sure," I say, calling him up in my mind. "Wears his baseball cap backward? Says 'yo' all the time?"

"Danny! He doesn't say it *all* the time."

"Good." Because it was seriously annoying. "He doesn't drink, does he?"

"Oh my God, you're almost as bad as Dad. No. Not much, anyway. And I won't ride with a drunk driver. I swear."

"Okay." I chuckle. "Sorry." There are a hundred other Big Brother things I feel like saying, but I hold 'em in. "I used to be around for stealth pickups, that's all." Whenever Vi found herself in an uncomfortable situation with her friends, she used to call me. Now that I'm not there, I worry that she'll do something dumb just to stay out of trouble with our parents.

While Leo was always perfectly behaved, Violet and I weren't. Covering for each other is a lifelong habit.

"You worry too much," she says. "I drive myself now. But I can't wait to visit. Will you take me to a party?"

"No," I say automatically. I'm happy to rescue Vi from trouble, but I'm not willing to help her find it in the first place.

"Kill joy."

"We'll have fun," I promise. "I'll take you to Gino's for pizza, and maybe we'll go skating."

"Yay! Just like when I was *seven*."

I snort. "But I'm fresh out of bail money."

"Danny? Did you get arrested?" Suddenly her tone is serious.

"No," I say a little too forcefully.

"There's a lawyer Dad's been talking to."

Shit. "I know, Vi. I'm sorry. It's just there's been a little...entanglement and Dad doesn't want you to worry."

She groans. "But you're going to tell me about it when I visit, right?"

"We'll see." I check the time and realize I have to get going. "I can't wait to see you, shrimp. Email me the date and time, okay? But now I have to go. I have a date. If it goes well, I'll tell you about her." I offer this bit of enticement so Vi won't feel so bad about my secrets.

"You'd better," she says.

After we hang up, it takes me a few minutes to find my Foreigner T-shirt. I need it as a joke for Lianne, but it hides in the bottom of my dresser drawer until the third time I look for it. So getting dressed takes three minutes instead of one. I stick my phone in my pocket, grab a jacket and I'm ready to roll.

Out in the living room, it's no surprise to find Orsen, Pepe and Leo wolfing down meatball grinders. My brother lives in Trindle House, but since Orsen's place is the de facto hockey team hangout, I see him here all the time.

"Hey!" Orsen says, giving me a wave. "Didn't know you were home. We would have ordered something for you."

I'd heard them come in an hour ago, but I've been more or less hiding in my room. "Thanks—I'm good. Just heading out for dinner now. You need anything from the outside world?"

Orsen shakes his head. "Can't send you out for beer, so I guess not."

He's twenty-one and I'm not. "Useless again, then. Bye ladies."

"Deej?" My brother stops me.

"Yeah?"

"You called the lawyer, right?"

Oh my fucking God. I'm so sick of the nagging. "Two days ago." I shove my phone in my pocket and grab my jacket, hoping for a quick exit.

"How did it go?"

Seriously? Who would want to talk about their legal troubles while the hockey team listens? "Fine. No—great. *Spectacular*."

"Danny..." he chides, but I'm already opening the door. When I'm clear of it, I slam it behind me.

It's cold outside, but the walk is short. In fact, Gino's pizza is one of the few destinations convenient to our house. At Harkness, most of the students live in one of the twelve dormitory buildings we call "houses." My brother is rounding out his fourth year in his.

I should be there, too. But instead I'm in exile. Like Napoleon.

At least my place is convenient to Gino's. I get there fifteen minutes early, because I want to put my name down for a table. Both times I've hung out with Lianne, I found her fun and easygoing. But she's probably used to fancy things. And while I'd warned her that Gino's Appizza was very *un*fancy, I don't want her to have to stand around waiting for a table in the divey little front section, either.

This part of Harkness isn't the prettiest, but I don't mind the gritty neighborhood because it has character. This pizza place has been here for seventy-five years. And there are actually pizza snobs who make hundred-mile treks just to eat here. I hope Gino's never upgrades the laminate tables and the black metal napkin dispensers. If the place suddenly starts looking slick, I'll fear for the quality.

As I approach the glass door, which is already steamed up from the night's first pies, I can smell it—that amazing combination of garlic and homemade tomato sauce and excellent cheese. By the time I open the door, I'm already getting a contact high. Lianne will *have* to love it. Nobody could smell that and remain unmoved.

I'm even smiling to myself a little as I do a quick scan of the room. It's not too busy, either. But then my eye snags on something. Some*one*.

She is here. Annie.

For a moment, it doesn't quite sink in that my night has been ruined. At first, I just study Annie's profile—the way her red hair falls behind her shoulder, and the way she smiles at her friends. People who used to be *my* friends, too. For an aching moment, I stand there trying to make sense of it all.

But then I realize my problem all at once.

According to the agreement that I've made with the dean's office, I am required to stay away from her. Fifty feet, to be exact. I don't think Gino's Apizza is fifty feet wide. And even if it was, I can't even *appear* to break my agreement. If she complains to the dean, it will make me look bad. And I can't afford that. Not at all.

The problem crackles quickly through my chest, the way a sheet of ice breaks in every direction at once. There is no way to save the evening that I'd planned.

I turn around and exit Gino's.

Walking away, I wonder what to do. I step under the awning of the check-cashing place across the street and pull out my phone. *Shit.* I don't want to cancel on Lianne. But what choice do I have? I could make up some stupid excuse and ask her to dine elsewhere with me. *It's too crowded. I don't feel like pizza.*

But I don't want to lie. And there's the real problem. If I go out with Lianne tonight, lying is exactly what I'll be doing. Even without the snafu at Gino's, I'll be pretending to be just another happy-go-lucky Harkness guy taking a girl out for dinner— not a guy with an ax hanging over his neck.

I tap Lianne's number and listen to it ring.

"Hello? Am I late? I thought I was early," Lianne says into my ear.

Just the sound of her voice makes me ache. She's so fucking cute. "You're fine," I say, and I mean it. There is nobody finer. I can't imagine why she wanted to go out with me, even for pizza, when she could have anyone. "But, uh, I can't make it tonight. I'm really sorry." More sorry than she'll ever know.

At the distant end of the square, movement catches my eye. I spot Lianne moving toward me. Her hair shines under the street lights. She stops walking, and there's a beat of silence on the line. "You're not coming? Why?"

The pressure in my chest redoubles. "I..." *I'm such an asshole.* "I can't. Something came up." Lamest excuse ever.

Her voice drops. "I see."

"I'm sorry," I repeat, as if it matters. You don't cancel on a girl, even if she's someone who has lots of better things to do. It's rude. But I have no choice.

"Right," she sighs. "I see. Then goodnight." The line goes dead, and I see her jam her phone into a little bag she holds. I expect her to turn around and disappear. But that's not what happens. Instead, she walks into the square, crossing the street, entering the tiny park. She stops for a second as if lost, her eyes on the glowing store-front of Gino's Appizza. Then she sits down on one of the cold benches. She puts her hands on either side of her knees and drops her chin.

Shit!

I can't even breathe now. Lianne shouldn't sit here in this dodgy little park alone. That's a terrible idea. She should get up and head back to campus. Or call a limo to take her to the city, to somewhere movie stars go on a Thursday night. She has better things to do than eat pizza with me, anyway. "Come on," I whisper under my breath.

But she doesn't move. And all at once, I understand that Lianne does not, in fact, exist on some higher plane. Celebrity or not, she feels the sting of rejection the same way anyone would. Even if it comes from the likes of me.

Her narrow shoulders droop, and I'm in fucking *agony*. Unlikely as it seems, I've hurt this girl, which is something I never wanted to do. I hurt her, and it's because I have to avoid *another* girl who *says* I hurt her. But I didn't.

Every time I try to get away from it, even for a couple of hours, it just drags me back down.

While my heart breaks into smaller and smaller pieces, I stay in the shadows watching Lianne, even though her defeated posture kills me. But I don't like her sitting there alone in the cold.

Please go home, I beg silently. *Please.*

Eventually she straightens up. *That's it*, I coach. She reaches up and unwinds the scarf she's wearing, which sparkles when it catches the light. Inexplicably, she tosses it onto the bench beside her. Then she stands, turns, and heads back toward campus.

After she's gotten half a block away, I cross the street and rescue her scarf off the bench. The fabric is light and gauzy, with a subtle shimmer. It looks expensive, and I don't have a clue why she'd leave it behind. I tuck the thing into my jacket and then follow her to the corner. From the shadow of another building, I watch as she reaches the art school, then passes a coffee shop with students spilling out of it.

She's safe now, and I don't have to worry. But my feet follow her anyway. I'm so torn up inside. If I go home now, I'll only end up on the bed in my room, staring at the ceiling.

Outside the coffee shop two students are hawking T-shirts. Last year I'd found their designs novel, so I have several of them. There's the Huck Farvard shirt, a perennial favorite. And another that reads, "Go ___!" And underneath: "(Harkness has no mascot, but we're very fierce. We swear.)"

A new shirt catches my eye, and I have to stop and stare. It says:

Yes, I go to Harkness.

No, I don't know Lianne Challice.

Seriously?

I turn my head abruptly, scanning for Lianne's retreating back. I don't see her anymore. I'd been watching when she walked past this spot, though. She'd passed these shirts without so much as a stutter step. Perhaps she didn't notice, or else she's seen them before.

Either way, it's freaky. I don't think I realized what she was up against before tonight. How *weird* it was to be her.

"See something you like?" one of the student vendors asks. She's wearing mittens and doing a fidgety dance to stay warm in the January chill.

"Nope," I say, and there's an edge in my voice. How could someone possibly think this shirt was funny?

Spinning around, I head home again. Where I have nothing to do and nobody to talk to.

Chapter Seven

THE BISCUIT IN THE BASKET

Lianne

I thought that moving to New England meant I'd experience four perfectly picturesque seasons. But apparently, that's not how it works. Harkness, Connecticut is its own weird climate, where winter brings a lot of dreary weather, but nothing you can make snowballs from.

As I walk to my art history class on Friday, it's raining. Or maybe it's almost snowing. As the little blobs of ice-cold precipitation begin to pelt me in the face, it's hard to say which.

Yippee, it's...snaining.

As I walk, I'm composing an item of hate mail. *Dear January. You are killing me, you know that? You and I have to have a talk before things get out of hand. Listen—I understand December was a tough act to follow. You're under pressure, and I think it's making you a little crazy.*

In December, I did Shakespeare at the Public Theater in New York, while staying at Bella's house on the Upper East Side. I went ice skating at Wollman Rink and went out for dim sum with Bella and her sister. Good times were had.

But, January? It's like you're not even trying. First you dump this whole sex scene thing in my lap. Thanks for that. And then I get stood up on the first date I've ever (not) had.

Really? That's just mean. Like Shawshank Redemption *mean. But without the redemption. Luckily it's only the tenth of the month, though. There's plenty of time to make it up to me. So see what you can do.*

I run through the snain and into the big old lecture hall. There are rows and rows of old wooden seats with red velvet cushions. The stained glass windows lining one wall depict scholars in mortarboard hats and Latin encouragements. The Harkness motto is lettered across the top. *Esse Quam Videri.* To be, rather than to seem.

When I'd chosen Harkness College, this is just what I'd pictured—a dusty old building, a mahogany lectern at the front of the room, and a professor in a lumpy sweater with elbow patches. I settle myself into a seat in the back row, notebook and pen at the ready, hoping the hiss I hear from the old heating system can dry me off before it's time to go back out into the January chill.

The professor is still adjusting his clip-on microphone when I hear the first hint of trouble—it's a sound that's dogged me my whole life. The rapid firing of a Nikon camera's shutter.

Oh no. Here?

My stomach drops to the floor, and I begin evasive maneuvers. I swivel my body away from the sound, then dig into my bag for my phone.

"Excuse me," the professor says into his microphone, addressing my harasser. "This is private property. You'll have to leave."

The asshole with the camera will never obey him, though. It's a lesson I learned early in life. Paparazzi make their money by *not* listening. They are professional assholes.

I tap on a number that's stored in my phone. I'd hoped to never use it, but when campus police picks up, I'm happy that my overbearing manager had thought to make me store it. "Hi," I tell the dispatcher who answers. "My name is Lianne Challice and I'm a freshman. I'm trying to attend a lecture in the Masterson building right now, but a photographer is disrupting the class, and he won't leave. The professor has already asked him to."

"A...photographer?" the dispatcher asks. I've confused him. Most calls to campus security are probably about lost wallets or drunkenness.

"He's a paparazzo," I try to explain. And he's coming closer. I can hear the camera sounds and nothing else, because the whole lecture hall has gone quiet.

My back is suddenly sweaty. Rising out of my chair, I abandon my bag, my notebook and my coat. My face is mostly hidden by my phone on one side and the brim of my trusty baseball cap, which I tug as low as I can. The asshole photographer knows exactly who's under here, but I don't want him to get any shots he can use.

Charging up the aisle, I see amusement on the faces of my classmates. This doesn't usually happen in a history of art survey on a Friday afternoon. I'm actually glad they find it funny instead of maddening. Though I'd like to bite someone.

"A paparazzo?" the dispatcher asks in my ear.

"Yes. He's trespassing. It's *illegal*," I point out.

"I've already sent a unit to Masterson Hall," the officer assures me. "ETA is two minutes."

I don't answer right away because I've picked up my pace. I shoot out of the lecture room and take a quick right down a gloomy old hallway. There's a ladies' room down here. Running now, I reach it ahead of the photographer and yank open the door. This will only work if it's the kind of bathroom with a lock on the inside—paparazzi don't care about rules.

Dashing inside, I push the door shut. And? No lock. This is a bathroom with three stalls.

Thanks January. Thanks a crap-ton.

I do not rush into one of the stalls. There's no point. At least now if I end up having to try to sue this guy or get a restraining order, I can say that he followed me into the ladies' room. That sounds pretty sleazy. Also? This room isn't that big, which means the asshole will have to refocus, maybe even switch lenses.

"The security officers have entered the building," the dispatcher says into my ear.

"I'm in the ladies..."

The door flies open in front of me, and a giant camera lens is shoved into my face. "Smile, Lianne."

I put my elbow in front of my face just as the shutter starts its machine-gun patter. I hear feet running toward us across the stone floors.

"Hey!" a masculine voice cries out. "You can't go in there!"

The shutter whirrs. Paparazzi don't care about the rules. They care about the shot and about their precious equipment. That's it.

"Step out or we will forcibly restrain you," the voice warns.

The clicking stops. I don't drop my arm, though, because it's probably just a pause.

"Step *out*. I'm arming the taser."

Now *that's* exciting. I've never seen a paparazzo tasered. I peek under the crook of my elbow to see what's happening.

The asshole has lowered his camera and is backing out of the room. "Don't touch my camera," he barks. "I always win my lawsuits."

A real charmer, my stalker. I recognize him, too. He's the one they call Buzz. To go with their stupid jobs, paparazzi tend to have stupid nicknames.

One of the policemen snaps handcuffs onto Buzz's wrist. "You have the right to remain silent. You have the right..."

"You cannot be serious," Buzz argues. "It's just a fucking picture."

"Step outside."

"You'll see me again soon, Lianne!" the photographer calls over his shoulder.

And I'm sure he's right. The paparazzi are like roaches. Nothing stamps them out.

They disappear, but the second officer stays with me. He's an older man with a grey military cut and friendly eyes. "You okay?"

"I'm fine," I assure him. What I am is *embarrassed*. So much for blending in.

"Good. I'm going to need your statement."

"Okay, but I really need to be in that lecture hall right now. Can I give it to you afterward? Please?"

I have succeeded in looking sufficiently pitiful, because he caves. "All right. But come to the station right after class, you hear?" He hands me a business card with an address on it and sends me back to class.

When I slink back into the room, a hundred pairs of eyes turn in my direction.

"Is it safe to begin the lecture?" my professor asks from the podium, his voice bouncing off every mahogany surface and then right into my very soul.

My head bobs with an awkward nod. "Must be a slow news day," I mutter.

Nobody laughs.

Damn it. You only get one chance to make a first impression. There went mine.

By that evening, I've never been so happy to see the backside of a week in my life. Seven o'clock finds me lying on my bed in sweatpants, perusing the menu of a Thai restaurant that delivers. And because I'm a wild and crazy girl this semester, I'm considering ordering noodles instead of steamed veggies.

A Hollywood girl knows how to live large, you feel me?

Just as I considered this sacrilege, Bella taps on my door and then opens it. "Let's go, Lianne! Hockey game starts in half an hour."

I'd forgotten about the hockey game I'd said I'd go to. "I'll have to pass. I'm beat."

Bella makes the sound of a buzzer. "Brrrrrp! Sorry. You do not get to flake out on me here. I've been waiting all week to watch my team beat Saint B's and to show you the glory that is hockey. And I already got your ticket. So put your skinny ass in some jeans because I don't want to miss the first faceoff."

"But I'm *comfortable* right now." Damn it, I'm whining now.

She lifts an eyebrow. "Did I mention they sell hot dogs and popcorn?"

Hmm... That does sound promising. "Does the popcorn have butter?" Weirdly, millions of people have eaten popcorn while watching one of my movies. But I'd been dieting for so long that smelling it at a premier was as close as I'd come to the stuff.

"Probably. Now hurry up."

Groaning, I get off the bed. "Remind me why I have to go with you?" It's not like Bella had never been to a game before.

"Because you're Fun Lianne now."

I pull on a pair of jeans. "It's cold in the rink, right? Do I need to bundle up?"

"You won't even notice because the players are so hot." She tosses me my coat. "Wear this. Let's roll."

Bella wasn't kidding when she said she wanted to see the puck drop. It wasn't enough that I'd gotten ready in all of five minutes. She soon has us practically sprinting up Science Hill toward the rink.

"I'm wearing only one coat of mascara for you. And you didn't mention there'd be a death march first," I complain as we speed-walk.

"Not my fault you have tiny little legs," she says. "And we're almost there."

Ahead of us, people are streaming into the arena. Bella leads me over to the student section door and pushes two tickets at the staffer guarding it.

"How much are tickets?" I don't want her to have to pay for me.

Bella waves off the question. "They're free if you pick them up ahead of time."

"What? I thought you meant that if I didn't go to the game, you'd be out money..."

She gives me a wink. "Got you here, didn't I? You can hit the concession stand if you want, I'm saving us seats."

An hour later, I'm having a hell of a lot more fun than I'd expected. Sitting in the student section with Bella, I eat a soft pretzel and a box of popcorn. Then I go back for a hot dog with all the fixings.

In between bouts of screaming at the players, Bella tries her best to explain the game. "There's two defensemen, and... HIT HIM TREVI! CRUSH HIM LIKE A BUG!"

I am probably going to end up deaf in one ear. But I'm not sure I mind, because hockey is exciting. Unlike baseball, which I consider to be a cure for insomnia, this game is nonstop action—the players flying past me at warp speed, the puck pinging from stick to stick so fast my eyes can't track it. And every few minutes a player slams another player into the boards, and my heart leaps into my throat. It sounds violent and yet I feel a very inappropriate thrill each time it happens.

"FUCK HIM UP!" Bella hollers beside me. Her voice is half gone already. "Come on guys!" she cheers, clapping. "Put the biscuit in the basket! Bring mama's cookies to the kitchen!"

Then I feel her go tense beside me, and the whole student section seems to lean forward. A Harkness player has broken away from his pursuers. It's just him and the puck and the other team's goalie, who also tenses.

Our guy—Rikker—feints to the left and then fires the puck

like a missile. I can't see it anymore, but a lamp lights on the plexi behind the net, and half the arena stands up and screams.

We scored! And now I'm hugging Bella and there's music and it's *thrilling!*

Omigod. Hockey. Who knew?

When we sit down again I'm flushed and happy, as if I did something right. All I did was watch, but it feels bigger than that. It's a strange sensation, and I file this away to think about later. I'm still holding the hot dog I bought. I lift it for a bite, and my eyes travel to the other side of the rink. Where a giant camera is pointed in my direction.

Shit.

I lower the hot dog, and the lens falls.

I raise the hot dog, and it rises.

"God damn it!"

"What's the matter?" Bella yelps.

"Fricking paparazzo. The one from History of Art —he's back."

"Where?"

I groan. "How could you miss him? And every time I try to take a bite, he takes a picture."

Bella's fair brow wrinkles. "Why?"

Sigh. "Because anyone looks like a pig with a bite of food in her mouth. When a photographer wants to make you look ridiculous, they catch you eating."

My friend's eyes widen. "That's a thing?"

"It is." A few minutes ago I was having a great time. Now I feel exposed.

Bella's face is full of concern. "Shit. I'm sorry, babe. Do you think we should call security?"

"No." I spent enough time in their offices filling out my incident report. "The hockey rink is a public place, so that asshole isn't even breaking any laws." But if I try to sneak out, he'll just follow me. And then I'd be alone out there with him. It's not like

I want to ask Bella to walk me home in the middle of the game, either.

"You didn't even get to eat your *food*. That's just wrong." She slaps her thighs, then turns to glance around the rink. "I have an idea. Follow me." She stands and begins edging past the other spectators, toward the aisle.

Clutching my hot dog, I trail after her. "Where are we going?"

She doesn't answer me. She just waves me up the stairs, then disappears behind a wall. I round the corner to see her opening a door signed PRESS BOX. She waves me over.

Inside the little room, which is sheltered on three sides but open to the rink at its front, I spot her friend Graham tapping on his laptop. "Psst," Bella says, and he turns his head. "Lianne needs to be out of sight for a little while." Graham nods, beckoning to me quickly before turning his attention back to the game.

Bella gives me a little shove into the room. Then she closes the door behind me.

The little room is long and skinny, with a desk spanning the front. Five heads are bent over computers, all in a row. At one end, an older gentleman wears headphones, and speaks into a microphone. Graham sits next to him. In the center are two guys wearing Saint B's jackets—obviously from the visiting team. Then the fifth guy...My heart trips over itself. Because DJ stands in the corner, his eyes on the ice, his hand on a computer mouse.

He hasn't noticed me yet. All his attention is funneled onto the game. As I watch, he clicks something on his screen. And then I hear a Green Day song begin to jam from the stadium speakers. DJ's hand moves to a lever on a sound mixing board, while his eyes stay trained on the action on the ice.

Below me, the players line up for another faceoff. "When I Come Around," thunders off the walls. But at the moment the ref drops the puck, the song quickly fades out while the skaters chase the puck toward Saint B's goal.

DJ's eyes drop to his computer screen while he taps furiously on a keyboard.

He still hasn't noticed me.

With my back against the press box wall, I feel handily invisible. I finish my hot dog in three bites. Then I dig some mints out of my purse and pop one in my mouth. Then? A fresh coating of cherry lip gloss.

Because hope springs eternal. And you just never know.

Chapter Eight

SURPRISINGLY COMPETENT FALSETTO

DJ

My awareness of Lianne is a gradual thing.

I hear the press box door open and shut, but I'm too busy to look. As I cue up my next couple of song ideas, I feel eyes on me. In my peripheral vision, I see a pair of shapely legs in skinny jeans, and a delicate hand, its thumb hooked into the pocket of a tailored wool jacket. Her fingernails are shiny and pink, like candies.

Below me, a whistle blows. I'm smiling—and then scrambling —because Saint B's is getting called for hooking. I hit "play" on Inner Circle's "Bad Boys."

This is good. We need the power play, and I fucking love this song. It's Friday night, we're winning the game and I'm in the zone, doing my job, thinking only positive thoughts.

And in spite of the fact that I let her down, the most amazing girl at Harkness is watching every move I make.

With one hand I beckon to Lianne, but I can't look at her yet because I have to pay attention to the action on the rink. It takes a few seconds for the penalized player to make his way over to the sin bin and for the opposing team to send out their penalty-killer shift. So the rasta beat plays on.

This is my moment of greatness, of course. Nobody knows it's me, and maybe only half the audience will even get the joke. ("Bad Boys" is perfect for when the other team gets a penalty.) But five-thousand people are nodding in time to the groove I've chosen for them, and it's a beautiful thing.

Not only does Lianne appear at my side, she peers over my screen to see what I'm doing. "Quite the setup you've got here."

I step back to make room for her, putting a hand on her shoulder to guide her past my body where she can see the sound-board. At even this small contact, my pulse kicks up a notch. She smells like flowers and mint.

The ref skates up to the centers, and the players lean in for the faceoff.

Lianne is bent over my sound board, examining it. So I take her hand and move it onto the master lever. "Ready?" I whisper.

She nods, and we're very close together now. Her hand is warm underneath mine. On the ice, the puck drops. I close my fingers over hers and together we slide the master down to zero, ending the sound clip.

"Oh, the power!" Lianne whispers. "Are you ever tempted to *accidentally* blast an airhorn when the other team is about to shoot for a goal?"

"All the time," I tease.

She drops into my chair, which I never sit in anyway. "What are you going to play next?"

"It depends what happens." I lean in closer to her, because I can't help myself. The pull I feel when she's nearby is so strong. "If we score again, I'll play something obnoxious."

"What if they tie it up? Wait..." She points at the list of songs on my screen. "You could play 'Are You Gonna Go My Way,' by Lenny Kravitz?"

"Now you're getting it," I say, giving her ponytail a playful tug. I need to stop touching her, but it's difficult. "How did you end up in here, anyway?" I know better than to think she was looking for me.

Lianne makes a face. "I needed to drop out of sight for a few minutes. I'm kind of hiding behind your computer screen right now."

"From who?"

She shakes her head. "Just...a jerk with nothing better to do on a Friday night than hassle me."

I do *not* like the sound of that. But for the moment, Lianne is perfectly safe right in front of me, and I need to keep my eyes on the game. The ref makes a weird call. He stops play on Harkness for icing, but the crowd saw the puck ricochet off a Saint B's stick. There is widespread unhappiness. Half the student section gets to its feet. They're yelling at the ref. Across the rink I see guys pounding on the plexi in their displeasure.

The music at a hockey game isn't just for fun. At tense moments like this, its job is to soothe the crowd. To remind the spectators that they're there to have fun and not to riot. And to express their emotional state in a lighthearted way.

I lean over Lianne and play "It's Tricky" by Run DMC.

"That's an oldie," she says, swiveling around to look up at me.

"True." I agree, making a quick adjustment to the bass output. "When a song is older than high school, that means we have to dance to it." Giving Lianne a nudge, I start to move my hips and wave my hands.

Lianne spins my rotating chair until she's facing me. But for a moment, she just lifts her chin and pins me with a look. Meanwhile, I'm dancing alone like a crazy man. We watch each other, and I can see her trying to decide whether she's going to play along, or let me twist for standing her up last night.

I deserve it. But I don't give up. Instead, I stick my ass out a little farther and shimmy. I'm the only one dancing in the press box, and I probably look ridiculous. But I'll look ridiculous for Lianne any day of the week.

A slow smile takes over her face, and then she caves. She lifts her hands to frame her face and begins to vogue, her slender arms posing and diving in time to the music. We're both going for it, as if the team's success tonight rests on our performance.

Six seconds later I'm sliding the master back down to zero as the team skates on, my chest grazing the top of Lianne's head. I get a whiff of her shampoo, and it's tempting to drop my face into her neck for a kiss.

Down, boy.

The buzzer rings, signaling the end of the second period. I lean over Lianne, my hand on her slender shoulder. "Double click on 'Brown Eyed Girl,' will you?"

She grabs the mouse and does as I ask, her movements swift and precise. "I like your job, Daniel."

Daniel. Nobody calls me by my real name, and I like the way it sounds on her lips. "It's a good time, right? Can't believe they pay me for this." *For now*, my subconscious jabs me. The ax that's hovering over my neck never quite goes away. Not even when I'm having fun.

Lianne tips her head back so she can look up at me. "Why did you stand me up last night?"

Oh, hell. I've never owed anyone an explanation as much as I owe her one. But that doesn't mean I know what to say. "This year isn't going so well for me. There are complications, and sometimes they have really bad timing. I'm really sorry. You have no idea."

Her eyes fall shut and she stands up. My gut plummets, because it seems like she's about to walk out. But instead she simply turns her back on the rink and folds her arms. "That's not the most articulate excuse I've ever heard. But since you sound sincere I'm inclined to let it slide."

"Okay," I whisper, feeling my sadness lift by a few ounces. Her forgiveness is an unexpected gift.

"You're not the only one having a shitty year, by the way." The words are challenging, but her expression is vulnerable. Her eyes shift to the side, as if she didn't intend to say that.

"No? I'm sorry." I am, too. *So* fucking sorry for being an asshole last night. Though I'm really not sure how I might have avoided it. Oh yeah—by staying away from her in the first place. I can't help but ask, "What goes wrong for you?"

She gives her pretty head a little irritated shake. "Harkness hasn't been easy. It's not the school work, though. That part is fine. It's just everything else."

Tell me about it. Somehow it feels natural to tuck her into a hug. So I pull her small body into my chest, and wrap my arms around her back. And it feels so fucking good to hold her. "Can we still be friends?" She nods into my shoulder. "Good," I rumble, trying not to notice how perfectly we fit together. We just stand there for a minute, and my mind is quiet again. She has that effect on me.

"Daniel?"

"Hmm?"

Lianne lifts her head. "Your song is ending."

Fuck. I release her and grab the computer mouse, executing a sloppy fade into "Sweet Child o' Mine" that's only a second or two off the mark. Nobody will notice except for me. And Lianne, of course. What kind of DJ almost leaves dead air?

Her eyes twinkle with humor, but she doesn't call me on it like I expect her to. "I do a mean Axl Rose," she says instead, as the opening guitar riff of the song bounces brightly through the stadium.

"No way," I challenge. "This I have to see."

She removes her baseball cap and flips it around in her hands. "You have to air guitar Slash's part. I'm not feeling it yet." The corners of her mouth twitch.

"Fine," I say a little huffily. As if I haven't spent months of my life on my air guitar technique. I mentally pick up a nice Telecaster, brace it against my body and begin pick out the riff.

The drums and the bass come in while Lianne shakes her head, tipping her face downward so that her hair falls forward. Then she puts the baseball cap on backwards and low on her forehead. As the music builds toward Axl's first line, she slowly lifts her chin, eyes closed, moves her shoulders and claps her hands once over her head. With a serious, pinched expression, my miniature Axl begins to sing the first line about a smile...

And Jesus Christ, she *is* Axl Rose. The way she holds her shoulders. The tense grip she has on an imaginary microphone. The way her hair swings when she moves. It's *hilarious*. My air-guitar accompaniment breaks down when I start to laugh.

She doesn't even complain when I quit my part of our act. She just carries on. I hear a snort from further down the press box, and now Michael Graham is clapping from his seat.

"Holy shit, do you see who that *is*..."

My gaze swings in the direction of the two guys from the visiting team. They're staring at Lianne with a mixture of surprise and amusement on their faces. Just as I realize what's happening, one of them aims his phone at Lianne.

She stops instantly, whipping the hat off her head and fixing him with a glare. "No pictures."

"Come on," the Saint B's guy urges. "That was awesome."

"Hey," I argue a little louder than necessary. "She said no pictures." Lianne must be so fucking tired of being everybody's celeb sighting. Their most-loved Instagram upload or their most-liked Facebook status update.

The asshole lets the moment linger, his eyes locking with mine. They say, *What are you going to do about it?*

"Put the phone away, pal," Michael Graham says quietly.

After one more arrogant beat of disobedience—just because he can—the Saint B's guy shoves his phone in his pocket again.

But the moment is ruined. Lianne is sitting in my seat again, scrolling through the list of songs on my screen, trying to look like she doesn't care. I'm starting to understand just how good an actress this girl really is. And it depresses the hell out of me. Who wants to be good at ignoring everyone?

She leans in, reading my playlists.

"You have everything arranged by mood!" She claps her hands, delighted by this idea. "Of course that makes sense, though."

It's true—I couldn't do my job without sorting the songs into emotions. There are songs under the headings "victory lap" and "time for a rally" and "penalty box."

"I don't get this choice," she says, her face quizzical. "Pat Benatar's 'Heartbreaker'?"

Ah. I give her a grin and then sing the line that makes the song perfect. I have to use a comically high voice for Patty B's line about the right kind of *sinner*. It's perfect for when one of our guys catches two minutes in the sin bin.

Watching me, Lianne's eyes go wide. "Holy shit, DJ. You have a surprisingly competent falsetto."

"Girls tell me that all the time," I deadpan, and she giggles.

I'm so tempted to kiss that smile off her face right now, but I can't. When I'd asked her if we could still be friends, I'd meant it. That's all I can offer her.

My heart didn't get the memo, though. I cue up the next song, but all I want to do is admire her smile and pull her into my arms again. I want to tell her some more silly jokes, and put on another song so old that we're required by my dorky little rules to dance to it. I could stand here all night talking to her, but the game will soon be over.

Happy moments like this are as rare as hat tricks. So all I can do is make the most of it.

"You pick the song we'll play when Harkness scores again," I offer. "Anything you want," I add.

"Yessss," she says, rubbing her hands together, as if I've offered her more than just the choice of a song.

That's all I've got to give her, though. And probably all I'll ever have.

Chapter Nine

I'M NOT OVER

Lianne

It's official. I'm having a blast tonight.

I've forgotten all about my paparazzo nemesis. I was supposed to be hiding from him in the press box, but I'm just here to have fun. DJ doesn't seem to mind, either.

A few minutes into the third period, the crowd makes an unhappy noise as Saint B's ties up the game. DJ's response is to play "I'm Not Over" by Carolina Liar.

"Good pick," I say as he hovers over the sound board. His smile is only inches from me, and the proximity makes me feel warm everywhere.

God, I like this boy. I mean—it isn't just *anyone* who gets to see my Axl Rose imitation.

While Harkness fights to break the tie, we play songs of encouragement at every opportunity. "How about 'Bust a Move.'"

"Cue it up!" he encourages me. So I do. And for the next break in play, he picks "Fight for your Right" by the Beastie Boys. They're both old, so we dance both times.

"We've got quite the classic rap thing going here," I say, sitting down afterwards. I've totally stolen his chair, but DJ doesn't care.

He gives my shoulder a squeeze. "That's right. Taste this good should come at a premium price." But then I lose his attention when his face tenses.

I scrutinize the play down on the rink, but I can't find the puck. "What's happening?"

"My brother is trying to... *YEAH!*"

Several thousand people roar as Harkness scores again. The student section goes crazy, and everyone in the press box leans over their computer screens, tweeting or recording or announcing the play. I hear the announcer credit Leo Trevi for the assist and John Rikker for another goal.

When I glance over at Michael Graham, he's typing and grinning at the same time. Rikker is his boyfriend, and Graham is the sports editor for the newspaper. They're both having a good night.

"Play your song, lady," DJ prompts me.

Ack! I'd been so distracted by the goal that I'd forgotten. But a half second later, Springsteen's "Glory Days" is blasting through the rink.

"That's cocky," DJ teases.

I give him a grin over my shoulder. "Sometimes it's just your turn to be cocky."

"Fair enough." He tenses his hand over the sound board again, waiting for the faceoff. I enjoy the view of his muscular forearm poised over the levers. DJ looks more like one of the jocks on the ice than a music geek. He's a study in contrasts, actually. Hockey nut. Music nerd. Great kisser.

Breaker of dates.

I've already forgiven him, though, which means either I'm an idiot or I'm just that smitten. The third period of the hockey game is going fast, and I'm not eager to hear the final buzzer. This is the most fun I've had at Harkness. Except for that kiss...

This boy likes me, I think. Maybe? The fact that he stood me up is confusing. Yet every time he looks at me, he smiles.

"Glory Days" plays on as the ref takes an extra moment to reset the position of the Saint B's net. DJ waits and watches for his cue.

"Can I do it?" I ask, my hand hovering over his.

"Sure," he says. "Fade out the second you see that puck drop, but not before." He retracts his hand, but doesn't move his body. We're so close that I can feel the warmth of him radiating over me.

The puck falls and I drag the lever down, fading The Boss down to silence. "Now I have the *power*," I brag.

"Nice job, smalls."

"What's *with* the short jokes?" I complain, and his answering chuckle is evil.

A few minutes later the game ends, and we've won 3-2. That makes me the only Harkness fan who wishes there were *more* time on the clock. "Do you ever play any going-away music?" I ask hopefully.

DJ shakes his head. "The management doesn't want me to give the crowd a reason to linger."

But I want to linger. Whoever runs this place is totally onto me.

My phone chimes from my pocket, and it's a text from Bella. *Your photographer is standing outside the front door. I told him you left already and then walked away. Get Graham to take you out the back door.*

Roger that, I reply. *Thank you!*

I watch DJ pack up his laptop. I'm in no hurry to leave him or to run into the paparazzo outside. At the other end of the desk, Graham slings a pack over his shoulder and stands. "Lianne? Bella texted me to walk you out the back door. Ready?"

Crap.

But DJ says, "I got it, man. I'll walk her home." So my heart starts doing the tango. "Who are we ducking, anyway?"

Graham rubs his chin. "A photographer with a camera the size of a tanker truck. Let's all go together."

"It's just not that big a deal," I argue. "Go ahead, Graham. I'm good."

A slow grin overtakes Graham's face, and I pray DJ is too busy packing up to see it. "Okay then. Goodnight."

When he walks out, DJ and I are alone in the booth. I have an irrational hope that he'll invite me out for drinks or something to make up for last night. Or ice cream. Or a walk around the parking lot. *Anything*.

He picks up his backpack. "Let's get you home, then."

Right.

I hold up my phone. "Bella said we should go out the back. If, um, that's no problem."

"Sure thing. Follow me."

I do, and it's a pleasure, because I love the way DJ fills out a pair of jeans. I like the way his shoulders move when he walks—his gait is tough but casual, like a soldier at ease. My whole life I've been surrounded by beautiful people. But many of them have a Hollywood sheen—a self-conscious beauty. DJ is a different brand of sexy. And it's a brand I like a lot.

I could be a very loyal customer of his brand.

He walks me down a set of stairs at the back of the mezzanine level. There are signs pointing toward the various locker rooms, and I notice there are women's as well as men's. "Who DJs the women's games?" I ask.

DJ turns around and winks at me. "Who do you think?"

"You?"

"But of course." He stops in front of a metal door. "Do you want me to take a look outside?"

God, I am sick to death of the drama. But there will only be more of it if that asshole is outside waiting for me. "That would be awesome. He's about forty, dirty blond hair, big camera resting on his beer gut. You can't miss him."

Before he steps outside, he turns around to give me the kind of smile that makes me forget my own name. "Be right back." Whistling to himself, he steps out the door.

Now I'm alone for a moment with my own thoughts. *Invite him over*, my heart whispers. But I'm not sure I'm that brave. Saying the words isn't all that difficult. But the follow-through is problematic. He would come upstairs to my room and...then what? I'll probably start babbling like a moron. I won't know where to sit. I'll just quietly freak out while I try to figure out whether he's going to kiss me...

There's the sound of a key in the lock, and the door opens. "Looks deserted," he says, and I follow him.

He's holding the door, and when I step outside he lets it close and then puts a wide hand in the center of my back. I like the feel of it. In fact, it's fair to say I've never felt this kind of sizzle for anyone before. It's unfamiliar, this fizzy brew of excitement swirling through my insides. Everything seems more intense when he's around.

It's a crisp January evening, but I want to walk slowly toward Beaumont House in spite of the chill. In the distance I can hear the murmur of happy voices in the dark — stragglers from the game, probably. It's Friday and our team won and a very attractive boy is walking beside me. I love the way this feels. The night is so full of possibility.

"So how was your week?" I ask, because that seems like a safe question.

"Eh. I've had better."

"Me too." But I realize part of the reason my week sucked was our date fiasco, and I don't want him to know how much it bothered me. So I change the subject to the first thing that pops into my head. We're passing a kiosk—a place where people hang flyers of all kinds. "I need to hire someone, like a drama student. To help me with some...homework. How much do you think tutors get paid?"

DJ thinks it over. I like the way the light from the street lamp slides over his handsome features. "Depends on the subject. If it's math or statistics, it could be like forty bucks an hour. But writing tutors get about half that much."

Of course, money isn't an issue for me. I just wanted to make sure I put the right amount on my flyer. "All right. What I need isn't exactly skilled labor."

"What are you hiring for?"

"Reading Shakespeare out loud."

He gives me a sidelong glance. "Can't you do that yourself?"

"Of course I can. But I need someone to read *with* me, a whole play, two or three times. I want to hear every line of it. That's the only way to really understand."

"Are you taking a Shakespeare course?"

I shake my head. "It's, uh, a personal project."

"A play?"

"The Scottish play." I give him a smile, because I probably sound like a crazy person. "There's a superstition against saying the name of it. But there's three witches, and the king gets murdered."

"MacBeth," DJ says, then he nudges me with his hip. "Is it unlucky for you if I say it?"

"I hope not."

"So this is a play you're doing? Like, for work?"

"Only if I'm lucky," I admit. "I want this part very, very badly. The film won't be made for a year, but the director is casting it soon, and if he calls me in I want to be so well versed that it's practically dripping off me. So he won't be able to *imagine* someone else playing her."

"One of the witches?" DJ asks.

I whirl on him. "Bite your tongue! I want Lady M."

He holds up two hands in submission. "Easy. You mentioned the witches a minute ago. I'm just trying to follow along."

We're standing under another street light, and I realize I probably sound as loopy as one of the weird sisters in the play. "Sorry.

I'm just a little nutty about being typecast. I've spent seven years waving a magic wand. It's a problem."

He doesn't seem offended, though. He's smiling at me again. "'Lady M,' huh? You can't say her name? Someone's a little superstitious."

I raise one hand toward the cold night sky. "Guilty."

He shrugs. "Athletes are superstitious, too. My brother used to have a pair of lucky skate laces. They broke, like, five times before he was finally willing to give up on them. But I've never been superstitious. I don't have a lucky mouthguard or any pre-game rituals."

"You play hockey?" I blurt out.

His expression flickers. "Used to," he says, jamming his hands in his pockets. He starts walking again, and his voice dips low. "I didn't get recruited for the Harkness team, though. Came close with a few Division One schools, but it didn't happen for me. Could have played Division Three, but it meant picking a college that just wasn't as good."

"Sorry," I say. See how good I am at flirting? I've got this boy talking about rejection.

"I'm over it," he chuckles. "I used to think that not playing college hockey would be my life's greatest disappointment." The mirth drains from his voice at the end of the sentence. There's a story there, but he doesn't volunteer it, and I don't ask.

Maybe it's bravery, or maybe it's foolishness. But I reach out and take one of the oversized hands I've been admiring all night. When his fingers close around mine, this little act of courage is vindicated. Yessss!

His hand swallows mine up. Then his thumb strokes my palm, and...holy cow. Who knew there were so many nerve endings in my hand?

"I could do it," he's saying.

"What?" I mumble. I'm too busy focusing on his touch to hear him.

"Reading out loud. Shakespeare. Even a dumb jock can read the lines of a play."

"You..." My brain cells realign themselves just enough to allow me to respond to his offer. "You'd take the job?"

He gives my hand a squeeze. "You don't have to *pay* me. Jesus. It's just some reading, right?"

"Well," I squeeze his hand back. "It's a bunch of hours, though. Maybe...six? But not all at once. And if you got sick of it I could just hire someone after all."

"I won't get sick of it," he murmurs.

Looking up, I'm startled to find we've reached the gate to Beaumont House. And I'm not ready to let him go. But he drops my hand anyway, presumably so I can dig out my ID.

Fumbling, I do that. And it's now or never. "You want to"—my voice squeaks—"come in?" It's probably not possible to deliver that line with less finesse than I just did. Seriously, Actor's Equity should yank my membership.

DJ's expression becomes so solemn that my heart drops into my shoes. "This is as far as I can go," he says.

That's an odd way to word a refusal. But I don't call him on it, because his face tells me that his answer is non-negotiable. So I pull myself together and stand as tall as my five-foot-one frame allows. "Thank you for walking me home." I look him in the eye, but I'm dying inside. What does a girl have to do for a little more of this guy's time? Whatever it is, I'll do it. I'll become it. I'll study up, and I'll ace the test.

Those long lashes blink at me once. Twice. "Goodnight, Lianne." Then he leans forward and I hold my breath.

The kiss lands on my forehead, lingering sweetly there for a moment.

Then he's gone. I watch his ridiculously attractive denim-clad backside retreat into the shadows of the walkway between Beaumont House and the architecture library.

Damn.

Damn damn damn.

I race up the stairs to my room, where I let the door fall shut with a frustrated crash. Then I'm kicking myself, because the noise will probably bring Bella through the bathroom door to see what's wrong.

It doesn't though, and in a few seconds I understand why.

"Ohhhhh, *Belleza*." It's a deep, resonant moan, and it's followed by some curses in Spanish.

Bella and Rafe are going at it again.

As I nudge my computer mouse to wake up the machine, he moans again. By the time I've double-clicked on the song I want, they're both moaning and grunting like a couple of wild boars during truffle season.

Maybe it's a good thing DJ did not come upstairs with me. Casual conversation is a lot trickier when you're chatting over the sounds of escalating sex in the next room. I would probably combust with embarrassment.

Pat Benatar's "Heartbreaker" begins to echo off the walls of my tiny room. So I sing along with all I've got, especially the high-pitched bit that DJ'd sung in the press box. I try to recapture the silly fun I had earlier, but it's harder alone. It's nine-thirty on a Friday night, and I'm pretty sure I'm the only one on campus who's alone tonight.

It doesn't help that Pat Benatar's "We Belong" comes on next. I've always loved the heavy-on-the-reverb opening riff, and the devastation in her voice. And just like that I'm a cliché, singing about loneliness in my dorm room.

Yikes.

By the time the song is over, it's quiet next door. So I shut everything off and get into bed with my copy of the Scottish play.

DJ had said he'd read this sucker with me, and I'm totally holding him to it. Watch me.

———

I don't see Bella and Rafe until the next morning. I'm on my third cup of coffee—and Act Three of the Scottish play—when they put their trays down at my table in the dining hall.

"Hey, *pequeña*," Rafe says. "A little light reading?"

"Sure." I clap the book shut as Bella sits down. "How about that win last night?"

"Wasn't it awesome? Aren't you glad you went?" She nudges Rafe. "Baby's first hockey game."

"Soccer is where it's at, Lianne." Rafe winks at me.

"Hush, hottie. That's not funny," Bella whispers, and her hand moves so I know she's touching him under the table.

The cloud of affection between them is so thick I can hardly draw breath, even from the other side of the table.

Bella must notice this, because she stops mauling her boyfriend and frowns at me. "Who walked you home?"

"Uh, DJ."

Her face lights up. "*Really*. Did he come upstairs?"

"Nope."

"Why?"

"What do you mean, *why?*"

Her eyes bug out. "Why didn't you invite him upstairs to see your collection?"

"My collection of what?"

"Oh, honey." She gives me an eye roll. "It doesn't matter what. Just invite him upstairs."

"I did!" I squeak. "He turned me down."

Her forehead creases. "Really? Are you sure?"

"Did you *see* him up there?" God, I know my game needs work. But does she really think I could get this wrong?

"Okay, *how* did you ask him?"

I sit back in my chair. "Really? You're going to make me relive it?"

"Yes I am," she says, cutting up a piece of sausage. "Something just doesn't compute."

My sigh sounds more diva-like than I'd wish. But it's extra-embarrassing to describe my pathetic life with Rafe listening, too. "I said, 'Want to come in?' And he said, 'This is as far as I go.'"

Bella squints at me, as if there must be something I'm missing. "And then?"

"He kissed me on the forehead, like you do with your little sister."

Bella doesn't bother to hide her cringe. "Ouch."

"Yeah."

She's quiet for a few seconds. "I don't get it. You two are totally into each other."

Oh, the mortification. I drop a hand over my eyes. "Apparently that's not the case."

Bella snorts. "Honey, I *saw* the way that boy looked at you the other night. Like he wanted to have you for dessert. Just watching the two of you size each other up got me all hot and bothered. I had to stop in Rafe's room on the way home and strip him naked and..."

I hold up a hand for silence at the same time that Rafe does, too. "I get it." No need to hear the details. And whatever Bella thought she saw at Capri's, it wasn't there. If it had been, I wouldn't be alone right now. Or, at the very least, I would have gotten a real kiss.

Damn it.

"Something is wrong with this picture," Bella muses, lifting her coffee cup.

I'm tired of thinking about it. "Obviously." Into my own coffee cup, I add, "I'm totally unfuckable."

"What?" she asks.

As it happens, three cups of coffee makes me really tetchy. "I *said*, I'm obviously totally unfuckable!"

Several heads turn in our direction, and Rafe claps a hand over his mouth and tries to stifle his laughter.

And all I can think is: *Thanks, January. Thanks a lot.*

DJ

Hockey players are good roommates, but they aren't tidy. I'm doing laps around the house I share with four other guys, cleaning up. This weekend the team has two away games—Brown last night and RPI tonight.

I could have asked them to put their shit away before they left on Friday, but I didn't want anyone to question my motives. So I've taken it upon myself to throw books and gym bags into bedrooms. I take a pair of dirty socks out from between two couch cushions and toss them into Orsen's room, though they may or may not belong to him. I stack up all the video game paraphernalia and wash every glass I find in the public areas of the house.

Lianne Challice is coming over. To my house.

Crazy.

When I texted her two days ago asking if she still wanted help reading MacBeth, she said she did. I'd suggested the library, but she'd pointed out that you're not supposed to perform Shakespeare at the library where people are trying to study.

But we're going to be really good at it, I'd teased.

Naturally, she'd replied. *But I'm not giving a free show. Come over here?*

I couldn't do that, of course. And I didn't want to explain. So I invited her over to my place instead. And since I needed a plausible excuse to switch the venue to my place—other than the truth, which is that I'm not allowed into her dorm—I'd added, *I'll make dinner.*

My heart palpitated after I hit send on that one. Because it sounded like a date. And I owed her a date.

But I can't fucking date. I can't.

That sounds great, she'd replied.

That had settled it. I would make her dinner just this once. So it had better be awesome.

My family is Italian, and I make a good lasagna. So I'd spent my morning picking up supplies at the grocery store, then making two lasagnas. My mom has a saying: never make just one lasagna. "It's an amazing dish, but it's a pain in the backside," she always says. "Only a fool makes one of them. Always make two. You can eat twice for the effort of cooking once."

So I did. One of them I wrapped up and froze. The other is in the oven now, making the house smell awesome. Lianne is due in ten minutes, so I'm spending that time panic-cleaning. The living room looks decent enough after my attentions so I head into my room and make my bed. Lianne won't be setting foot in my bedroom tonight, of course, but if she sticks her head in here I don't want her to think I'm a slob.

This year I seem to spend ninety percent of my time worrying about what other people think of me. It's exhausting.

From my back pocket, my phone rings. "Hello?" I answer, wishing I didn't sound winded. I might clean my house to impress a girl, but I sure didn't want her to know.

"Daniel? It's Jack."

Jack is the lawyer, and the last person I want to talk to right now. "It's Saturday night," I blurt out. Why the hell would he call now?

"I know," he chuckles. "But I'm having one of *those* weeks. I was in court all day yesterday and didn't get a chance to tell you that the college gave us the meeting I asked for."

That stops me cold. "They did? The other lawyer couldn't get them to do that."

Jack chuckles again. "I told them we would sue for discrimination and slander if they didn't give you a forum to tell your side of the story."

Fuck. "But I don't want to sue anyone." I just want it to all go away.

"I know that. But the college needed a reminder that the rest of your life hangs in the balance. And threat of a countersuit was the best way for me to make that point."

This whole thing is such a fucking disaster. Who sues their own college and then later holds out his hand for a diploma?

"Daniel, look—they understand that I'm the bad guy here. My role is to be the one who agitates. They don't think you're sitting in your dorm room plotting a revolution."

"I don't have a dorm room," I mutter.

"*Exactly*. And I'm the one whose job it is to point out that they've been unfair."

"Okay," I say, my chest tightening with misery. I hate this, but I'll hate being kicked out of school more.

"They gave us February twelfth. That's in less than a month."

My gut clenches. This is just like scheduling surgery. You're supposed to be glad to get it over with, but who wants to be cut open in the first place? "June would be better," I say. If I could just get one more semester under my belt...

"The girl will sue if they put off her case until June."

Of course she will.

"You and I need to meet next weekend. I'm going to ask you questions and give you some tips. We're going to rehearse your testimony. I know you're a busy guy. We can do this on either Saturday or Sunday. Which one works best for you?"

"Uh..." I close my eyes and think of the hockey schedule. Luckily, the men's hockey team has another road trip planned. "I guess Saturday is okay."

"All right—I'm putting you in for Saturday the twenty-fifth. You'll get an email from my assistant confirming the location and time. And let me say one more thing—you need to be very careful for the next couple of weeks. Squeaky clean. No complaints against you for anything, no matter how trivial."

That just makes me ornery. "I never had a single complaint against me." *Just this one enormous one.*

"Of course you haven't." My lawyer's voice is low and quiet. "Just be mindful that you can't afford to be part of anything questionable. If your friends are stirring up trouble, just remove yourself from the situation."

"Okay."

"Hang in there, Daniel. This is progress."

Too bad progress feels like being run over by a Zamboni. "Thank you. I'll look for that email."

We disconnect, and I kick one of the old armchairs that Orsen and his teammates found to furnish the house.

I do *not* want to tell a room full of college administrators what happened in my bedroom on a random night last April. How I had sex with my neighbor (and lab partner) even though I wasn't very attracted to her. Even though it was all her idea, and we weren't drunk. It was perfectly consensual and perfectly legal and still not a moment I'm looking forward to describing.

I'll have to admit to the whole world that I'd been kind of a shit, even if it wasn't the kind she'd accused me of being. In the interest of defending myself, I was *still* going to sound like the world's biggest asshole. It was just a hookup. My family will be sitting there listening to me describe who removed whose clothes, and who first brought up the idea of a condom.

Afterward, I never called this girl. Didn't ask her out. Didn't bring up that night again. It wasn't my proudest moment, and everyone I love will know all about it.

Even if I win, I'll lose.

My phone rings again. I take it out of my pocket warily. If it's the lawyer, I'm not answering again. Let him leave a voicemail if there's something he forgot to say.

LIANNE the display reads. And goddamn, I'd forgotten she was on her way over. I'd actually forgotten. "Hello?"

"Can you do me a favor?" She's breathing hard like someone who's been running. "Open your door in about sixty seconds. But don't show your face."

"Why?"

"Photographer."

Five seconds later my hands are on the deadbolt. I pull the door open a crack and wait.

"Thank you," her voice says into my ear. Then, "Go fuck yourself," she says a little louder, to someone else.

"You kiss your mother with that mouth?" a male voice asks.

"My mother? Why don't you go stalk her? She likes attention, even from assholes."

I want to look out the door, but she told me not to. And there's no peep hole.

Lianne has ended our call, but now I hear feet on the front steps. A small hand pushes the door open. She steps into the room and slams the door behind herself. "Fucker," she grumbles.

I try a joke. "Aw, but I think so highly of *you*."

She gives a little frustrated shriek. "Sometimes I hate my life."

"Sing it to me, sister." I cross the room to the picture window. The guy outside is studying the house, but for the moment his camera hangs loosely on his chest. "What does he want?"

Lianne shakes her head. "Just pictures. He'll sell them to a tabloid, and they'll write a fake story. Princess Vindi's near-death experience. Her bout with bulimia. Her alien love child. Whatever. I'm not very interesting so they have to make their own news."

"Should you call the police?"

She shakes her head. "He's not on private property. These guys know their rights and they're really good at making sure they can't get into any real trouble."

Out the window, the photographer just stands there, a patient expression on his face. "So what do we do?"

"We read the Scottish play," Lianne says, peeling off her coat. "He'll get bored and cold eventually."

"Okay. But dinner first, right? I made lasagna."

Lianne's face lights up. "Is that what smells so good?"

"Yeah, I think it's done, too." She follows me into the kitchen, where I peek into the oven. The cheese is bubbling everywhere, and the top has browned. "My mother made sure that my brother and I knew how to make three dishes."

"What are the other two?" Lianne asks, coming to stand beside me. Because of the dramatic entrance she'd made, I hadn't gotten a good look at her yet. Every time I see Lianne she looks better than the last. Tonight she's wearing skinny jeans that make her waist look tiny, and a sweater that feels ridiculously soft when she brushes up against me.

I have to fight the urge to measure both the sweater's softness and the size of her waist with my hands. "Um..." What was the question? "I make a nice frittata, and I can do roast chicken."

"I can't cook at all," she confesses. "But I suppose if you want to live off campus, it's handy to learn."

I never wanted to live off campus, but I'm not going to bring that up. "Want a soda? I have Coke and diet."

She opens the refrigerator and grabs a can of diet. "Thanks!"

Shot scored. I bought those just for her.

I plate up two big squares of lasagna. There's Caesar salad, too, though I bought it at Gino's on my way home. I divide that onto our two plates. It's a nice meal. I let this girl down once already, and I need her to know that it's not personal.

Nobody ever wants to hear, "It's not you, baby, it's me." But in this case, that's one hundred percent true.

Our plates are ready, but now I don't know where we should sit. The kitchen table is tiny and wedged into the corner. We rarely sit there.

But the couch is right in front of the window, where the asshole photographer probably still waits. We don't have curtains or blinds. My roommates walk around in their underwear all the time anyway—they just don't care. Although there's a curtain rod hanging at the ready. "Hang on a second, okay? I want to cover the living room window."

I duck into Orsen's room. He's got a banner tacked up to his wall. CONGRATULATIONS HARKNESS HOCKEY, CONFERENCE CHAMPS, it reads. The college hung one in each of the houses' dining halls last spring after his team made it all the way to the national championships.

It only takes me a second to pull it down. After carrying it into the living room, I stand on the back of the sofa and drape it over the lonely curtain rod. "There."

When I climb down, Lianne is watching me, her plate in her hands, her face turning red. "I'm sorry, DJ. I shouldn't have come. This is so..." She shakes her head, and her exasperated expression makes my heart give a tug. "One wonders why I don't have any friends, right?"

"Come on, now," I whisper, taking the plate out of her hands. I carry it over to the coffee table. "Forget about the asshole with the telephoto. *He's* the pathetic one, right?"

She plops down on our couch with a groan. "I guess."

"Eat up. We have a play to read." I dash into the kitchen again for my own plate and a Coke. When I return, Lianne is tucking in to her dinner. "This is awesome. I didn't eat pasta for about ten years, and now I don't know how I survived."

I sit down beside her on the sofa. "You didn't eat pasta?" Was that even possible? "My family would starve if it wasn't for pasta."

"Yeah? I've met your brother. Are there more of you?"

I nod my head and swallow a mouthful of lasagna. "We have a little sister, too. Still in high school."

"Who does she look like?" Lianne tilts her head and studies me, and warmth creeps across my face under the heat of her gaze. "You don't look much like your brother. I mean, I can see it in the shape of your face, a little..."

I give her a grin. "You're seeing things then, smalls. I'm adopted."

"Oh, geez." She sets her fork down on her plate. "Sorry! I'm such an idiot."

"Why? People have been saying that to me my whole life."

She's studying me now. "You must get sick of hearing it, though."

I shrug it off. I don't like anyone knowing that it gets to me. I wasn't adopted until I was two. My adoptive parents knew my birth mother from church. She was struggling on Long Island, away from her family back in Colombia. I don't know all the details, but she gave me up and then moved back to her country.

I don't remember her at all.

Time to change the subject. "Do you have siblings?"

"Sort of. Not really." Lianne uses her fork to cut another bite of my lasagna. I'm happy to see that it's disappearing from her plate.

"Sort of? Not really?"

"I have two half brothers. They're in their thirties. The last time I saw them was ten years ago. I'm not even on the Christmas card list."

It's my turn to stare. "Jesus. Sorry."

She lifts her perfect chin to look at me. "Don't be. My father was on his fourth marriage. I was born when he was sixty-five. My brothers were teenagers before I could talk. And my mom made sure that they weren't ever invited to be with us. She didn't like competition of any kind."

"And your dad just put up with that?"

She tilts her head to the side, considering the question. "I think he did whatever he wanted. My family was *never* normal. My dad had acting jobs all over the world, and my mom was a costume designer. So my parents never spent much time together in the same house. I'm pretty sure my father saw at least as much of my brothers as he saw of me..." Her eyes go soft. "He was a lot of fun, my dad. The life of the party. I always knew he was interested in me, but only up to a point. Nobody ever got more than a tiny fraction of his attention, but when it was your turn, there was nobody better."

"He passed away, right?" I ask.

She nods. "I was eleven. There was some big scandal, of course. He was with some other woman when he died." She rolls her eyes. "My mother had three memorials for him. One in France. One in Hollywood. One in New York. There's nothing that woman won't milk."

Yikes. "Your family is a little more colorful than mine."

"That's a kind way to put it." She smiles at me, and I feel it in the center of my chest. This girl's smile is something else. All that perfection lit up. It's powerful stuff.

After we've eaten our fill, Lianne carries our plates to the kitchen and returns with two glasses of water. "Reading out loud makes you thirsty," she says, setting down the glasses and settling onto the sofa next to me. "Just tell me if you need a break, okay? We don't want to strain your voice." She kicks off her shoes and tucks her slender feet beneath her body. Then she hands me one of two identical paperback copies of Macbeth. "Ready?"

"Yeah." I open mine and flip past the introduction. This feels more intimate than I'd expected. But of course we'd sit close together. We don't want to shout across the room at each other.

Though at this distance I can smell the sweet scent of her shampoo.

We're studying, asshole, I remind myself. "So how do you want this to go?" I ask, settling my thumb on Act 1, Scene 1.

"At the beginning we'll take turns alternating lines, regardless of who they belong to. But whenever Lady M is in a scene, I'll do her part."

"Okay."

She purses her perfect, pink lips and begins to read the first line, which belongs to Witch #1. "When shall we three meet again? In thunder lightning or in rain?"

Feeling slightly self-conscious, I read the second witch's line. "When the hurlyburly's done, when the battle's lost and won."

"That will be ere the set of sun," she returns.

It takes only a couple of minutes until I forget to feel self-conscious, because it takes a lot of concentration to pronounce Shakespeare's verse. I relax into the sound of our two voices, and in the next scene I'm better able to sink into the story. Three Scotsmen recount a battle they've just won, and it's exciting. "If I say sooth, I must report they were as cannons overcharged with double cracks, so they doubly redoubled strokes upon the foe."

I haven't read Macbeth since high school English, and I'd forgotten how creepy it is. Witches. Death. Dark poetry. Whenever I finish a line, I'm rewarded with the sound of Lianne's voice. She reads in a calm and measured tone. She isn't acting out the parts, just stepping through the language like I am, listening to the words as they come.

When Macbeth meets the witches, they tell him he'll be king. But he doesn't trust it. Then Lady Macbeth finally takes the stage, and Lianne sits up straighter beside me. The scene has her reading a letter from Macbeth, and then worrying that he'll be afraid to seize the crown and fulfill the witches' prophecy. "Yet I do fear thy nature; it is too full o' the milk of human kindness to catch the nearest way."

We've only been reading for a few minutes when Lady Macbeth plots the king's murder.

I stop Lianne after we read that scene, handing her a drink of water. "Quite a part you've picked out, smalls. I'd forgotten that the whole thing was her idea. Mr. M doesn't even *agree* to do it. Not really."

"He does so!" In her excitement, Lianne wiggles closer to me, flipping the pages of her book. "Here—he says, 'We will speak further.'"

"No way." I laugh. "That's just something a husband says to get rid of his wife before the hockey game comes on TV. 'Honey, we'll talk about it later.' It's not the same as saying, 'You're right, I need to murder the king.'"

Lianne turns her face away and laughs, and I love the sound of it, and the weight of her knee against my thigh. She's near enough to me that all my senses are on high alert. "You make a good point, sir."

Since I'd do anything to make this girl smile at me again, I make a goofy fist pump. Then I poke her in the side. "Your line, Lady Mac..."

She moves fast, reaching up to clamp a hand over my mouth. "Don't say it, unless you're reading it right from the script. It's bad luck."

I can't help it. Pure instinct makes me kiss the palm that's pressed against my lips before lifting it away. "Fine. I'm not very superstitious. But I don't need any bad luck right now, either."

"Why?" she whispers.

Whoops. The urge to unburden myself of my problems is so fucking strong. I haven't felt so comfortable with anyone in a long time. And Lianne is everything I like in a girl—she's smart and fun, with a great sense of humor. And I'm so attracted to her that I ache when she looks up at me with her warm, intelligent gaze.

But I don't stay a word. "Your line," I prompt.

We get through Act One, and then take a short break. Lianne

peeks out the window, peering around the edge of my makeshift curtain. "I think he gave up. I hope he did, anyway."

"Wouldn't he have better luck stalking famous people in New York or L.A.?" I wonder aloud.

She drops the curtain. "Absolutely. And I'm not very newsworthy. So I really can't figure out why he's here. I was thinking of asking my manager to look into it."

I hate the idea of this weirdo following her around campus. I mean—what if he's some crackpot with a thing for her? "No point in waiting. Why don't you call him now?"

She bites her lip, and I wish I could bite it for her. "Okay, you're right. Thanks."

I go into the kitchen to give her some privacy. I'd bought brownies at the grocery store, and I cut them into bite-sized squares and put them on a plate. When I return, Lianne is already off the phone. "What did he say?"

Lianne shrugs. "I left a message. He isn't great about following up when I ask for help. But maybe he'll ask his assistant to look into it. I'll probably get a lecture about security. He never wanted me to come to Harkness in the first place."

"Why?"

"Money, of course. I'm a better paycheck when I'm working. And I'm harder to control when I'm not in California. That's why I chose this place, actually. Because I couldn't see him showing up in Connecticut to boss me around." Her grin is sweet and evil at the same time.

"Well." I nudge her knee with mine. "I'm glad you did."

She gives me a happy smile, and I inwardly kick myself. I can't flirt with this girl. I can make her dinner and be a good friend. The fact that she's even sitting here beside me means more to me than I'll ever let on. A year ago, I had a million friends, a fun job at the rink, and another three years at Harkness ahead of me.

Now? I've got the job and that's all. And even that will end if they kick my ass out.

Lianne smooths her copy of the play open to the start of Act II. She nudges me with a slender knee. "You're Banquo."

I deliver the line. "How goes the night, boy?"

Lianne's voice is low and steady. "The moon is down. I have not heard the clock."

Banquo's next line is, "And she goes down at twelve." For some reason this line sounds dirty to me, and my stomach contracts with a laugh that I hold in.

"I take 't 'tis later, sir."

Wouldn't you know it? My next line is: "Hold my sword." I choke it out, but it's a struggle.

Lianne uses her book to slap me on the belly. "Mind out of the gutter, DJ. This is serious business." But then she bursts out laughing.

"Sorry," I sputter. "Maybe you should have hired a theater student."

Grinning, she rolls her eyes. "You're not the first guy to ever turn the bard into a dirty joke. I'll bet there's even Shakespeare porn."

There's something distracting about the word "porn" coming from her exquisite little mouth. "You mean like..." I wrack my brain for a good title. "*The Taming of the Screw?*"

"Sure. Or *Two Gentlemen Do Verona?*"

"Good one. And don't forget *As You Lick It.*" Lianne giggles, and now I've made her face turn red. "Your turn."

"Uh, *King Rear.*"

"Yeah!" I high-five her. "And *Coriolanus!* You don't even have to change the title. Unless it's to *Coriolanal.*"

Lianne snorts, and her hands fly to her mouth. "Oh my God. You are *way* too good at this. And bonus points for obscurity. Nobody knows that play." She wipes her eyes. "Come on. Back to work. Read Banquo's line."

So I do. And I manage not to laugh again, even when Banquo

says the king went to bed after having been "in unusual pleasure." Not even when I declare I've kept "my bosom franchised."

Since we're home alone, it's awfully quiet. And when rain starts pounding the window behind us, we have to speak up a little. But Lianne doesn't stop. She reads the famous speech by Macbeth, "is this a dagger I see before me?" And I forget about our jokes and the rain and everything else, because she really gets into it. The highly paid actress sitting beside me has wrapped the language all around herself like a coat. I close my eyes and hear only a tortured man trying to decide if he can plunge a dagger into his king and seize the crown. The speech is perfect, and the last line arrives before I'm ready. "I go, and it is done. The bell invites me. Hear it not, Duncan, for it is a knell that summons thee to heaven or to hell."

I have chills when I open my eyes to find her looking up at me.

Chapter Eleven

WHAT? LIKE THAT'S WEIRD?

Lianne

I can't interpret the expression on DJ's face. He's studying me, as if he'll be quizzed later on the details of my features. I don't understand the intensity of his gaze, but I don't mind it, either.

Then he smiles at me in that way of his—like he sees me all the way through.

In my life, I've been some exciting places—red carpet ceremonies. Movie debuts. Yachts in the south of France. I've met more movie stars than you can shake a wand at. But I've never had as much fun as I do whenever DJ and I are in the same room. It doesn't matter if we're drinking watery beer at the pizza place or sitting on his roommate's old sofa with books. Wherever I can see his lopsided smile, I feel happier than if I'd just won an Oscar.

Then he opens his mouth and says the perfect thing. "You really want this part, huh? This plot is so sinister."

It takes me a second to answer, because I'm so touched that someone is interested in what I do. Even my asshole agent has never asked why I want this part—or any part. And here's DJ, waiting to hear what's on my mind. He leans forward, listening with his whole self. And we're so close together! If I leaned forward, we'd be...

Wait. What was the question? *Focus, Lianne!* "The fact that it's sinister is what I like about it. Shakespeare didn't write any other female parts like this one. Lady M is much more interesting than Juliet. The plot is messy and complicated. Just like real life. There's no magic fix."

"No kidding." DJ's eyes drop to the page and stay there.

Now, I'm a decent actress. And all good acting is the interpretation of emotion. He's got this whole dark and broody vibe working. But he doesn't revel in it. It's not intentional. I can see so clearly that this boy is troubled. Those big, expressive eyes don't always shine with joy. There are shadows there, too. Something's bothering him, but he's not going to tell me what it is.

We probably don't know each other well enough yet for me to ask. He's so close to me, though. I feel our awareness of each other grow loud. It's like the scratchy silence between tracks on an old vinyl record. Giving in to temptation, I reach up and palm my favorite part of his jaw—the squared-off bit where the stubble looks dark against his smooth skin. His eyes fall shut when I touch him, and unless I'm crazy, he leans into my hand.

A roll of thunder startles me, and my hand twitches. DJ's eyes fly open and he gives me an amused smile.

He's *right there*. We are as close together as two people can be who aren't kissing. I've never planted a kiss on a guy before. But DJ makes me feel brave. And he won't mind, right? He made me dinner. He's reading the world's most depressing play as a favor to me. On a Saturday night!

Yes, I can do this. I can kiss him, and it won't end in disaster.

But I don't do it. Too scary.

DJ watches me think about it, his smile growing wider the whole time. Then he reaches his hand out and cups my jaw. We're mirroring each other.

Before I can finish the thought, he slides his big hand around to the back of my head and tugs me closer. And strong arms pull me against a hard chest before I can get my panic on.

Yessssss. He dips his chin and presses hungry lips against mine. Happiness is being wrapped into a kiss.

I make a ridiculous whimpering sound, but maybe DJ doesn't notice. He gathers me closer as he deepens our kiss. His mouth is both soft and demanding at the same time. I sort of ooze against him, melting into a puddle of helpless goo as he gently parts my lips and tastes me. All I can do is lean into it. His next kiss is deep and warm and everything I ever wanted. He tastes like cola and Shakespeare and Saturday nights. I'm greedy, like Veruca Salt at the chocolate factory. But without that bitchy voice.

Loud rain beats against the window, or maybe that's my pounding heart. DJ is kissing me and I might *expire* from wanting him. In fact, my hands have begun to explore his chest, which makes him groan. And I love that sound.

But then there's another noise, and it takes my lust-fogged brain a moment to register the voices outside and the clatter of keys in the front door. I leap away from DJ, back to my own cushion of the couch.

I pick up my book just as the front door bursts open. Orsen lumbers into the room, shaking himself like a big wet dog. He's quickly followed by DJ's brother. They're both carrying giant duffel bags—big enough to stuff a body inside. Before he passes us, Leo Trevi notices us on the couch, then quickly looks away. Then he looks back again in a classic double take. "Whoa! Hey, you're—" His eyebrow quirks. "—Reading *Shakespeare* on the couch?"

"What. Like that's weird?" I snap. I'm quite grumpy that he's just interrupted the hottest kiss of my life.

Leo's mouth opens. Then closes. Then opens. "Uh... I guess not."

"Why was the door locked?" Orsen asks. Then he looks from

me to DJ and shakes his head. "Never mind." Then he disappears into his room.

The door was locked because of the asshole photographer. But the fact that Orsen believes otherwise makes my face flame. All of me is pretty much on fire at the moment, and I sure hope it doesn't show.

DJ frowns up at his brother. "Why are you here?"

"Where is the love?" His brother chuckles. "Can I throw my gear in your room?"

DJ grunts his assent. "I meant—how are you back from Providence already?"

Leo disappears momentarily to toss a giant hockey bag into one of the doorways at the back of the house. "It was a four o'clock game. Perfect, right?" He reappears, grinning. "We finish a two-game sweep and still have time to party. Feel like setting up your stuff and spinning some discs? Orsen just invited the whole team over."

"Oh." DJ closes his book and turns to me. "Maybe we should hit the library."

Nooooo! Not hardly. I've made it half way through my freshman year without attending an actual college party. It's time to peel the big L off my forehead. "I'd rather play with your DJ equipment."

It takes me a second to figure out why Leo doubles over with laughter. I replay the sentence in my head, and a flush creeps up my shoulders and neck. *Play with DJ's equipment...* Just shoot me. "For *music!*" I sputter.

But Trevi the elder has already laughed himself into the kitchen. "Lasagna!" he yells from the other room. "Hell yes! Deej, I can have a piece, right?"

"Sure," DJ grumbles.

My face is still on fire, but I don't have to look at DJ yet because the front door opens again, and another trio of hockey players come trundling in, but without their gear. "Hey!" the first one says. His jacket reads RIKKER. The second jacket says

O'HANE. The third face is one I know. It's one of Bella's besties, Pepe. "Bonsoir," the big Canadian greets me.

"*Avez-vous gagné votre jeu?*" I ask. *Did you win your game?*

"*Naturellement*," he replies.

"*Merveilleux!*"

"You speak French?" DJ asks me.

"Sure. One of the benefits of getting dragged around Europe as a child."

He smiles, then stands and reaches a hand toward me. When I take it, he pulls me to my feet. "Let's get out the turntable. I'll teach you to beatmatch."

"Cool! I've done that a few times." I'm not letting go of his hand until he makes me.

He tugs me toward his room, presumably for the turntable and computer. "Of course you have."

DJ's room is small, like a little monk's cell. The double bed takes up most of the space, and the place isn't decorated at all. There are no posters on the wall. It's tidy, though. The books on the desk are stacked into a square pile, and all the pens in the pencil cup point downward.

I open my mouth to remark on it, but I don't get the chance. DJ takes my face in two hands and kisses me. *Hard.* It's sudden and the way he steps into my space until our bodies are aligned is impossibly hot. He gives a sort of growl that rumbles through my chest in a happy wave.

Just as I'm really getting into the swing of it, he releases me, steps back, and leans down to fish for something under the bed. "Haven't used this stuff in a while," he says in a completely normal voice. A coil of cable lands on the bed where he tosses it. He kicks his brother's hockey bag out of the way and reaches under the bed for what must be a portable turntable in its case.

Meanwhile, I'm just standing there trembling, mouth open, face flushed. I mean—after a kiss like that, I need a cold shower or at least a few minutes alone to cool down. He's actually whistling now, going about his business as if the room didn't just tilt a minute ago when we tried to climb in each other's mouths.

"You coming, smalls?" DJ gives me a smile, which doesn't help matters. Because those dimples make my insides feel squishy.

"S...sure," I say shakily, following him out of the room.

Chapter Twelve

CHERRY LIP GLOSS

DJ

An hour later, the house is full of people, and the doorbell is still ringing. I keep opening it, wondering when the cops are going to show. I didn't used to be a worrier, but my lawyer's advice to stay out of trouble is ringing in my ears. Though I couldn't bail on this party, because Lianne is here at my invitation and she's having a blast.

We set up my gear on a table in the corner beside the sofa. I've let Lianne choose all the music, and she's on a classic rap kick. At the moment, she's dancing on the coffee table with Pepe, everyone's favorite tipsy Canadian. I've already removed all the hockey magazines and empty cups, so she won't stumble. And I've tucked my brother's banner around the window more carefully. If that reporter is still out there, I don't want him capturing this. And every time she sets down a half-empty drink, I take a big gulp of it, because I'm not sure she understands that there's a pretty hefty dose of vodka in this punch that Orsen whipped up. Lianne must weigh about ninety-eight pounds soaking wet.

Okay—that's really not the image I need right now.

A few kisses with Lianne and my head is spun around like the records on the turntable. It's not wise to start something with her. My rational brain knows this. But she's ridiculously attractive to me. She's also a natural dancer; my eyes keep drifting to the sway of her hips and the shake of her pert little ass.

It's been a while since I felt this kind of attraction. A *long* while. Like, I wondered if my dick was broken. I didn't have a sexual thought all last semester. That's pretty freaking weird, and if I didn't have a hundred other problems I'd probably be worried about it.

Lianne though...she just kills me. Up on the coffee table, she and Pepe shake their butts to a funny part in a Public Enemy song, conversing in a language I don't speak. She's wearing a silly smile, and I just want to haul her off of there and kiss her again.

She's having too much fun, though. And why shouldn't she? Except for me, all the people in this room will still be at Harkness after the midterm break. She should make friends who might actually stick around.

When I look around the room, though, I notice that not everyone is friendly to her. Lianne is clearly a source of curiosity. From some people there are sidelong glances and whispered asides, as if Lianne is an alien species or a zoo animal. One girl is downright nasty, and unfortunately that girl is Amy, my brother's girlfriend.

At first, I hoped I was imagining it when Amy elbowed her puck bunny friends every time Lianne bent over the turntable. But then I heard her make a snarky comment about Lianne's powers of sorcery, and I realized Amy really has nothing better to do with her time than to poke fun at someone she doesn't know.

My brother's girlfriend is a bitch on wheels, and while I have my theories about Leo's choices, I still don't know how he puts up with her. He's too easygoing to enjoy someone so high mainte- nance. Every time I hear another insult fall from her carefully made-up face, I can only assume that she's more fun in bed than out of it. When I cross the room again, I hear Amy say, "If I were her, I'd use my magic powers to increase my cup size to at least a B."

I give her an ornery glare, but she doesn't even notice. My opinion doesn't even register with her because I don't play for her favorite hockey team.

"DJ," she says, grabbing my biceps as I walk past. "Play me something from this decade?"

She always speaks to me like I'm the help. Not even a *please*. "You'll have to talk to Lianne," I say. "She's the DJ tonight." I'm not trying to complicate Lianne's evening, but I'll bet Amy is too self-absorbed to actually go and make eye contact with my favorite freshman.

But it turns out I'm wrong about the girl. (This is a theme in my life.) She marches over to Lianne and taps her hand. Lianne hops off the coffee table and cocks her head to hear better. Amy makes her request, and I watch as Lianne gives her a once-over, trying to decide whether or not to give in.

"'Centuries' is the team's win song," I hear Amy whine. "It's by Fall Out Boy. The team will expect you to play it."

This is laughable, because most of the guys she's referring to are at the other end of the room playing video games. They don't give a fuck.

"Interesting pick," Lianne says, hopping off the coffee table. "The riff in the middle almost makes it eligible for the jukebox at Capri's. That bit by Suzanne Vega."

"Who?" Amy asks, scrunching up her perfect nose.

Lianne only shakes her head. "They're just not teaching nineties hits to the kiddies anymore. You can cue it up if you want. Knock yourself out. I'm going to see what they're playing." She points at the boys at the other end of the room.

I'm a little bummed she gave in. Amy is wealthy and attractive and used to getting people to do her bidding. People should say no to her more often.

But Lianne gives me a little, secret smile and drifts toward the other end of the room.

The front door opens for the millionth time, admitting Bella and her boyfriend Rafe. A cheer goes up among the hockey team. As the former team manager, Bella is very popular. "Nice win tonight, guys!" she calls. Then she does a double take. "Lianne Challice! I've been looking all over for you."

"By 'all over' I assume you mean my room?" Lianne asks. She's squinting at the TV screen, a studious frown on her beautiful face.

"And I texted!" Bella walks over to give her a soft swat on the head. "Thanks for telling me about the party. What kind of a friend are you?"

"Didn't know about the party until it started," Lianne mutters. She's leaning over Orsen's shoulder now, captivated by whatever game he's playing.

"Huh," Bella grunts, her forehead wrinkling. "Then you owe me a few other details."

"Hey man," Rafe says, high-fiving me. "How are you?"

"All right. Drinks are in the kitchen. Help yourself to whatever." Hell, Rafe is underage, too. But what's one more? This party had better not get busted. I feel like I'm seconds away from turning down the music like somebody's grandpa.

I decide to watch Lianne some more, because that always takes my blues away.

She's biting one of her small fingers now, like someone who wants to say something but isn't sure she should. I watch her eyes go from worried to exasperated. "Gah," she says. Then she leans on the back of Orsen's chair. "Okay, NO! Don't go that way. You *just* saw the troll sweat on the floor, right?"

Four heads swivel around to look at her. "What?" my brother says, which is exactly what the rest of them are thinking. They're trying to wrap their heads around the idea that a girl knows something about their gory video game.

Lianne rolls her eyes, pointing at the screen. "That shimmer in the corner? A troll passed through here. You need an x-force weapon or you're toast."

"Um..." O'Hane chuckles. "Okay, that's probably why we're always biting it on this level. Who has an x-force?" He looked from one player to another. "Bueller? Bueller?"

"I could...uh...lend you one," Lianne says. "I mean, I don't want to hone in on your game."

My brother reaches over the back of the big chair he's sitting on, grabs Lianne's hand and tugs her around toward him, while Orsen starts laughing. "Come here and teach us more about troll sweat," he says.

Lianne perches on the generous roll-arm of Leo's chair. He puts the controller in her hands. Those small fingers fly over the buttons as she logs into the game under her player name—Vindikator. A new avatar leaps onto the screen. It's a young man with golden hair and impeccable armor.

There's a chorus of approval. "Nice," Orsen says.

"Your avatar is a dude!" says someone else.

"Holy shit—you're Vindikator?" O'Hane yelps.

"Don't tell *anyone*," Lianne says sharply. "It's my little secret."

"Wow," O'Hane breathes. "Vindikator is...he's like... *famous*."

Messages start popping up on one side of the screen. "VKA-TOR! Where you been tonight?" And, "You're back, bro!"

"Oh my God." Orsen chuckles. "You have a following."

Without comment, Lianne does something that clears all the messages off the screen. "Okay, who wants the X-grade weapon? You can use a sword or a spear. There are advantages and disadvantages to both."

In the silence that follows, four hockey players exchange amused glances. It's clear they have no idea what she's talking about.

"Um, which one is bigger?" O'Hane asks. "Size matters." The others chuckle.

"The sword. And mine is *lengthy*." She taps the buttons until a gleaming sword appears on the screen. "Step right up, boys. Who's man enough to use this thing?"

My brother raises his hand, so Lianne does something which transfers the sword to Leo.

"Whoa," he says. "I look fierce."

"Yes, you're very intimidating," Lianne agrees. "Just don't cut off your feet, okay? I've seen that happen and it ain't pretty."

"Good to know," my brother says with a grin, giving Lianne's knee a friendly squeeze.

I'm surprised at the strength of my inappropriate jealousy when my brother touches her. He didn't mean anything by it, and Leo would never make a move on a girl I liked. But I hate seeing it nonetheless.

Jesus. As if I have *any* claim on her. Our friendship is probably toast after Harkness makes a decision about me. At least when I'm gone, and Lianne finds a great guy, I won't be around to watch it happen.

The only silver lining is that I'm not the most jealous person in the room. Amy has changed the music to Fall Out Boy, like she said she would. Now she's swinging her hips around, looking for a little attention. And not finding it.

Every dude in the room is staring at the screen, where my brother's avatar has gone troll hunting. His pals follow him down a corridor, where there are creepy shadows between the torches on the walls. "Come out wherever you are!" Leo taunts the screen. "Imma gonna mow you down for once." He heads toward a turn at the end of the tunnel.

"Wait." Lianne grabs his hand, preventing him from advancing. "He's right around that corner. Let him come to you. Then go for the heart, it's quicker. It will cost you less energy."

Amy is standing beside me now, watching Lianne and my brother. She's stopped shaking her hips and started glaring.

Everyone stares at the screen expectantly. Nothing happens.

"Um, I think..." Leo starts. Then a giant, sweating beast lunges into view, coming for him. "Fuuuuuuck!" my brother says, laughing. On the screen he raises the sword and hits the troll in its gut.

It roars as blood gushes out and onto the floor.

"Ew," Amy pouts.

"You have to hit the heart," Lianne repeats just as the troll lifts its arm to club my brother.

Leo maneuvers the controller until his avatar can take another swing. This time he hits higher.

The troll crumples into a disgusting heap on the floor.

"Awesome," several hockey players say at once.

All at once Lianne's avatar perks up and begins to moon walk like Michael Jackson. And "Beat It" is playing in the background.

Orsen points at the screen and roars with laughter, and Lianne buries her face in her hands.

Chuckling, my brother puts the controller onto her lap. "What's the matter?"

"I forgot I wrote that script," she says, looking up at the screen. "It was just a little joke for whenever a troll bites it."

"Wait," Leo stops her. "You wrote a script? Like...you *changed* the game?"

"Sure." She shrugs. "That's how I feed my dragons, too. I automate things."

"You have dragons?" Orsen asks. "Like, plural?"

"Yeah." Lianne smiles. "A few."

"How many?" he presses.

"Well, eighty."

There are sounds of disbelief. "Show us," Orsen demands. "That's so cool."

"Okay." She presses a button on the controller and the scene dissolves onto a sunny hillside, with a castle in the distance. The viewpoint seems to fly over the rolling terrain, as if in a dream.

"Whoa," Leo says, reaching over to give Lianne's elbow a squeeze. "You can *fly?* That's cool."

"Trevi!" Amy whines. "Come and dance with me." She walks over to the other side of his chair, takes his hand and tugs. "I put on a great playlist."

"In a bit, babe. I want to see Lianne's dragons."

"Do you want to play?" Lianne asks sweetly. "I could probably fashion up some designer armor for you so you don't hurt yourself too badly."

Amy gives her a sneer, looking quite capable of spitting fire, like one of Lianne's dragons. "No thanks." She stomps off, while all the other eyes are focused on the screen. There's a sound of awe as the camera sweeps over the castle wall and into what looks like a medieval zoo, with a different colorful dragon in every stall.

The beasts lift their heads as Lianne's avatar floats down on a set of hidden wings, landing among them. "Hi babies! I'm home!" the avatar exclaims.

The Harkness hockey team laughs while Orsen passes around fresh bottles of beer.

While Lianne and her newest fans talk about DragonFire, I do some tidying up. I carry a bunch of empties into the kitchen. My plan is to take them out the back door to the recycling bin, but when I open the door to the back hall, there are two figures making out in the dark. One of them has the other one pushed up against the wall, wrists trapped by strong hands.

It's my brother's teammate Rikker, kissing the hell out of his boyfriend, Graham. The back hall is a small space, and they're in the way of my errand. So I drop the bag of empties to the floor with a jingle. "Take these out back when you're done, kids."

One of them grunts his acknowledgment, and I retreat, leaving them to it.

Just another day with the Harkness Hockey team.

I finally get Lianne back about a half-hour later, after my

brother and his friends have taken a few dragons on test drives into battle. She looks flushed and happy.

"That looked fun," I tell her. "I'm not much for gaming, but I did enjoy watching Amy get all jealous."

Lianne grins. "I'll bet she put on this Miley Cyrus tune just to torture me. My ears are bleeding."

"You better fix that," I say. "Can't have that."

She leans over my laptop. My eye is drawn to a creamy inch of Lianne's neck just below her ear, and I'm thinking about kissing it. But Bella and Scarlet Crowley run up and thrust out a drink for Lianne. "For that, you win a margarita."

Lianne straightens up. "For what? Troll hunting?"

Scarlet tilts her head subtly toward whiny Amy, who has taken residence on the chair's arm in exactly the same spot where Lianne had sat before. Staking her territory, obviously. "Yeah, *troll* hunting. Let's just say I'm a fan of your work."

Lianne winks, taking the cup. "I've never had a margarita."

That makes Bella gasp and clutch her heart. "That is *terrible*. A girl's first margarita shouldn't be in a plastic cup. But it's better than nothing."

"Tasty!" Lianne declares after her first sip.

"I'm Scarlet," the other girl says, thrusting out a hand. "And where were you a year ago? That wench has been giving me hell since I started going to hockey team events with Bridger."

Lianne takes a deep pull of her margarita. "Maybe she hates women. I thought it was just me."

"Nope," I argue, my thumb massaging the small of her back. "She only hates the pretty ones."

"Well, yay," Bella says. "I must be very attractive. Because she's never been able to stand me, either."

"And here I thought she only hated sorceresses," Lianne says, leaning into my touch. "If I was a real sorceress, I'd cast a spell on Amy. I'd stun her into next Tuesday."

We all laugh. Pepe walks up with a pitcher of margaritas and tops up Lianne's cup. "Come dance *avec moi*."

She takes his hand and off they go. Lianne changes the music to "Baby Got Back," and they're just goofing around, talking and dancing half-heartedly so that nobody spills his drink. Pepe is a great guy, but now I wish he'd twist an ankle.

Where is all this jealousy coming from?

The party goes on, and I know my lawyer would tell me to get out of here—to take myself out for a nice cup of coffee somewhere, far from this bastion of dance music and underage drinking. But there's no way I'm leaving Lianne here, and she doesn't look like someone who wants to go home.

I collect a couple of used cups and ferry them into the kitchen, feeling like an outsider. I'm like somebody's grouchy dad, surveying the party, looking for things that could go wrong.

Lianne is still dancing with the happy-go-lucky Frenchman, and I can't watch. I'm jealous, and it's not just because he's got his big paw on the waist of the girl I want. On any given Saturday, I used to look as carefree as Pepe does right now. That used to be my life, too.

I tidy up the kitchen, which is a pretty pathetic move. There's a freshman D-man making out with one of Amy's singing-group friends against the refrigerator. They don't even notice as I put the now-empty lasagna pan in the sink to soak. By the time I'm wiping down the counters, they've stumbled off, probably looking for a more private spot, which hopefully will not turn out to be my bedroom.

"There you are!"

The sound of Lianne's happy voice makes me smile immediately. She breezes into the kitchen and hops up onto the counter beside me. But it's a pretty good distance off the floor for someone so short, and maybe the edge where she puts her hand is still wet, because she doesn't quite manage it. My hockey reflexes kick in and I step in front of her before she can tumble off and onto the floor.

Her body pitches against my chest with a warm thud, her chin landing at my shoulder. My arms are full of a pretty girl in a soft sweater.

"Whoops," she whispers. But instead of struggling backward, she puts her hands up to cup the back of my neck. Then she turns her face into my neck and takes a deep breath. "Mmm."

My hands land at her hips, and I give a shiver. She has no idea how potent it is to stand here pressed against her. Each of my senses leaps to attention. And when her lips press against my jaw, I let out a quiet groan.

Lianne lifts her head to look into my eyes at close range. "Hi," she says with a shy grin.

I don't get a chance to answer, because that's when she kisses me, her soft smile landing on mine. "Mmh," I hear myself say as she presses closer. And holy God, we're off to the races. I take over, deepening the kiss. When I part her lips with my tongue, she whimpers into my mouth. She tastes like limes and happiness.

Kissing Lianne is magic. Her soft lips turn down the volume on all my worries. Even the party fades from my consciousness as my tongue begins to stroke hers.

My hips press forward as we kiss, and Lianne's knees tighten around my body, as if she wants to make sure I'm not about to leave her. I'm pressed into the warm center of her, diving into her mouth while she melts like butter against my body. She makes a needy sound in the back of her throat, and I feel it everywhere. Her hands weave into my hair and I pull her closer. We've extinguished all the empty places between our bodies. But still we shift against one another, just double-checking that there's no way we could get any closer without losing all our clothes.

I'm standing in my kitchen and so turned on it's ridiculous.

Then her lips disappear from mine, and for a split second I'm crestfallen. But then she's worshipping my neck with soft, open-mouthed kisses. And Jesus H, it's amazing. The sweep of her tongue at my throat brings me more alive than I've felt in months.

Somebody moans, and I'm pretty sure it's me. My body is screaming for more. And I can't remember why I ever resisted her.

"I like that," Lianne sighs between kisses.

"Hmm?" It's hard to listen when she's setting me on fire.

"You made a noise. A good one." Then she giggles.

Oh, hell. I cup the back of her head and slowly pull away, getting a good look at her. And, damn it, all the signs are there— her eyes aren't focusing well, and her smile is blurry. "Aw, buddy," I say, kissing her once more, softly. "How many margaritas did you have?"

She gives me a sloppy grin. "Doesn't take much. I'm a cheap date. Can we go into your bedroom now?" She punctuates this request with a little burp, and then another giggle. "Please?" She leans against me, running a hand down my chest. "Mmm, I just want to lick you everywhere."

This time when I groan, it's with disappointment. Because no licking is about to happen. I'd never get busy with a drunk girl. And I shouldn't get busy with Lianne, anyway. The timing is terrible, no matter how much I like her. "Smalls, we can't do this tonight," I say gently. But I can't back away, because if I do, she'll tumble off the counter.

"Why?" she yelps. "Is it because I'm socially awkward? Is it because I'm fun sized?"

"It's because you're wasted." Chuckling, I give her one last kiss, this one on the nose.

"But I want to," she argues, her small hand torturing me. Fingers spread wide, she sweeps down my stomach until that naughty hand lands on the bulge in my jeans.

And now I'm biting the inside of my cheek to keep from letting her know how much I wish we could fool around. I catch her slim hand in mine and give it a single kiss. "It's time to take you home."

———

It's a good thing I stopped drinking hours ago.

Bella and Rafe have already left the party. So I borrow Orsen's car. Lianne sobers up a little by the time I explain that we're going to make a run for the garage together, "in case that asshole photographer is out there somewhere."

"It *rained*. I hope his fancy camera got soaked," Lianne grumbles.

"He probably packed it in hours ago," I agree. "But we'll be careful anyway." Lianne seems a little unsteady on her feet as she puts on her coat. "Piggyback ride?" I offer.

"Heck yeah."

I crouch down until she puts her arms around me, then I stand up again, my hands under her knees. I open the door with an elbow and then trot across the darkened driveway and into the open garage.

Lianne kisses the back of my neck before I reluctantly set her down beside the passenger door of Orsen's car. "Hop in, smalls," I say, opening the door for her and eyeing the driveway. There's nobody out there, though.

When she's buckled in, I run around and get into the driver's seat. A minute later we're backing out of the driveway for the two-minute drive to Beaumont House. Lianne is quiet, looking out the window.

I assume she's sleepy, but she turns to me when I pull up at the curb. "I had so much fun tonight," she whispers. "Thank you."

"Don't mention it," I say, my voice rough. God, this girl kills me.

"More Shakespeare later this week?" She smiles when she asks it—an awkward little grin. It promises that Shakespeare won't be our only topic.

"Absolutely."

She opens the door and slides one foot out. I give her left hand a gentle tug. Lianne turns to me with a smile that turns shy when I hold her gaze. I can't resist it. Leaning in, I pull her toward me. We meet above the gearbox for a kiss. And the happy sound she makes when our lips connect lights me up inside.

Ours is a kiss that wishes the night weren't over. We're in an idling car that's parked in the fire lane. All we've got is this one last moment, so we make it a good one. Jesus H, she's like honey on my tongue. "You taste so good," I mumble between kisses.

She grips the back of my head and lets out a shaky sigh. "Cherry lip gloss," she whispers before diving in for another.

Smiling, I suck her tongue into my mouth while my palms skim over her breasts, and she moans. I break it off, practically panting just from a few kisses. "It's not your lip gloss, babe." I know I need to say goodnight and let her go, but every time we're together the chemistry is thick. As if Macbeth's weird sisters have stirred up something in their cauldron that glues her tight body against mine.

Against my better judgment, I give her ass a suggestive squeeze. She moans again. I fucking love that sound.

But then there's another noise and not a good one. It's the insistent repetition of a camera's shutter.

Fuck, I curse under my breath as I pull back.

It occurs to me that Lianne could close the car door again so we can drive off together. But that's not what happens.

The next moment Lianne is gone. Before one whole second has passed, she's exited the car, crossed to the Beaumont gate and swiped her ID past the reader.

My heart crawls into my throat as the fucking photographer follows her all the way to the gate. I cut the engine, because if that asshole tries to follow her into Beaumont, he's going to have to go through me.

But he doesn't. When the big iron gate slams shut, Lianne is on the inside and he's peering in after her, calling her name, asking, "Who's your boyfriend?"

Fuck.

My hands are squeezed into fists that I'd happily pound him with. And I'm considering the idea when he puts the lens cap back on his camera and backs away from the gate. Then he melts into the darkness of the pedestrian walkway that passes between Beaumont and the English building.

Only when I'm sure he's gone do I restart Orsen's car and drive back home.

Chapter Thirteen

MY DRAGONS ARE HUNGRY

Lianne

Note to self: anger and adrenaline can make even a drunk girl move fast.

By the time I make it inside my entryway door, I'm seething. Stomping up the steps to the fourth floor does nothing to improve my mood. The asshole paparazzo has *ruined* a perfectly good kiss. And there aren't that many kisses in my life. It's not like I have kisses to spare.

What must DJ think? It's a pain in the ass to hang around with me, that's for sure.

I'm still angry as I brush my teeth, still irritated as I climb into bed.

Falling asleep is difficult, too, as my mind runs through a blurry reel of the evening's spectacular events. Maybe they're not spectacular to anyone else. But look at me! I hung out on a Saturday night, just like anyone would do. I made an a cappella singer jealous with video game weaponry. I drank a margarita or four. I rehearsed Lady M's part with the hottest boy at Harkness.

And he kissed me again. Many times. But even when I was

brave and kissing the stuffing out of him, he wouldn't take me to bed. He brought me home instead.

Damn.

In my mind, I replay the kisses several more times, because that's more fun than worrying. Then I sleep.

———

It's noise that wakes me up in the morning, as usual. I almost wrap my pillow around my head in the standard evasive maneuver. Then I realize that the noise I'm hearing isn't the sound of Bella and Rafe in the mad throes of passion, but my phone ringing.

Grabbing it off my bedside table, I see DJ's name on the display. "Hello?" I squawk after swiping the screen.

"Aw, you're sleeping?" he asks.

"No." I clear my throat. "Okay, yes."

He chuckles into my ear. "It's late. I thought it was safe to call."

"Damn." No wonder the room is so bright, and there's nobody yelling, *pound me, Rafe! Harder!* I'd slept through it. "What time is it?"

"Eleven."

"Wow, really?" I don't know if I'd ever slept so late before. "My dragons must be hungry."

DJ barks out a laugh and says something under his breath. It may or may not end with *so fucking cute.* "How's your head?"

I give this some thought. My head is perfectly fine. But why is he asking? "Um... It's okay. Shouldn't it be?"

There's that chuckle again, low and soft in my ear. I just want to climb through the phone and rub that sound all over my body. But I guess that would be weird.

"You got a little tipsy, that's all," DJ says softly. "I think it was the tequila."

"Right." Now that I've had a moment to wake up, the details

of last night are coming into focus. The video game and Amy's ornery face. The tasty margarita Bella and Scarlet gave me. And the one Pepe poured me after that. The dancing. And then DJ in the kitchen... *Oh my God.* I groan out loud.

"I thought you said your head was okay," DJ prompts.

"It's not that."

"Your stomach?"

"Ugh, no." *It's my poor injured dignity.* "Did we...talk in the kitchen?" I remember sitting on the counter. We kissed, and I said... *Holy hell.* Please, Jesus, let me not have said those things out loud.

DJ's silence is not encouraging. And when he speaks, the amusement in his voice is unmistakable. "We may have talked in the kitchen."

"Right." *And I said I wanted to treat your body like my own personal lollipop.* "Oh man. So that's what happens when I drink tequila." DJ's chuckle is audible through the phone. "Hey, can you do me a favor?"

"Sure," he says, his voice amused.

"Can we never speak of this again?"

"Okay?"

"I'd better run," I say quickly. I need to get off the phone and hide under something. Preferably forever.

"Wait." DJ laughs. "There's a favor I need to ask, too."

"Really?" I can't imagine what. And if he's going to make a joke about *licking*, I will *die*.

"I have, uh, something I have to do next Saturday. And there's a women's hockey game I'm supposed to DJ at five o'clock. There's a sub I called once last year, and he was okay. But I wondered if you wanted to do it."

I'm listening so hard for him to tease me that it takes a minute to sink in. "Really? You'd let me DJ a game?"

"Of course. You'd be great. The pay isn't much, though. Fifty bucks. I'm sure you usually work for a lot more than that."

"I don't want the *money*," I scoff. "I want the *power*."

He laughs. "Don't ever run for office, babe. Or if you do? Pick another slogan."

"This is going to be *great*." Seriously. I can't wait. "Saturday, right? I have six days to prepare."

He rewards me with another warm laugh. "Don't spend too much time on it. I know you're busy."

DJ may know me better than any other guy at Harkness. But he clearly hasn't witnessed me on a tear. And I have so much to do before Saturday. *So much*. "Can I choose my own playlists?"

"Of course."

"Thank you!" I squeak. "Gotta go now." I need to find some sporty, ass-kicking songs by *women*. Like, dozens of them.

"Okay, sweetheart. Have a good morning."

"I will. Later!" We hang up, and I'm halfway to my computer before I remember again that I told DJ I wanted to lick him everywhere.

The groan I let out probably shakes the walls. Because Bella opens my door and sticks her head in the room. "What is it now? Another bad sex scene?"

I wish. "No. Just regrets."

Her eyes widen. "Really? How's your head, anyway?"

Why does everyone keep asking that? "It's fine, actually. I might be one of those people who doesn't get hungover."

"Of course you don't. Then how's your sex life?"

"Bella!" The question catches me off guard, and my cheeks immediately flame like the coils in a toaster.

My neighbor grins at me. "Ah ha! You two finally did it! Your number just *doubled*, you hussy. How was he? DJ has that quiet, serious thing going on. I'll bet he's a very focused lover. And good with his hands..."

I clap my hands over my face. "Stop! Even if there were juicy details, I wouldn't share them."

"Wait—no details? You *didn't* make the monster with two backs?"

"Ugh. Nice image." I fling myself on the desk chair. "We didn't. For a minute I thought maybe we would. But then we didn't, and he brought me home."

"Well, okay," Bella says, twirling the end of her bathrobe tie. "That's progress, right?"

"Right."

"You could always ask for it, you know."

"Um…" Actually I don't know. "Not sure I could put it into words. Not sober, anyway." Too embarrassing.

Bella snorts. "Sure you could. Repeat after me, okay? 'DJ, let's get naked. I want to bounce on your dick.'"

Yuh! "That is not a sentence you will ever hear me say."

"Never say never," Bella chides me. "If you can't say what you want, how do you expect him to give it to you?"

I made a grumbly noise. "It's so obnoxious of you to make sense."

"Honey, I *know*. Now get dressed. If you don't have juicy details, I need brunch. Right now."

"I need a shower," I whine.

"Then take it already. Feed me food or sexual exploits. It's one or the other."

I'm hungry too, I discover. So I do as she suggests and head for the shower.

Chapter Fourteen

NICE CATCH

DJ

For Harkness students, Sunday is not a day of rest.

I have to choose a paper topic for French History and a set of calculus problems to do. But every five minutes or so my mind drifts off my books and onto certain other topics. Like the way Lianne's lips felt against mine. And the way she wrapped her whole body around me while we kissed in the kitchen. And it's not only her looks that attract me. I love her buoyant attitude, and the contrast between that giant personality which is somehow encased in a tiny body.

It's been a long time since I allowed myself to want someone, let alone touch anyone. It's hard to think sexy thoughts when the last time you took your clothes off the result was a nasty accusation.

But Lianne's small, smooth hands have flipped some kind of sexual switch for me. I just want to kiss her again, to find out if her mouth is as sweet as I remember it. I want to strip off all her clothes and hold her narrow hips in my hands.

It's a terrible idea for me to get involved with her right now. I know this. But she's so fucking cute and twice as sexy. And somehow I trust her, even though we haven't known each other long. There's something just so forthright about her—the way she squares her small shoulders and refuses to take any crap from anyone.

I want her, even though the timing is awful.

These are my thoughts as I labor through Sunday. I do homework and then I hit the gym. And in between sets on the squat rack, I think of making out with Lianne and of the way she sighed when I touched her.

I can't wait to see her again. It's so freaking nice to look forward to something for once.

The coming week is going to stink, what with my lawyer powwow and everything. But still, I get a whiff of enthusiasm when I realize I can call Lianne tonight just to hear her voice.

I do two extra sets on the bench, just because I can.

On Monday I call Lianne to see how she's doing. Maybe it makes me a sap, but I want her to know that I'm thinking about her. She doesn't pick me up, though, so I leave a voicemail asking how she's doing and whether the asshole photographer had decided to leave her alone.

That night I'm reading a homework assignment on my bed when I get an email from her.

Daniel—

Today I'm rereading the beginning of the Scottish play, and I can't help but hear your voice as Banquo. So that's distracting.

Anyway, I'm sorry about that photographer. He sold a photo to this rag (link). And you'll laugh when you see the caption. But I think this means he'll leave me alone now.

—Lady M

I click on the link and the website for a tabloid comes up. And there we are—Lianne's foot is outside the car, but the rest of her is in my arms. We are in a goddamn clinch—a deep kiss, with our hands gripping each other. The picture causes something to go wrong in my gut, because anyone who sees this can read me like a book. I look about two seconds away from hauling her back into the car and holding her forever.

Jesus H.

The caption *is* funny. She's right. It reads: "Silver screen sorceress-turned-college-student Lianne Challice leaving her boyfriend's car. She's dating James Orsen, senior and star goalie for the Harkness hockey team. At 6-1 and 200 pounds, the NHL prospect's save percentage is an impressive 91%. Nice catch, Princess Vindi."

"Holy shit!" I snort to myself. The photographer must have run the plates on Orsen's car, or maybe the deed to his house, then Googled him. Lianne was right when she said the gossip rags didn't care about the truth. I slide off my bed and carry my tablet to the goalie's door. "Hey, Orsen?"

"Come in, dude."

I push his door open. "Your car is having its fifteen minutes of fame."

He looks up from a chemistry textbook. "What?"

"I'm sorry about this." I hand over the tablet.

"*Aw!*" he teases. "Look at the lovesick boy in my car."

Ugh. "Read the caption."

Orsen's howl of laughter is loud and immediate. "No fucking way!" Then he's tapping on my screen.

"What are you doing?"

"Sending myself the link. I'm a *catch*, Deej! And the NHL wants me. I look a lot like you, which is a fucking shame, though." He laughs some more.

I shouldn't have shown it to him, because now he's going to pass it around. But most players have a Google alert on their own names in case sportswriters mention them in the press. So he probably would have found it. And anyway, what can I really expect?

While Orsen forwards the link to everyone we know, I head back to my room. This will be today's little humiliation. Compared to the other shit swirling around in my life, it's not a big deal.

Except I'm wrong about that. So wrong.

While I study calculus, the photo makes the rounds. It reaches my brother, of course. And sometime during the next twenty-four hours, he mentions it to my father. Because when my phone rings on Tuesday afternoon, there's a whole lot of *what the fuck* on the other end of the line.

"Danny. What the hell are you doing with this girl?"

Ouch. "She's a nice girl, Dad. We're friends." Even as the words came out of my mouth, I know how I sound. The kiss in the picture… That asshole photographer is unfortunately talented. He'd captured the moment with too much clarity.

So I can practically feel my father's sneer all the way across the Long Island Sound. "Why would you even *try* to tell me that? Not only are you involved with a girl, you picked one that gets you in the newspapers? Don't you ever *learn*?"

His words are a direct hit to the gut—the kind that knocks your breath away. Maybe it's terrible timing for me to get involved with Lianne, but being with her isn't *wrong*. I'm not a fucking criminal. And I'm so tired of people thinking I'm either stupid or a bad person. With the mess I'm in, there's no door number three.

"Danny," my father says my name as a gasp, as if it pains him to go through this with me. "Nothing else matters but your case. *Nothing.* I'm trying to save your life. You need to at least act like you're paying attention."

There's a bang, and the line goes dead.

He hung up on me. My own father hung up on me. That's a Trevi family first.

Stunned, I sit there for a few minutes just weighed down by how isolated I really am.

The worst part is that I can totally see his point. We can't have the college viewing me as some kind of playboy. That picture doesn't make me look like a nice boy at the center of a big misunderstanding. The jackass photographer may have gotten my name wrong this time. But the next one? He might not make the same mistake again.

And then I have a *really* ugly thought. Lianne has no idea she's been hanging out with a guy who's been accused of hurting a woman. If the next magazine bothers to get the real story on me, *that* would be an ugly little photo caption. The thought makes me feel suddenly sick to my stomach. If it got out, Lianne would be right there in the middle of my scandal. I'd be dragging her down into the muck with me.

Defeated by this idea, I roll onto my stomach, burying my face in my pillow.

When my email dings a moment later, I open up the app, expecting to see my father's name. He's not a screamer—never has been. Who ever heard of a hot-headed forensic accountant?

But the new email isn't from my dad. It's from the grad student who runs my French history seminar on Thursday nights. I wouldn't bother to open it right now, except that something in the subject line catches my eye. So I click.

Dear students,

Due to the renovation of Cruxley Hall, our weekly meeting place has been reassigned. Please find me tomorrow at our usual time in the Trindle House seminar room, which is located off the dining hall. Enter the Trindle House courtyard at the College Street gate and take the first entryway on the left. Text me if you can't get in the gate, and someone will come out to fetch you.

   Until tomorrow,
   Davis

I reread it three times, hoping it doesn't say what I think it says. But it does.

For anyone else at Harkness, this room reassignment is just a tiny adjustment in their daily routine. For me? A huge problem. Attending the weekly seminar is twenty percent of my French history grade. And now that hour-long session has been relocated to a residential house, where I'm not permitted to go. Even worse it's Trindle, which is *my* house. And my accuser's.

That's it. My limit is hit. That's all the bullshit I can take in one day.

My temper flares so hot and bright that before I know what I'm doing, I've yanked the calculus textbook off my bed and hurled it across the all-too-narrow expanse of my room, where it smacks the doorframe with a thunderous crash, and then drops loudly to the floor.

And what's worse? This display of toddlerhood hasn't even made me feel better. Getting off the bed, I kick the book out of my way and head for the kitchen. I'm neither hungry or thirsty, but I just can't sit in that little cell any longer.

In the living room, my brother looks up from the video game he's playing with Orsen. It's like he fucking lives here. "Hey, Deej," he says. "Want to play a round of RealStix?"

No, actually. I'd rather beat you with the controller. "Why the fuck did you show that picture to Dad?" I demand. "Like he's not already on my case? You had to make my pile of bullshit deeper?"

He pauses the game, setting the controller aside, and Orsen doesn't say a word. "I didn't show him. I told him about it, though. Look—maybe that wasn't too smart of me. But I thought it was a moment of levity, you know?"

"I don't *have* those," I say through gritted teeth. Leo wouldn't understand, anyway. His greatest challenges are which video game to play before practice, and what's on the menu in the dining hall.

Leo cringes. "Dude, I'm sorry."

"He's *so* pissed. He hung up on me."

"Dad?" His voice is incredulous. "You sure?"

"Am I *sure*?" Yeah, I want to punch Leo. A nice uppercut to his smug jaw, maybe. "Like I don't know when someone hangs up on me? I think Dad is worried I'll sully the family name. That maybe your NHL recruiters will run away." It's more truth-telling than I'd planned on. But Dad's concern eats at me sometimes. He's always cared a lot about how things look.

"What?" Leo frowns up at me. "That's ridiculous."

Except I don't think it is. "Really? You want to tell me you *never* had that thought?"

Now my brother looks guilty. "I have a lot of stupid thoughts, Deej. I mean—I worry I'm going to lose the game if I put my right skate on before my left one."

"Oh, the horror," I scoff. Then I stomp back into my room. Fucking Leo. His team might get another shot at the Frozen Four in ten weeks. After that he's going to graduate and move up to an NHL farm team, probably.

I'll be looking forward to a summer job at the seafood place again. And maybe staying there for the rest of my life.

My calculus book is still on the floor, so I bend down to retrieve it. A pair of high-tops appears in my line of vision. When I stand up, I find they belong to Orsen. "Hey, Deej?"

"Yeah," I grunt, expecting him to ask, *what's your fucking problem?*

"I need an extra hour of practice. Grab your bag, man. Come take some shots at me."

"Can't," I say automatically. Though I haven't worn a pair of skates in a long time—too long. There's probably nothing I'd enjoy more than spending the next hour firing pucks at Orsen.

"Need the help, man," he says, tapping the old molding. He frowns at me, his big face stern underneath three days of scruff. "Let's go. Meet me in the car in five." He walks away.

"Hey!" I call after him, still feeling belligerent. "I didn't say I'd go!"

The only response is the back door opening and closing again. What the hell? Just because he's rented me this room, now I'm his slave?

After another moment standing there seething, I realize there's no way I can do more school work right now. The walls of my little room are practically closing in on me. Once again I'm feeling my Napoleon complex. Not because I'm short—because I'm exiled.

I get my hockey gear out from under my bed and I follow him out to the car.

Chapter Fifteen

CRAZY IN LOVE

Lianne

All I want to do is see DJ. Or text him. Or call him. My mind has become a continuous loop of craving, punctuated by blushing and the occasional giggle. I sound like Janice from *Friends*. At least I don't have that eighties hairdo.

The good news is that my photographer has fled Connecticut. I hacked into his website to find a bunch of photos he'd taken at his sister's wedding in New London on Sunday, an event that explained his showing up in this part of the state. Even better— the next set of pictures, taken yesterday, were of Justin Bieber arriving at LAX.

Good riddance, Buzz.

In the minus column, twentieth-century theater class continues to be a grind, though I manage to arrive to the next class early to snag a good seat. I'm so early, in fact, that the only people in the room are the skinny professor and Hosanna, the redhead who'd said she wanted to read Neil Simon. She's standing with the professor, and they're looking over the syllabus together. But the conversation is not going well.

"I don't understand why you took this class if you can't do all the reading," he says in a grumpy voice.

"We, um..." She glances in my direction, as if wishing she did not have an audience. "It's just these two plays. You can assign me something else instead."

"Hosanna, when I assign Harvey Fierstein to my students, it's not a political act. It's not a moral decision. We read about Arnold's homosexuality not to push an agenda but to understand where American theater was in the nineteen-eighties."

"I know that, sir," she says in a voice so low that I almost cannot hear her. "But I follow my church's rules to keep peace with my father. It's a compromise I make so that I can stay at this school."

Fascinated, I am hanging on their every word, staring down at my phone in my hand, though the screen is dark.

"It's not a compromise at *all* when you let someone else tell you what you can read," he presses. "The point of a liberal arts education is to learn to think for yourself. And to do that, you have to read things that expand your experience."

Neither the professor nor Hosanna says anything for a moment, and I have no idea who will cave in.

"I won't be reading those two plays," she says finally. "If it won't work to assign me something else, I'll lose points on my grade instead. That's my only choice."

She takes a step backward, as if finishing the conversation. But he holds up a hand. "I'll make a deal with you. You don't have to read those two plays, but I don't want you skipping the discussions. You don't have to contribute, but you should listen."

"Okay," she agrees quietly.

After that weird little drama, the class itself is as dull as usual. In fact, nothing else holds my attention at all. Not my school work. Not DragonFire. Not even the Scottish play. I've basically stumbled through the last forty-eight hours, looking for DJ whenever I'm walking around campus. And lord help me if I actually find him. I'm a little afraid of my own reaction. Hopefully I'll be able to keep cool enough to avoid blurting out, "Forget Shakespeare, let's rehearse a sex scene!"

The only task I can focus on is the one DJ gave me. I've compiled an excellent playlist for the women's hockey game on Saturday. All that's left is practicing with the rink's soundboard.

The rink schedule shows a gap from three to four o'clock, between the women's team practice and the men's. I needed a few minutes alone with the sound system so if there is anything confusing, I can ask DJ before Saturday.

I don't want to ask, though. I just want to impress him with my competence. People don't expect me to be competent. They think that because I've done a lot of smiling into the camera, that's all I can manage.

DJ's different. He listens when I talk. And he gave me this little DJ gig without a moment's hesitation. So I'm going to do the best damn job that's ever been done at a women's game.

My playlist? It's epic. I have all the music figured out. But I have to make sure I know how the soundboard works, or nobody will hear it.

The main doors to the rink are open, so getting into the building is no problem. The last hurdle is getting into the press box. But I've found that if you walk around like you belong somewhere—with your shoulders thrown back and your chin held high—people rarely stop you.

So I "screw my courage to the sticking place," as Lady M says, and I march around the mezzanine level toward the press box.

But, damn it, the ice isn't empty like I thought it would be. There are two guys down there practicing. Are they going to be pissed if I test the sound system?

Pausing in the student section, I try to figure out who they are. Since they're suited up from head to toe in hockey gear, it's not easy to guess. But I decide the goalie is Orsen, since he's the only goalie I know. The other guy? It's hard to say. He's wearing a plain red jersey, which tells me nothing. His skating is so fast and fluid it looks like flying. He skates backward in a perfect arc, dribbling a puck with his stick, then reverses direction, crossing the ice in front of the goal.

He shoots so suddenly that I almost miss it. Before I register what's happening, his arm sweeps forward and the puck is airborne. Orsen reacts at superhuman speed and snatches the puck out of the air. Then he chuckles.

I don't hear the other guy's response, because he's skating backward again, facing away from me. He picks up another puck from the blue line. But then a third player sweeps onto the ice and challenges him for it. So red jersey changes tack, stickhandling the puck away from the new guy, zipping incredibly fast across the gleaming surface. His pursuer can't quite catch him.

Watching hockey is like watching a high-speed car chase, and I'm loving it.

Red jersey evades his challenger, changes direction, then snaps the puck at Orsen. The goalie dives, but he's too late. The puck whistles into the corner of the net.

"Fuck," Orsen complains as red jersey hoots in victory. "Yeah, yeah." The goalie chuckles.

The new guy punches red jersey in the arm, then points up into the stands at me.

Whoops. I'm busted for ogling hockey players.

But then it gets worse. When red jersey lifts off his helmet, I realize that I'm *really* busted. Because it's DJ staring up at me.

My face is beginning to turn the same color as his jersey as I give the three of them a stiff wave and then stumble along toward the press box.

Luckily, the door opens for me, and I duck inside and close it behind me. I never expected to see DJ here. He's going to think I'm a crazy stalker lady.

I get right down to business, hooking up my laptop to the soundboard. The connections work exactly the way I'd expect.

Yet when I start up a playlist, no sound booms from the rink's speaker system.

It's probably just a software problem, and those are my specialty. I let the playlist run, and I begin checking my computer's output settings. When that doesn't work, I take a closer look at the soundboard, fiddling with the levers.

Finally, I hear music. Unfortunately, the song suddenly blasting through the speakers is Beyoncé's *Crazy in Love*. Whoa. Paging Dr. Freud. I scramble to change it to something. *Anything*. I double click on Chelsea Dagger and slump into the chair in relief. That's when the door flies open and DJ walks in, his hair wet from the shower.

"Nice Beyoncé tune," he says with a smirk.

Damn. "I prepped an all-female playlist for the women's game," I say quickly.

His eyes open a little wider. "Hey, that's a great idea. They're going to love it."

The praise makes me feel all squishy inside. Or maybe it's just the sound of his smoky voice. Either way, I'm humming inside and out. "They might not even notice."

"They will." DJ crosses to the desk that runs the length of the press box and parks his hip against it. "How are things with you?"

"With me?" *I think about you night and day*. "Fine. I just wanted to look over the system again before the game."

"Graham can help you if you run into any snags," he says, folding his gorgeous arms across his chest. "I made sure he was planning to be in here on Saturday."

See? Even DJ has a plan for my incompetence. "But Graham has a job to do. I'll get it right without his help."

"I have no doubt." The words are soft, and I like the sound of them. But I don't like that he's way over there, practically in the next zip code.

"I've been studying," I add. "For Saturday."

"Yeah? Working on your playlist?"

"Well, of course. But I don't think you understand what I'm like when I get my hooks into a project. I've been studying the *game*, because the music between plays depends on what's happening down on the ice."

DJ's lips twitch. "That's true, my little apprentice."

"What did I *say* about the short jokes?" But it's a false complaint. He can call me whatever he wants as long as I get more kisses. "Go on, then. Quiz me on the hand signals."

Smiling now, DJ hops off the desk. "Okay. What does this mean?" He lifts one bent arm and touches his elbow.

"Easy one. That's the penalty call for elbowing."

His eyebrows lift. "Look at you! Okay. What's this?" He makes the washout sign, both palms facing the ice, arms spread wide.

"No goal!"

DJ nods appreciatively. "You aren't easy to stump. One more." He makes the letter C with one hand then lifts it toward his face.

"Um..." God, I don't know that one. "Contact to the head?" I guess.

"Nope." He grins. "It means I really need a drink."

I tear a page from my notebook, wad it up and throw it at him. He ducks just in time for the ball to fly over his head.

We're both smiling at each other now, but he's still several feet further away than I want him. "You want to get some coffee?" I blurt out. "I'm done here."

His face falls, and my heart bobbles. "I can't. I'm sorry."

"Too busy today?" There's something in his expression which tells me I don't really want to hear the answer.

DJ pulls out one of the desk chairs and sits on it. "Can we talk for a minute?"

I shrug, feeling more miserable by the second. I thought we had something good. And now I'm about to get the brush off.

"It's sort of about that picture, but sort of not."

"I'm *sorry* about the picture," I say quickly. "The guy left town, too. I'm pretty sure."

"The thing is, my father ripped me a new one for that picture." DJ pinches the bridge of his nose. "I'm in some trouble with the college. And my father is working really hard to get me out of it. When I said it wasn't a good time for me to be with anybody, I really wasn't kidding."

My temper spikes. "I see. I'm the trashy friend you have to scrape off your shoe until your reputation recovers." It comes out sounding even bitchier than I'd intended.

I expect DJ to get angry with this characterization, but that's not what happens. He only looks defeated. With an elbow on the desk, he props his face in one hand. "You're the classiest person I know, smalls. There is nobody in this whole fucking town I'd rather spend my time with than you. But I can't. It isn't fair. But there's no such thing as fair, anyway."

My eyes feel hot. The only guy I've wanted in a long time is basically breaking up with me. And why does he have to be so freaking nice while he does it? "Will you at least tell me why?"

His face is a stone. "I never wanted to have that conversation, because I care what you think of me. I mean..." He rubs the back of his neck and stares at the floor. "I did something a little stupid, and kind of insensitive. And now I'm in a lot of trouble for something that I didn't do at all."

He doesn't want me to press him on it. I can feel his reluctance from across the room. "Please tell me what's the matter," I whisper anyway. Because I'm stubborn. And I'm afraid that if I don't get answers now, there won't be another chance.

But he just shakes his head. "I'm not supposed to talk about it," he says, and my heart crumbles a little more. Because we both know that's just an excuse. If he trusted me as much as I trust him, he'd tell me the problem.

DJ stands up, and I know he's about to leave. "I'm sorry," he whispers. "There's just no other way." He reaches for the door.

"Wait," I say instinctively. There's something final about the way he's turned away from me. *Exit, stage left.* "I still need to read

Shakespeare," I blurt out. "You're kind of leaving me in the lurch, here." It's the weakest excuse in the world, but I am not ready for him to just walk out of my life.

He stops, glancing back at me. "Well." He clears his throat. "Can we do it over the phone?"

Do it over the phone. My stupid brain turns that into something dirty. *Phone Shakespeare.* Gah. How ridiculous. And how completely unsatisfying. "I guess," I say, still disappointed.

"This weekend, maybe," he says.

"Okay," I whisper. I know DJ has a problem, and that everything isn't about me. But he won't tell me what it is, and that hurts. And I don't have to be happy about it, either.

"Goodbye," he says, his voice rough.

"Later," I answer, just to be difficult.

He smiles, an unexpected parting gift. And then he's gone.

Chapter Sixteen

FULL OF SCORPIONS

DJ

The night before my lawyer interview, I can't sleep.

I find myself awake at four-thirty in the morning, thumbing through my copy of Macbeth. Most people wouldn't consider it a comfort read. But I hear Lianne's voice while I read. And I like imagining her copy is beside her bed somewhere in Beaumont House where she's sleeping peacefully.

Besides, Macbeth is a verifiable tragedy. And it takes me out of my head.

I'm fascinated by the funny scene with the drunk porter, because it comes at such a weird moment in the play. The king has just been killed, but the porter doesn't know that. So he's drunk and full of bawdy jokes. But that's how life really is. Sometimes you're the fool who believes everything will be fine in the morning.

Giving up on sleep, I keep reading. The hardest scene to read is the one where Macbeth is half out of his mind at the dinner party. He keeps seeing the ghost of Banquo. The guilt is making him crazy, and Lady M just pleads with him to keep it together. He can't do it, though, no matter how much she begs. "Full of scorpions is my mind," he says.

Mine too, buddy. Only I'm going mad because people *think* I'm guilty.

Eventually I fall asleep with the paperback on my chest. When I wake up a few hours later, I'm still clutching my place in Act Four.

I've skipped breakfast, but that's okay because I have never been less hungry. After a shower and a careful shave, I put on some khakis and a button-down shirt. There's probably no reason to dress up for my own lawyer, but I can't help but play the kiss-ass. If I've learned anything this year, it's that telling the truth isn't enough. The universe works on another set of rules, and I don't own the manual. So all I can do is make sure my face is smooth and my shoes aren't scuffed, and hope it somehow makes a difference.

I've borrowed my brother's car for this adventure. At ten o'clock I'm behind the wheel of Leo's Jetta. At a few minutes to noon, I'm pulling up in front of a suburban law office in Westchester County. There is exactly one other car in the parking lot—a shiny BMW. I'm sure my father is making one of the lawyer's car payments today. It can't be cheap to have this man's Saturday.

God, I hope he's worth whatever I'm costing my dad.

There's a sticky note on the glass door to the law firm's office. "Come on back, Daniel. Second door on the left." I pocket this note and go inside, removing my wool overcoat and tossing it onto a lobby chair on my way toward what turns out to be a rather fancy office. The big oak desk and oriental rug practically shout "SUCCESSFUL ATTORNEY."

"Afternoon," a well-dressed man says, standing up to brush muffin crumbs off his tie. "I got us some sandwiches."

"Thank you, sir," I say, leaning over the desk to shake his hand.

He's a little younger than I'd pictured. I have to wonder what his usual case load looks like. Does he specialize in rape accusations? Is that a thing?

Everything about this case makes me feel dirty. If there's an industry niche for getting young jocks out of trouble, I don't really want to know. For the millionth time, I wish I could just wash my hands of the whole episode.

Out, out damned spot, as Lady M would say.

"You can just call me Jack, okay?" He passes me a paper plate with a club sandwich. "Now, Daniel," he says, sipping his coffee. "Let's get started. We have a lot of ground to cover. I'm going to ask you some questions. There's a lot in your file, but I need to fine tune some things. Lots of little, picky details. And sometimes you're going to say, 'I don't remember.' And that's fine. You're going to find my level of detail annoying, but it's my job to ask you every little thing. Because one of these details is going to matter, okay?"

"Okay." Sounds like a fun time.

"You mentioned the last time we spoke that on the night in question, you and the girl were at a party. Can you tell me about this party?"

I clear my throat. "We call it an Around the World party. There's, uh, a different drink served in every dorm suite. And you go around and try them all." And since we were all nineteen when this happened, I'm incriminating myself.

"Uh huh," he says, unfazed. "Did your room serve any drinks?"

"No sir. The party was in the next entryway over from mine. We were just, uh, guests."

"You and the girl were both guests. Because you live in the same entryway?"

"Right."

"Okay. Did you serve anyone an alcoholic beverage that night?"

"No. That night I only drank other people's liquor." I'm a criminal *and* a mooch. Awesome. My lawyer actually chuckles, but I have more to add. "At that kind of party they only serve in these tiny cups. So you can taste everything without bankrupting the hosts."

"Got it. Do you think you could find some of those cups if I needed you to?"

"You mean...at a store?"

"Yes. If we had to figure out how many ounces you drank."

"Sure. I could find the cups, but I don't know how many drinks I had. And I don't know how alcoholic they were." Probably not very alcoholic, actually. Because making drinks is expensive. And it's not that easy for freshmen to buy liquor from a store.

"I know we can't be precise," my lawyer admits. "But we could figure out the maximum you drank—the number of rooms in the entryway times the volume of the cup. Is that right?"

"Yeah. It's not polite to double dip, although I'm sure some people do it."

"But not you."

"No."

"Were you drunk?"

"Not really. I had a little buzz, maybe. But those cups are small, and we did a lot of standing around talking."

"Was Annie drunk?"

The sound of her name makes me feel cold inside. "No—she doesn't drink."

"She said that?"

"Maybe?" Did she? "I never saw her with a drink in her hand. Ever."

"Was anyone drunk that night?"

"Yeah, sure. One guy from my entryway had a flask he kept using to refill his cup. But my little group didn't get sloshed."

"All right. At what point did Annie ask to stay the night in your room?"

"I don't know what time it was. We were standing in the stair-well of the entryway that was hosting the party. There were a few people there. And she said her sister was there for the night because she was being recruited by the crew team."

"So this is a younger sister. Did you meet her?"

I thought about that. "Yeah, but only for a second. It was when we were all about to go next door for the party. The sister was running off with her rowing buddies, but I remember being introduced."

"Okay. How did Annie ask you if she could stay with you? Did she ask you by yourself, or did she ask you and your roommate at the same time?"

Jesus Christ, I have no idea. "It was a long time ago. And at the time, it was not that interesting of a question." Little did I know... "I... I just have no idea if my roommate heard the question. I think I answered it by myself, though."

"Okay. Do you remember what words she used when she asked?"

"She said, 'I told my sister she could have my bed tonight.' Then she asked if she could use the camping mat we keep in our room for when visitors come. My roommate Jake had most of the visitors. But it's my mat."

The lawyer is quiet for a second. "The way you put that sounds as if she meant to borrow it and take it back to her room."

"I know. That's what I thought she'd do."

"Okay. When did it become clear that she intended to sleep in your room?"

"Um, I'd already brushed my teeth when she knocked on our door. She was wearing a nightgown and she had a sleeping bag under her arm. She said that since she and her roommate had taken apart their bunkbeds, there wasn't enough room on the floor for her to unroll it. She said, 'I'm going to sleep here if you don't mind.'"

"What did you think about that?"

"I felt like a dick for letting a girl sleep on the floor while I stayed in my bed. But I didn't say anything, because she seemed happy with the arrangement."

We've been talking for maybe ten minutes. And now I have a splitting headache. I hate the way I sound when I explain myself. And I hate the way we sound like a courtroom drama.

I hate everything about this discussion, and if I could rewind my life I would have avoided what came next that night.

"What happened next, Daniel?"

We were here to practice, so practice I did. I told him how Annie initiated everything. A girl climbs into my bed and starts kissing me. I kiss her back. She starts touching me. So I touch her, too.

I guzzled the whole cup of coffee while I'm telling it, because it all sounds so fucking sordid. *Sure, I never looked twice at you before. But let's get it on.*

We had sex. Unremarkable sex. It wasn't worth it. In hindsight it sure wasn't worth spending a Saturday telling my very expensive lawyer the blow-by-blow of my sex life.

Next come his questions.

"Let me back up to the kissing," my lawyer says. "When she kissed you, how did she position her body?"

"Uh..." My head stabs me. "Like, half on my body."

"Did she say anything when she climbed in your bed?"

"She said 'hi.'"

He makes me walk through everything again—when Annie kissed me. When I kissed her back. When I grabbed her ass. When she started grinding on me.

The lawyer stops for clarification. "She pushed her pelvis up and down on your pelvis, as if for sexual stimulation?" he asks.

Uh, yeah, dude. Grinding. "That's correct."

My head is practically splitting apart when I tell him that I put my hands under her nightgown. She sheds her nightgown. I lose the flannel pants I'm wearing. She asks if I have a condom.

"She vocalized this question?"

"Yes she did." This is one of the details that keeps me sane. Even if it's deeply confusing to me why I'm here, I'm not confused about what happened that night.

"And did you vocalize your answer?"

"I'm not sure. I know I opened the bedside table, but she had to fish them out."

"Why?"

"Because I was on my back, and I couldn't see them."

"Okay—at what point did you flip over?"

"I didn't. I took the condom from her and I put it on."

"Did she help you put it on?"

"No. I always do that myself."

"Why?"

"So it goes on the right way." Because I used to think it mattered. Before this year, I thought I could prevent disaster by being careful.

"Then what happened?"

I already told you. "We had sex."

"In what position?"

Shoot me. "I was on my back. She was on top of me."

"The whole time?"

"Sure."

"At any point did you move from that position?"

"When I got up to throw the condom away."

For a long moment, the lawyer is perfectly silent. "She brings up the condoms. And you're always on your *back*. What I wouldn't give to cross-examine this girl." He sighs. "Sorry. I got side-tracked. We can't prove your innocence without the young woman's help. We really need to figure out why she's saying this wasn't consensual..." He flips a folder open on his desk and starts sifting through the papers inside.

Meanwhile, I'm trying to picture telling a room full of people —including my family—the details of how we did it cowgirl style. And isn't that what a guilty man would say, anyway—that everything was her idea? Will anyone believe me?

He looks up at me with a serious expression, then sets his pen down. "Was there *any* point during this encounter when the young woman hesitated? If she said 'yes,' then 'maybe not,' then 'yes,' I need to know that. If you discussed it at all, I need the details."

I just shake my head. "There wasn't any discussion. She never stopped. She never even slowed down."

"Did you..." He clears his throat. "Hold her in a way that restricted her movements? Where were your hands? I'm still trying to figure out the basis of the dispute."

Me too, buddy. "Not at all. I mean..." I clear my throat, too. "I, uh, had my hands on her, um, breasts, I think."

He makes a note on his pad, and I stare into the bottom of my empty coffee cup, praying for the end of this inquisition.

———

"Let's move on," my lawyer says a few minutes later, after we've literally discussed the dismount. "I want to ask you about her state of mind afterward."

I should be relieved to change the subject, but the truth was I was more embarrassed about this than anything else.

"We didn't discuss it," I say. "I mean...at bio lab the following Tuesday, we just worked on the assignment."

My lawyer nods. "Did she do anything weird? Anything at all?"

That's a tough question to answer. I didn't really know Annie well enough to say whether she was acting weird. "I don't think so. But I really didn't want to talk about what happened. So I wasn't the most attentive lab partner that first day."

"You were nervous?" he probes.

That sounds guilty, too. "Nervous isn't the right word. How about sheepish?"

"All right. Tell me why you didn't want to discuss what happened."

"Because it's stupid to sleep with your lab partner, especially if you're not really into her." *Into her.* Ugh. I wish I'd chosen different words. I wish I'd chosen not to sleep with her at all.

"So you and Annie didn't talk about it. Who *did* you discuss it with?"

"My roommate."

"Why?"

"Because he woke up at some point during, um..."

"He heard you having sex."

"Yeah."

"And he was in the bunk above you."

"Yes."

"What did he say?"

"He said, 'You and Annie? I didn't know you were into her.' And I said 'I'm not, and it was probably a stupid thing to do.'"

My lawyer clears his throat. "I'm going to need to speak to your roommate."

Good luck with that. "He's in Tibet this year."

I swear the lawyer says "fuck" under his breath. "Okay. I'll need his email address. They have email there, right? And maybe Skype?"

"Probably." I haven't spoken to my roommate all year, though. He's not here, and I'm too embarrassed. *Hey man, how's Tibet? Remember that night I had sex in front of you?*

Talk about awkward.

The questions last for hours. And then finally we're done. Jack is packing up his papers, and I unfold my stiff body from my chair.

"Let me run something by you," he says, tucking yet another folder onto his stack. "You weren't really planning to have sex that night."

"No, I wasn't."

"But you let it happen."

"Yes." Didn't we just spend three hours on this?

"Did she force you?"

"What? No!" That's the most ridiculous idea ever. If he's even half serious, I need a new lawyer. Because this one is cracked.

"But you regret it," he says.

"Of course I do. How could I not?"

His nod is serious. "You regretted it *before* she accused you, though."

"Yeah. I regretted it because it was awkward. And I wasn't interested in her. What's your point?" Maybe that sounded rude, but I was seriously running out of patience.

My lawyer taps his fingers on the desktop. "I have a suspicion that this whole case boils down to regret, which is not the same as force. But I don't know how to prove it if the college won't let me interview her."

In other words, this whole session was for nothing. "But even if they do let you talk to her, I'm still the guy who's accusing a girl of lying." It's hard to imagine a worse position to be in. I watch the news. No matter which side prevails, nobody ever wins. The guy comes across looking shady as hell, and the woman gets harassed all over social media. Disaster for everyone.

"Unless she withdraws her complaint, or else Harkness dismisses it," my lawyer says, rising from his chair. "We have to let the college know that they've dropped the ball all over the place. That they didn't bother gathering any of the facts. That's my only play here."

He comes around the desk, but I'm still rooted to his rug.

Because there's one thing that neither of us has said yet. "It's probably not going to work, is it?"

Jack stops in front of me, offering me his hand. We shake before he answers. "No guarantees. But we won't go down quietly."

That's exactly what I'm afraid of.

————

We both climb into our cars, and Jack drives away first. For a few minutes I just sit there, too spent to drive myself back. It's five o'clock. Right now the women's game is just starting. Lianne has texted me a picture of the women warming up on the ice. "I'm ready," she's added. "Don't worry about a thing."

As if.

I drive back to Harkness, and there's traffic. By the time I park my brother's car behind the rink where he keeps it, people are already streaming out of the game. I check my phone again and find a stream of text messages from Lianne. *Having a great time*, she wrote during the first period. *Played "Girls Just Wanna Have Fun" when we scored. Played "Shake it Off" when they scored.*

Yep. She totally has the hang of it.

My phone buzzes in my hand with a text from goalie Scarlet Crowley. *DJ! You are awesome! We loved the 100% chick music.*

Of course they had. *Don't thank me*, I reply. *It was Lianne in the booth today*. I get out of the car and lock it, thinking about my shaky future at Harkness. Then I text Scarlet again. *You should ask Lianne if she wants the job permanently. She might enjoy that*. I add Lianne's email address and then shove the phone in my pocket.

An hour later I'm home in our silent house. The guys are in Boston tonight to play Harvard. It practically echoes with silence, and I could be getting a lot of school work done. But I'm ridiculously tired from being grilled all day. And my classwork seems even more pointless than usual.

I turn the TV on and flip a few channels. My phone lights up with messages from my parents—both of them separately—asking how it went. Since they're paying the lawyer a big chunk of change to try to extract me from my troubles, I really ought to call them back. But I can't seem to make myself do it. They want to hear of progress, and all I can hear is Jack saying, "We won't go down quietly."

Tonight the fight is all out of me.

Chapter Seventeen

I DIDN'T ORDER A PIZZA

Lianne

I love Scarlet's email at first. *We loved the music! Thank you so much!* But when she mentions that DJ said something about giving me the job permanently, I'm instantly steamed.

What was that boy thinking? I'm not stealing his *paycheck*. He loves that job.

So I call him up to give him a hard time. The first two times he doesn't pick up. But I'm very persistent.

"Hi," he says warily the third time I call. "Are you okay?"

"Yes. Well, no! Why would you want to give away your job?"

There is a brief silence. "I probably can't keep it much longer, actually. Somebody will have to DJ all the games if I leave."

"Leave and go where?" That doesn't make any sense. Hockey season ends in April. It's almost February already.

"I..." He stops talking. "Lianne, I know I'm being a dick about this. But can we just drop it? I had a really shitty day."

The sound of his voice tells me that's true. But I persist. "We were supposed to have Phone Shakespeare."

"Yeah." He sighs. "I just... Another night, okay?"

"Okay," I say, because what is my choice?

But after we hang up, I'm not so sure I did the right thing. DJ sounds lonely and in desperate need of distraction. And I'm lonely and in desperate need of DJ.

And I know just where to find him.

I mull this over for a few minutes. Getting caught on camera with DJ is not an option, though. The odds are low, but I won't risk it. Getting off my bed, I go through our bathroom to knock on Bella's door. "Are you in there? I need wardrobe help again."

"I'm here," she says. When I open the door she adds from the bed, "But didn't we establish that I'm not very helpful?"

"This time you will be. I need some hockey gear."

Bella sits up. "Then you've come to the right place."

———

An hour later I walk up DJ's street. I look pretty awful, and there aren't any photographers around for miles. But better safe than sorry. The big box in my hands makes it hard to knock on the door, but I can't exactly set it down. There's a doorbell button, but it looks a hundred years old. I angle my body and lean into it with my elbow. The satisfying yodel of a bell echoes through the door. I make my voice deep and call out, "Pizza delivery!"

Someone stomps over to the door, and it swings open to reveal DJ wearing sweatpants and a scowl. "I didn't order a pizza."

"You should have," I say, stepping into the house, forcing him backwards. "Because you weren't kidding about Gino's. I almost starved to death just smelling this."

His mouth falls open. Shock is not his sexiest look, but I like it anyway. "You brought me a Gino's pie?"

"I brought *us* a Gino's pie. Because one of us still hasn't gotten to try any." He recovers from his shock just enough to lift the box from my hands and carry it over to the coffee table. I use the opportunity to yank the hideous stick-on mustache off my face.

"Where'd you find that getup, smalls?" he asks. He helps me out of the Harkness Hockey jacket and hat I'm wearing. My copy of the Scottish play falls out of the pocket, and DJ scoops it up off the floor.

"Bella. Duh." When I'm free of the jacket, I make a move toward the sofa and the pizza in front of it, but DJ catches me by the hand.

When I look up into his eyes, there's a volatile brew swirling around in there. It's warmth and seriousness mixed with sadness, too. "I'm sorry I was a grouch earlier," he says. "But I am ridiculously glad to see you right now."

"That's more like it," I whisper. He gives me a smile, and I wonder if I'm about to get a kiss. Instead, he plants a warm hand on my back and steers me toward the sofa. "I'll try to find you a soda. Unless you want a beer?"

"No thanks. Water is fine, too."

I open the lid of the pizza box and inhale. It smells amazing. A moment later DJ puts two plates and two glasses of water down, as well as two napkins. "You got the MOR pie!" he says happily. "That's a great pick."

His approval makes me float. I might drift up to the ceiling, I'm so light inside. I'm like that scene in Mary Poppins where the children float, except without the British accent. "Well, I asked Gino what to get for one of his biggest fans, and he said 'You can't go wrong with the *more*.' And I was, like, *more what* until I read the menu and saw meatball, onion, ricotta."

DJ passes me a slice on a plate and then grabs one for himself. We are both starving, so we eat in silence for an entire slice. Then he grabs another one. "Jesus H, that's good. I haven't eaten much today. Too stressed out."

I don't ask why, because he probably won't say, and I don't want to be shot down. "Well, I wish you could have seen my faceoff fades. They were tight. And I beat-matched the songs in the breaks between periods."

Chewing, he sets down his plate and studies me. His eyes glitter with humor. I know I've just said yet another dorkalicious thing, but I don't even care. Because DJ *gets* me.

When I've finished my slice, he takes the plate out of my hands and sets it beside his. Then he reaches over to slide one muscular forearm beneath my knees, and he slides me onto his lap as if I weigh no more than the TV remote. Strong arms wrap around me, and my chin lands at his collar bone. I tuck my face into his neck and take a deep breath. He relaxes back against the sofa and sighs. As if we sit cuddling like this all the time.

It would be nice if we did.

It's peaceful hearing DJ's heart *glug-glugging* under my ear. One of his big hands strokes my hair slowly. "Thank you," he says, his voice a low scrape in my ear.

I don't know if he's thanking me for subbing at the rink or for feeding him pizza. Or maybe for just showing up—I hope that's why.

Sitting curled in his lap is doing strange things to my senses. His body heat seems to singe me everywhere we touch. I'm acutely aware of the fresh scent of laundry detergent and clean boy under my nose. I want to scrape my face against his evening whiskers and run my hands down his strong chest. The thighs under my body are surprisingly firm, and I'm tempted to explore their shape with my hands.

I think it's inevitable that I'm finally getting another kiss. But I'm too chicken to just go straight in. Instead, I lift my chin a couple of degrees, until my lips find the underside of his jaw. I place one soft kiss there, and then another. I trace the ridge of his jaw with my nose and then kiss him right under the ear.

DJ says nothing. But when I suck his earlobe into my mouth, his breath catches. I'm pretty far out on a limb right now, nibbling on a boy who isn't kissing me back. But since I've spent so much of the last week fantasizing about being with him again, my fear of rejection can't sing loudly enough to be heard over the drum solo of my lust.

Again he shifts my body as if I weigh nothing, turning me around to face him properly. One easy move with my knee and then I'm actually straddling him. My behavior shocks me a little. But apparently it does not shock DJ. He pulls my hips in tight against his and wraps his arms around my waist.

Then he kisses me as if he's just invented kissing and wants to give me a thorough demonstration of how it's done. Apparently it's done with full, hungry lips that press firmly against mine and a gentle tongue that teases the seam of my lips just once before I open for him. And it's done with his hands skimming my back and with the low, throaty sound of longing he makes when I deepen our kiss.

I let my palms wander down his chest and then under his T-shirt. He groans when I pass featherweight fingertips low across his belly. I skim a hand up the ridges of his abs, wishing I could see them. Nibble on them. But I don't know how to ask for more.

Usually, I blame my lack of experience on my strange lifestyle, but the truth is that I'm just gutless. Bella would agree with me in a hot second. If she were in my shoes, she'd have this boy naked and moaning her name in ten seconds flat.

I'm not that kind of girl, although I aspire to be.

DJ's T-shirt is in the way. That's just obvious. So I tug it upward until he gets the message, breaking our kiss to shuck it over his head.

Now I have what I want—an unencumbered expanse of DJ's chest and abs. I dive back into his mouth while my hands skate around all that smooth, tight skin. He groans beneath my touch, and his hands come to rest around my waist, his thumbs gently stroking my belly. I'm turning into a puddle of pure want. Our kisses take on a hot rhythm. Push and pull. Parry and retreat. It's glorious, and I can feel how hard he is between my legs, and it makes me giddy. Because it's me who made him that way.

DJ breaks our kiss by cupping my jaw, his dark eyes appraising me from very close range. "What do you want, sweetheart?" he asks softly.

You. Everything. Please.

God, isn't it obvious? But he actually wants me to answer. I've never asked a boy for sex before, and I don't know the script. And apparently it takes several margaritas to break through my inhibitions. The last time we were here in this house, I offered to massage him with my very drunk tongue. And the only result was embarrassment.

What to do?

In the end, I take the cheaters' way out. I lift my top part way up until DJ catches on and pulls it off.

Achievement unlocked.

In celebration, DJ pulls me against his warm body so that we're skin to skin. Then he sweeps the hair off my shoulder and begins to kiss my collarbone.

Now, I was home-schooled, so there are likely gaps in my scientific education. And I've just discovered a doozy. Nobody ever taught me that there was an electric wire running from my neck to my lady bits. As DJ worships my neck with his mouth, I feel myself grow hot and slick between my legs.

Meanwhile, my happy fingers wander his abs, especially the thickening trail of hair beneath his belly button. When I stroke the skin just north of his waistband, his abs clench under my hand, and he gives a throaty groan.

God, that sound. I can't wait to hear it again.

I'm not brave enough to push my hand inside his waistband. So I trail it down the fabric, cupping the hard bulge I find there.

He takes a deep breath, then leans back against the sofa. "Lianne, sweetheart." His voice is strained, and I love the tint of pink on his face. I put it there. "Tell me what you want." He cups my cheek in his hand.

I lean into his palm. It's much easier to touch him than to answer the question.

"We can't have any misunderstandings," he says quietly.

Damn it all—he's not going to let me be my usual chicken-hearted self. But how does someone like me ever learn to navigate these tricky waters, anyway? There has to be a way, or else all the shy people would be bred out of the species.

DJ holds my gaze, waiting. I lay my head on his shoulder and kiss his neck once. Twice. He strokes my hair, but I know he's still listening for me to explain myself. "Act five, scene one," I whisper finally.

"You want to read the Scottish play?" His voice is low and growly and *very* amused. With one of his roughened palms, he skims my bare arm, and I close my eyes to better appreciate it.

"Read just one line. Five-one, line seventy-one."

Cupping my head to hold me in place, DJ leans forward just far enough to grab my paperback off the table. I keep my face buried in his neck while he flips to the scene I've given him.

I can tell when he finds it, because his stomach contracts in surprise. "It's Lady M's line," he says. "You're supposed to read those."

"Read it for me," I insist, my face burning up.

He lowers his lips until they're brushing the shell of my ear. "To bed," he says in a husky voice. "To bed, to bed."

I hold my breath, wondering if I've made myself clear.

Big hands grasp my rib cage, and DJ rights me gently so I'm forced to look him in the eye. My face burns with the knowledge that I've just propositioned him. But in the positive column, the view from his lap is pretty damned good right now. He's staring back at me with tousled hair and kiss-bitten lips. He looks hot and turned on and all mine. "I'm crazy about you," he says.

"I know," I tease. But it's all bravado.

He chuckles anyway. His fingertips trace up and down my bare back, and it's heaven. "I'm having a terrible year, Lianne. You're the only good thing in it."

"It will get better," I insist.

For a moment he's quiet. "The thing is, I'm not sure it will." Instinctively I tighten my arms around DJ. But he doesn't dive in for a kiss like I want him to. "Christ," he whispers. "I'm sorry."

"Why?" My voice comes out all breathy and weird. Like I've just run a race. My heart wobbles on the edge of the diving board, wondering if we're about to get thrown over.

"I'm a bad bet right now, smalls. I might not be around much longer."

My scalp tingles. "Daniel, am I trapped in a John Green novel? Do you have three weeks to live?"

His abs shake as he chuckles at me. "It's nothing like that, but thanks for the dose of perspective. I might not finish the semester, though." His smile fades immediately, and he reaches up to my face, his thumb gliding across the cheekbone. Even this PG-rated touch gives me tingles. "And I'm done with one-night stands. So I wasn't going to go there with you."

Well, damn. It's not that I don't appreciate the chivalry. But it isn't every day I decide to sleep with someone. And I know he wants to. At least part of him does. I put two hands on his firm chest, and I lay my head on his shoulder again, just because I can. "Look," I whisper. "I've never Shakespeare-propositioned anyone before. I wouldn't do that unless I was sure."

DJ hugs me again, giving me a gentle kiss on the temple. I hold my breath, waiting to see what he'll decide. I tilt my head to the side so his kiss lands again on the delicate skin near my collar bone. And then he's sucking gently, kissing me, while I melt like a cheap lipstick over his body. Two hands slide down my back, landing on my ass. Then he squeezes, and it's so wonderfully dirty that I hear myself whimper.

He groans. Then he stands up, lifting me, slinging an arm underneath my backside. While I cling to him, he carries me on a short trip to his darkened room. A few seconds later my back hits the bed, and I pull him down, too.

As DJ's weight settles onto my body, he lets out a husky sound of approval, and it vibrates down my body, boomeranging at my toes and zipping upward again. I let my hands slide up DJ's smooth back, enjoying the dip of the centerline and every single muscle along the way. Meanwhile, he's kissing his way up my neck and onto my throat.

Suddenly, it's just not naked enough in here, though the weight of his hard body is glorious. He's winding his fingers into my hair while his mouth worships my skin. I am a puddle of need underneath him, and nothing he does is quite enough. The clothes that separate us are my new enemy. I want them gone, but it's a problem. Because I refuse to push DJ even one millimeter away in order to fix it.

All I can do is roll my hips upward, willing my jeans and his sweatpants to vanish, like a bit of Princess Vindi sorcery. If there was a spell for getting naked, I'd utter it.

Luckily, DJ understands. In between scorching kisses, he presses up off my body and puts a hand on my fly. "Are these coming off?" he asks.

In answer, I pop the button myself and lower the zipper. DJ tugs the fabric and the jeans are history. I give his sweats a tug and *whoosh!* They disappear, along with his boxers.

My eyes are adjusting to the dark room. The streetlights beam through his one window, and it's just enough to appreciate how beautiful he is. His abs could be featured in a fitness magazine, and that V of muscle diving down past his hip bones... Yum. Is it terrible if I just stare?

Two strong arms reach out and pull me against his body. He dips his head and begins dropping kisses at the top of my breast, just above the skimpy bra I'm wearing. Then he noses beneath the fabric and takes my nipple into his mouth.

I'm not expecting that, or the bolt of desire that rips through me. My gasp causes DJ's head to pop up in surprise. We stare at each other for a second, until I shake off my stupor and flick apart the bra's front clasp. Slowly, he lowers his head again, nudging the cups of my bra out of the way, grazing my overheated skin with his lips. "Mmm," he rumbles.

"They're small," I can't help pointing out.

He shakes his head, his aquiline nose brushing the swell of my breast. "They're perfect. Just like the rest of you." He cups one breast, then lowers his mouth and sucks.

God. With a loud moan, I practically leap off the bed like a patient who's been shocked with a defibrillator. DJ answers me with a sexy rumble. Then his hand slips straight down my tummy and into the underwear that I've already soaked through. Thick fingers slide low between my legs, coming to rest exactly where I want them. He begins to touch and tease me, and I'm trembling beneath him as he kisses his way across my chest.

It's so, so sexy. I don't even know what to do with so much desire. So I roll toward him, and we're on our sides now, facing each other, and kissing again. Always kissing. His big hand keeps up its ministrations between my legs, until I'm full-fledged vibrating with arousal. His fingertips shove down my panties and I hold my breath.

"This okay?" he rasps, and my answer is a moan.

My panties disappear. He's removed them with some kind of ninja move. I'm finally nekkid with the only man I've ever really wanted. There are nervous butterflies in my stomach, but only because I don't want to do this wrong. But DJ takes my hand and places it right onto a very hard dick. I'm surprised at how satin-smooth he is and how *hot*. I give him an exploratory stroke, and he growls into my mouth. So I do it again. Every sound he makes seems to vibrate deep in my core.

His tongue pushes into my hungry mouth just as his hips roll me back into the bed. And... wow. A loud moan escapes from my mouth, and I decide to be embarrassed about it later.

DJ chuckles, and it's the most beautiful sound, all low and sexy. "Lianne?"

"Mmm?"

"Are we having sex?"

Just hearing the words in his gravelly, turned-on voice gives me a spasm of nervous excitement. "Yes," I whisper. I'm about ten seconds from spontaneous combustion.

The next sound I hear is the glide of his bedside table opening, and the crinkle of a condom packet. He tosses the packet onto the bed. Then he kisses me on the forehead. "You sure?" he whispers. "There are a lot of other ways I can make you feel good."

I give a happy shiver, wondering if I could get him to start at the top of the list and tick them off one by one. But since I can finally have what I really want, I pick up the condom and hand it to him.

He takes it, holding my gaze. Then he leans down and gives me a single, serious kiss. "All right," he says, as if deciding something. When he kisses me again, I grab him with both arms and both legs and hold on tight.

Chapter Eighteen

TOTALLY SPOILED FOREVER

DJ

Using the moment to cool down, I sit up and rip open the condom packet. Sheathing myself carefully, I take a couple of deep breaths.

I haven't trusted anyone with my body in months. But nobody else gets to me the way Lianne does. When she looks up at me with those pretty, intelligent eyes, there isn't a thing in the world I wouldn't do for her if she asked me. And she's asking for this. It's in her shy smile and the way her body responds every time I touch her.

For the first time in months, I'm buzzing with both desire and optimism. Trusting someone enough to take her to bed isn't easy for me anymore. But this is Lianne. She's smart and fierce and lovely. And she's reaching for me not just with her arms but with her entire being.

Lianne puts one of her small, soft hands on my hip, her thumb grazing my ass. There is love in her touch, and I close my eyes and focus on that. Tonight she's pulling me back across this threshold.

The way she showed up at my door with pizza and a smile when I really needed her.

I lie down beside her, pulling her into my arms for a hug. And as she sighs against my chest, I realize something important—it's not just Lianne who I trust right now, it's *me*. I know what mutual desire looks like. It looks a lot like the panting, happy girl in my bed. Her eagerness feeds my own. The volume on the confusion I've felt all year is lowered just a fraction of a decibel every time Lianne touches me. Because I'm not crazy, I'm not blind, and I'm not deaf to nuance. Not tonight, and not before.

Lianne kisses my neck, and it's true joy that I experience as I roll her closer to my body. We are skin on skin, and it's the best thing ever. "You make me happy," I whisper, because it's true.

"You make me crazy," she returns.

"Crazy bad?" I kiss her neck. "Or crazy good?" I suck gently on her sensitive skin and she whimpers in my arms. When I slide one of my knees between her two smooth ones, she throws her head back and lets her legs fall apart. It's the sexiest thing I've ever seen. I'm going to burst from wanting her.

I settle myself in the cradle of her body. We line up perfectly together, and I wonder if she's noticed. Bracing myself on my elbows, I lean in for more kisses. No matter what, I will never get enough of her.

Her eyes lift to mine, and they're heavy-lidded. Even in the dark I can make out a flush on her cheeks. Her lips are swollen from my kisses. She's waiting, but I stop to watch her for a moment. Not because I'm uncertain. Just because I *cherish* this. While it's damn hard to find a silver lining in anything that's happened to me lately, I'm positive that I appreciate Lianne more right now than I would if my life were easier.

After one more doozy of a kiss—it's almost impossible to stop at one—I take one of her hands and wrap it around my erection. Then I lower myself so that I'm right at heaven's doorstep. On a sigh she pulls me into her body. When she removes her hand, I kiss her palm and then slide the rest of the way inside. And it's beautiful. She's soft and tight and gripping my hips with her knees.

I have to drop my head into the shelter of her shoulder for a moment to regroup. It's been a long time since I dared to get so close to anyone, and I didn't realize letting down my guard could ache like this. I'm facedown in the ocean, and she's the lifeboat. I'm devastated by the way she's holding me everywhere at once.

"Daniel," she whispers, straining to hold me closer.

Hearing my name on her lips makes my heart skip a beat. "You good?" I ask, giving my hips an experimental roll.

"So much better than good." When I roll my hips again, she lets out a shuddering moan.

Jesus H.

I work it slowly, because I want this to last. It won't, though, if Lianne keeps making those irresistible noises. I love how she sounds so out of control. Right now, she's not the cautious girl who hides under her baseball cap. She's eager and a little crazy, and I love it. Nobody gets this version of Lianne but me. Tonight, no one exists except the two of us. I would keep it this way forever if I could.

Kissing my way down her hairline, I pause at her ear. "First time I ever saw you, I wanted a kiss," I whisper, punctuating it with a kiss on her cheekbone. "Now I'm totally spoiled. Forever."

It was true, too. Lianne tugs my head down for another deep kiss as I sink into her once again. This is how it feels to get just what you need when you didn't even know you needed it. It's not just the shock of pleasure I feel every time I move. It's the soothing beat of her heart against mine and the way she holds on as though she's never letting go.

We meet again and again, and it's beautiful.

Her breathing shifts, becoming hot and desperate. Her hands

grip my arms, then my sides, then my back, as if she's searching for something and not quite finding it. I take a deep breath, trying to hold myself together a little longer. Reaching back, I grab one of her smooth legs in my hand and bend it, kissing her knee and holding it tightly to my chest.

"*Oh*." She grips my ribcage.

I bear down, closing my eyes, trying to resist the pull. But the erotic look on her face is burned on my brain, the way her mouth makes a perfect O of surprise. I groan against the pressure to burst from so much desire.

"Oh, D..." She bites off my name on a gasp. Then she gasps again. And the sound of her coming apart ruins me. She grips my body everywhere and I let myself go, chasing down my own release with more urgency than elegance. Sensation clobbers me, and I let it all go—all the tension, all my anger. Like a burning arrow, I let it all fly. It singes me clean through, until there's nothing left but our rapid breathing and sweaty limbs.

Heavy-limbed and spent, I roll to the side and pull Lianne with me. She wraps her arms around my neck and burrows in with a comfortable sigh. I don't ask how she is because I already know the answer. A small, soft hand traces quiet patterns on my back, while her breathing evens out.

We hold each other for a while, until exhaustion weighs me down. I give her a tight hug, but then I struggle to sit up, leaving one hand on her perfect ass. "Be right back," I practically slur. I stumble into the bathroom. After a necessary minute in there, I remember that I left half a pizza on the coffee table, so I shuffle out to put it away in the fridge.

A minute later I slide back into bed and pull Lianne's small body against mine. "I've been awake since four," I tell her as my eyes fall closed. "I have to sleep. I'm sorry."

Her slim hand caresses my hair. "Can I stay?"

"Of course," I mumble. "You got somewhere else you need to be?"

"No," she laughs.

I try to give her a sleepy smile, but I'm too tired. The last thing I feel before falling asleep is her head on my bare chest.

Chapter Nineteen

THE SOUND

Lianne

Consciousness comes to me slowly.

At first I'm only ten percent awake, and I discover that I'm lying on my side in bed. That's nice. Somehow I know it's Sunday, and there's nothing on my calendar.

When my consciousness approaches the fifty percent mark, I realize I'm not in *my* bed. The light is all wrong, and the pillow too thick.

None of that matters, though, because I'm tucked against a deliciously hard body. When I glance down, I find a strong forearm wrapped over my hip. And a broad hand is splayed on my belly. The sight of it gives me a little spasm of happiness.

I'm in *DJ's* bed.

I'm in DJ's *bed!*

Yay!

I reach one hundred percent consciousness in a hurry and then overshoot, clocking in at a hundred and fifty. There are voices outside DJ's bedroom. My face heats at the idea of being caught naked in bed with a guy. Thank God the door is closed. I'd pulled it shut last night after I slipped away from a sleeping DJ for a drink of water and to borrow his toothpaste.

Just as I'm worrying about this, someone knocks. "Deej? Can I come in?" It's his brother's voice.

I'm frozen with indecision. If I answer, I'll out myself. But if I don't answer, that door is going to swing open.

DJ saves us by waking up enough to respond. "Not if you want to live," he grunts.

"Okayyy..." Leo chuckles. "But I need to ask you how it went yesterday."

"Why?" DJ sounds irritated.

"What do you mean, *why?* Because I care about your case."

"Not now," DJ growls, sitting up. "Jesus."

"Sorry," Leo says after a beat. Then he moves away from the door.

DJ tips himself back onto the bed, throwing a forearm over his eyes and sighing into the silence.

"Your case?" I echo before I can think better of it.

He grunts. "We'll talk about that."

"We will?" I roll toward him, and I'm rewarded with a view of his spectacular six-pack. But when I look up, he's frowning.

DJ pulls me in against his chest. An impressive proportion of our skin is touching and it's kind of glorious. "I don't want you to hear it from anyone but me," he says softly. "But we'll get dressed and go out for coffee. Not talking about that here."

I lay my cheek on his shoulder. "Okay." Now that he's promised to tell me, I feel a tingle of fear. For a short time I'd been wrapped in the DJ cocoon, where there was only sex and sharing his bed.

He holds me close, one hand stroking my back. I've never woken up nekkid in a man's bed before, and it's pretty great. The luxury of rolling over for cuddles? I want this every morning.

I don't speak, because I don't want to break the spell. But I wonder where DJ's head is. I can almost hear the creak of his gears turning. After a little while he startles me by saying, "I hope you know I'm crazy about you."

Squeak! I barely restrain myself from blurting out any number of embarrassing echoes of this sentiment. But I stay quiet because I'm afraid of over-sharing, and also because DJ sounds sad. Like he's saying it because he might not get another chance.

Instead of answering, I nestle closer, nuzzling his shoulder.

He pushes the hair away from my face, kisses my forehead and sighs. And I let myself drift.

"I'll check to make sure the bathroom is empty for you," he says after a while.

I take the hint and finally untangle my limbs from his.

My dignity is mostly preserved as DJ escorts me to an empty bathroom. And while I'm trying to make myself presentable, he gets dressed and borrows Orsen's car keys.

I'm putting on my socks when I hear DJ's brother stop him in the living room. "Aren't we going to talk?"

"Not now we're not," DJ says.

Luckily I'd fetched my shirt from the sofa last night before I fell asleep. But my shoes are still in that room. So I have to go in there. I've only ever done the walk of shame once before—from Kevin Mung's trailer to mine. We were filming in Australia, and one of the catering people saw me. The next day, two hundred actors, filmmakers, costume and makeup people and key grips were talking about it.

That's how it felt, at least.

I try to affect a blasé attitude when I walk into the living room. "Hey," I say to Leo Trevi. "Morning."

It doesn't help that he's visibly shocked to see me. "Hey," he says after a beat.

DJ lingers in the doorway. "I've got Orsen's keys. Ready?"

"All right." I take my shoes with as much nonchalance as I can muster. As if sleeping over at a guy's house and then looking his brother in the eye were perfectly routine.

"We're going out for breakfast," DJ says in the direction of his brother.

Leo recovers enough to give us a cheery wave. "Have fun! Just in case you didn't, uh, catch the game on the radio, we won last night."

"You score?"

"Twice."

"Awesome," DJ says, but his face is pained.

We get into the car together, and DJ drives us to a neighborhood I don't recognize. It's not far away, it's just that I never leave the confines of the Harkness campus.

He is silent behind the wheel. But between shifts of the gearstick, he palms my hand where I've rested it on top of my knee.

"You know Harkness a lot better than I do," I point out as he turns into the parking lot of a cute little diner with a neon sign in front. Through the plate-glass windows I see a bustling Sunday morning crowd, and I realize that for the first time in weeks I may have to deal with fans.

Who knew I'd grow to appreciate the shunning of my Harkness classmates?

DJ kills the engine. "Been coming up here for years now with Leo and to see his games. Paid attention because I thought I'd be around for a while."

"Won't you be?"

He snaps the keys from the ignition before turning to me. "Maybe not," he says softly. "That's what I have to talk to you about."

"Okay."

Neither of us makes a move to get out. We sit for a moment listening to the engine tick. "There's this sophomore girl," he says eventually.

My heart does a dive off a cliff, with a triple flip, full twist.

DJ sighs. "See, I don't even know where to start. With the shitty thing I did? Or the shitty thing she *says* I did."

"What if you started at the beginning?"

"Right. Okay. She, um." His eyes lift to mine. "She lived in my entryway last year. You know how it is on Fresh Court—the other freshmen are the only people you know at first. They become your first friends."

I nod, even though I don't really know this. Because my brilliant manager decided that Fresh Court wasn't secure enough for Princess Vindi. That's why I live in Beaumont House already, across the bathroom from Bella. The rest of my class won't join me there until next year.

"She was my lab partner in Bio 114. We were friendly, but..." He clears his throat. "That's all. Until April eleventh."

He watches me for a reaction, but I'm only confused. "What happened on April eleventh?"

"Well, her sister was visiting, so she asked if she could stay in my room." DJ swallows hard. "My roommate and I kept a camping mat for visitors. She brought her own sleeping bag and everything."

After he falls silent, I wait a moment. But his reluctance is stubborn. "Then what happened?"

"Well, my roommate fell asleep. And he started to snore. Like really loudly. That happens when he's been drinking. And Annie starts giggling. We're both awake."

Annie. I have a feeling I'm going to wish I'd never heard this name. "Then?"

His eyes are on the gear shift. "She got up off the floor and climbed into my bed. She started kissing me, and I let her. Things went on from there. We had sex." His voice is completely flat. The words "we had sex" are uttered with the same enthusiasm as a guy would use to say, "They gave me the death sentence."

"That happens," I lie. To me, sex with DJ was a Very Big Deal. But for him it might be just another Saturday night. I don't like knowing that.

"And afterward she got into her sleeping bag on the floor. And when I woke up the next morning she was gone. I thought that was the end of the story. I mean...we didn't talk about it afterward. I, uh..." He sighs. "I steered clear of the topic, because I wasn't really interested in starting something up."

That part sounds familiar. That's *exactly* how it was between Kevin and me—we did it once. It was awkward. We never spoke of it again. "But you were still lab partners," I point out. The awkwardness goes away eventually. Kevin and I are still good friends.

"Yeah. We got a B-plus on our final project. I felt like a dick for awhile, though. Like maybe she was waiting for me to ask her out. But I wasn't interested in dating her. Maybe that sounds mean, but she wasn't really on my radar. And if she hadn't climbed into my bed, nothing would have happened." He gave his head a violent shake. "I thought that was the end of it."

"But it wasn't?"

He squeezes his eyes shut. "I got a call four months later. In August. From the assistant dean of students. Turns out this girl told the dean's office that it wasn't consensual."

At first I'm not sure I'd heard him correctly. It takes a moment for his words to play back in my mind. And when they do, a chill spreads across my shoulder blades. "She *what?*"

His eyes still closed, he nods. "But it did *not* happen like that. I've thought about that night a thousand times since. There are all these details I use to hold on to my sanity." His eyes snap open. "She *wasn't* drunk, either."

"Okay," I whisper.

And DJ keeps talking now, the words tumbling out. "She initiated *everything*. The kissing. Then the touching. She's the one who asked me if I had a condom." He pushes the heels of his hands into his eye sockets. "I didn't force *anything*. I would never do that."

That's when I remember to breathe. "I know that," I gasp.

Because, on a gut level, I *do* know it. But I'm also confused. How could two people have such a different version of events?

DJ pushes his body back against the car door. "Like I said, I'm telling you this so you don't hear it from someone else. But I know how crazy it sounds."

"So..." I'm still trying to wrap my head around it. "What's going to happen?" If the college really thought he raped someone nine months ago, why was he still here?

He gives his head a shake. "I wish I knew. The college has me on a kind of probation until they decide whether or not they believe me. There's no criminal case against me. Harkness can handle me however they want. I have a lawyer, and he's trying to get them to do a thorough investigation. But they don't have to."

I swallow, and my throat is dry. "Why do you think the girl would do this? Who wants that kind of attention?"

His expression flattens, as if someone suddenly turned out all the lights. My heart is thumping like crazy, and I realize my question sounds like an accusation. But I'm really just trying to understand.

DJ's dark gaze travels to the ceiling of the car and stays there. "I don't know, Lianne," he says carefully. "But I've spent a thousand hours thinking about it. And I can't *ask* her. I can't even stand in the same room with her. The college has ordered me to keep back fifty yards."

That gives me a shiver down my spine, because it sounds like something on *Cops*. It's hard for me to reconcile the boy I slept with last night with someone who basically has a restraining order against him. But nothing of what he's told me makes sense. "Okay, if she's seriously telling the college you..." I bite off the end of my sentence, unwilling to put that word next to DJ's name. "If that's what she says happened, then why aren't the cops involved? And why did she wait—" I do the math, "—four months to say something? That's got to look weird, right?"

He shakes his head. "Real rapes are underreported all the

time. Because girls are scared or embarrassed." He has to stop and take a breath. DJ looks almost as stressed as I feel. "The college wouldn't think the lag was weird. But the whole thing makes me feel insane."

"I bet."

"I mean *really* insane." His voice cracks. "In the middle of the night I get all these wacko ideas. Like—what if she got raped for real, and was too traumatized to remember the details? Maybe her memory only offered up this random night in April. Or what if someone snuck into my dorm room that same night and hurt her? And I know I sound like a fucking crazy person right now. But these are the things I think about when I can't sleep."

Macbeth hath murdered sleep, my brain offers up.

"And the worst part is that I can feel all my friends wondering, too. And my family. My parents say they believe me. But I can hear them wondering—if I'm innocent, how the *fuck* did I get into this situation?"

"I can't even imagine."

One of DJ's hands grips the steering wheel, and his knuckles are white. I don't think he even knows he's doing it. His other hand fidgets with Orsen's keys. "I know this is a lot to dump in your lap. I wanted to take you out for pancakes. You..." He frowns. "The only time I feel like myself is when I'm with you. But if you want me to drive you home instead, it's really okay."

He stares out the front windshield now, looking at nothing. I'm good at reading people's emotions, and I can feel the stress pouring off him. Right now I have to decide what to do—are we going to try to have a semi-normal breakfast, like lovers do on a Sunday? Or are we going to go home?

And that's when I realize why DJ didn't tell me about this before. Because I can't sit here without forming my own theories and opinions about what happened. Just like everyone else in his life, I have to decide whether I believe he's telling the truth or not.

God, how does he get through the day?

"Let's have breakfast," I hear myself say. "Can we order bacon?"

He tips his head back against the window, and I get a small, weary smile. But no dimples. "Of course we can." He has the air of a man who's ordering his last meal. But it will have to do.

We get out of the car and walk silently to the front door. It swings open suddenly, and when I take a quick step backwards, my back collides with DJ's chest. He tucks me into his side almost absently, his arm circling my back. And while we wait for a family to make their way outside, he brushes a kiss against my cheekbone.

I was *this close* to having an ordinary lovers' Morning After. But now we're only acting those parts.

And the room is full of people. Too full. "Can we have that booth in the back corner?" I ask the hostess quickly.

"Sure, hon," she says, grabbing two laminated menus.

I pull my hat down ridiculously far and follow her in a hurry.

DJ does the gentlemanly thing and takes the seat that faces the door to the kitchen. But that's actually the seat I want, because then I don't have to worry about making accidental eye contact with someone who will ask me to take a selfie with them. I take off Bella's hockey jacket and my trusty baseball cap and toss them on the empty seat. Then I say, "Scoot in."

After aiming a look of surprise at me, he complies, making room for me.

I sit down beside his big body. When I pick up my menu, our elbows touch. The fact that we had actual full-on, bare-naked sex last night is both weird and not weird. Here I am scanning the breakfast choices beside a man who was recently inside me. This idea heats me up, and I lose my focus between the western omelet and the quiche Lorraine.

DJ puts his hand on my knee, and I start to tingle.

"Um, what?" I ask after a beat, realizing that he's asked me a question. I look up into his slightly amused face.

"Which do you prefer, blueberry or plain?"

It takes me a second to realize we're talking about pancakes. "I don't know. I haven't had pancakes in a decade. I'm more of an egg-white omelet kind of girl."

"Wow," he says, dropping his menu on the table. "Scary revelations all around today." He smiles, but it doesn't make it all the way to his eyes. The boy beside me is drowning in his troubles. They're here in the booth with us and sucking down all the available oxygen. I wish I could rewind twelve hours or so to when I didn't know. But that isn't really fair. DJ told me a couple of times he needed to keep his distance, and I pursued him anyway.

Now I tip my head to the side, resting it on his bulky shoulder. He turns to me and brushes a quick kiss on my temple. "What if we go halvsies?" I offer. "A big omelet and pancakes?"

He gives me a little elbow nudge. "An egg-white omelet? I don't know if I can choke that down."

"A real one," I compromise. "But with vegetables in it."

"Deal," he says.

All the food is surprisingly good. Or maybe I'm just starved. But soon my mood is shored up by eggs, pancakes and the side of bacon DJ ordered. I check my phone and find a couple messages from female hockey players thanking me for my "all-chick playlist," as one of them calls it.

When I show DJ, he gives my knee a squeeze. "You don't have to do it. I know you're busy. But if I get kicked out, they'd love to have you for the rest of the season."

The coffee I've drunk goes sour in my stomach. "You're *not* getting kicked out."

"That's my girl." He gives me another sad smile. "*Feisty* Lianne. Maybe you should be my lawyer. I'd rather spend four hours with you than him, too. That's where I was yesterday. He's still hoping to get me a real hearing."

"What if they don't? What's his plan B?"

DJ actually winces. "He wants to sue the college for violating my rights. I'm not allowed to set foot in the residences. You may have noticed that I, uh, never walk you upstairs."

"That's why you live in Orsen's house."

He nods. "I'm hanging by a thread, smalls. I'm sorry to dump the whole sordid tale in your lap. But I need you to know why I'm a shitty date most of the time. It's not because I don't like you."

I grab his hand under the table and squeeze. DJ finishes his pancakes left-handed so that he doesn't have to let go of me. And even though we haven't had the most conventional lovers' Sunday morning breakfast, it will just have to do.

When the waitress drops the check on our table, DJ snatches it up. And I don't pull out my wallet and try to pay half, because I know he doesn't want me to. Maybe I don't date, but I watch films about people who do. I know the most basic rituals. The dude gets to pay sometimes, even if the chick got two million dollars for her last film.

"Thank you for breakfast," I say as I slip out of the booth after he's paid.

DJ gets out, too. Then he reaches for my things on the opposite seat. "It was nothing, smalls," he says quietly, holding out my coat for me to put on.

That's when I hear The Sound.

Sometimes it's a sharp intake of breath. Sometimes it's followed by laughter, or a little shriek. But after a while all the forms of The Sound are easily recognizable. Because you know you've been spotted, and the next ten minutes of your life have been rescheduled, and there's not a damned thing you can do about it.

Today it comes from two tables away, where three teenaged girls and perhaps their grandmother are having brunch together.

One of the girls has clapped her hand over her mouth, and the beads on the ends of several dozen braids are swinging around in her shock. Behind a pair of bright pink glasses, her eyes bug out and then light up.

She is adorable, and yet she brings out my inner sociopath. Because the timing? Not good.

"Omigod!" she yells, jumping up so fast that the glasses of orange juice on their table wobble. Her sisters' eyes travel over to see what she's staring at.

In their excitement, the girls practically leap their table to get to me. I turn to warn DJ and watch as his eyes widen in alarm. Then, in the span of a fangirl shriek, he moves with freakish precision, somehow sliding his body between me and the charging girls.

"Um," I say, putting a hand on his back. "It's okay."

He looks over his shoulder with one eyebrow raised, as if asking how a thundering herd of girls could ever be okay. But he doesn't know how it is with me.

"Omigod," the girl with the pink glasses says again, peering around DJ. "I saw on the news that you lived in Harkness now and I've been looking ALL OVER THE PLACE! Please? Can we have a picture?" She whips out a phone, and DJ eyes it like it's a rattlesnake in the desert.

I give him a gentle shove out of the way, because I know the only way out is through. I take the camera from the girl's hand and pass it to my freaked-out-looking date. "Take a couple, please?"

The girls swarm around me, giggling and touching me. I smile as best I can and try not to think too hard about my unwashed hair and yesterday's walk-of-shame clothes. *They don't care that you're not wearing any makeup*, I promise myself.

I'm almost free when someone mentions autographs.

Digging into my pocketbook for one of the Sharpies that I

always keep there, I tell DJ that he can warm up the car if he wants. "I'll just be a second."

He eases toward the door, but his face is wary.

I sign a napkin, a phone case and a library card before making my excuses. By some miracle, nobody else stops me, and I'm shooting for the door of the diner a minute later.

DJ yanks it open and we're free.

We hurry over to Orsen's car and climb inside, slamming the doors. He cranks the engine and then lets it warm up. "Shit," he says finally. "Does that happen a lot?"

I shrug, because it does, but I don't want to admit it. That wasn't even so bad—those girls approached me when I was putting on my coat. But people have sat down *at my restaurant table*. They've followed me into the ladies' room. They've gotten off the elevator at my hotel room floor just to see where I'm sleeping.

"People are really fucking scary," DJ says suddenly, echoing my own thoughts.

"This is true."

Our ride back to Beaumont House is subdued. I don't know where DJ's head is, but I'm wondering about a girl named Annie. Who she is. And why she'd accuse him.

"Are you okay?" he asks when we pull up outside.

"Yeah," I say immediately. "Are you?"

He regards me with those dark eyes. At least now I know how he comes by his brooding. "Sure," he says, fooling nobody. But this is a ritual too. The man says he's fine. He has a big strong body, ergo he is not allowed to crumble.

Today I feel like telling ritual to go suck it.

Quickly, I lean over and kiss him. He makes a little, bitten-off sound of surprise. "Thank you for telling me," I say.

"Thank you for being awesome," he says, his voice all gravel.

"You owe me a couple of hours of Shakespeare," I remind him.

"I'll pay up." I see the flicker of a real smile when he says it. There was even the ghost of a dimple.

"You'd better," is the last bit of bravado I fling at him before getting out, waving and closing the door.

Inside the Beaumont gate, I take the flagstones two at a time. I whip over to our entryway door and then up the stairs. In my room, I throw Bella's jacket on my floor and climb onto the bed where nobody slept last night. I put my face in the crook of my elbow and take a deep breath.

I don't know what to think about the bomb DJ just dropped on me. I asked him to, of course. And before that, he'd tried to warn me away. Now I understood why he'd been holding that story in. To hear it *required* you to choose a side, and I kind of hated myself for thinking about it like that.

Every moment I'd spent with DJ I'd felt absolutely safe with him. And if anyone asked me right this second whether DJ was a terrific guy, I'd say yes in a heartbeat.

So what the hell happened last April eleventh?

My computers were just across the room, their screen-savers scrolling through a slideshow of my dragon corral. I know at some point in the next couple of hours, my curiosity will win, and I'll be Googling the heck out of all the girls at Harkness named Annie. But first I will bathe.

I'm humming one of the DragonFire themes (it's a sickness) when I shut off the water after my shower. Shoving the curtain aside, I'm startled to find Bella standing there. She hands me my towel, one eyebrow raised.

"Morning," I say as my cheeks begin to heat.

"You are so busted. I knocked on your door an hour ago and there was nobody home."

"That happens," I try. "I had an early breakfast."

She grins. "With who?"

Jeez. I wrap the towel around myself and duck past her and into my room.

She follows me, of course. "Come on, babe. Did you or didn't you?"

See, I've pictured this moment before. I've actually been looking forward to the time I'd finally have to confess to Bella that DJ had rocked my world. And he had, of course. But this moment isn't sweet like I'd imagined, because it's been overshadowed by everything I've learned since.

"Well?" Bella demands. "Look, I know you're a private person, but the suspense is killing me. Did you do the deed? Wait—I know you're shy. So you don't even have to say it out loud. Blink once for yes or twice for no."

That makes me giggle, because I love Bella to death. And nobody at Harkness has been more generous to me than she has. "We did it." My smile fades, though, and she notices.

"Omigod." Bella claps her hands to her cheeks. "Why aren't you happier? Was it awful? No—it couldn't have been awful. They're a very talented family..." She's pacing my tiny rug, then stops, a look of horror on her face. "Oh, *hell*. Does he have a fun-sized dick?"

"No!" I squeal. "And even if he did, I'd still love him." Then it was my turn to clap a hand over my mouth. DJ wasn't even my boyfriend. I'd basically seduced him after feeding him pizza. Listen to me, jumping the gun.

Her eyes widen. "Hold on, sister. So what's the problem?"

"He's perfect. But..." I stop. Can I even tell Bella? Was that betraying DJ's trust? He hadn't asked me to keep it a secret, though.

"Sweetie, you're scaring me," she says, sitting down on the bed. "Did something happen? Did the condom break?"

"It's nothing like that." I sit beside her. "DJ has a problem, and I don't know what to think. But it doesn't leave this room."

Bella makes a heart-crossing motion in front of her chest. "I know that most of the time I have no filter. But I am capable of keeping my trap shut. Especially for you, shorty."

"I know. There's a weird story I need to tell you..."

Five minutes later, Bella's eyes are bugging out. "I just can't picture that at all."

"Me neither."

"I mean..." Bella stares up at my ceiling. "He's such a good guy. Of course, I can't really picture *any* guy doing that. Yet it happens all the time..."

Ugh. Bella's twisty train of thought runs a lot like mine.

"And if he didn't do it, why would anyone say he did? Not just *say* it either—say it to the dean's office. That place intimidates the hell out of me. You'd have to be totally insane to waltz in there for fun and lie about something like that."

The pancakes I ate earlier twist in my stomach. "It's just weird, right?"

Bella gives me the side eye. "So who is this Annie?"

"No idea."

"Really? You haven't hacked into the college database yet to run a background check on her? You're slipping, my friend."

"You know I want to," I say slowly. "But I shouldn't stick my nose in."

Bella chuckles. "You will, though. Have you met you?"

Indeed I have.

Chapter Twenty

CAPTAIN OBVIOUS

DJ

After I drop off Lianne, I fill Orsen's gas tank to thank him for the loan of his car. The gray sky over the town of Harkness is a perfect reflection of my mood.

When I get home, my freaking brother is still sitting on the couch in the living room, drinking a cup of coffee out of my mug. I skirt him and head into my room.

But he appears in the doorway a minute later. Shit. The dude spends more time in this house than I do. If I get kicked out in a couple weeks, he can just take over my room. Maybe that's his plan, anyway.

"Hey," he says.

"Hey." I wait.

It only takes him a moment to go right for the jugular. "Dude," he says. "I didn't know you and Lianne..."

"What do *you* care?" I ask through gritted teeth. "Are you going to tattle to Dad?"

"Whoa." Leo holds up a hand in a sign of surrender. "Jesus, no. I don't fucking care if you're hooking up with her. No, that's not true. I *do* care. Good for *you*, dude. I'm dead serious. If I was in your shoes, I think I'd have, like, chick-induced PTSD."

"Who says I don't?" I grunt, not trusting his enthusiasm. Not trusting *anything*.

Even though I wish he would leave, Leo sits down on the end of the bed. "You're awful grumpy for somebody who got laid."

"You think?" I push my hand over my eyes. "She's probably running for the hills right now." Last night was perfect, but I hadn't done the math. This morning it's so obvious that I've fucked everything up with Lianne. She was the best thing that had happened to me in months. But getting so close to her meant I had to confess my troubles.

So now she's no longer the only person who won't look at me like maybe I'm a terrible person.

"Why is she running for the hills?" Leo asked quietly.

"Because I told her at breakfast. You know. The whole ugly tale."

"Nice timing."

I give him a little jab with my foot. "Thanks, Captain Obvious. But I didn't have a choice. I need to explain why I never walk her home. Why she was covering for me in the booth at the women's game..."

Leo is so quiet that I check his face. "She didn't take it well?"

"She took it fine over breakfast. But she's probably in her room right now starting to wonder. Everyone does, right?"

My brother shakes his head. "Not everyone."

"Don't say that," I hiss. "You *seriously* want to sit here and tell me that you never wondered whether I was guilty?"

"Danny, I never have."

"*Liar.*"

His head snaps back as if I've punched him. "Look, jackass. I *get* why you're angry. But save it for the people who are screwing you over. I never doubted you. Not for a second."

Bullshit. How could anyone *never* doubt? I know better than anyone what happened that night. And all I do is sit around wondering what the hell happened. And what I missed.

My brother nudges the calculus book beside him on the bed. "You got a lot of work to do today?"

"Does it matter if I do it? My semester is circling the drain."

"Then let's go to the rink. I need to loosen up before practice."

"Nah." I grab the book. "Don't feel like it."

"Danny, don't be like this."

He grabs the book out of my hand. And it's such an annoying big brother thing to do that my blood pressure shoots up immediately. "Don't be like *what?* You think I'm lazy?"

"I think you're *depressed*, Danny. Like—the real thing." He hands me the book again.

"Naw."

"*Yes.* This isn't you. You don't sit around in your room. You always have a thousand projects, a DJ loop you're making, party to go to."

"I have *seventeen days* until this meeting. What's the point of anything if I'm not here? Do you not hear me?"

"I do hear you," my brother says. "And I feel like telling Dad that you need help."

"Help with *what?*" My voice cracks. "What's Dad going to do, other than get on my case?"

"Maybe you need to see someone," my brother says, his face grave.

Swear to God, the whole world has lost its mind when it comes to me. "Leo, I *do* see someone. He's called a lawyer, and he costs three hundred an hour. And Dad reminds me of that every chance he gets. Just *go* already. You've done your duty as the good kid. Tell Dad you checked up on me and I'm fine."

"Except you're not."

"Would *you* be? I seriously don't know what you want from me."

And maybe he doesn't know either. Because at that, Leo finally gets up and leaves my room.

I shut the door behind him. The next couple of hours are hell as I try and fail to keep my head on homework. Finally I lie down on my bed and pull out my copy of the Scottish play, because it makes me think of Lianne. She and I never got around to reading any of it last night. I'm probably the only guy on earth who's going to start associating Macbeth with foreplay. *Is that a dagger I see before me? Yeah baby. Hold my dagger.*

Smiling for the first time in an hour, I grab my phone and prepare to text her. But I stop myself before sending any dirty Shakespeare quotes. After what I told her this morning, I don't know how she'll take it. Does a dagger joke make me sound like a creeper?

Great. I can officially add her to the list of people who are likely to overanalyze everything I say.

I miss you already, I text instead. Because it's true.

———

The following week, my father calls a lot. He wants to talk about the case. As if talking about it is useful. And I can't even duck him, because my sister's visit is coming up, and if she needs to reach me, I have to take calls from home.

Conversations with my dad have been tense all year, but lately they're downright unbearable.

"We need to talk about this potential lawsuit," he says. "Jack wants to do some groundwork so he's ready to file if the hearing doesn't go your way."

"Bad idea," I insist. "Why pay his hourly rate to plan a lawsuit we might not need?"

"Son, we need to be prepared for the worst."

Great. So I'm not the only one with a dim opinion of my chances.

"There's something more. Jack shared a new idea with me."

The wobble in the pit of my stomach suggests I won't like it. "Such as?"

"He knows a group of lawyers who are trying to put together a class-action lawsuit that seeks to set a tough precedent for colleges who try to adjudicate their own rape cases. He thinks your case is perfect."

Perfect. The word bounces around inside my gut. Only an asshole would use that word to describe the hell that is my year. "No way."

"Don't say that until you've heard what he has to say," my father snapped.

"Dad, I don't want to be anyone's test case. Ever."

"You have to clear your name!" my father bellows.

When he says that, I just hear *our* name. His name. Shit. "I think you have *no idea* what would happen if we sued the college over this. The whole world is going to just assume that I did it, and that I'm suing to try to find a loophole."

"But if you *didn't* do it," my father fires back, "you should never be afraid to say so."

All I could hear was the word "if" in that sentence. It strikes me dumb.

"Danny," he says. "Don't ever be afraid to tell the truth."

"I am not. Afraid. Of the truth," I grind out. "But thanks for the show of support."

Then, for the first time in my life, I hang up on my father. But it's either that or lose it completely. He's still convinced there's a magic solution that makes the whole thing go away.

There isn't. Yet I'm the only one who sees that.

Chapter Twenty-One

THE WONDER CHILD

Lianne

The days that follow are like a roller coaster. Whenever I try to concentrate on my coursework, my mind drifts to the R-rated scenes we played out in DJ's bed. It's hard to read Brecht when I'm picturing that perfect moment when DJ laid me down on his bed. Rawrrrr. I catch myself staring into space, grinning like a fool.

But whenever I remember he might be kicked out of school, I'm full of despair.

There are sweet texts from DJ that make me smile. But when he calls me to say hello, he sounds blue. And reserved, too. It scares me, because I'm afraid we won't get another chance to be together in the same happy way we were on Saturday night. I'm haunted by the things he told me before we went into his bedroom. "I'm not a good bet." And, "I'm done with one-night stands, so I wasn't going to go there with you."

I didn't listen, did I? Now I want things from him. Big things. And he's already warned me he may not be able to deliver.

My coping mechanism is research. And not all of it healthy.

Of course I've already given in to the urge to search for every Anne, Ann and Anna at Harkness. But she's proved surprisingly elusive. I have a few clues. He said she's a sophomore and in Trindle House.

"Whatcha doing?" Bella says from over my shoulder while I'm in the middle of this task. My screen shows the script I've written to parse every girl at Harkness whose name begins with A.

"God!" I leap in my seat. "You scared me."

"I noticed." My neighbor peers at the screen. "Did you find her?"

There's no point in pretending I don't know who she means. "Nope."

"Stop looking, babe. Eat a bunch of ice cream or get drunk. But obsessing about her is not a good plan."

As if I don't know that. I close the browser window. "I've been researching the politics, too. DJ told me that the college didn't bother to investigate his case. And apparently that's a thing."

"It is?"

I nod. "It's a big problem. Women report a sexual assault to their school, and then the school drops the ball. Because they don't know how to do it right."

Bella lies down on my bed. "When I made my complaint to the dean, they videotaped the whole thing. Did they do the same for DJ?"

"He got a phone call, out of the blue. They're not giving him a chance to defend himself."

"Fuck," Bella empathizes. "Have you seen him lately? Where do you two stand?"

Isn't that the question? "I don't want to be the kind of girl who demands to talk about the relationship. After...you know."

"Sex?" Bella props her chin in the crook of one arm and looks up at me. "But maybe you're the kind of girl who needs to know.

Doesn't make you a bad person. If you need exclusivity to be comfortable, there's no shame in saying so."

Coming out of her mouth, it sounds mature and completely rational. But whenever DJ and I speak on the phone, I can't make myself bring it up. "Maybe I should have thought about that beforehand. And he's got so much on his mind."

"So do you, now," Bella points out.

Right. "But he's got this huge problem to solve. It seems rude to bang down his door and ask if he'll be my boyfriend now."

"But maybe you need to do that before any more banging happens."

"Maybe," I hedge. Wanting a label from him makes me feel needy, though.

"So can we order Thai food and drink cheap white wine tonight?"

The question catches me off guard. "Sure? Well, yes to the Thai food. No to the wine." I've never been a fan.

Bella gets up to get her credit card. It's her turn to pay. I'm firing up the order page online when my phone rings. I answer immediately, of course, hoping it's DJ.

"Lianne," Bob says. "I called you today."

Right. He had. "Sorry," I say, wondering why my calls to him are never returned as promptly as his are supposed to be.

"Did you sign it yet?"

That's Bob for you. He's a charmer. "Any news on the Scottish play?" It's not nice of me to hold this contract hostage. But the minute I sign it I'm going to lose his attention again. Sometimes a girl's gotta do what a girl's gotta do.

"It's not the only good role in Hollywood," he snaps.

"True," I say carefully. I want Lady M. More than life itself. But if Bob wants to talk about other good roles for me, that's a conversation worth having. "What else did you have in mind?"

"After you're done with Princess Vindi, we need to age you up. That's why this sex scene isn't so bad for your career. Directors want to be able to picture you as a female lead. We can't keep peddling you as the wonder child forever."

"I'm listening." It wasn't often that Bob wasted any brain cells trying to think Big Thoughts about my career. I pressed the phone closer to my ear, wondering if any juicy roles have crossed his desk lately.

"Have you considered an enlargement?"

"What?" For a second I don't understand. An enlargement for...photos?

"I think you should consider it," he suggests. "If you want to play the ingenue, you need to have the body."

Shock makes me unable to speak for a moment. "Bob," I finally choke. "I'm not getting bigger boobs. There have to be roles I can play without double Ds."

"A C-cup would be fine," he says. "Lots of parts for those. I mean you."

"I have to go," I manage to say. And somehow I don't throw my phone against the wall. Though I want to.

"Think about it," he says before nuking our call.

Oh, I'll *think* about it. Probably while throwing darts at Bob's picture and grinding my teeth.

"Bella!" I call. "I changed my mind about the wine! I want some."

"Poured it for you already," she returns.

Bella is the best kind of friend. That is all.

———

On Thursday night, I get a chance to see DJ live and in person. He's got an odd gig playing music for a skating party. Harkness College has donated rink time on a Wednesday night for a Boys and Girls Club skating party. He asks me to meet him in the booth and to come hungry.

When I get there, I find that he's brought us Gino's calzones and Caesar salad. And cannoli for dessert.

"Wow," I say, stripping off my coat and putting it over the back of a chair. "Fancy."

"Are you hungry? I'm starved." DJ is bent over his computer, probably cuing up songs. He's already laid out two place-settings, one for each of us. I take off my trusty baseball cap and worry it in my hands. I'm having a dork moment, wondering if I'm supposed to kiss him hello.

He looks up after a minute and smiles. "Hi, smalls. Good to see you."

"Likewise."

DJ drops his eyes to the screen again. "Wasn't sure you'd come."

"Why?"

He gives a half shrug and busies himself again. Below us on the ice, teenagers are circling to a Lady Gaga tune. "Okay," he says eventually, moving away from the keyboard. "This is easier than a game. I've got forty minutes of continuous music cued up. But if you get the urge to be creative, go for it." He comes around to stand beside me, then leans down to kiss my forehead. "Let's eat," he says.

So we do. And we watch the teenagers on the ice. Some of them are skating in earnest, while others cling to the side, laughing at their own attempts to stay vertical. When a slow song comes on, they pair up, holding hands while they circle. The song is John Legend's "All of Me," which is such an over-the-top love song it makes me feel self-conscious. "That guy right there," I say, pointing at a kid in a green jacket. "He's going to ask that girl to skate. The one in the pink hat. I'll put five bucks on it."

DJ snorts. "Okay, I'll take that bet. I don't like your chances, though. The song is half over."

"True." We watch together, waiting to see what happens. I can't see the boy's face, but it's obvious he keeps looking over to where the girl stands. And every time he does, her friends poke each other and giggle.

"I'm not taking your money, smalls," DJ says as the track plays on and on, and John Legend proclaims his undying love. "Our man would probably be brave enough to do it, but her posse is kind of a tough audience."

Down on the ice, our guy shoves his hands in his pockets. I'm about to concede when he pushes off and skates unsteadily toward the clump of girls. "Omigod!" I squeak, grabbing DJ's hand. It closes around mine.

I hold my breath while the boy speaks to them and John Legend croons through the sound system. Finally it happens. The girl turns her back on her friends and wobbles further onto the ice. Our boy reaches for her hand, and then they both wobble. It looks scary there for a second, but then they recover, skating off in a counter-clockwise oval with all the other brave couples.

When I catch DJ watching me, he looks away.

"What?" I ask, my voice thick.

He smiles. "You're just so freaking cute, smalls."

"Would you have asked me to skate? If we met in high school?" That sounds like I'm fishing for compliments. But it pleases me to think about a younger DJ and a high school me. I never went to high school. With my big life and my even bigger paycheck, nobody ever wants to hear me ask what I might have missed.

"I'd have asked you in a hot second," he answers, chuckling. "We didn't have ice skating parties at my school, and it's a damn shame, because this would have been my event, right? And if you couldn't skate, that would make it even better. Because then you'd have to hold on tight." He squeezes my hand. "Wish I'd met you in high school. Everything would be different."

Now I'm sad again.

The song ends, and an uptempo Katy Perry song comes on.

Our couple splits apart. They were together for probably ninety seconds. I hope it's not the end for them.

When the party ends, I help DJ pack up his stuff. "Can I walk you home?" he asks. "I'm headed to the library. With all that's going on, I'm a little behind."

I swallow my disappointment. I'd been hoping for more alone time with DJ. "Sure."

Chapter Twenty-Two

TOOTHBRUSH AND MACBETH

Lianne

Sunday is the next chance I get to have some private time with DJ. I've made the case that I really need to catch up on some Shakespeare. But it's a foil, of course. It's just an excuse for another magic night with him. He invites me over for eight o'clock.

By seven-thirty I've already done my face with subtle *do me* eyes and just a whisper of my favorite cherry lip gloss. But then I make three laps around my tiny dorm room without finding the book I'm looking for. "Hey, Bella?" I call through my open bathroom door. "By any chance have you seen my copy of Macbeth?"

A moment later she appears in my doorway holding it. "Sorry, I was reading it."

"Really? Don't you have your own work to do?" I snatch the book from her hands, frustrated that I just spent twenty minutes looking for it.

"Well if you want to get all technical about it." She tosses herself onto my bed, then watches me stuff the book into my backpack. "Going to DJ's?"

I'm so busted. "Um, why would you ask?"

"Macbeth and your toothbrush? It's a strange combination. Wait..." She lunges for my bag before I can react, her hand closing on something I've stashed in there. She squeals with glee. "Oh MY God! You're bringing lingerie!"

I grab the nightgown out of her hand before she can inspect it further. "It's not lingerie. It's cotton."

"I saw lace."

"You're nosy."

Bella cackles. "Don't forget the condoms. Hey—I have some flavored ones. You want a sample? I have cherry and watermelon. And vanilla, but those are gross."

"I'm good," I say tightly. The fact that I'm hoping for a fun night in DJ's bed embarrasses me, even if Bella doesn't understand my hesitation to say so. It's easy for me to tell DJ that I like him. A lot. But it's still impossible for me to say out loud that I hope he removes all my clothes the second I arrive at his house.

I drop the nightgown on the bed and leave it there. I'd wavered mightily on bringing it, and now it seems pushy of me. Bella hands me my coat with a smile. Then she sweeps the night-gown up, folds it twice and tucks it into my bag.

Without a word, I jam it a little further down so it's not visible from the top.

"Have a fun night," Bella says. "I won't wait up."

"Thanks," I mumble, while Bella snickers.

DJ had said he'd be free to hang out after eight, and it's quarter 'til when I arrive on his street. Hopefully he won't be irritated that I'm early.

Eager much? I tease myself as I climb the stoop.

The other two times I've visited DJ's house, there was nobody else home. But tonight is different. Orsen answers when I knock. "Hey," he says, opening the door wide to admit me. "DJ!" he yells. "Company!"

As I step forward into the living room, several heads swivel around to see who's arrived. There are one or two hockey players I don't know very well and some girls. One of them is wearing that stupid shirt, proclaiming herself to be a student of Harkness who doesn't know me.

Guess that's accurate.

"Hi," I say into that hush that's fallen over them.

"Hey, Lianne," says the freshman O'Hane, but the rest just stare. It's like any day on campus for me. I shift my bag a little higher on my shoulder and hope DJ emerges from wherever he is soon.

"Thought he was in the kitchen," Orsen mutters. "Deej!"

"I'll check," I say, eager to get away from all the eyes on me.

But when I duck around the corner I hear a girl's laughter, and then DJ's low voice saying something teasing to her. Then she laughs again. Though I feel a chill on my neck, I keep going, rounding the refrigerator, spotting DJ at the little table in the corner with a smiling girl with dark, wavy hair.

They look very cozy.

DJ looks up to discover me standing there. And I swear to God, the smile drops right off his face. "Lianne," he says. "Hi."

"Hi," I manage. But I feel like turning around and running out.

He stands up quickly, just as the girl turns her head. "This is my sister, Violet."

His...what?

"Oh my *GOD!*" the girl squeals. "Danny! You didn't tell me you knew Lianne Challice! *I love her!*"

He comes around the table and gives me a one-armed hug, which I return awkwardly. I don't get a kiss, either.

"Sorry I'm early," I say.

Violet is grinning wildly. "Omigod, Danny! You weren't *going* to tell me, were you? Jesus, are you *dating?*"

"Um," DJ says while I die a little inside. He said *um*. So I guess we're not, in fact, dating. I paste what I hope is a neutral expression on my face. And I think I can hear the lacy nightgown in my backpack laughing at me.

Fortunately, Violet is still making The Sound, and doesn't seem to notice her brother dodged the question. She's jumped up to grab my hand, pumping it up and down. "This is *epic*. I've seen *all* your movies. Twice. And I'm totally acting like a moron right now, aren't I? But..." Her smile is so hopeful. "You probably hate it when people ask. But could I *please* have a picture?"

"Sure," I say at the exact same time that DJ says "No."

Ouch. I mean...I know what happened the last time I got caught in a photo with one of the Trevi family. But, geez.

Violet whips out her phone anyway. She stands beside me and aims the selfie cam at us. I smile, sort of, and she takes the shot. Then she turns on her brother. "Okay, this is *crazy*. I know I need to calm down."

"You've been cray cray for eighteen years, Violet. Why stop now?"

She makes a face at her brother. "*You* have so much explaining to do. Like, *months'* worth."

They exchange a long glance I can't quite read. "I know," he says quietly.

Violet crosses her arms in front of her chest. "And yet you just spent the whole day not answering my questions."

DJ's wince is so big it would be visible from space.

"Violet!" Orsen yells from the living room. "Your friends are here!"

"Thanks!" she returns. Then she gives her brother a thump on the chest with her fist. "You are saved by the bell. For *now*. But after this concert—" She nudges him with her elbow. "—and then after I go to a *rave* with strangers, and drop ecstasy and get wasted, we're going to talk."

"Right after I bail you out of jail," he deadpans. "Don't forget that part."

"Exactly." She reaches up and musses his hair before turning toward the door. "I'll see you in a few hours."

"Call me when it's time to walk home," he says, following her. "I'll come and meet you."

"Danny, I'm not going to get lost," she scoffs over her shoulder.

"Just do it, will you? You don't know this neighborhood."

"Lianne Challice made it here alive," she fires back.

Whatever he says next, I don't hear it. I take off my coat and drape it over a chair. Then I wait in the kitchen for him to reappear, leaning against the refrigerator, wondering what just happened. Maybe it's juvenile of me, but I'm feeling kind of crushed by how that all went down. If I had siblings who actually spoke to me, I'd be on the phone in a heartbeat, telling them I'd met the most awesome guy...

He reappears a moment later, his face serious. "Sorry, smalls," he says. "That was..." He sighs. "My sister doesn't know about my mess, in case that wasn't obvious. Or that *picture*, or my dad freaking out about it. So..." He rubs the back of his neck. "Sorry."

"Why doesn't she know about your case?" That's the weirdest thing he's just said. "Your brother does, though, right?"

"Oh, yeah." He opens the fridge and pulls out a Diet Coke for me. "Vi put a hurting on the soda supply, but I saved you one."

"Thanks?" I'm still ornery. Still not sure where I stand. And maybe it's selfish of me to care so much about labels when DJ's world is half collapsed. He has less space in his life for me than I have for him. I get it. But I've never done any of this before, and it stings that it means less to him than it does to me.

"Come on," he says, ready to change the subject. "Let's find somewhere we can read. The living room seems occupied."

There's a giggle from the sofa as I follow him out of the kitchen. "Yep."

"We could always stay in the kitchen," he says, jerking a

thumb toward the tiny table in the corner. "But it's not very quiet. And there's my room. You pick."

"Well..." I clear my throat. "I'd rather not have an audience."

"Okay," he agrees. Then he leads the way into his room.

I wait in the doorway while he moves his sister's flowered duffel to the floor and tosses a copy of Macbeth onto the quilt. I toss its twin beside it, taking care to zip my backpack shut immediately. I had big expectations tonight, and now that my hopes are dashed, I sure don't want to advertise them. I climb up to sit on the bed, my back to the wall. There's room for him to sit close to me or far away, and I wait to see what he'll do.

DJ sits at the head of the bed, which is certainly further away than I'd like. But then he scoops my feet into his lap. "Okay, smalls. What are we reading today?" He grabs a paperback.

"I need to hear Act Five," I tell him because it's true. Also, it doesn't hurt that it's the last act in the play, which will quickly bring us to the ending. Because hope springs eternal.

"Okay," DJ says, flipping open the cover.

He's all business. So I gamely pick up the other book. It's his copy, but that's okay. I like seeing which pages he's dog-eared. His book is more broken-in than I'd expect. Looks like DJ has been studying the Scottish play as much as I have.

"I have two nights watched with you, but can perceive no truth in your report," DJ begins, reading the part of Lady Macbeth's doctor.

We settle in. And shortly I read Lady M's iconic "out, damned spot" speech.

The rhythmic trading of lines soothes me, and I love hearing DJ's low voice answer back in Shakespeare's verse. We both relax. And in the fourth scene, DJ even begins to grin.

I enjoy his smile, so I don't bother to point out that we aren't exactly reading a happy scene. Then, on the next page, he laughs outright.

"What is it?" I can't help but ask. "Are you thinking up more Shakespeare porn?"

He eyes me over the edge of his book. "You should talk. Your highlights are hilarious. I mean—they're no *As You Lick It*. But still."

"What highlights?"

He gives me the side eye. Then he flips back a page and passes over my copy of the book. I find a bright pink line underneath a quote. *What wood is this before us?* There's a pink smiley in the margin. When I turn the page, there's another one: *The wood began to move.* And finally, *Thou comest to use thy tongue.*

My groan is loud. "That's *Bella's* handiwork. Not mine."

"Sure it is," he chuckles.

"No, really!" I flip through the book and find several more. *I have given suck*, and *I have done the deed.* And, funniest of all, *I hear a knocking at the south entry.* I snort. When DJ grabs the book to see why, he bursts out laughing. "It's not me!" I protest. "I swear!"

"I believe you! Almost."

I give his knee a swat, and he grabs my hand and kisses it. When his eyes meet mine, I find all the warmth there I've been looking for. "I missed you," I blurt out.

His smile slips away. "I missed you, too. I'm sorry. It's been a busy week. Lots of calls with the lawyer. And my father."

Ouch. "Are you okay?"

He tilts his head to the side and sighs. "I'll be all right. I liked it better when you didn't know to ask me that."

I scoot closer to him on the quilt. I want to hug him so badly, but there's a new sort of distance between us that I don't know how to bridge. "I care about you. Is that so wrong?" There's a tremor in my stomach, because I don't know how much is safe to reveal. Does he even want to know how much I like him?

He leans over, hooking me around the waist and hauling me onto his lap. "I care about you, too," he says, pushing the hair off my shoulder and kissing my neck. "That's why I hate dragging you into my disaster."

My brain goes a little fuzzy, because I'm finally right where I wanted to be. "Maybe it won't be a disaster."

"Maybe," he echoes. But he's not convinced.

He kisses my neck again, and I close my eyes. Life is just better when DJ is nearby. I wish I could keep him always within arm's reach. "Hey," I say as a big hand settles onto my tummy. I could sit like this forever. "My friend Kevin has a movie coming out next month. There's a big premier in New York. You want to come with me? It will be an over-the-top kind of party. We might have fun."

"Next month?" he says between kisses. "Sounds like fun, smalls. But I can't plan that far ahead. You should ask Pepe or someone who knows they'll be around."

My heart teeters, and just when things were going so well. "I don't want to go with Pepe. If you're not available, I'm not going at all."

DJ goes very still. But I plunge ahead anyway.

"I mean... You'll still be *alive* next month. So you could plan ahead. If you *wanted* to." DJ's from Long Island. Even if he's left Harkness—God forbid—it's just a commuter train ride into the city.

In other words, DJ and I are still possible even if he's kicked out of school.

I hadn't meant to bring that up, but there it is. And now I forget to breathe while I wait for him to speak.

Before answering, he removes his hand from my back. "When is it?"

Exhale. "I'll look it up and text you the date."

"Okay."

We sit still for a bit. He doesn't reach for his copy of the book, and neither do I. It's a perfect quiet moment. Until I wreck it. "I read about something, and I thought you'd find it interesting."

"What?" He nuzzles the back of my neck with his nose.

"One of the largest sororities in the country is backing this piece of legislation which would make it illegal for colleges to adjudicate rape cases. Colleges aren't very good at it, and people are starting to get pissed off."

He sighs. "Et tu, smalls?"

I shift a bit in his lap so I can see his face. "Seems kind of important. There are women as well as men who think that colleges aren't providing justice. I read about a case where a rape case was assigned to a faculty member who'd just landed on the disciplinary committee. He was an *entomologist*."

DJ slides me off his lap, setting me down on the mattress beside him. Then he bends his knees up toward his chest. "I've heard these stories. And I absolutely want my chance to tell the college that they've fucked up my case. But I am not comfortable telling them how to run the place."

"Why not? You know better than anybody they aren't getting the job done."

DJ tips his head back against the wall, and I panic, realizing that I've made him angry. "Nobody wants to hear that from me," he says tightly.

"They should."

"No," he says more forcefully. "You of all people should be able to understand how twisted it would look." He holds up two hands, as if hanging a banner. "White guy from the suburbs tells Harkness College how a rape case should be handled." He shakes his head. "They'll look at me and see a guy who's found a new way to get away with it."

"You are very trustworthy," I say in a shaky voice. But DJ is probably right. If his case hit the media, all the usual fun rules would apply. He'd be clickbait for sure.

DJ turns his head to look at me with irritation in his eyes. "It's not that easy, Lianne."

But I can't stop myself from pushing. "What if..."

"*Stop*," he says. "Maybe I can't be one of your projects."

"What can you be, then?" The words slip out before I can take them back.

His mouth opens and then closes. "You think it's even up to me? What I want and what I can have aren't even in the same time zone."

I wait for him to say more, but he doesn't. I've effed up the entire evening by shooting off my big mouth. "I shouldn't have pushed."

He hugs his knees with the same arms that should be hugging me. "It's not your fault, smalls. None of this is. We have really shitty timing, is all."

There's more silence, which I fill by worrying. "What's supposed to happen next, anyway?"

"My lawyer wants me to sue the college, and I'm supposed to decide by next week. But I'm really not comfortable being some kind of crusader against the way they're allowed to handle sexual assault. I mean—right this second my sister and her doofus friends are painting the campus red. And I'm sitting here hoping that a couple of meatheads don't try to take advantage of them. And, Jesus, then there's *Georgia*..." He lets the sentence die.

"What about her?" I'd forgotten that story he'd told me about Leo's ex.

DJ shakes his head. "I just wish I knew what she'd make of this whole mess. The lawsuit. The politics."

"Then why don't you *ask* her? She might really be able to help you." He'd said they were once close...

"Nah," he says, leaning back against the wall. "I don't want to trouble her with my bullshit."

"DJ!" It comes out as a gasp. "It's not bullshit. It's your *life* we're talking about here." And I'm part of that life, or at least I wish I was. But he's not going to look at it that way, no matter how badly I wish he would.

Am I being selfish? Am I being crazy? I've never wanted

anything as badly as I want him. And the flat look on his face right now makes me want to scream. So I begin evacuation procedures. I grab my copy of the play and scramble off the bed. "You're not Macbeth," I whisper. "But you play him so well."

His head snaps back, actually thudding against the wall behind him. "That's easy for *you* to say." And now I know I've overstepped, because his face flushes with anger. "But my parents look at me and wonder if I *raped someone*. My brother looks at me and sees Georgia's attacker. The college treats me like a leper. The whole world thinks you fart glitter, babe. Not sure you can understand."

My blood pressure doubling, I grab my backpack off the floor, toss it on my shoulder, then look at DJ.

The dark eyes that look back at me are pained. "I'm sorry," he says quickly. "That was uncalled for."

I can't even respond, because then he'll be able to hear how much those words hurt me. Instead, I turn the doorknob and slip out of his room.

He doesn't call me back.

Closing his bedroom door behind me, I lurch forward then halt as peals of laughter come from the living room. There's no way I'm passing through there. My coat is still in the kitchen, so I go in and grab it off the chair. Then I sneak out the back door.

It's a cold, damp night, but I trot away from the house without even stopping to put on my coat.

He's under too much pressure, I tell myself. *Anyone would snap.* But I'd thought he was the only one at Harkness who didn't think of me as a spoiled brat. Now I know he does.

I'm halfway home before I realize the mistake I made when we argued. I'd *said* it. I actually said it out loud—the Scottish play's title character's name. The ill-fated king who is vanquished in Act Five. Done in by fate.

God damn it. God damn everything.

Chapter Twenty-Three

OMIGOD THE HYPOCRISY

DJ

When the back door slams shut, I flinch.

I hate the idea of Lianne walking back to campus alone, mad at me. Gripping the quilt underneath me in two hands, I fight the urge to chase her down and apologize again. There is nobody in my life so amazing. I've never met a girl like Lianne—never felt so much attraction to anyone. Ever. But it's not fair for me to string her along. Nothing I could possibly say tonight would fix the mess I'm in.

I'm a guy with nothing to offer her except scandal. So I stay put.

After a little while I pull out my phone and text my sister. *We need to talk. Sorry I didn't do that earlier when I had the chance.* At least there's one little wrinkle in my life I can smooth out.

She replies immediately. *I can be back in an hour. Love you!*

Aw. I miss my sister. Unlike me and Leo, Vi and I have always been close. It's probably because she was just a baby when I joined the family. Leo was older, and he resented me, I think. I remember so clearly the kindergarten-aged Leo standing in the center of our bedroom, telling me that I was not, in fact, his brother. We were probably fighting over a toy or something, and surely Mom leapt in and shut down that line of argument. But you never really forget those words after you hear them even once.

Speaking of our mom...

I dial her next. "Danny," she answers, her voice full of surprise. "Is everything okay? Violet got there all right?"

Clearly I don't call Mom very often. Whoops. "Everything is fine. Vi is at a concert with her friends for another hour. But..." I clear my throat. "Mom, I gotta tell her tonight. She's not stupid. She knows something is wrong, and I hate lying."

Mom is quiet for a second. "You do what you think is right," she says softly.

"Look, I know the whole thing embarrasses you. But Vi can keep a secret."

"Oh, Danny." She sighs. "That's not the reason we didn't tell her."

"It's not?" I croak. "Seemed like it."

"*No*, honey! Your sister is just *so* emotional. She loves you so much, and she'll be so angry for you. We just... She's a senior, and we were trying to keep her focused on school until we knew more. I'm sorry if I gave you the wrong impression."

"Uh, okay." The back of my throat has begun to ache. "Vi is tough, Mom. She isn't going to fall apart just because I'm having some trouble."

"No, she won't fall apart. But she'll try to throw herself into finding a solution. She'll wage a campaign or plan a revolution before breakfast time. I'm going to brace myself for the T-shirt-making and the drama."

I laugh, but it comes out like choking. "I'll try to calm her down before she goes home tomorrow."

"I'm sorry, sweetie. I should have leveled with her already."

"It's okay," I say automatically. Though it isn't really.

"She was just thirteen when poor Georgia was..." Mom sighs. "Vi was so upset. She didn't sleep for a week."

"None of us did," I say a little too sharply. The night we got the call was rough. Georgia's father flew down to Florida to be with her. And Leo spent the next several days pacing our house and punching the heavy bag in the basement. He kept trying to get Georgia on the phone, but she wasn't speaking much. It was brutal. I haven't thought about those dark days for a long time.

"Anyway, I love you, Danny. I never want you to think that I'm ashamed of you. That's just not true."

My eyes feel hot now. I didn't know how badly I've needed to hear her say that. "Love you, too," I grind out.

"If your sister wants to call home tonight, I'll keep my phone on. Even if it's late, you can tell her to call me."

"Thanks. Love you."

I lie on my back staring at the ceiling for a while after we hang up. Not for the first time I wonder where Georgia is tonight. Last I knew, she'd been heading for Duke and a spot on their women's tennis team. Lianne told me to call her, and I'd sneered at the idea. But really, I'm just a coward.

Which is not something I want to be.

I pick up my phone again. Scrolling through my list of contacts, Georgia's name is still there. I used to call this number if I needed a ride and couldn't find my brother. She always had an extra minute to say hello to me. We also had a game going for a while where we texted each other lyrics to songs, and the recipient had to name the album and the year it came out, without cheating.

Smiling at my ceiling, I know what to do. Though it takes me a few minutes to settle on a song, I text her two lines from "Where Are U Now" and wait.

The reply doesn't take more than a minute. *Really, D? A Bieber song?*

You didn't give the year, I protest. *Or the album.*

My phone rings a second later. "I'm rusty," Georgia says immediately when I answered. "It's been a while."

The happy sound of her voice is like a shock to my system. "You sound *good*, Gigi."

"You too, Danny boy! How *are* you?"

"Good," I say immediately. Although that's a big goddamn lie. "Okay, not good. Do you have a few minutes?"

"Of course I do," she says, her voice serious now. "What's the matter? Is everyone okay?"

By "everyone" I'm pretty sure she means my brother. But talk of Leo will have to wait. "Yeah nobody's dying. But I'm in a tight spot, and I wanted your advice about something. I mean, only if you're comfortable talking about it. It's a really weird story." I can feel myself backing away from the conversation already. I'm just so tired of admitting I've been accused of doing something awful.

"Spill, Danny," she says.

———

An hour later, we're still on the phone when Vi waltzes into my room and sits on my feet. I hold the phone away from my ear for a second. "Can you give me just a minute? I'll be right with you."

She rolls her eyes. "Yes, your highness. Where's your movie star girlfriend?"

"I was an ass and she left."

Vi's face falls. "I'm getting a drink. And then you're going to tell me everything."

"Sorry," I say to Georgia. "It's a little crazy around here."

"Must be. You have a girlfriend?"

"Well..." I sigh. "I'm crazy about this girl. But if I get kicked out, that will be the end of it."

She's quiet for a second. "I hope that doesn't happen, D."

"Me too. But enough about my shitty life. We didn't talk enough about you."

"That's okay. I'm in the running for an awesome job with a professional sports team."

"Really?" I laugh. "That's great! Which one?"

"I'm not going to tell you the details, because in the first place you need to go, and in the second place I don't want to jinx it. But if I get this thing, I promise to call you up and spill."

"You better. Call me if you don't, too."

"It's a deal. And please let me know if they hold a public hearing for your case? Because I want to come up and support you."

"You're the best, Gigi. I'll let you know what happens."

"Love you, Danny."

My heart gives a stab. "Love you too, babe. Sorry it took so long to call."

"Me too, you. Goodnight!"

I hang up with Georgia, and my head is spinning. It sucked telling her about my case. But apparently it's Make Danny Feel Better Night, because she showered me with support. I think I expected her to say something like, "You must be a terrible person if this girl pointed her finger at you." But she didn't say that at all. She said, "Oh my God, I'm so sorry." And then she said something that wasn't exactly uplifting, but it made me feel better anyway. "Tread carefully, sweetie. There is no issue thornier than this one. You have to stick up for yourself—I insist. But if the lawsuit turns your stomach, then don't let them push you around."

"But does their lawsuit offend *you*?" I'd asked. That's what I'd really called to ask.

She thought about it a while before answering. "Yes and no. I don't like the idea of a bunch of men deciding how rape cases are handled. That's not cool. But it sure sounds like your college needs an ass-kicking. Here's a big fat irony—you and I are home tonight, having a serious conversation about sexual politics. Meanwhile, half a mile from you I'll bet there's a bunch of guys in a frat-house basement getting girls wasted to improve their chances tonight. There's work to do, that's for sure. But I think education is a better tool than a class-action suit."

I let out a breath. "Okay, I'm going to tell my lawyer to shove it on the lawsuit. It just hits me the wrong way."

"Follow your gut, Danny Boy. You're a good guy, and I know you'll make the right decision."

That made me smile. And I'm still smiling now as Violet comes back into my room holding a beer. "Okay, what happened?"

I try to take the beer from her hand, but she holds it out of my reach. "That's for me, right? You're eighteen."

"Omigod, the hypocrisy." She takes a swig. "We'll split it. And you'll tell me what the hell is going on."

I make room for her on the bed. "My news sucks. But it's not the end of the world." *Even if it sometimes feels like it.*

"Are you in trouble, Danny?" My sister's eyes were wide with worry.

"Yeah. But not, like, with the cops or anything. The college thinks I did something ugly, but they're wrong."

Violet moves closer to me on the bed, then hands me the beer. "Okay. Take a sip and then tell me. I can take it."

I take a modest sip and hand it back, thinking the women in my life were all pretty amazing.

Chapter Twenty-Four

GLITTER FARTS

Smalls—

I'm so sorry I was a dick the other night. It turns out that wallowing in your problems turns you into an asshole.

You're the best thing about this whole year. I don't know what's going to happen to us, but I want you to know that I'm doing my best to figure it out. I called Georgia last night after you left. You told me to do it, so I did. She was really helpful to me, and so thank you for kicking me in the ass when I needed it.

I also told my sister everything. Not only did I tell her about my mess with Annie, but I told her all about meeting you at Capri's. The way you played "I Wanna Sex You Up," and then said it was an accident. :) I told her every (g-rated) thing about you, and then she ripped me a new one for losing my cool when you were just trying to help me.

I'm sorry. In case you missed that the first time, I'm really, really sorry.

My sister is awesome, and if everything goes my way, I hope she'll visit again so we can all go out somewhere together.

But if it doesn't go my way, I'm really going to miss you. So please return one of my calls so I can apologize in person.

D.

———

Lianne

"So *that* explains why you've been in a mood this week," Bella says from over my shoulder. "Are you going to call him?"

I ignore the question, because I don't feel like talking about it. "Let me ask you something, and I want you to be honest." I stand up and face her.

"Kay," Bella says, sipping her coffee.

"Do I need implants?"

Bella chokes on her coffee. "What?" she asks between choking sounds. "Who said that?"

"My asshole manager."

My neighbor's hands begin waving in the air because she's coughing too much to speak, yet she has a lot to say. I think.

"Do you need the hug of life?" I ask.

Her eyes are watering when she answers me. "No—to both questions. Don't get a boob job. Your future nurse practitioner does *not* approve of unnecessary surgery just to please a man." Bella is starting nursing school in the fall so she can be a nurse midwife and talk about vaginas professionally. "Are you seriously considering it?"

"Not *seriously*. I know I shouldn't listen. But it is Hollywood. And my boobs are—"

"—Fun-sized," Bella finishes.

Ugh. "My head is not in a good place," I admit.

"Is this because DJ was an ass?" Bella probes. I haven't told her the whole story, so she's digging.

"No." I click my email shut so I don't have to read his apology for the tenth time. "Okay, yes. That's part of it."

"What did he do?" she asks softly.

"He got mad at me for meddling. I told him I'd been

researching the way colleges handle sexual assault, and he kind of lost it." I open up DragonFire to see how my dragons are holding up. I feel a video-game binge coming on. Forget my ninety-minute rule. It didn't do me any good.

"Men aren't always good at accepting help," she says.

"Pretty sure he had a point," I grumble. "He shouldn't let me tell him what to do. I'm not even a little bit impartial."

"You care about him, though. That counts for something."

I pick up the game controller and fire it up. "I care too much. And if he leaves, I'm going to be really hacked off at the universe."

Bella nudges my chair with her toe so it swings me a little bit. "I know, *pequeña*. You aren't very good at taking chances on people. So you need to make sure they stick around."

"I take chances," I growl while staring at a bunch of dragons which are nothing but pixels of light on a very expensive screen.

"Come to Capri's with me," she says. "A little pizza and some weak beer will cleanse your spirit."

"Can't," I say automatically.

"DJ will probably be there. And I've got a stack of quarters you could use in the jukebox."

The pull is so strong. I want to see DJ's smile so badly it aches. But to what end? He's probably going to get snatched away from me. And that will just suck for both of us. Why should I put us through that any longer?

The screen lights up with messages. *Vindikator! You're back again tonight! Awesome.* These are the friends who won't desert me. We're not close in the real sense of the word. But it's better this way.

"Really?" Bella sighs. "You're going to spend the night with your dragons?"

"And Brecht. I'm writing a paper on my least favorite playwright. It's due next week."

"Okay..." she says slowly. "Work hard."

"Will do," I say without looking away from my screen.

Bella leaves, and I'm not even sorry to be alone. Maybe Hark-ness really wasn't a good choice for me. I should go somewhere people really do think I fart glitter.

Chapter Twenty-Five

SELFIES WITH BONO

DJ

I stare into the depths of the juke box, wondering what to play. I'm sick of the eighties and nineties tunes. If Lianne were here, we'd have fun joking about the lack of selection. We'd marvel at the one-hit-wonders. We'd argue about the classics.

Without her, it's just a bunch of so-so tracks, and a long night to fill with them.

I know I pushed Lianne away last weekend. At the time, it seemed like the right thing to do. Who wants a guy on the verge of becoming a college dropout?

Except that I miss her terribly.

"Hey," a female voice says, and I look up fast. It's Bella. I don't even try to disguise my disappointment or the way my eyes go right over her shoulder, hoping to find Lianne. "She didn't come," Bella says, reading my not-very-opaque mind. "I tried. But she's kind of down in the dumps."

"That's my fault," I grunt.

"No," she says, patting my shoulder. "It's not. But there's something I want to explain to you." Bella flips a chair around backwards and straddles it. Then she sips her beer. "Okay, I know Lianne seems like the most sophisticated girl in the world. And, yeah, she could hack into NASA and launch a spacecraft from those computers in her room. And she has a selfie of herself with Bono on her phone."

"Bono? Really?"

Bella nods. "She puts up a big front. But the people in her life? They're shit, DJ." She holds up a hand. "Present company excepted." She gives me a smile and I try to return it. "Her mother is a world-class narcissist. I mean—the woman was too busy with her new twenty-five-year-old French pool boy to come to New York over Christmas to watch her only child perform Shakespeare at a famous theater. And I've *met* that creep she calls her manager." Bella gives an exaggerated shudder. "Lianne doesn't trust people, because she's been burned. A lot. So I know you've done right by her, except for the one argument. But you just need to try a little harder. It's like, she needs proof that you'll stick by her."

"Okay," I say slowly. I'm pretty sure I just learned something important. If only I knew what to do with it.

Bella grins. "I know you won't let her down." She stands up, pats me on the head, and heads straight to the rowdiest table, where two of my brother's teammates move aside for her to sit down and join their game.

I'm not in the mood to play quarters. Or for smack talk. So I grab my coat and duck out the back way. I walk home slowly, wondering what I could do for Lianne. It's a nice thought—a project that has nothing to do with my lawyer and the case. They've been keeping me busy all week. Phone calls. Emails. Words they want me to use when I explain what happened that night. Phrases they want me to avoid.

Nobody's asking me to lie, of course. But they want the truth to come out in a certain way. And that's hard, because the truth is a messy, untidy thing.

So it's a relief to brainstorm ways to make Lianne smile. Even if she and I are going to be separated, I can still make the effort. There are six days left until my meeting. Lianne had accused me of behaving like someone who had three weeks to live. And now I could finally admit she was right. A week from now, I'll still be a guy who likes a girl named Lianne, no matter what. And she'd still be lonely.

I turn the corner onto York, and the T-shirt vendor is there, bundled up against the cold. The offensive shirt with Lianne's name is still there, too. I'm half a block past when something occurs to me. Backtracking, I hurry back until I'm in front of the guy. "Can you make a custom shirt?" I ask without preamble.

"Sure. Would take me a day, maybe two. Costs twenty bucks, forty if you want two-sided."

I pull out my wallet. "One side will do."

Chapter Twenty-Six

LYLE LOVETT AND LISA LOEB

Lianne

Bella sticks her head into my room for the third time this evening. "Are you preparing for a role as a vampire?"

"What? Why?" I don't bother taking my eyes off my screen.

"Because you never leave your room. It's like you think the outside air will burn your skin off."

"Uh huh," I say. I'm battling a new kind of droid-troll that's been cropping up in DragonFire this week. They're hard to kill, even with an X-level weapon. But I think I'm making progress. Words of encouragement from my online buddies scroll past. *Hit 'im again, Vindikator! I think it's working!*

"What's that shirt you're wearing? Oh my God. Did you have that made?"

I knew Bella would notice, but I wore it anyway. Because it's too good not to wear. It reads, *Yes, I go to Harkness. Just deal with it.*

Bella does something drastic then. She puts her body between me and the screen.

"Shit!" I scream, freezing the game because she's going to get me killed.

"Now you're listening," she says. "Great shirt. That's showing them."

"Thanks." DJ sent it to me. I found it in a gift bag hanging from my doorknob. He couldn't have been the one to put it there, though, because he's not allowed in the building. I suspect one of the hockey players. There was a note, too. It read, "Thought you needed this. Love, D."

Love. It's not a word people use when they write to me. I'm ashamed to admit I tucked his note into my nightstand drawer.

The previous night there'd been a delivery from Gino's pizza. It was a MOR pie, and I also received two Diet Cokes. Then I got a text which read, "I was thinking of you when I ordered mine. And you showing up at my door with a pie was one of the nicest things anyone ever did for me. Hope you're hungry. —D."

Bella and I feasted. I texted him a polite thank you instead of calling. I would have rather heard his voice, but I was afraid of what I might say. *Pizza is fine, but I just want you.* And that would only make him feel bad the week before his big appointment with the dean. So what was the use?

Tonight I hadn't heard from him. Yet.

"Hockey game starts in thirty minutes," Bella says. "It's weird that they're having a Monday game, but it's because of the midterm break."

I'd forgotten she was there. "I'm not going tonight."

She heaves a sigh. "Please? There's pretzels and hot dogs. And your paparazzo hasn't been back."

"I still have that paper to write." It's a dodge, and she knows it. But Bella disappears without a word.

DJ texts me later. *Hockey game tonight. The booth makes me think of you now. Wish you were here with me.*

I feel the floor bobble beneath me as the diving board adjusts to the weight of my heart. I picture myself slipping into the press box just like I did that first time and choosing songs with DJ as the players slice across the ice below. This could be his last hockey game. He didn't say that in the text, but we both know that in less than forty-eight hours, he might be finished here.

So when the final buzzer rings tonight, what would we find to say to each other? *Hey, it's been nice knowing you.*

I don't want to have that conversation unless it's really necessary. So I stay in my room like I'd planned.

Later, I get another text. *In your honor, I'm playing only artists that start with L tonight. I've cued up Los Lobos, Lynyrd Skynyrd, and Linkin Park. It's the weirdest playlist ever. The guys are going to think I've lost it. Unless you come up here and make it better.*

This makes me smile so hard. I know he's teasing, but it's kind of adorable. I reply: *Don't forget Lyle Lovett. Lisa Loeb. Led Zeppelin.*

Two hours later, Bella bursts into my room. This time, I'm actually working on my Brecht paper when I look up to see her face, red from running up the stairs. "Lianne, seriously? For the good of hockey fans everywhere, will you call that boy? His music has gone to shit."

"Wait," I say, sitting up. "What happened?"

"He played Linda Ronstadt. At a fucking hockey game," she fumes. "And that's on you!"

Yikes. "I thought he was teasing!" Which makes my text—adding three artists to the list—kind of a *fuck you.*

Bella shakes her head. "When I went into the booth to complain, he just said to give you this." She pulled a scarf out of her pocket. My scarf—the itchy one I'd abandoned on the park bench the night he stood me up. "Here." She thrust an envelope at me, too.

"Thanks," I say, taking it.

She gives me a disappointed look and then leaves. I open the envelope and unfold a piece of notebook paper.

Dear Lianne,

I was doing a little cleaning in my room this week, just in case I won't need it after spring break. And I found this. That night when I stood you up at Gino's, I watched you walk into the square. I only bailed on our date because my accuser was inside the restaurant when I got there. I panicked and cancelled on you.

That was the theme of this winter, and I'm sorry.

You're the best thing that happened to me all year, smalls. I'm sorry if my panic made it seem like I was always blowing hot and cold. You're the most amazing girl I've ever met, and I'm crazy about you. I hope I get many more chances to tell you in person. But if I don't, I wanted to say it tonight.

I understand why you didn't come to the game, though. We can keep those memories happy if you want. It's okay.

Miss you,

D.

Well, damn.

Now my eyes are hot, and the sounds of foreplay are bleeding through the bathroom door. Great.

I wake up my computer and flip over to Spotify, where I begin to blast the first song I see from the playlist I made for the women's game. It's "Real Gone" by Sheryl Crow.

Pushing my copy of Brecht aside, I curl up on top of my bed alone. The upbeat tempo of the song does not match my mood. I lie there and wonder what it would be like to have a boyfriend sharing my bed. Why did I have to fall for the guy who can't?

Chapter Twenty-Seven

A LAP AROUND CAMPUS

DJ

I thought I'd be a wreck the night before the big meeting. To my surprise, I'm really not. What I am is ready for this to be over. Whatever happens, I can take it. I just want to know.

It's after eight, and I'm sitting on the couch in the living room of Orsen's house. Leo showed up a couple of hours ago with Chinese food. Now the two of us are sitting in front of a basketball game that neither of us is very invested in.

His phone rings, and he answers it. "Hey babe. I'm hanging with DJ." There's a pause while he listens. "That's not a great idea. I'll catch you tomorrow, okay? Night."

Thank God he didn't invite Amy over. If this is my last night at Harkness, so be it. But I don't need her to be part of it. Leo hasn't said much tonight. He's just here for me. He's appointed himself my keeper for the night. For once I'm comforted instead of annoyed.

We stare at the game a little longer, but when it goes to the ten-millionth commercial break, Leo mutes it and tosses the remote onto the coffee table. "I'd get you drunk tonight," he says, "but I don't think the hungover look is what your lawyer wants for tomorrow."

Chuckling, I try to picture that. "Good point."

"You need anything, though?"

I shake my head. "I just want it over. This has been a really long year."

"No kidding." We're quiet for a second, and then he says, "I think it's going to be okay."

"Why?"

"I just do," my brother says.

"Hope you're right. But even if you're not, I just want an answer. I'm so sick of wondering what's coming. I followed all their weird little rules. I haven't been inside the gates of a House or in any of the Houses' dining halls. I was so careful, because I'd do anything to prove I was a good guy. And the shitty thing? There's no way they've noticed."

"Right?" my brother agrees.

"Made me feel like a criminal every day, too. Hey—remember that guy who worked at the drug store across from the middle school? He'd follow us around when we went in to buy candy after school."

"The creepy dude with the mustache?"

"Yeah, him. I never stole a thing from that shop, but he made me feel like a delinquent anyway. That's how this year has been. Times a million."

"Sorry, man."

"I know." The game comes back on, but I don't feel like watching it. "I think I need to get out of here. Maybe go for a run."

"Okay." Leo stands up. "I'll do a lap around campus with you. Then I'm going to go pack for my trip." Leo is going away with Amy for three days before he has to come back for hockey.

I put on my shoes and a fleece vest, and we head outside. We take off down the street at an easy pace, running in and out of the streetlights' pooling glow. Leo tells me his itinerary—three days on a beach. "Don't forget your sunscreen," I say. "You don't want to burn your white ass before playoffs." Leo and the rest of the family are paler than I am. Whoever my father was, he tanned easily.

"Thanks for the tip."

We run on, past fraternity row, which is lively tonight. People are celebrating the coming break. We loop around Science Hill and then head back toward campus. The Houses come into view one by one, yellow lights shining from their decorative old windows. Beaumont House is the prettiest of them all. One of those lights is Lianne's, probably. When our route takes us past the Beaumont gate, my feet stop, unbidden.

Leo circles around to where I'm standing in front of the gate, peering inside. "D?" he asks.

I just point inside. "I'll see you tomorrow?"

He doesn't try to talk me out of it. He just nods and runs off down the street, toward his own House.

From inside, a student walks toward the gate, backpack over his shoulder. On his way out, he lets me in without a second glance. That's how it always works. A student's ID only opens his own House gate, but we let each other in all day long. It's just the easy trust that one student gives to another without thinking too hard about it. I used to take that for granted.

I don't even know if my ID opens Trindle gate this year. I never checked.

Lianne's room number is 317. I had to look it up when I sent the T-shirt over with Corey Callihan. So it's easy to find her entryway. And luck is with me, because someone's coming down the stairs and opening the door.

Chapter Twenty-Eight

NOT A JOHN GREEN NOVEL

Lianne

The knock on my door surprises me, because it can't be either Bella or Rafe. The low murmur of their post-coital conversation is audible from the other room. I've just finished blasting a dance playlist to muffle their shenanigans, and now it's back to reading Brecht.

When the knock comes again, I get up and open the door, and DJ is standing *right there*. You could knock me over with a feather, I'm so surprised.

"Hi," he says, his big dark eyes taking me in. "I just had to see you, smalls." He leaves off the words *one more time*, but we both hear them anyway. "Can I come in for a minute? I won't stay long if you don't want me to."

I don't answer this question. Instead I just *fling* myself at him. "I'm sorry," I gasp as I wrap my arms around his neck and squeeze. He smells like winter air and clean sweat. And I just want to climb inside his jacket and stay there forever.

"Hey, it's okay," he says, catching me in strong arms.

But it isn't. It's *not at all okay*. I thought it would hurt less if I kept my distance these last couple weeks. But I was wrong. I *ache*. And now I'm scaling him like a tree, wrapping my legs around his waist and clinging to him like drowning passengers to flotsam in the *Titanic* movie.

DJ actually chuckles, but I don't see what's funny. He carries me into my room and kicks the door shut. "Oh, smalls. I missed you so much." He sits carefully on my bed and buries his face in my hair.

I take another deep breath of him, and then a giant convulsive sob comes heaving out of me. I try to gulp it back, but that only makes it worse. My eyes erupt like fountains.

"Oh, noooo!" he croons. "Don't cry. It's like you said. This isn't a John Green novel. Nobody's dying."

But my heart is unconvinced. And now I'm ugly-crying. I'm like Claire Danes on *Homeland*, but without the dignity. And I can't even wipe my face because I still have an octopus hold on DJ, so that he can't leave before I can get over myself.

The bathroom door flies open and Bella sticks her head in. "What's the matter... Oh. Sorry." The door closes again before either of us bothers to answer. Somehow DJ manages to extract a hand from my embrace and reach for my tissue box. And then he's dabbing at my tears and shushing me gently. When the mess has been mopped up, he sits back and looks at me for a moment, his brown eyes almost twinkling.

Beneath me he kicks off his shoes. And he unzips his fleece jacket and I relax the death grip I have on him so he can toss it on the floor. "Come here," he whispers, pulling me down until he's lying on his side on my bed, and I'm tucked against him, my face buried in the hollow between his neck and shoulder. "Shh," he says again, rubbing my back with one big hand.

I calm down slowly, listening to the beat of his steady heart until mine matches it. We are cuddled up together in exactly the way I've always wanted to be.

Nobody says anything, and that's okay. We're soothing each

other without words. I brace my hand on his tight chest. I love the feel of him, and he knows it. And he cradles me in strong arms.

After a while, DJ leans in and places a soft, thoughtful kiss on my cheekbone. It's so sweet that I have to take a deep breath to keep from crying again. But then he kisses me a second time, and I make myself focus on the softness of his lips on my face, and the scrape of the evening whiskers on his chin.

I turn like a flower toward the sun, fitting my mouth against his where it belongs. Our first kiss is slow and sweet. We both just savor the connection. It's like finding an object I thought I'd lost —I have to stop and admire it for a moment, wondering how something can be both familiar and unexpected.

But then DJ makes a hungry, bitten-off noise at the back of his throat. His next kiss is deeper. And then deeper still. And I'm waving him in like those guys on the tarmac beckoning the jetliner with those orange...things. Whatever they are. And where was that thought going? Because...*oh. Oh, yeah*. His mouth is the only place I want to be. I'm going to climb inside and never leave. I'm about to start picking out curtains and rearranging the furniture.

He opens for me on a sigh, his palms warming my lower back.

But I want more. Much more. So I plunge my hands down his abs, lifting the hem of his T-shirt so that I can connect with skin. My fingernails scrape lightly across his belly, sifting through his happy trail, and he lets out a happy moan.

That sound is all it takes to turn me into a crazy, desperate person. I tug at his T-shirt until he gives in and yanks it off. The bare-chested DJ stops to kiss me again. Big hands cup my face while he worships my mouth. His tongue makes long, drugging pulls against mine. Then—finally—he lifts my top over my head. When he discovers I'm not wearing a bra, he makes a low sound of approval. His fingers trail up my skin, leaving shivers in their wake, until the pad of one of his thumbs teases my nipple. I practically leap off the bed because I'd forgotten how incredible his touch feels.

I've spent too many days hiding from all the affection I feel for DJ. What a waste. Now I only have tonight to make up for lost time.

DJ isn't chuckling anymore. He's admiring my body with such tenderness that I feel a tightness in my chest. I love it, but it steals my breath. So I drop my eyes, allowing my hands to slide down to the waistband of his athletic pants and push them down. He raises his hips to let me strip them off. While he's still kicking out of them, I push down my yoga pants and my underwear in one go.

"Jesus H," he breathes, taking my waist in his hands. He rolls to his back, lifting me on top of him with as much ease as he'd lift a pillow. And—wow. I'm stretched out on a gorgeous nearly nekkid man. He's still wearing his black briefs. But his hardness is right between my legs. I'm kissing him and touching him everywhere while practically panting into his mouth. Losing myself in all this wanting.

"Please," I say after many more kisses. There's no doubt in my mind where this is headed, so I'd like to get there sooner rather than later. (There must be no doubt in my neighbors' minds, either, because Daft Punk's "Get Lucky" is suddenly playing next door. Loudly.)

"Please what?" DJ asks, smiling up at me. "You don't like saying what you want, do you?"

Busted. I shake my head.

"Why not?" he asks, ruffling my hair playfully, as if now was a convenient time for a chat. Meanwhile, I'm ready to combust.

"Because," I gasp. "If I say it, I won't sound like a nice girl."

His eyes go soft. "You are a nice girl—the nicest one. And that will still be true even if you scream along with the soundtrack for *As You Lick It.*"

This makes me snort with laughter, and it's not sexy. But DJ smiles anyway. And, God, there's nothing quite so potent as DJ smiling up at me from under my nekkid body. He's still smiling while he runs both hands down my bare sides onto my hips. And he's still smiling as he reaches between my legs to caress me with one smooth, slick sweep of his fingers.

"Oh geez," I gasp, and he grins. "Ohhhh," I moan. My hips can't resist the urge to move, increasing the contact with his hand. So I give in, shifting and practically writhing against him. It's so dirty but so irresistible that I just don't care.

With his free hand, DJ gathers up my hair which has fallen in my face. Holding onto it, he kisses me again, then sucks on my tongue. The moan I make is probably loud enough to be heard over Daft Punk.

It takes all my willpower to shift off DJ and dive for the drawer to my nightstand. I plunge my hand inside and find one of the Welcome to Harkness condoms I received on move-in day. DJ sits up and takes it from me, and a few seconds later he's shed his briefs and the condom wrapper. The second he's covered, he lifts me into his lap. Straddling him, I brace my hands on his shoulders and slide him exactly where I want him.

There's a pause while we stare into each other's eyes, just getting used to the idea that we're here and this is real and it's *wonderful*. It's like a brilliant moment in slo-mo, with golden light and a perfect view of his warm eyes. There's a whole lot of naked affection looking up at me, too.

And then? It's as if someone fired a starting gun. Our lips crash together and I lever up on my knees, straining against him. And it's not just me who's suddenly urgent. DJ pumps his hips as we reach for each other in every conceivable way. It's not graceful, but energetic. We're like that last chase scene at the end of *Speed*, where the bus knocks everything out of its path. We are arms and legs and heat and friction.

"Jesus," he grunts out, but I muffle it with another of my kisses.

Somehow I end up on my back without even knowing how I got there. DJ over me is at least as amazing as DJ under me, because I can see each muscle flex as he moves and trace the precious crease in his forehead as he works us closer together. But when he slips a hand between our bodies, everything gets so much more amazing that I forget how to think. I just let it all go, arching up to him, cresting and then sliding down a wave of pure pleasure. I'm vaguely aware of DJ making a sound that's half growl, half grunt, and then all the muscles tense in his neck and chest.

Seconds later, he's collapsed onto the bed, breathing hard into my hair.

It's a really long time before either of us speaks. But it's a good kind of quiet, and not at all sad. He shifts on the bed to make us more comfortable, and then I'm drifting on happiness and the smooth skin of his shoulder.

"I need you in my life, smalls," he says in a whisper. "No matter what happens tomorrow, that won't change."

"Mmm," is all I can say. Some minutes later I decide to contribute to the conversation. "I'm still worried," I admit. "Aren't you?"

"Yes and no. I don't want to lose. But I'm not panicked anymore. It took me a while to get over the fact that sometimes shitty things just happen."

"But..." It's hard to put into words how much this bothers me. "This shitty thing must have an explanation. Doesn't it kill you to not know *why?*"

"It did," he admits. "But then I realized that it was killing me to be so angry about it. If I never get to know why, I still have to keep going, you know?"

"I guess." Personally, I doubt I could ever be so Zen. "What's the plan for tomorrow?"

"The meeting is at eleven-fifteen. My family is coming up. Even Violet, though I wish she didn't have to hear me tell what happened. My cynical lawyer says that family is good, though. And Violet called me a sexist pig for wanting to exclude her."

This makes me smile, because I can picture it.

"The dean's office has been really vague about who will be there—the dean, or the full disciplinary board. My lawyer's plan is to get them to listen to all the ways they've dropped the ball on the investigation. And he's got a statement from my roommate in support of my side of the story."

"Your roommate?"

"He's in Tibet this year. But he was, uh, there when it happened."

I don't press for more details because I do not want to picture him with another girl. "That's good, right?"

"Yeah, but it might not be enough to convince 'em that they don't have the story straight. My lawyer also reached out to Annie's sister, but he didn't get a response. If this were a trial, he could interview her, no question. But it isn't."

I give him a squeeze. "Will you let me know what happens? Because I won't be able to think of anything else."

"Of course I will. But enough about tomorrow. Come here and kiss me. There's still twelve hours until I face the firing squad."

I do exactly as requested, and he smiles as I lower a kiss to the corner of his mouth and tease him. I kiss my way up the side of his face, and he closes his eyes and pulls me closer.

"Will you stay tonight? I mean..." That sounded awfully eager. "I know you're not supposed to be here."

"But I want to be," he says. "Can I set my alarm for six? Nobody will see me leave. And I have more packing to do in the morning." When he catches my panicked expression, he kisses me on the nose. "For midterm break, remember? It might not be permanent. And even if it is, you're not allowed to panic yet. Not tonight."

"Okay," I promise. And then I kiss him again, because it's easier to be happy when we're making out.

———

Later, we get up and take a shower together, which is funny because it used to piss me off when Bella let guys use our shower. Hello, hypocrisy. And with DJ and I all wet and slippery together, things got a little heated. We have to go back to bed to finish the job.

After one more clean-up, it's late and we finally tuck ourselves into bed. DJ folds me against his chest, and it's perfect. "I like you here," I whisper.

"I like it here, too."

Neither of us says *I hope we get a chance to do this again*. But we both hear it anyway.

Chapter Twenty-Nine

NOBODY WANTS TO TALK ABOUT FIERSTEIN

Lianne

My goal was to get to twentieth-century theater early today, so I can ask the professor a question. But after DJ kisses me goodbye at six, I roll over and sleep for another three hours. Who knew that good sex was so exhausting?

So when I eventually arrive in the classroom, I'm only ten minutes early instead of twenty. But at least there's nobody else around yet. "I have a question for my paper about Brecht," I say without preamble.

The professor looks up to squint at me through his wire-rimmed glasses. "*You're* writing about Brecht?"

He sounds amused, and I am immediately pissed off. "What, you've already decided that I can only handle Neil Simon?"

The professor holds up two hands in surrender. "First, let's not bash Neil Simon. He has more Oscar and Tony nominations than any other playwright. And I didn't mean to imply that Brecht is over your head. It's just that I'm bound to get a dozen Brecht papers, most of which will be regurgitations of my own work. I thought I could count on you to break it up a little."

"Oh," I say slowly. "Too bad I didn't consider that."

He smiles. "Now what is your question?"

I've only begun to explain when the next student arrives. It's Hosanna, and she's out of breath. "So sorry to interrupt," she gasps. "But I have a situation."

"Is your *situation* the fact that we're discussing the Fierstein today?"

She flinches. "I said I'd attend, and I want to. I swear. But there's a meeting in the dean's office. My parents flew in for it. I'm really sorry."

The professor's annoyance shows through in his tone. "Get a dean's excuse, then. If your meeting is legit, it shouldn't be a problem."

"Okay. Thank you. Maybe I can...come to office hours and review the Fierstein discussion?"

It takes me way too long to realize who Hosanna is. But just as all the right connections are firing in my brain, a greying man appears in the doorway and snaps, "Annie. We're going to be late."

I can actually feel my jaw dropping. Mr. Impatient wears a preacher's collar and an ash-gray suit. He's the dad who forbade his daughter to read a play containing gay sex. And his daughter is Annie. *That* Annie.

After one more muttered apology, Annie follows her father out. The professor asks me if we can discuss Brecht another time. "During office hours?"

"Sure," I say slowly. Other students are streaming into the room now. In slow motion, I drop my bag onto the conference table and then stare again at the doorway where Annie and her father just disappeared. It takes a moment for me to reconcile my idea of Annie with the girl who was just here. I'd imagined DJ's Annie to be quite obviously evil, probably with horns and a tail. The college equivalent of Meryl Streep in *The Devil Wears Prada*.

But she's not. And now several more ideas are crowding my brain. DJ said he might never get an answer to his "why." But maybe he can. That conversation I overheard...it's a clue. It has to be. And the fact that her father forbade her to read the course-work? That's just weird.

Isn't it?

With shaking hands I pull out my phone. But DJ isn't going to read his texts while facing the dean. So I jump out of my chair.

The professor looks up, cocking an eyebrow at me. "I..." *Breathe.* "Sorry, I forgot to do something."

He squints. "*Nobody* wants to talk about Fiersten?"

"That's not true," I say, my voice shaking. "I loved the Fier-stein." But I turn my back on him anyway, dodging the incoming students. I run out into the hall and then out of the building.

That's when I come to a screeching halt, because I realize I don't know where the dean's office is. Another three minutes are lost as I tap on the screen of my phone, consulting the Harkness website.

Then I run.

Eventually I'm pounding up the marble steps of an imposing building. I press on through a big foyer, finding an assistant at a desk. "Um, there's a meeting? Uh, Daniel Trevi?" I stammer.

She directs me down a corridor toward the chapel room. I try to slow down, so I won't be panting like an Iditarod contestant when I find him.

I'm late, though. The door is mostly closed, and I can hear a man's voice already addressing the room. "This is highly irregular. My client and I need some clarification before we begin. Since the complainant and her family have suddenly appeared at our meet-ing, should I assume I'll be allowed to question Ms. Stevens?"

"No!" another man's voice shouts. That's probably Hosanna's father.

"Then why is she here?" the lawyer presses.

"Gentlemen!" a woman's stern voice cuts in. With a pounding heart I peek through the crack in the door. At the front of the room I see Dean Wilma Waite, affectionately called Whomping

Wilma by the students. "The complainant's family became available on short notice. And since it's in everyone's best interest to clear up this case in a timely fashion, I asked the Stevens family to appear today."

"That doesn't answer my question," the first man insists. I can only see the back of him. But it *has* to be DJ's lawyer.

"I have not yet decided who—besides your client—will be addressing me today," the dean says. "So why don't we begin?"

"There's only one way this works." I can almost feel DJ's lawyer's irritation through the oak-paneled door. "My client is here to tell the truth and clear the air. But he can only do that if the other party remains silent. If they can't do that, we can't proceed."

"Fair enough," the dean says.

"If the complainant's family is allowed to jump in with questions, that amounts to a de facto cross examination," the lawyer continues. "After which we should be entitled to *our own* cross exam."

Ooh, tricky. I like this guy.

There's a rumble of whispers and disgruntled voices from inside the room. I swear I hear someone say, "total shit show," and I wonder if it's DJ's dad.

I sink to a bench outside the door. There's no way I'm bursting in there now. But neither can I leave without knowing what happens.

"Now let's get started," the dean says. "We'll begin by asking Mr. Trevi to recount the night of last April eleventh. So please come up to the front where we can all hear you."

I look up fast, because I hear footsteps approaching me. There's a girl pounding her way down the hall. I'm so jumpy that I automatically assume she's here to bust me for eavesdropping.

But she's not dressed like an employee of the dean's office. She skids to a stop in front of me, wearing a leather jacket and tight jeans. I notice the streak of blue in her hair and the stud in her nose as she demands, "Is this the meeting? Hosanna Stevens?"

I nod like a ninny.

Satisfied, she pushes open the door, and I hear her say, "Sorry I'm late."

"Caroline!" The preacher sounds startled. "What are you doing here?"

"Stopping Annie from doing something stupid."

I'm on my feet, my toe wedged in the door so I have an even better view inside. But then I pull my head back quickly because everyone has turned to stare at the newcomer, even Annie's own family. "You're not supposed to be here," her father says. "Get out."

"No way. I just took a three hour bus ride to tell Annie something important." I risk another look inside, and see the newcomer staring her sister down. "Don't let Dad do this. You'll regret it."

"Who are you?" DJ's lawyer asks.

"Caroline Stevens. The sister."

"Shut your mouth! Shut it right now!" the preacher yells.

"I want to hear this," the lawyer argues.

So do I.

The gutsy leather-clad sister circles the room away from her father, approaching the dean at the front. "Listen, it's my fault that this happened. I really want to tell you why."

"All right," the dean says. "Please sit here." She motions toward the chair where DJ is seated beside her. It's the first time I've gotten a look at him all gussied up in his suit. I'd say he looks terrific except for his ashen skin. When Caroline approaches, DJ leaps out of the chair and walks back to sit beside his family.

Caroline takes his seat and crosses her legs. "Okay, I stayed in Annie's room the night of April eleventh. And I saw her in the morning when she came back downstairs."

"Hush!" her father shouts. "This is none of your business."

His younger daughter shakes her head. "Not true. Your brainwashing bullshit is absolutely my business. You made her do this." She points at Annie in her seat.

That's all her father can take. He jumps from his chair and lurches over to his daughter, almost too angry to walk. He grabs Caroline's arm and tugs her out of the chair.

I'm watching with my mouth hanging open when someone puts a hand on my shoulder, causing me to leap into the air. When I whirl around, I find two uniformed security guards. "Excuse me," one of them says.

I duck out of the way, my heart flailing from panic. But the guard disregards me, entering the room. By the time I've resumed my spying position, Mr. Stevens has unhanded his daughter and is receiving a stern warning from the security guard. They convince him to sit down, but he's still wearing a snarl. "You cannot interrogate my daughter. She's just a child."

"I'm eighteen!" Caroline says quickly. "Ask me anything."

The dean is unflusterable, I have to give her that. "Please tell us your full name and your birthdate. Then I'd like to hear all that you remember of April eleventh and twelfth."

Caroline leans forward and gives the introductory information. Then she says, "But I heard Daniel's name *before* April eleventh. Over the midterm break last year, my sister told me how much she liked him." She turns her chin toward her sister. "Sorry. But you know it's relevant."

Annie's face is downcast, and I felt my first real wave of empathy for her. Liking DJ is something I can certainly relate to.

"So, she said she didn't know how to get his attention. And that was always Annie's problem. She's too quiet. So I said, look, you can just kiss him. Boys are a little slow on the uptake." She turns in DJ's direction. "Sorry."

Half the people in the room chuckle, probably desperate for even a shred of levity.

"I told her to just go for it. That it might not work, but then at least she'd know if there was any potential. And you can't ignore a kiss. When I came to campus in April I asked her if she'd taken my advice, and she said, 'Maybe I'll try it tonight.'"

"None of this is relevant!" her father shouts.

"One more word Mr. Stevens," the dean snaps. "And you're gone."

"I wasn't at the party," Caroline continues. "And when I let myself into Annie's room later, she wasn't there. I went to sleep. She woke me up about six when she came back."

"What did she say about her night?" the dean asks.

Caroline looks at her sister while I hold my breath. "She said it was the best night of her life."

"No it wasn't!" her father yells, leaping from his chair. "You lying little whore! Both of you!"

The security guards have had it with him. They step forward and yank him out of the chair. "Let's go. You can wait in the foyer."

"Hands off me!" he protests. But they march toward the door and I jump out of the way. That door is about to swing open and reveal me.

So I turn and go, my heart pounding. I shouldn't have been snooping, anyway. But I can't say I'm sorry I did.

Chapter Thirty

GOOD NEWS

DJ

It's over. It's really over. And I'm off the hook.

My family isn't exactly rejoicing, though. We're all kind of freaked out by everything we just learned.

And me? I'm just limp with relief.

It's quiet on the walk to Orsen's house, where I'm to pick up my stuff before driving back to Long Island with my family. "I need a few minutes," I say after I unlock the door. Immediately I head into my room. I open my laptop so I can text Lianne on the full keyboard. Because this won't be easy to explain in just a few words.

Good news, I say first. *The college dropped the case.*

My fingers hover over the keyboard while I try to find the best way to explain what happened. Even though I'm happy to be cleared, I feel sick about that meeting, because I'm pretty sure that Annie's troubles aren't over. I begin fumbling through my explanation.

Turns out Annie's father overheard his daughters talking about me over the summer. And Annie wasn't wearing her purity ring anymore.

(Do you know what that is? I didn't until Vi explained it to me a few minutes ago.) The dad freaked.

I stop typing for a second just imagining the scene at their house. *From what I can gather, after he heard their conversation he was verbally abusive. Like, awful. He said either she was guilty of a major crime, or I was. So after a while she broke down and chose me. After screaming at her for a week or so, he handed her the phone and stood over her while she reported to the college that it wasn't consensual.*

Maybe she even believed it, too, by the time he was through with her. I still have no idea what was going through her head. Yet it's a lot easier to forgive her than it was a few hours ago. *Anyway —her sister showed up to tell the dean that Annie was not unhappy after spending the night in my room.* I read that last sentence a few times before hitting send. It's hard to talk to Lianne about this. Texting is probably the chicken way out. *I was right about one thing, though*, I add. *She was upset that I didn't want to start dating. That's what she told her sister, and that's when their dad overheard.*

In other words, if I'd been more careful with her feelings, it's entirely possible that I could have avoided the whole mess.

While I'm thinking this over, Lianne texts. *I'm just happy that you're okay. Can I call you in five mins?*

Of course.

I carry my duffel bag into the living room. I leave the boxes I'd packed behind—turns out I'm going to need that stuff to finish the semester. Maybe I should be giddy about that, but I'm too emotionally drained to celebrate.

"That poor girl," my mother says. "Imagine growing up with people who equate religion with shame."

"That poor girl almost stole your son's future," my father returns. But that sounds dramatic, even to me.

"Hey, Dad?" Vi asks, and I can tell from her tone that she's going to tease him. "How come I never got a purity ring? I like gold jewelry. I mean, it's a little weird to wear your *hymen* on your finger. But bling is bling."

My dad looks up from his phone. "If you stop dating losers, I'll buy you one."

Leo snorts and high fives our father. "Wait—is it that lacrosse player who says 'yo' every third word?"

"It's not every third word," Vi argues.

"He could at least drop it at the dinner table," my father grumbles. "Yo, pass the carrots."

"Leo should talk." Vi pouts. "Amy is the worst."

"She's okay," Leo grumbles, which is hardly a ringing endorsement.

Vi's gaze cuts to me, and she smiles. "You know who's having the best luck in the dating pool right now?" I give her a warning look, but it's no good. "Danny is."

All the parental eyes in the room turn to me, while Leo and Vi smirk.

"The girl from the picture?" my father asks.

"What picture?" my mother asks.

Fine. I guess we're doing this now. "Her name is Lianne. And I want to ask her to visit over the midterm break."

My mom's eyebrows shoot up. "All right," she says. "I didn't know you had a girlfriend."

"It's new," I say at the same moment Vi says, "He's keeping her a *secret*."

Thanks, sis. Thanks a lot. I tug on her ponytail in retribution. But it really doesn't matter, of course. Before today I didn't know some of my classmates had families where this sort of announcement would be like dropping a bomb.

That's when my phone rings, of course. And I'm definitely answering, because it's Lianne on the line. "Excuse me," I say, while Vi giggles and yells after me to say hi for her.

"Hey, smalls," I say into the phone. Then I close my eyes so I can hear her better. I can hardly believe it's really over. Lianne and I can have pizza wherever we want to.

Or have other things.

"Hi," she breathes. "Are you headed out of town?"

"Yeah. But only for a week. And I want to see you anyway. What are you doing for the break?"

She clears her throat. "Well, I'm staying here. But I've been summoned to New York on Wednesday night."

"For that premier?"

"No, I'm skipping that. But my manager is coming to town for it, and he asked me to meet up for drinks. He knows I'm on break, so I don't have an excuse. And I'm hoping he'll finally listen to me about the Scottish play."

"I'll go with you," I offer. "I mean, if I wouldn't be in the way."

"Really?" she squeals. "I'd love that."

"Why don't you come to Long Island before that? Monday or Tuesday. Hell—come right now if you want."

"Won't *I* be in the way?"

"Not a chance. I already told my mom I wanted to invite you."

"Wow. How about this—I'll finish my Brecht paper this weekend, then come down on Monday. If it's really okay."

"It's better than okay." I catch myself smiling into my phone. "If you take a car service to the ferry in Bridgeport, I'll pick you up in Huntington."

"Wow, okay. I can't wait."

"DJ!" my brother yells from the living room. "Let's go!"

"I heard that." Lianne sighs. "Call me tonight?"

"Absolutely."

When I go back into the living room, my sister is tapping her foot. "Well? Is she visiting."

"Yeah, Monday."

Violet squeals. "This is awesome. My friends will *die*."

"Why?" my mother asks, bewildered.

"I have a little picture to show you," Vi says, scrolling through her phone as she and my mother head for the front door. "See if you can identify this girl..."

"Oh my goodness," Mom says. "Isn't that...Princess Vindi?"

"Yes it is!"

Leo just shakes his head and follows them.

My dad waits for me to shoulder my bag. "Feeling better, D?"

"Hell yes."

He squeezes my shoulder. "I'm sorry we've had a rough time, you and me." He holds the door.

"Me too, Dad."

"I wasn't ever giving up on you, though."

"I know," I say, and find that it's true.

Then I get in the car with my family.

Lianne

I've just had a manicure while drinking a cappuccino from Starbucks. Violet and her two friends took me out for nail treatments and gossip. It was like *Sex and the City*, but without the liquor.

Really, life could be worse.

Now we're in the car again, heading back to the house. I'm riding shotgun because the girls treat me like visiting royalty.

"Lianne is not a show pony," DJ had warned his sister. "Maybe she doesn't want to hang out with your friends."

"I kind of need a manicure," I'd said to put him at ease. "It will be fun."

And really, it was. The girls grilled me about Kevin Mung, his famous singer girlfriend and the Sorceress set, of course. But then they'd moved on to other topics, like what to wear to their upcoming prom.

The three of them are so comfortable with each other that it's adorable. "We've known each other since kindergarten," Vi's friend Jenny said earlier. I never had those friendships, and it seems so nice.

"What kind of a car do you drive, Lianne?" Vi asks, bringing me out of my reverie. The topic has switched again, and I've failed to notice. "Wait, let me guess. A Mini Cooper."

"What did I say about short jokes?" I complain, and they all laugh.

"I didn't mean it like that!" Vi protests. "Fine. You drive a Hummer."

More laughter.

"A Porsche," Jenny guesses.

"A Mercedes E-class," guesses the one they call Jazz.

"You are all wrong," I tease. "Because I don't drive."

"Wait, ever?"

"Nope. Don't know how. Never got around to learning," I explain. When you're shooting in Australia half the time and traveling with your fickle mom on three continents, driving lessons just aren't practical.

"Wow." A hush falls over the car, as if I've just revealed an important failing. Jenny pipes up eventually, "DJ could teach you. He's a good driver."

Now there's an interesting idea. "I wouldn't want to scare him." Driving with me might not be a ton of fun.

The car makes a quick turn as Violet steers into what looks like a church parking lot. "Who needs him? Men always think they understand driving better than women. It's ridic." She comes to a full stop. "You can have your first lesson right now."

"What?" *What?*

There's a squeal from the backseat. "This is so cool. Princess Vindi drives on Long Island."

I start to sweat. "We can't, Vi. What if something goes wrong?" Just what I need is to dent my new boyfriend's parents' car. That ought to cement the status of our relationship.

"It won't." She gives my elbow a poke. "Gotta start somewhere. Everybody drives."

This is true. And three girls are waiting to see what I'll do. So even though my hands are starting to sweat, I get out of the car and walk around to the other side.

Vi climbs over the gearbox and plops into my seat. "Okay. Put your foot on the brake to start."

"Which pedal is it?"

There's a squeal of laughter from the backseat.

"The big one," Vi says calmly. "Makes sense, right?"

It does. But my toe barely grazes it. "Um..."

Vi grins. Then she leans over my body and pushes a knob forward, and my seat begins to advance toward the steering wheel.

"Okay. That's better." I depress the brake as far as it will go.

"Now, use this to put the car in D for drive." She points at the gear selector, and I do as she asks. "Great. When you let up on the brake, the car will idle forward. We've got some space here, so you can touch the gas, and then maybe turn right to drive toward that corner of the lot." She points.

Seems simple enough. So I let up on the brake, and the car slowly inches forward.

"Okay, good," Vi says encouragingly. "Now a little gas."

I move my foot to the other pedal and we leap ahead. The sudden motion *freaks me right out* so I slam on the brake again, and all our bodies lurch forward. "I'm sorry," I say quickly.

"That happens to everyone," Vi says, pushing the hair out of her face. "Not so much heat this time, okay?"

Shit. I've just learned two things. 1) Driving is harder than it looks. 2) Vi is a saint. "Okay," I promise. "Or we could just quit while we're ahead."

"You can do better," she insists.

Well then. I let up on the brake again and just let the car idle for a few moments. Then I apply gentle pressure to the gas, and lo, an easy forward movement.

"Awesome," Vi says. "Slow down just a smidgen and turn."

I let off the gas and just touch the brake. Then I turn the wheel to the right. I'm driving! I mean—I'm still scared. The car still feels like a giant metal beast that might run away from me at any time. But I'm doing it. Just like normal people.

"Ready to turn again?" she prompts as we approach the end of the lot.

I turn the wheel and execute the turn. And things are going so well that I tap the gas again. I think I could really get the hang of this.

"Deer!" Jenny shrieks.

And she's not lying. From the shady area at the end of the lot, a doe has stepped out on the asphalt, and I'm heading straight for her. Panicking, I jab my foot forward. But I miss the brake and clip the gas pedal instead. The car lurches forward, and the deer is just twenty feet away.

That's when Violet grabs the wheel and turns us away from Bambi, while I search for and eventually locate the brake pedal. We come to a rapid stop, but my heart is about to explode.

"Well," Vi says eventually. "That wasn't supposed to happen. Sorry."

From the backseat comes a hiccup and then a gut-bursting honk of laughter. Followed by howls.

Vi turns her big eyes on me, and I watch her lips twitch. And then she bursts out laughing, too. "Oh, *God*. Wouldn't that have been awful to have to explain?" She puts her face in her hands. "Fuck. That was close."

I'm shaking, but I feel a hysterical giggle coming on. "DJ is not going to like this story," I say, my voice wobbling.

"We are NOT telling him," Violet insists. "This is going to be our little secret."

"Really? Okay."

We switch seats again. And the last giggles don't stop until we're back in the Trevi family driveway.

Luckily I'm able to calm down, though, because DJ's mom is in the kitchen of their generous colonial when we enter through the garage. "Hey Mom!" Violet calls and then marches right past.

But I can see that Mrs. Trevi is making dinner by herself. "Can I help you with that?"

She looks up from where she's dicing an onion into perfect tiny cubes. "How are your knife skills?"

"Well..." God. "Pretty terrible. But I can wash and peel things."

Mrs. Trevi beams. "I'm just teasing. This is actually the last step—it's one of the toppings for chili. I don't even need help setting the table, because I was going to let everyone eat it in front of the basketball game instead of dragging them to the table like I usually do."

"Oh." Last night we'd had pot roast in the dining room, and I'd been nervous about sitting down with the whole family, but it turned out to be fun. They have an easy way about them.

It's a little weird staying in their house, though. His mom set me up in the guest room, which makes it a *little* easier. I don't think I could wander out of her son's bed in the morning without bursting into self-conscious flames. It was bad enough this afternoon when he gave me a hug and a slow kiss before I left to go out with Violet. Violet made a catcall and yelled, "Get a room!" then cracked up.

I pretty much wanted to die.

"I'm still happy to help. Maybe the cleanup, then."

Mrs. Trevi winks. "Perfect. Because I'll be at my book club. That's why I'm serving dinner in the den. Actually, you could pour some drinks. Ice water for Violet and milk for DJ and Leo."

"I can manage that," I say, heading for the cabinet where I'd seen glasses earlier. "But cooking is something I haven't gotten around to yet."

"You've been busy," Mrs. Trevi says lightly.

"That is true."

"I don't know any other nineteen-year-olds who work full time."

"Not all year," I protest. But I'm secretly glad to hear her say it. People think acting is just prancing around, looking important. But it's really four AM wakeups and shoots that go until midnight because the sound guys are arguing about where to place the boom.

It's not like I dig ditches for a living. But it's not bonbon-eating, either.

"Where does your mother live?" she asks, scraping her onions into a serving bowl. She places it alongside another bowl of avocado chunks and another of shredded cheese.

"It depends on..." *Who she's fucking.* That good girl complex I've got? It comes from never wanting to become my mother. "The season, I guess. She's always said she never wants to be tied down anywhere. Lately she's dividing her time between France and Palm Springs."

"Huh. So where's your home base?"

I chuckle. "Um, I have some things in storage in LA. And a PO Box. And a dorm room. I mean—there's a room for me in Palm Springs, but I don't think of it as home."

When I look up, DJ's mom is studying me with big brown eyes. I know there's no biological relationship between her and DJ, but they have a similar gaze. "And you're an only child?"

"Mostly. It's complicated."

DJ walks into the room then, smiling when he sees me. "Hey! Is my mom grilling you? That's not cool."

Mrs. Trevi tips her head back and laughs. "I totally was. Lianne honey, I'm sorry."

"No!" I protest. "Don't be."

He walks around to stand beside me, putting an arm around my waist. "How was the salon? Were you painted and squealed over?"

"Only in all the right ways." I lean into his side, and his clean laundry and aftershave scent is all I want out of life. I hold up my hands so he can see. "Big decision. I went with purple instead of pink."

"Nice." He kisses my hand. "So when are we leaving for the city? It takes about an hour to get there. Ninety minutes if the traffic is bad."

"Let's see..." I do the math. "We leave at seven and get there after eight or eight-thirty? Is that okay?"

"Sure." He squeezes my shoulder. "What am I wearing to this thing?"

"Whatever you want. Seriously. There is nobody we need to impress."

He chuckles. "Let me rephrase the question. What are *you* wearing to this thing?"

"Because you want to be twinsies?"

He gives me a grin. "Sure, smalls."

"I'm wearing dark jeans and a fancyish sweater. No baseball cap. And eyes done in I-only-see-you-every-few-months-so-I'll-make-a-little-effort."

His mom laughs, but DJ raises an eyebrow. "What was that last part?"

"Never mind. Just wear New York casual."

"Gotcha."

I pat him on the back. "Now let's pour some drinks. Your mother has a book club to get to."

Then the three of us move around their comfortable kitchen, dishing up chili, counting spoons, and just generally being nice to each other. I could get used to visiting here.

Chapter Thirty-Two

THE WEAKEST HANDSHAKE IN THE WORLD

DJ

At seven o'clock a navy blue limousine pulls up in front of my house. "Lianne?" I call up the stairs. "Either the car service is here or the queen is visiting."

"Be right down," she says.

I peek again through the curtains and wonder how much that rig is costing her for the night. Maybe I don't want to know.

"Sorry," Lianne says, her feet light on the stairs.

I turn to watch her descend, and, *damn*. She really has no idea how beautiful she is bouncing down the last few stairs in tight jeans and a soft sweater which drapes from shoulder to shoulder. I want to smooth my hands across it, taking in the creamy skin exposed by that feminine neckline.

She comes to a stop in front of me, tilting her perfect chin up to look at me. "Is something wrong?"

I'd like to take her right to bed. But I have to be content with grabbing her for a quick hug. "Not a thing, gorgeous." I kiss her forehead and take a breath of her vanilla scent. "Where's your coat?"

"By the back door. I'll get it." She darts away, and I'm just standing here like a dolt, smiling at the empty room. This is the effect Lianne has on me. Every damn day.

When she returns, I open the door for her and follow her out to the car. The chauffeur extracts himself from the driver's seat. "Miss Lianne!" he says. "How are you?"

"Hi Reggie. Thanks for driving out here."

He opens the rear door. "My pleasure."

The pleasure, of course, is in the paycheck I'm sure.

I follow Lianne into the back. The only time I've ridden in a limo was at my high school prom. And this car is a hell of a lot nicer than the garish white stretch we'd hired back in the day. It smells of leather and money.

Even the click of the door closing sounds expensive.

"I would have driven you to the city," I say quietly, putting an arm around her slim shoulders.

She looks up at me with a little smile. "I know, and I appreciate it. But then you wouldn't be able to drink, which I encourage. In the first place, you can be sure that my friends have excellent taste in liquor. And I think they'll be easier for you to tolerate if you're holding a glass of their overpriced single malt. I have to stay sharp, but there's no reason you shouldn't indulge."

"That's an interesting theory." I pull her a little closer to me. "But then we could have trained it in."

"Daniel." She snuggles up against my side. "I know you probably think I'm crazy to drop a few hundred bucks on this car for the night. But the train isn't fun for me if I'm asked to sit for a dozen selfies when I really just want to spend time with you. So would you do me the favor of just enjoying it? I hired the car so that we could be together in the least stressful way. I really think we're *due* for that, don't you?"

Ah, tonight I have the feisty Lianne. My favorite one. "Yeah, sweetheart. I can do that for you."

"Good," she says, folding her small hands. Her nails gleam with a light purple polish.

I can't resist bending down to kiss her collarbone. "You are delicious," I say before kissing her again. "And if you want to rent a fucking jet for a trip into the city, I promise not to argue."

"Billy Joel takes a helicopter to his concerts," she says, lifting her chin to give me better access to her jawline. "But it's not door to door."

I chuckle into her neck. "Good to know." God, she feels so good in my arms. These past twenty-four hours have been torture. I'd hoped she'd sneak into my room last night, but she'd stayed put in the guest room. "You look beautiful tonight," I whisper, and she gives an unmistakable shiver.

"Have to put on my game face," she says, her hand warming a spot in the center of my chest. "So you can't mess me up until afterward. But in the meantime, we can play the button game."

"What?" I ask, stealing one more kiss just below her ear. *The button game* sounds dirty to me, which probably means that Lianne and I need more time alone.

"What do you think this one does?" She points at a switch on the console overhead.

I squint at it. "Opens the moon roof?"

She pushes it and a bank of soft lights comes on. "Not quite."

"Fine," I laugh. "What's this for?" I tap a button beside the switch.

"The television."

I push it, and when the moon roof opens and we both laugh.

———

An hour later we're inching through midtown, just a few blocks from our destination. Lianne has begun to look uncomfortable. She's backed into the corner of the long seat, her arms folded across her chest.

"You okay over there, smalls?"

She sighs. "Yes and no. This could be a disaster."

"Why?"

"I dunno. I'm starting to think this was a bad idea. If my manager is not in the mood to talk about the Scottish play, it will be a wasted trip."

I stretch a foot out and hook it under hers. "It won't be a total loss, right? We just watched an episode of Jimmy Fallon on the hidden satellite TV. And we found two secret compartments."

But she doesn't even smile. "DJ, do we need a safe word?"

"What?" I sputter.

"Not for sex. For this party. Like if you say 'hippopotamus' I'll know we should leave. Okay—not that word. That wouldn't come up in polite conversation. But if my friends are assholes, you might be completely miserable. And I'm happy to bail at any moment if Kevin is being an asshole or Bob drops more names than a Kardashian before we even get our coats off."

"Aw, sweetheart—I don't care what they do. And if they're really as bad as you say, there's the entertainment value to fall back on."

"Ugh. But your family is *so* nice, D! And it's been so much fun to meet them all. But now we're walking away from the freaking Waltons into my really dysfunctional proto-family. When they get out of hand, they can be despicable. I've learned to tune them out, but I'm afraid you'll just hate it."

"Smalls?" I wait until she looks up at me. "For most of the last eight months, my middle name was dysfunctional. And how bad could it really be?"

She picks at a fingernail cuticle. "If it's really bad—like *The Great Gatsby*, but without the groovy flapper dresses—will you still love me?" Her chin snaps up and there's panic in her eyes. "I mean *like* me. You know what I mean."

I slide all the way over to sit beside her and kiss her on the temple. "Even if your friends are the most obnoxious people I've ever met, I'm still falling for you, smalls. Because you're the best one there is." I palm the side of her head and press my lips to her hairline. It humbles me to know she's worried what I'll think.

Her breath catches, and she slides her arms around my waist. I'm engulfed in the sweet smell of her hair, and the press of her body against mine is giving me big ideas. But then the car slides to a smooth stop at the curb, and Lianne and I let each other go as the door clicks open.

"You have my number, Miss Lianne?" the chauffeur asks, offering her his hand.

"I do," she promises, stepping outside.

"Call me if your plans change. Otherwise I'll see you here at ten-thirty."

I duck my head and step out of the car. And when I straighten up, the first thing I see is the exploding flash of a camera in my face. Jesus H, that's blinding.

A small hand closes on mine and tugs me forward. I follow Lianne past a snarl of people on the sidewalk. A burly doorman yanks the hotel's door open and sort of shovels us inside, putting his body between the photographer and us.

Everything is black. I blink several times, but my vision barely improves. "What the fuck? I can't see anything."

"I know," she sighs. "They painted everything black in this hotel's lobby. Because that's hip. Give it a second." She guides me to the side where I can make out a female hotel clerk behind the desk. "Excuse me," she says, and the female clerk's eyes widen in recognition. "I'm here to visit Kevin Mung. But I forgot to ask him which ridiculous superhero he registered under this time. It's usually Captain America or Thor."

The knowing clerk smiles. "Well, Miss Challice, I can't tell you if Mr. Mung is a guest of our hotel. But there is a superhero registered to the Suite Royale on the penthouse level."

"Of course there is," Lianne says under her breath. "Thank you." With a vice grip on my hand, she leads me to the elevators.

There aren't many people around, but heads turn anyway, lingering on my gorgeous girlfriend. She doesn't seem to notice. The elevator doors slide open and we get inside. "Okay, I've decided we do need a safe word. It has to be something that might come up in conversation. I know—that French history class you hate. What are you studying?"

"Balzac."

"Perfect," she says, watching the elevator display climb all the way to "PH." When you're really rich, it's not good enough to stay on a numbered floor.

We find the right suite by choosing the door with music thumping from behind it. I hang Lianne's jacket on a coat tree beside the door, and take in the scene. There are maybe twenty people, but some of them are at work while others are at play. There's a uniformed hotel worker clearing away dinner dishes from a table. And another one passing out drinks on a tray. Lianne flags her down and asks me what I'd like to drink.

"Whatever ale you have in a bottle," I say, just to be easy.

"Right away, sir."

Okay. I could get used to that.

I recognize Kevin Mung from his movies with Lianne. He's sort of splayed on a showy, velvet sofa. Two women are sitting on tufted footstools at his feet, giggling at everything he says. When he spots Lianne, he beckons lazily. It's not how a man should greet his guests, let alone his friends. But the rules are probably different if you're him.

Lianne holds up a finger to tell him just a second. Then she waves to someone else, who comes bouncing over. He's a skinny... trans woman. *She's* a skinny trans woman, I mean. "Hiiiiiiii baby!" she says, kissing Lianne on the cheek. "Good to see you, girl. I miss you."

"Lightmare, this is DJ, my boyfriend. DJ, this is Lightmare, who does makeup for me sometimes."

"Lianne, honey, your boyfriend is a cutie! And it's always a pleasure to see you. Baby, I need some new music. It's all the same old playlists because I haven't seen you for a while."

"Fine," Lianne says, smiling. "I'll make you some new stuff, but we have to keep to our usual deal."

"Gawd," the flamboyant woman with the weird name complains. "Getting the shakedown from a movie star. And it's only nine-fifteen." But she winks, so I know it's all in fun. Then she digs into the big bag on her shoulder and fishes around for a minute before emerging with a tube of lipstick. "Here's a down payment. Brand new color from Yves St. Laurent's fall line. It's not even for sale yet."

"Ooh!" Lianne squeals, opening the tube. Then she touches the lipstick to the back of her hand and holds it up to the light. "Nice shine. And it's cool, but the undertones aren't too blue."

"That's my girl."

To me it's just a pink dot on Lianne's hand. I don't really get it, but Lianne's face suggests she's just won the lottery. "Really? I can keep it?"

"That color will look better on you than me." Her friend sniffs. "But don't tell Kevin's bitch, because she's been pawing through my stuff all night and I didn't give her shit."

Lianne giggles. "Where is her highness anyway?"

"Probably in the bathroom, because that's where the biggest mirror is."

My beer arrives, along with a soda for Lianne. After the server walks away, Lianne blows out a breath and leans to whisper in my ear. "Unfortunately, looks like we've got Drunk Kevin tonight. I apologize in advance. The sober one is more fun."

I squeeze her hand and take a deep sip from my bottle. "Doesn't matter, smalls. The beer is cold."

"And I don't see Bob anywhere. If he blows me off tonight, I will not be a happy camper. This was his idea," she grumbles. "Come on. Let's talk to Drunk Kevin."

The ridiculous footstools are vacant for the moment, so Lianne and I sit there.

"Hey!" her friend Kevin slurs. "You look good, babe."

"Thanks?" Lianne's voice is cautious. "I want you to meet DJ, Kev. He's made my second semester bearable."

The guy offers me the weakest handshake in the world. "Pleasure," he slurs, like an imbecile. And I don't miss Lianne's wince. I wish she wouldn't worry about what I think. She's a class act, even when she's surrounded by assholes.

"How was the premier?" she asks him, nudging his foot with hers.

"Fun. But we're celebrating a new deal tonight. Did you hear?"

She shakes her head. "You got a new part?"

"Yeah, man. I'm playing The Saber in the next Flash Man movie."

"Wow, Kev." Lianne sits back a few inches. "That must pay well."

"I know, right? And I did it, babe. I made the jump. Playing a grownup and everything. It'll be your turn soon." He takes a sloppy sip of whatever he's drinking. "Seven months from now we'll be done with sorcery. Just have to get through one more."

"Yeah," Lianne agrees, crossing her arms over her chest. She's sort of shrinking in on herself, and I don't know why.

"Looks like you found someone to help rehearse your scene with." His bleary eyes cut over to me, and he grins.

I don't know why that's funny. "We've done some reading."

A snort erupts from the asshole lounging on the sofa. "Is *that* what we're calling it? Fuck. Only Lianne would rehearse a sex scene. Cool that she wants to do you, though, because she said she's done doing me!"

"Kevin!" Lianne gasps.

"What? I can't make a little joke?" He starts laughing his drunk ass off.

Cue the super-awkward silence, while Lianne turns white, like she might throw up.

I stand, resting one hand on her hair. "I think your friend needs a moment alone with you to apologize for being a tool. I'm going to find another beer, okay?"

She looks up at me, wide-eyed, and nods.

And I force myself to walk away for a moment. It's either that or punch the guy for making Lianne feel so embarrassed.

Chapter Thirty-Three

OH-WHAT-THE-HOLY-OMIGOD

Lianne

I want to just lie down on the ground and *die*. Like Eponine in *Les Miserables*, but without the singing. And there's no way that DJ is going to throw himself onto the French cobblestones and sing an ode to my spirit, because he looks really ornery right now.

And Kevin just made me sound like a total slut.

"You ass," I hiss at him. "I *finally* have a boyfriend, and you have to go and bring that up? I seriously want to knee you in the nuts right now."

Kevin snorts. "We're all friends here, right?"

"I don't think that word means what you think it means."

He only gives me another stupid grin.

"Where the hell is Bob, anyway?" It's time to see my manager and cut my losses.

"Smoking on the private patio." He points toward a door I hadn't noticed before. "This suite is killer."

I get up without another word. Man, Kevin is going to wake up to a nasty email from me, where I tell him there's something called boundaries, and if he doesn't figure out what those are, I'm going to make his life *hell*. It's seriously tempting to take a picture of him with his shirt mis-buttoned and his eyes crossed from liquor and email it to the tabloids. They'd invent a story about rushing him to detox on death's door.

That would be so, so evil and I wouldn't really do it. But God I want to.

DJ is across the room, taking a beer from the server, and I maneuver between two of Kevin's fan girls to reach him. When I try to see this party through DJ's eyes, I'm embarrassed for myself and everyone in the room. They all look self-consciously hip. And it seems the celebration of Kevin's new contract started hours ago, because everyone is three sheets to the wind.

And the sad thing? I really don't fit in here. Several months away from this scene only makes that more obvious. Which is weird, because I've spent this year feeling like I don't fit at Harkness.

So where the hell do I belong?

DJ moves to my side and puts a hand on my back, and for a half second it seems I've found my answer. We fit together like puzzle pieces. But only if he doesn't change his mind about me after an hour in the company of my closest friends. And I'm just waiting for him to ask me about Kevin... Ugh.

I don't look up into his eyes, because I'm afraid of what I'll see there. "Let's find Bob so I can talk to him. And then we can get the hell out of here."

He gives my waist a reassuring squeeze. "Deep breath, smalls."

Outside on the patio, the air is quite cold. But I don't mind because it's bracing. And there's Bob with a cigarette, leaning against the railing and chatting up some bottle-blonde half his age.

"Sorry to interrupt," I say, giving him a wave.

"Omigod, you're Lianne Challice!" the woman squeals. "This party is just so amazing!"

Yep, and not in a good way.

"Lianne, honey! Didn't know I'd see you tonight!"

For the love of God. "Well, Bob, demanding that I show up improved your chances somewhat."

"Yeah?" he says, scratching his chin. And that's when my sinking feeling kicks in again. Because Bob is kind of drunk, too. He's not a big drinker, not like Kevin. But if he and his new super-hero action star just inked a seven figure deal, it makes sense he'd tie one on tonight.

But it sucks for me, because I need this man's undivided attention. And at the moment I'm pretty sure most of his brain has leaked into the nearly empty whiskey bottle on the table. I march up to stand right in front of him, and I don't bother to introduce DJ because my manager can't multitask. I need the jerk focused on me so we can get out of here and I can apologize and then we can make out in the limo. Like in *Say Anything*, but without the Peter Gabriel soundtrack.

"Bob, seriously," I try. "We were supposed to talk tonight. About the Scottish play, for starters. And the future. I mean— it's great you've gotten Kevin all sorted out. But now it's *my turn*."

That came out more bitterly than I'd planned. Though it *was* my turn. Bob made a fortune off me every year. And all I wanted was one focused hour of his time. Okay, more than an hour. More like a day or a week. But for fifteen percent of my millions, he could *focus for longer than a fricking phone call, right?*

I feel myself getting *all* riled up. Like the Hulk, but not green.

Bob just tilts his head, as if he heard a small buzzing in his ear and couldn't place the sound. "We'll talk," he says. "There's time. And you're the one who insisted on going to college, which complicates things."

"Fricking college. Such a waste of time, right?" I quip.

"Exackly," he slurs. "Hey—" His eyes narrow. "—have you been eating carbs? You look bigger." He raises his hand and catches the draped neckline of my sweater. "Except for here. You need to upgrade these." I feel the pad of his thumb skim across the skin just above my strapless bra.

"Not cool!" I yell. It's like I'm suddenly caught in a slow-mo nightmare moment, because it's hard to get away from him. I've kind of trapped myself between Bob and the table. I do an awkward elbow slash toward him, because I don't want to drop my soda or my purse. "Hands off your investment," I manage to sputter.

Bob laughs.

"The lady said *hands off*." A millisecond second later, Bob's arm is gone, and so is the table. DJ's body is now between Bob and me. My boyfriend looks down at me, his eyes dark with something that looks like fury. "How about we leave now? Before I punch someone in the Balzac?"

"Okay?"

He slides the soda glass from my hand and puts it on the relocated table next to the whiskey bottle. Then he gently steers me toward the patio door.

"Lianne?" Bob calls after me. My good-girl streak shrieks on, and I almost *can't* walk away without answering the authority figure who's been at the helm of my career for a decade. But DJ is making a low sound in his throat, like a growl. He's got my coat in hand and a foot out the door of the suite before I can even blink.

Out in the hallway, I check his face. His jaw is hard, and he practically lunges for the elevator. The doors spring open when he pushes the button. And after we're inside with the doors closed, he leans on the lobby button.

"Jesus," he finally breathes.

"Are you pissed?" I ask, uselessly.

"Of course I'm pissed," he mutters.

"I'm so sorry," I say quickly.

His head snaps to face me. "Sweetheart, don't you dare apologize. *You* are not the one who needs to do that." I watch as he takes a deep breath and lets it out slowly. "Shit, I'm sorry. I was seriously close to punching that tool. *Both* those tools."

"Well..." I don't know what to say. "I'm sorry I subjected you to them."

He shakes his head and the elevator opens to the lobby. DJ takes my hand and steps out. I follow like a puppy as he looks around then leads me deeper into the lobby bar. It's done up like a dimly lit library, with floor to ceiling books and decorative old furniture. He guides me to a set of two oddball chairs in the corner. The fact that this room is so weirdly dark makes the place feel private, which is useful to me. Because the last thing I need tonight is one more scene.

We sit, and DJ puts his elbows onto the tiny little table between us. "Come here," he whispers. "Please."

I'm worried about what he thinks of me, my career, my so-called friends and pretty much everything. But I could never resist a request from DJ to get closer to him. So I lean in.

He reaches up to catch my face in both his hands. "Are you all right?"

The question surprises me a little. "Sure?"

His big thumb gently strokes my cheekbone. "Baby, I know I started the night saying that I didn't care if the party sucked, that it didn't matter. But I was wrong. I'll still follow you anywhere you need to go, and I don't scare easy. But I won't stay quiet when someone treats you like shit. You are too important to me, smalls."

I swallow hard and just stare into his eyes, while he cradles my face as if I were a treasure.

"...But I hope you don't mind me saying that you need some new friends. The only person in that room who was good to you was the, uh, makeup person with the funny name. She's a keeper. The rest of them don't deserve you."

"I know, I..." My voice cracks. "They were really in rare form tonight. It's not usually that bad."

He chews his lip. "I hope you're right. But I wish you wouldn't let them off that easily. When that guy grabbed you..." He closed his eyes for a second and gave his head a little shake, as if clearing away the image. "Your face said that you were not okay with it."

"I wasn't," I admit.

"Is he always handsy?"

I shake my head. "Nope. But he's always indifferent to my feelings." It feels good to finally say that out loud. For too long I've just put up with it.

"So why do you stay with him? I mean—it's your decision. And you know the business better than anybody. But if it were me, I'd be asking myself if there wasn't somebody else who'd be nicer to me in between movie deals."

"See, he was my father's friend." In fact, I couldn't remember a time when I didn't know Bob. He was always just there. "So Dad hired Bob when I got my first movie deal. He's a great negotiator when he wants to be. But then my father died and then..." It's hard to explain. "There wasn't a lot of my dad left. His other kids ignore me. His house was sold. But Bob was still there, still telling me stories about my dad." Come to think of it, he hadn't told me one in a long time.

"I understand," DJ says softly.

"No, I hate him," I hear myself blurt. "You're right. He's just a vestigial organ. Like an appendix. But meaner."

DJ smiles suddenly, and it's like the sun has come out. God, the boy is attractive. "You're so fucking cute. Would it be pushy of me to ask if you know any other managers? If you really want that part as Lady M, you need to find someone who will chase it down for you."

Sad but true. And why have I wasted so much time hoping he'd help me? I got my December gig myself, just by calling up the producer at the Public Theater. But movie people were tougher. You couldn't really tell who was pulling the strings unless you knew somebody who knew somebody.

"There are lots of managers," I say slowly. "I'll have to poke around a little and figure out who's well-respected. Like I need a new project. One of the reasons I put up with Bob for so long is because switching is going to be a pain. You know what's funny?"

"What's funny?" DJ asks.

"My eldest brother is a manager."

"The one who doesn't send Christmas cards?"

"Yeah, good memory. Rick was just starting out when my father died. But I hear he's pretty good at his job."

"Well..." DJ asks the obvious question. "Shouldn't he be your first call? What do you have to lose?"

"Plenty," I blurt out before thinking better of the idea. DJ's eyes are questioning me, so now I have to explain. "Okay, you have a brother and sister who love you, right? I've *thought* about calling Rick. But if he says, 'I don't have the time,' or 'my list is full...'" Ugh. "I don't want to know, okay? It's easier to just call a stranger than hear my own brother won't help me out of a hole."

DJ's face goes soft. "Smalls, sometimes I forget."

"Forget what?"

He gets up out of his chair and comes around to mine. It isn't really big enough for both of us, so I hop up and he sits, and then I sit in his lap. DJ puts his arms around me. "You are amazing, and I forget that some people don't bother to see that. If you have a brother who won't take your call, that is just his utter loss."

I lean back against DJ, suddenly exhausted. "That is nice of you to say, especially since I brought you out for the worst night ever. Forget the boob grab. There was also that awful bit where we had to rehash my disastrous one-night stand." DJ doesn't say anything for a second, so I turn around to check his face. He looks thoughtful. "What?"

"Well..." He chuckles. "One night, huh?"

"Yeah, why? Surely you don't think there's anything wrong with that."

His eyes widen. "*Hell* no. I like that better. If you were dating

a movie star, then you stepped down to the ice rink disc jockey..."
He lets the sentence die.

But now I'm annoyed. "*Daniel*, really? A step down? Did you
not learn anything tonight? The guy couldn't even sit up straight."

DJ snorts. "Okay. You're right. Tonight has been a little crazy."

"This sore night hath trifled former knowings."

"Amen, sister." He kisses me on the ear. "The night isn't over,
though. It's only ten. There's still time to save it."

"Well, there's thirty minutes until the car comes back. Should
we order a drink? No—not a drink. Dessert. Something with a
million calories. Bob would make me feel guilty about it. But fuck
that guy."

DJ shakes his head. "He tells you what to *eat?*"

"Not anymore," I say firmly.

"Good. Is there any way you could cancel that car?"

"I suppose. But it's a long walk to Huntington."

DJ scoops me off his lap and gets up, setting me back down.
"Stay here a second, smalls. I'll be right back."

————

An hour later I'm full of hot-fudge brownie sundae. And DJ is
escorting me down a corridor on the hotel's fifth floor. He hums
as he opens the door to a room that's all ours.

I'd protested the expense, but he laughed it off. "My brother is
in the Bahamas on some beach with his evil girlfriend drinking
out of a coconut. I can spring for one night in New York."

So here we were, stepping into a uniquely shaped room with
crazy velvet wallpaper and—weirdly—a claw-foot tub in the
corner. "What the...?" I turn a corner and find the real bathroom,
complete with walk-in shower and high-end fixtures. So that tub is
just trying to be eccentric. Of course it is.

DJ tosses his coat on the bed. Then he stands over the tub,
peering over the side. "It's like a challenge, really. Fine. Then I

accept." He drops the bath mat onto the floor beside it and cranks the faucet on. The sound of running water burbles into the room.

"What are you doing?"

He looks up, grinning. "We have to get in the tub, smalls. It's eight feet from our bed. How could we not try it?" Whistling, he picks up a bottle of something off the ledge beside it, unscrews the top and then pours it in.

I wander over in time to see bubbles forming on the surface of the water. "Wow." It does look inviting.

DJ winks at me. Then he starts unbuttoning his shirt. His belt is next.

The rest of his clothes follow, and he drapes them neatly over the luggage rack. We have no luggage, of course.

A very naked DJ, still whistling, bends over to test the water with his fingertips. I admire the powerful body on display, and the fact that he isn't self-conscious in his nudity. "Coming, smalls?" He twists off the taps, then lifts one muscular leg over the side, stepping in.

I can't stop ogling him until almost all of DJ disappears under the surface of the water.

Finally turning away, I lift my sweater over my head. Then I drop my jeans. That leaves me wearing a skimpy little black bra and panties, and DJ whistles his appreciation. "Jesus H. Is this my best idea ever, or what?"

Slowly I turn to face him. He's sitting in the bath, sculpted shoulders visible above the bubbles, and he's eyeing me like he'd like to take a spoon and gobble me up like I just did to the brownie sundae.

I lift my chin, trying not to remember the shortcomings I see whenever I look in the mirror. Because DJ seems to like the view. So I focus on his face, and the way his eyes track my every movement. There's heat there, and I feed off it.

Since I'm down to my underwear now, I'm basically

performing a strip tease whether I'd planned to or not. I slip a thumb under the skinny elastic band at the hip of my panties and inch it down. When they finally fall to the wood floor, DJ lets out a groan. The sound of it is like liquid courage.

Taking my time, I find a hair clip in my bag, then gather up my hair and pin it high on my head, while he watches appreciatively.

Then, reaching behind me, I unhook my bra. But when it falls, I take my (small) breasts in my hands, my thumbs just grazing my rapidly hardening nipples.

"You're killing me, smalls." His voice is like gravel. "Get in, would you?"

But now that I'm comfortable with his eyes on me, I'm not ready for it to be over. Turning around, I bend over and grab my underwear off the floor, while DJ lets out a grunt of pure shock and desire.

I'm a little shocked, too. In a good way.

After tossing my things on the bed, I finally make my way over to the tub. I step in and sink down into the warm, soapy water on the unoccupied end. I sit down between DJ's outstretched feet. There's nowhere to put mine except over his legs.

DJ grasps my feet, one in each hand, and squeezes the arches. Then powerful thumbs go to work massaging the muscle there.

"Ohhhhhh sweet-holy-mother-Mary-omigod," I mumble while he works on my feet. Since I like it so much, he drops my left and uses both hands to knead my right. It's perfection. It's amazing. I tilt my head back and moan.

"Jesus, smalls." He chuckles. "That's some really intense moaning for feet." He switches my right for my left and starts in again.

"Goddamn-just-don't-stop-ever," I beg.

"Uh huh," he says, and I can hear the smile in his voice. But I can't see it, because my eyes are closed. I'm in heaven. It's warm, and lots of parts of a very wet DJ are touching me right now. I can feel the roughness of the hair on his legs beneath mine, and then there's the sweet torture of his ambitious foot massage.

He's got my ankles in his hands now, and his fingers are slowly working their way up to my calves, rubbing and smoothing the muscles in my legs. Warm, slippery fingers press and glide until he's passed my knees, and my thighs are wrapped in his big hands. And I'm suddenly so ridiculously turned on. With my legs spread as they are, my body feels open to him. And clever hands are working their delicious way up...up...

They stop mid-thigh on a gentle squeeze. I open my eyes in protest.

The look of love in DJ's eyes is unmistakable. "If you want me to touch you, come here and show me," he whispers. "But you've had a really shitty day, so if you just want to soak, that's okay, too."

Oh, *hell* no.

My lazy body agrees to stir just enough to tuck my feet under me so I can kneel in between DJ's legs. He reaches for me, pulling me down on his chest. "Hi, sexy," he says.

"Hi."

Then he pulls me into a kiss, and it's the best one ever. It's like that perfect kiss in *The Princess Bride*, but without the pirates or giant eels or the fire swamp. DJ cups my backside in two hands while I crush my mouth to his. The kiss goes wild immediately, his tongue seeking out mine, then worshiping me. Meanwhile, wet, slippery skin is sliding over wet, slippery skin. As he kisses me, I press down onto his big, strong frame. He's hard between my legs, and I brace my feet against the end of the tub and begin to slowly rock against him, back and forth, until we're both panting.

On a groan, DJ pulls his head back a bit, breaking our kiss. "You're trying to kill me, aren't you?"

"No," I murmur, dizzy from the kissing. "I'm trying to fuck you."

He gives a grunt of surprise. "Smalls! You said it."

I did, and not daintily. But do we have to rehash it? "You want to chat about it some more, or what?"

He laughs. "Sit up a little."

I do, and he slips out of the bath, dripping on the mat. He grabs two fluffy towels and spreads them out on the bed. Then he offers me a hand, which I take. When I'm out of the tub, he steers me over to the bed and sits me down. I scramble backwards, lying down on the towels.

Now it's my turn to stare.

I watch as a gleaming, nekkid DJ fishes his wallet out of his discarded pants and removes a condom. And I keep watching as he takes his erection in hand and sheathes himself.

My good-girl complex must have fled the building entirely, because when he walks back over to the bed, planting one knee on the edge, I spread my legs.

"Ungh," DJ says, closing his eyes for a hot second. I expect him to finish climbing onto the bed, but that's not what happens. Instead, he ducks his head and kisses me where I've never been kissed before. Just a soft kiss, and tender.

"Oh-what-the-holy-omigod-yes," I babble, melting back onto the towel like a puddle of fudge.

A warm, soft tongue begins to tease my lady bits, and I gasp. And who knows what I say next? Nothing intelligible. Because he's grasped my thigh and buried his mouth between my legs, licking and teasing and gently sucking. There has never been anything as good as this.

I'm wild for it, grasping his hair and speaking in tongues. But just when I sense that sweet release is imminent, he backs off. This happens twice more, and I finally realize that he's doing it on purpose. "DJ," I croak. "Come *here*."

"What do you want?" he asks in a husky voice.

"You. Right now."

He kisses my thigh very sweetly. "We have all night."

"But I'm not that patient!"

"Hmm," he says to the juncture between my leg and my pelvis. "I see," he says to my belly button. He kisses his way up my body, then rises up to kneel above me. He lifts one of my legs, bending my knee up to my body. I busy myself by watching every muscle in his chest flex as he straddles my other leg and leans forward. His gorgeous hips give one smooth push. And just like that, he fills me.

"Yesssss," I gasp. *Finally*.

"Mmm," my boyfriend agrees. He begins to move, but his pace is slow. DJ is in the mood to take his time. So I kick my leg free of his grip and pull him down onto my body, where he can kiss me. And when he does, it's so, so good.

I try to relax and enjoy every sensation. But after several lovely minutes, the pull of my own lust is too strong. It's coming, and it's going to be epic. Gripping DJ's back, I arch my hips into his and groan.

"Aw, yeah," he pants. "Use me."

That sounds wonderfully dirty. I grip him everywhere, with everything I've got. Another gravelly groan from DJ pushes me over the edge at last. And I'm like a film at double speed, everything happening at once. And the soundtrack is DJ making his own set of erotic noises, until a few moments later when we both flicker and fade to black, collapsing together in a steamy, satisfied heap.

"Best night ever," I pant.

DJ grins, his dimple showing. "See?"

"Mmm..." I'm rapidly turning immobile and weary. "Sleepy."

He pats me on the hip. "Get into the bed if you're going to crash, smalls."

I make a brief trip to the sleek bathroom then collapse in the bed.

Beside me, DJ texts his parents to let them know we stayed in the city, so they won't worry.

By the time he stretches out beside me, I'm already asleep.

————

I'm not sure why I wake up in the night. I'm exquisitely comfortable, parked against DJ's chest, his hand curled around my hip. We've only got the sheet over us, because DJ's body is like a furnace.

I love it so much. This sweet moment together is our reward for all the awful stuff we've been through. So even though I'll be tired tomorrow, I lie awake, listening to DJ's heartbeat.

"How goes the night, smalls?" he whispers a few minutes later, startling me.

"Good," I say. "Really good. Didn't know you were awake."

"Love being here with you," he says, kissing my hair.

I roll over to face him. "Something's on your mind, though."

He smiles. "Yeah, sorry."

"Don't be sorry," I say immediately. "What's wrong?"

His smile slips. "I don't know if you want to hear it."

"I do. No matter what it is. Aren't we done having this conversation?"

He smiles again. "Yeah. But it's sort of wrong to talk about *her* when I'm in bed with you."

Oh. For a second I feel a familiar wave of discomfort, because I know exactly what he's thinking about. But then common sense prevails. There's only one girl in this bed with DJ, and it's me. "That was a long time ago now," I point out.

"True," he sighs. "Before I got into bed I found an email from her."

"Really? What did it say?"

"It was an apology. She said, 'I'm sorry I dragged you into my awful family drama. Blaming you is the worst thing I've ever done, and I hope you'll forgive me.'"

"Wow. That's awfully brave."

"Sure is. Because I'll bet we're having a much better midterm break than she is. I can't even imagine living in that family. Her sister got up there and repeated all these awful things their father had told them—that if they had sex before marriage, it was like becoming a used tissue. That no man would ever want something ruined and dirty."

"Ew!"

"I know. The sister—Caroline—she cried. She pointed her finger at her father and said she wouldn't listen to him anymore. That nobody should. She said she was in therapy at U Mass for depression because their family and their wacko church was so oppressive, and she had all this shame for wanting things she wasn't supposed to want."

"God." I can't even imagine. "DJ? I have a small confession to make."

"You do?"

"Yeah. The day of your meeting I figured out who Annie was, and I saw her sister. I didn't hear much, though." I tell DJ everything about Hosanna's hurried visit to class to excuse her absence, and how I stumbled around campus to try to tell him what I'd learned. Only it didn't matter.

"She couldn't read the plays?"

"Nope."

"I never knew," he says, rolling onto his back. "I mean, she dressed kind of conservative, but some people do, right? She didn't, like, wear a sign that said, *I grew up with crazy people who do mean shit and call it Christian.* I mean—I went to church my whole life. But it wasn't like that."

"Yikes. Do you think they'll let her return to school? And are you going to reply to her apology?"

"That's what's keeping me awake. I want to reply. At the very least I want to tell her not to worry about me, that I'm fine now. The thing is, I kind of want to apologize, too. But that won't be easy to word."

"Also? Your lawyer would kill you."

He groans. "You're right. I mean—I know I didn't do anything like what she accused me of doing. But just because it was consensual doesn't mean it was a great idea. I wish I could say, 'I'm sorry I didn't care enough to wonder if you'd end up sad about it.'"

"Ouch."

"I know. But that's how it was. I just took what was offered, and I didn't ask questions."

"A lot of people would have done the same thing," I remind him.

"Yeah? A lot of people are assholes."

This makes me giggle, and that makes him chuckle. So there we are at three in the morning, laughing and snuggling in the dark.

It really is the best night ever.

CHAPTER THIRTY-FOUR

From: the Office of the Dean of Students

To: the Harkness College faculty, fellows, and student body

Dear colleagues,

One of the most important goals of the dean's office is to ensure that all members of the Harkness College community can live and study together in a safe and supportive atmosphere. As part of our commitment to equality and safety, our efforts against sexual harassment and sexual violence are ongoing and constantly under review. We take our commitment very seriously.

As part of our continued effort to improve our policies and procedures, I write to you today to announce that Harkness College has retained the services of Dreyfus and Arlington, Inc. This firm, staffed mainly by retired judges and other legal experts, will be occasionally engaged to assist in the college's efforts to investigate and adjudicate cases of suspected sexual assault and misconduct.

While the college retains the certainty that we are the last best arbiters *of our own systems and beliefs, certain cases may require timely interven-tion and investigation by persons with lifelong experience in these matters.*

By contracting their expertise, we can make our campus and commu-nity even safer and more equitable than it already is.

Any questions regarding this decision may be forwarded to my office. Thank you.

Sincerely,
  Dean Wilma Waite, PhD

Chapter Thirty-Five

TWO MONTHS LATER

Epilogue

Lianne

The hockey game starts in two minutes, and I am still hoofing it toward the rink. Tardiness is inexcusable, because this is a quarter-finals game. Harkness men's hockey is trying to squeak into the Eastern championships, and then hopefully into the NCAA finals. And I have become nearly as rabid a hockey fan as Bella these past couple of months.

It's a sickness, and I don't want to be cured.

As I trot across campus, I try to keep my mind on Harkness's chances. The team has been hit hard by injury the last two weeks, and I'm worried. Our Boston opponents are having the same problems. I know it's bad karma to wish injury on anyone. But it would be really nice of God to keep these things even. All the talk at Orsen's house this week has been about whether or not O'Hane will be able to play this weekend. He's nursing a shoulder injury. And we've already benched Big-D for a stress fracture.

Our defense could be a problem.

These are my thoughts as I hurry toward the rink. Because the other thing that's on my mind is an email I received a little while ago out of the blue. And I feel a shiver of nervous excitement thinking of it.

Dear Lianne,

A couple of weeks ago I received a letter from your college friend Daniel Trevi. He told me that you might be considering a change of management, and he thought you could use my help. And he suggested I reach out to you.

I have to tell you, I felt really guilty when I got this note, because I should have asked you long ago whether there was any way I could help. And to be honest, I'd lost track of the fact that you're all grown up and making your own decisions now. Every Christmas when I call your mother to say hello and ask about you, she gives me a big fat brush-off, which didn't encourage me to keep asking questions.

That's no excuse, though. I'm sorry. I can't believe it's been eight years since I've seen you.

I went home and I told my girlfriend the whole story. She called me an asshole, and I'm sure I had it coming.

Lianne—if you need any help or advice on the management side, or if you'd just like to have lunch next week when I'm next in New York, please let me know. I'm on the East Coast about a third of the time. I have an office in Union Square. So if next week doesn't work, I'm sure we can find another time.

Sincerely,

Rick Challice

There are several mind-blowing things about this letter, not the least of which is the fact that leaving Bob might turn out to be easier than I thought. And that Rick speaks to my mom. Every year. And my mom has failed to tell me. Every year.

But also, when I first read it, I couldn't imagine what possessed DJ to hunt down Rick and then ask for his help without consulting me. But then I remembered the conversation we'd had in the hotel lobby, and how I'd said I was afraid to ask Rick to help me.

I'd forgotten all about that chat, but obviously DJ had not. Then the logic became clear—if DJ asked Rick for help and Rick blew him off, I'd never have to know. DJ did this for me because I needed help, and he wanted to fix it.

I got a little teary over it. Like J. Lo on American Idol, but without the highlights. Then I realized I was going to be late for the hockey game, and my makeup was starting to run. So I had to fix it.

Even as I scamper across campus, I'm thinking warm, happy thoughts about DJ. Some of those thoughts include various ways we might celebrate later. I've gotten better at expressing my appreciation lately. It got easier to say sexy things to DJ when I realized how much he liked it. So I've been practicing with little things that I'll whisper in his ear.

Tonight seems like the perfect time to step up my game. So I pull out my phone, taking a page out of Bella's book. She'd told me what to say once before, and I'd refused. But now I'm so full of gratitude, it's time to surprise my man.

The phone rang only once before he answered, and the sounds of a very full hockey stadium were suddenly in my ear. "'Lo?"

"DJ," I sort of shout into the phone so he can hear me. "I want to strip you naked and bounce on your dick."

"Lianne?"

I yank the phone away from my ear and stare at the call screen. It says "DJ" on it, just as it should. "DJ?" I yell into the mouthpiece.

"It's Graham. DJ had to—"

I don't give him a chance to finish. Instead, I hang up, my heart pounding.

Holy God.

Two minutes later I show my ID at the door and scurry through the student entrance. I don't bother looking for Bella in the stands, because I'll be watching the game from the press box. That's where I sit for every game now, watching DJ work and interfering with his playlist when I see fit.

But Graham will be in there.

What have I done?

I open the press-box door a couple of inches, just to make sure Graham is busy at his computer. If I'm going to be avoiding him for the rest of my life, I kind of need to start now.

But he isn't in front of his computer. Instead, he's standing over DJ's setup, poking at the sound board.

And DJ is nowhere in sight.

Graham turns around and catches me watching him. "Hey! Could you please get over here? I can't find the introduction music."

Damn it.

I scurry over, and there's no time, because the players are circling the ice to silence. Bending over DJ's computer, I flip between playlists until I find U2's "I Still Haven't Found What I'm Looking For."

The crowd actually cheers when the music starts up, and Graham heaves a sigh of relief.

"Where's DJ?" I ask.

"My God, do you two not talk?" He slides out of the way. "He said you'd cover for him."

"We *would* have talked except..." Gah! *Why did you have to answer his phone?*

A slow smile spreads across Graham's face. "Right. You know, it's a shame, but the last call to DJ's phone was a terrible connection. I couldn't hear a *thing*."

I roll my eyes. "Good. We shall never speak of this again."

"Fine. But anyway—DJ needs you to back him up tonight." He waves at the equipment.

"Why?"

"The players are lining up, Lianne."

Shit! I whip around and fade out the song so the announcer can call for the national anthem. A women's a cappella singing group does the honors while I slip into the seat and check everything over. DJ's computer is all cued up and ready to go. But where is he?

Down on the ice, players circle into position for the first face-off. I hit play on Santana's "Smooth" while they get into position. They crouch in readiness. The ref drops the puck, and I fade out the song.

Again I turn around. "Seriously—is something wrong? Where's DJ?"

"Not a thing is wrong. Not really." Graham's smile is strange.

"Okay? Then...?"

"You'll figure it out."

"What?"

He only gives me that odd smile and moves down the row to sit in his seat.

Below me the game is in progress, and I have to pay attention. Harkness looks strong tonight. Leo and John Rikker execute a number of fast passes which leave the other team struggling to keep up. But two minutes in, they haven't gotten off a shot. There's a line change, and then we lose possession. Fortunately the other guys get called for icing. I play "Ice Ice Baby" for the faceoff, and wonder where DJ is.

I've gotten good at this, and my hockey knowledge is a whole lot better than it used to be. DJing the game is easy now, though I still wish I weren't doing it alone. These past couple of months together have been a lot of fun. I've always loved DJ's company, but after his problems were resolved, he became lighter. Sillier. We have a great time both in and out of the press box.

Things are going pretty well down on the ice, too. Boston gets called for high sticking, so I play "Hard to Handle" by the Black

Crowes. I'm squinting at the line change when I notice something odd. One of our defensive players is much shorter than the other one. Who is that?

"Oh my God," I say suddenly. "Oh my GOD!"

"Now she gets it," Graham mutters from two seats down.

"DJ!" I squeal. I'm so excited that I forget to fade out the Black Crowes and the song plays three seconds too long before I jam down the fade lever. Then I plant my hands on the desk and lean so far over for a better view of the ice that falling into the stands would be a real risk if I weren't so short.

DJ is chasing down a Boston player on the backcheck. "GET IT!" I scream. He makes several attempts before successfully lifting the other player's stick and knocking the puck out of the other guy's control.

The skidding puck goes wide until it's picked up by another Harkness D-man, who barely gets the pass off to a forward before getting slammed into the plexi. It's not the cleanest play, but THAT WAS MY BOYFRIEND WHO STOLE THE PUCK!

I'm practically in defib from the excitement.

Harkness charges around, looking for a scoring opportunity while the penalty clock ticks down on the opponent. Coach calls for an unlikely line change of forwards at the forty-second mark, and I can barely breathe. The fresh legs take a run at the net, but it's a fake-out. Leo Trevi flicks the puck backward under his own skate to his brother. My heart is in my mouth when DJ fires it back immediately to Rikker.

Who *scores*.

My scream could shatter windows.

I'm jumping around and shouting, tearing my way over to Graham. He's on his feet too, because his boyfriend just scored the goal that mine assisted. "Oh my GOD!" I shriek, throwing myself at him. I've probably shattered his eardrum. Down on the ice they're having a proper celly, high-fiving Rikker and rubbing DJ's helmet. "This is awesome! I love you, Graham."

Laughing, he sets me on my feet. "You know there's dead air right now, right?"

"FUCK!" I skid back over and double click on "Moves Like Jagger." I'm the worst DJ ever tonight. And it's totally worth it.

————

During the break between periods, I finally get the story from Graham.

"It's O'Hane's shoulder," our resident sportswriter explains. "Coach wants to take it easy on him if he can. And Bridger has a stomach bug."

"Oh!" Bridger is the senior who filled in last year in the postseason when Graham got injured. I try not to think too hard about how dangerous hockey really is. "So they just came up to the press box and said, 'DJ where are your skates?'"

Graham laughs. "I think they caught him at home when he was packing up his computer to come here. But, yeah. Pretty much. He dropped his computer here, plugged it in and told me to have you take over. Meanwhile, Leo was practically dragging him out of here by the collar. He looked a little stressed out."

"I bet." I *hope* DJ is enjoying himself. Skating in a Harkness playoff game wasn't something he ever thought he'd do. I hope this night is everything for him.

Also, I resolve to be a better DJ for the rest of the game. If he hears me slipping up, it will stress him out.

This gives me an idea.

There are six minutes left in the break, and already the Zamboni is halfway done surfacing the ice. So I'll have to work fast.

————

My next batch of songs is eclectic, to put it mildly. There won't be any calls to give me the job permanently after tonight's game. But I don't care. This is for DJ. The first time I ever watched a game from the booth I was already on my way to falling for him. So if nobody but DJ understands my picks tonight, it's really okay with me.

My choices might sound weird. But my cues are all perfect, no matter how nervous I am. Even when DJ is crosschecked into the boards, I keep it together, and he's back on his feet before I have the song cued up. I play:

"Dynamite" by Taio Cruz.

"Jump" by Van Halen.

"Dancing in the Streets," the Bowie and Mick Jagger version.

"Jenny" by Tommy Tutone, the only song that made the world memorize a phone number.

"Dancing with Myself" (The Green Day Cover, because what is a hockey game without Green Day?)

"Just What I Needed," the old Cars tune.

"Daughter" by Pearl Jam.

"Justify My Love." Thank you Madonna.

"Dancing in the Dark."

"Jailhouse Rock."

"Dark Horse" by Katy Perry.

"Jet Airliner" by the Steve Miller Band.

In other words: D J D J D J D J... I spell out my boyfriend's nickname over and over with the starting letter of the songs I choose. And even if they throw tomatoes at me afterward, it's worth it.

Three periods seem to last three years, and DJ doesn't get anymore shots at greatness. But when it's over, Harkness has won the game, 3-1.

I'm sweaty and high on adrenaline by the time the buzzer sounds. With shaky hands I carefully pack up DJ's computer and cables in the bag he's tucked under the desk.

"Good game, right?"

I look up to find Graham waiting for me. "The best."

He winks. "You need anything?"

"I'm good. Except..." This is weird. "Where do I wait for him?" I've never been a puck bunny before. I don't know the protocol. Too bad there isn't any time to make a stupid sign. Like MEET ME BEHIND THE ZAMBONI or YOU CAN HOOK ME ANYTIME YOU WANT.

"In the hallway downstairs. C'mon. I'll show you."

I follow Graham down a staircase and into the bowels of the rink. It's the same place we went the night DJ walked me out the back to keep out of the photographer's way. Except we turn right instead of left, and the corridor is stuffed with people. Girls, mostly. "So this is puck bunny central," I say, eyeing all the swinging ponytails and Harkness Hockey T-shirts.

"Watch it," Graham says, elbowing me. "I don't like that term." He crosses his big arms in an exaggerated way and gives me a comical face.

"Sorry!" I laugh. "Present company excepted. Obvs."

"Obvs."

"Is it weird to wait here? I mean...last year you were in there." I point to the locker room door.

He grins. "I *never* wait here. I was just showing you the ropes. After the game I have a story to file. My editor reads 'em all to make sure I mention other players besides Rik."

"But he had a goal and an assist tonight. It's not like you can leave him out of the article."

"See my problem?" He winks.

"What is taking so long, anyway?" I can't wait for DJ to come out here so the celebrating can begin.

"They have to beat on their chests and dance around to 'Centuries.' These things take a while. Then there's showering and slapping each other with towels. And words from Coach."

"Huh." I stand up on my tiptoes, but there are a lot of people between me and the door. I don't see any players yet. Although one head of long red hair makes me do a double-take. I try to raise myself up even higher, but there's only so much a short girl can do. Then a pair of hands grasps my ribcage and lifts me a few extra inches into the air. "Thanks," I huff as Graham offers me a better look of the girl leaning against the wall outside the locker room.

Hosanna.

When Graham sets me down, I don't know what to think. Who is she here to congratulate?

"Here they come," Graham says.

Leo is the first one to emerge from the locker room, and Amy pops out of the scrum to take a flying leap at him. She then holds up traffic by trying to eat Leo's face.

Lovely.

Rikker is the next to emerge, and he grins when he sees Graham waiting for him. "This is a surprise."

Graham holds up his fist for a bump, but Rikker grabs Graham's outstretched hand and pulls him into a headlock, then proceeds to give him a world-class noogie.

"Christ," Graham complains, shaking his boyfriend off. "And you wonder why I don't wait for you here in estrogen alley."

Chuckling, Rikker heads for the door, and I see Graham pinch his ass as he follows him out.

That was cute. But where's mine?

Other players begin to stream from the door, and I wait with a goofy smile on my face. The hallway begins to clear somewhat, giving me a better view of the door. None of the freshly showered heads that emerge are the one I'm waiting for. And then, finally, DJ emerges from the doorway, and he's the only one with a big bag of equipment on his shoulder. "Sorry," he says quickly to the girl closest to the door, because the bag nudges her in the chest.

That girl is Hosanna.

I watch while DJ does the same double-take as I did. "Hey," he says, with an awkward wave.

"Hey," she replies with a nervous smile. "Good game."

"Thanks." He moves forward with an uncertain look on his face.

Behind DJ, the injured freshman O'Hane emerges. His hair isn't wet from the shower, and he looks a little bummed.

"There you are!" Hosanna says brightly.

Immediately O'Hane's face lights up. "Hey! You're a sight for sore eyes." He scoops her up into a hug.

"Careful of your shoulder," she says immediately.

"Nah, it's okay."

I tear my eyes off this little surprise when DJ stops in front of me, a funny smile on his face. "Hi, smalls."

The sight of him triggers my inner Amy. Springing forward, I wrap my arms around his neck. "Oh my God, that was fun to watch. You were awesome! Was it amazing? What did Leo say? Did you hear my playlist?"

Chuckling, DJ drops his bag and braces himself against my onslaught. "What's with those sloppy fades in the first period?"

I punch him in the arm. "You asshole! I was in shock!"

"*Kidding*, smalls." He backs me up against the wall and kisses me. "Thank you for the interesting musical selections at the end there. I loved it."

"That was me cheering."

"I know." He kisses me again, and the slide of his lips against mine sends a ripple through my insides. Then he says, "Let's get out of here, sweetheart," and the ripple turns to a quake. I'd better stop making fun of puck bunnies. I think I just became one.

He grabs his giant bag and I skip along in front of him to get the door. "I want to hear everything! Did you even get to warm up? And do you think they'll need you in the semi-finals?"

We emerge into the dark April night. "I had no prep time at all, but it was almost better that way. No expectations, you know?

Just 'Get in here, we need a warm body because O'Hane needs another night off and Bridger's puking.'"

Ahead of us on the sidewalk are Hosanna and O'Hane, holding hands. I reach over and nudge DJ. "That's a surprise."

"Who knew, right?" He gives me a big smile with both dimples.

I wink. "Okay, I'm still not over this game, though. That assist blew my mind. Just...no hesitation!"

His smile is truly beautiful. "I think I'll be remembering that when I'm old. Maybe it's because I played with Leo my whole life, but I just *knew* he was going to flick the puck back to me like that. And I guess Rikker did too, because he got open." He shakes his gorgeous head. "It was just *perfect*."

I sigh. "It *was*. And I effed up the victory music because I was busy freaking out."

"I didn't even notice, because I was freaking out, too."

We turn toward DJ's house and walk half a block. But then he stops and turns to me. "Are you up for a party? Because I'm pretty sure that's what we'll find at my house. If you're not, we can go to your place after I drop off this bag."

I take his hand in mine. "We'll just see. Maybe Bella will make me a margarita."

DJ squeezes my hand. "Sounds like fun, but I'm cutting you off after one."

"And why's that?" I tease.

"Gonna need you sober later."

My ripple becomes a shimmy, and I pick up our pace toward the house.

———

In Orsen's living room there is much rejoicing.

There's music and dancing on the coffee table courtesy of

Pepe. Alas, there are no margaritas. Bella is on a gin and tonic kick, and I'm not a fan. So sobriety is not an issue.

"Lianne! Come fight trolls with us!" Leo calls from across the living room.

Amy gives me a bitchy stare and I almost say yes just to teach her a lesson. But I'm not in the mood. These days, I rarely play DragonFire except with Leo. And we had a game just yesterday. "Another time!" I call. "You need the practice, anyway."

He gives me the finger.

I love Leo, and now that DJ is less stressed out, we spend more time with him. I don't know why, but he and DJ are sharing a beanbag chair right now. It's a really cute picture, so I pull out my phone to get the shot. The phone opens to my email app, which makes me remember—for the first time in four hours—the email I received from my brother.

Only a wild night watching my boyfriend play hockey could have made me forget.

I take the picture and then walk over to ruffle DJ's hair. "Can I talk to you a minute?"

He looks up immediately. "Sure, smalls. Hang on." He struggles out of the beanbag and follows me to his room, where I sit on the bed. Playfully, he pushes me back onto the mattress. "So. Is *talking* code for something else?" He kisses my ear.

"Not in this case. Although you can feel free to hold that thought for just a few minutes."

He gives me a wicked grin and rolls onto his back, tucking both his arms behind his head. "Okay. Then what's on your mind?"

But now I'm distracted because his shirt rides up to reveal a nasty scratch on his belly. I lift the shirt and see red skin and the beginnings of bruising. Everywhere. "What happened?"

He pulls the shirt down. "That's just payment for all the fun I had tonight. Boston wanted it bad. If they ask me to fill in again, I might borrow some newer pads."

"Are they going to?" That's an exciting idea.

"No idea. Depends on everybody's injuries and the risks that coach chooses to take." He gives me a tired shrug. "I'm not even going to worry about it. It was great to be asked, and even better to play. Tonight was like a victory for the short people of the world. I'm just happy I got to do it. I'm a pretty lucky guy these days." He gives me a sexy wink.

Aw. "Does this hurt?" I lay a hand gently onto his abs.

"Not there." He gives my hand a little shove down his belly. "*Lower*, baby." When I roll my eyes, he grabs my hand and kisses it. "Really, I'm fine. Let's talk about your thing."

Right. "My thing is that I got an email from my brother Rick today, inviting me to lunch."

His eyes widen and he sits up on his elbows. "Smalls, I gotta tell you—"

I silence him with a raised hand. "It's okay. I know you wrote to him."

"I'm sorry I went behind your back. That was nosy, but I couldn't figure out another way to feel him out."

"I get it." I pat his chest gently, mindful of the bruises. "I know exactly why you did it. It was actually a really *kind* thing to do."

He catches my hand, covering it with his larger one. "It was supposed to be. I'm glad he answered you. Are you going to meet him?"

"Definitely. It was a really nice note. Do you think you could come along, too? I mean, if it's not at a bad time..."

"Of course I will. Already told you that, smalls. I'll go anywhere you lead me."

His smile and those big brown eyes, they just break my heart. "Listen, I'm worried about one thing." I put my free hand on his cheek. "If you play any more games, isn't there a pad you could put over your dimples?" I put my thumb right there in its favorite place, feeling his evening whiskers tickle my finger. "Don't hurt the dimples."

He pulls me down onto his chest. "You got it bad, babe."

I really do.

His kiss is soft, and I sink into it, still mindful of his midsection. "Is there anything I should kiss to make it better?"

"Um..." He laughs and kisses me again. "I can think of a few places."

"Funny, so can I." I kiss down the side of his face and into his neck. He smells like soap and DJ.

With a happy groan, he tightens his grip on my body, pulling my hips against his.

Life is good. And getting better all the time.

Chapter Thirty-Six

FIVE DAYS LATER

DJ

When my phone rings, we're in the back of another limo sliding through Midtown.

Just like last time, Lianne is looking nervous. She's fidgeting and shifting in her seat.

So I don't answer the call. But I get a text anyway. It's from Leo. *Be at practice today, bro! We need you again! Four o'clock.*

Jesus H. It's noon and I'm ninety minutes away. But if this lunch doesn't go too long...

"DJ?" Lianne says suddenly. "There's something I need to tell you."

Forgetting about Leo, I slide across the leather seat to her. "Hit me, smalls. What is it?"

She pulls an envelope out of her bag. "This is a rider that Bob wanted to put on my contract with the Sentry Sorcerer people. It's a nudity clause. They want me to do a sex scene. Does that freak you out?"

"Um...what?" There's a topic of conversation I never saw coming. Then again, I never dated anyone who showed up every eighteen months or so on movie screens all over the world. "Do you want to do it? It's your career, smalls. I'm never going to tell you what to do."

"I don't want to do it."

"Okay. Are you thinking your brother can help you figure out your options?"

"That would be nice." She sighs. "God, I'm *so* nervous."

Why? I stop myself from asking. It's hard for me to comprehend the fact that Lianne's family hasn't really been there for her and how sharply that must sting.

I spent the better part of a year feeling like the most unlucky guy in the world. But now I know better.

My arm slides around her back. "This is going to be fine," I say, hoping I'm right. And if I'm not, I'll ply her with dessert, music trivia, words of encouragement and sex until she smiles again. Lianne is a buoyant personality, and I know she'd do the same for me.

It's good, this thing we've got. Really good.

The car slides to a stop in front of a restaurant called Lexington Brass in Midtown. The name sounds stuffy, but when we step into the place, it's brighter and more relaxed than I'd imagined, even if some of the clientele are dressed in suits. There are a couple of people checking in ahead of us, so we'll need to wait a moment.

"This is nice." When I'd read the menu on my phone, it said something about buttermilk-fried chicken. So now I'm ready to chew off my own arm.

The hostess's eyes open wide when Lianne steps forward to give her brother's name.

"Wow. Right this way Miss Challice."

I whisper into her ear. "That's him, isn't it?" She leads us toward a man seated in the center of the room beside a woman who might be his girlfriend. He looks a little like Lianne. He has her same clever eyes.

"Yeah," she breathes. "I think I might puke."

"Really?"

"No," she says quickly. "But this is weird. It's kind of *Little Orphan Annie* meets her folks. But without the red wig."

"Aw. The sun will come out tomorrow."

She looks up in surprise. "You know *Annie?* And yet you keep your man card?"

"I have a little sister, thank you very much. And I know music. Duh."

"Duh," she echoes, and we share a smile.

We reach the table, and Lianne's brother stands up. "Hi," he says, his voice soft. Then he surprises us both by hugging Lianne. "I'm sorry it's been so long."

Okay, I might be able to like this dude after all. Maybe.

"It's okay," Lianne says, her voice wobbling.

And now heads are starting to turn our direction, and I see a couple onlookers nudge each other in recognition.

"Excuse me," I say to the hostess, who's hovering until we sit down. "This table is just a little too public. Is there any way you could put us in a corner somewhere?"

"Oh! I think I could do that." She looks around quickly. "Do you mind being in the back room?"

"We love being in the back room," I say truthfully. I've gotten better at figuring out how to eat out with Lianne without encouraging interruption. The details are everything. "Do you mind?" I ask her brother. "Sorry to make it complicated."

"Not at all," he says quickly. "I should have realized."

We follow the hostess around a corner to a table in a quieter section of the restaurant. Lianne and I are seated on a banquette side by side, with her brother and his girlfriend Mary opposite. After a round of handshakes, and placing orders for drinks, it's finally quiet. We're reading our menus when Mary speaks up.

"Thanks for nudging him," she says. "This is fun, and I've always wondered why we never saw you."

"Well, it's nobody's fault," Lianne says. "Except my mother's, maybe. She never told me you always call her around the holidays."

Rick shrugs. "She's a tough cookie. This past season I didn't manage to catch her. So it was more of a holiday voicemail. And I don't even know if our wedding invitation reached you."

Lianne sits back. "No. Of course not. I'm going to kill her. Congratulations."

"Thank you." Mary beams. "We'll send you another one. It's next fall on Cape Cod."

"Sounds pretty." She clears her throat a little self-consciously. "You must think it's weird that DJ wrote to you. But I didn't know what to do, and I was all pissed off at Bob and not thinking clearly."

"Sorry to hear that," her brother says. "But I didn't mind getting a letter from DJ. Calling would have been quicker, though. Because I travel a lot."

"I'll remember that for next time," I joke, finding Lianne's hand under the table.

She squeezes it. "I'm truly done with Bob. He isn't good to me, except on payday."

Rick flinches. "Sorry. Then I hope you'll look elsewhere for help. If you're not comfortable at my firm, I'll send you to a friend."

Lianne gives me a little sideways smile. "Well, that's easy. Can you just...take over? Or assign someone to do it? There's a part I want and I don't think Bob has even called them. He keeps stringing me along."

Our drinks arrive, and Rick takes a sip of his beer. "What's the part? I might know if it's been cast yet."

"Well..." Lianne looks self-conscious. "I really want Lady M in Jared Swanson's production of the Scottish play."

"Ah," Rick says. "Good pick."

"I did Juliet at the Public Theater this winter," Lianne says in a rush. "And I've been working really hard on the script. All I want is a meeting. I think I can sell it."

Rick lets out a breath. "I will make any phone call you want me to. But I can't say your odds are good. Sure hate saying so, though."

Lianne pales. "Damn. Is it already cast?"

"No and yes," he says. "I will call this afternoon and ask all the questions I can. But the problem is the male lead is cast. He's going to be played by Dermott DeAgostino. You know of him? British guy but he looks Italian?"

"Oh, *hell*," Lianne swears, tipping her head back against the wall behind us. "I never had a chance."

"Why?" I ask. I must be two steps behind, because her disappointment doesn't make sense to me.

Lianne turns in her seat and puts a hand to my chest. "Thank you for reading the Scottish play out loud with me ten times. I don't regret it, because it was so much fun, but I'm sorry I wasted your time."

"Why?" I ask again.

"Dermott DeAgostino," she says, and now her lips twitch. "He's..." She heaves a sigh.

"Six-foot-five," her brother finishes.

"Oh," I say slowly. I think I understand. "They wouldn't match you two together?"

"No." Lianne shakes her head. I can see her trying to hold it together.

Damn it. I wrap an arm around her back and pull her in. "Sorry, baby. You'll get the next one." But after how hard she's worked, that's inadequately comforting. Lianne's back heaves under my hand, and my heart breaks for her. "Shh," I say uselessly.

But it shakes harder, and I realize she's *laughing*. No, it's more than that. She's been seized by a giggle. "Omigod, Deej," she gasps. "It's not a good day for the short people of the world."

I feel a bark of laughter contract my stomach. Her silliness is kind of contagious. It never occurred to me that Lianne and I could have the same disappointments. I thought it was only men who had to be super-sized.

Now I'm laughing, too.

She presses her forehead to my shoulder and giggles into my shirt. "We read that play *so* many times. 'Let this pernicious hour stand aye accursed in the calendar!'"

"No!" I argue. "Lay it to thy heart, and farewell."

Lianne snorts, and we have to laugh some more. We are ridiculous. But then I have an ugly thought. "Do you think this happened because you said his name that time when we were arguing? I don't want this to be my fault."

"No way," she gasps. "Whatever."

"Whatever." I kiss the top of her head.

Lianne's brother is watching us with fascination. "I'll still call the director. Just in case."

She wipes her eyes with her napkin. "I appreciate it. But I'll live to fight another day either way. There has to be another juicy part out there for someone who wants to get out of sorcery."

"Oh, I can think of a dozen things," Rick says. "And if your goal is to do something more serious, you can probably hold out for just the right thing. Especially if you want to finish school, right? Seems like the perfect time to be picky."

Lianne takes a deep breath. "Thank you for saying that. I'm not used to people listening to me. Except DJ." She slides out of the booth. "I'm going to fix my face. Be right back."

She slips away toward the back, and I watch her go. Even after a disappointment, there's a bounce in her step. The girl just kills me. I love her so hard.

"Is Bob really awful?" Rick asks in a low voice. "One of the reasons I let Lianne's mom keep me away is that I didn't want anyone to think that I was after a cut of Lianne's star power."

I take a drink of my soda so I don't have to answer immediately. "You should tell her that," I say after thinking it over. "She thinks you don't care."

"Shit." He takes a swig of beer. "She was only eleven when our dad died, and she lived on another continent. There wasn't much chance of me being involved."

Mary puts a hand on his arm. "But now's your chance."

"She needs your help," I say, in case he hasn't already taken the hint. "And Bob is awful, since you asked. She hung on too long because he knew stories about your father."

Rick looks thoughtful. "I know a few of those, too. They're not all good, though."

"Doesn't matter," I insist. "She'd like to hear them."

"Have you two been together a long time?" Mary asks.

The question makes me chuckle. "Not exactly. Three or four months, depending how you count. But it's been a really tough few months for both of us. Like dog years. But we're hanging in there." It's true, too—I feel like I've been close to Lianne for years. And I plan to be.

"I like the way you stick up for her," Mary says.

"Who wouldn't stick up for her?" I ask. Lianne appears again, and when she reaches the table I raise my arm to let her slide in next to me.

Then a waitress appears and asks to take our order. "I'll go last," Lianne says, scanning the menu. "I can choose quickly."

I let Mary and Rick order first.

"I'll have the fried chicken," I say, passing my menu to the waitress. "And it comes with some kind of fancy mac and cheese?"

The waitress winks. "You don't want to miss it."

"I'll have the salmon salad," Lianne says, handing the menu over.

"Excuse me," I say before the waitress can walk away. "Could I have a side of mac and cheese?"

She frowns. "You have one coming already?"

"Yes, but I believe I need a second one."

"Yessir," she says, turning away.

"That's for me, isn't it?" Lianne asks, reaching for her Diet Coke.

"Uh huh. I'm happy to share with you, but only up to a point."

She looks up at Mary. "I just started eating carbs again. And sometimes I get a little frenzied."

Rick laughs. "I dragged you all the way to the city for lunch. Seems as good a time as any to indulge."

"Good point." Lianne relaxes against me. "Now let's hear all about your wedding."

———

Two hours later, we are cuddling in the back of Reggie's limo on the way back to Harkness. Lianne is talking to me, telling me her plans.

I'm kissing her neck.

"—And then maybe something by an independent director. Somebody who takes risks."

"Mmm hmm." I kiss the spot just under her ear.

"Are you listening?"

"Yup. Independent director. Taking risks." I suck her earlobe into my mouth, and she melts against me.

"That is so distracting."

"Mmm hmm." I skim the shell of her ear with my lips.

"Deej," she whispers, shivering. "What are you doing?"

"Just celebrating. A little bit."

"We can't...in the back of Reggie's car." She moves a little closer anyway.

"M'kay. But we can pre-party."

"Pre-party?"

"You know—loosen up. Do some stretches."

She giggles. "And then when we get home..."

"Nope," I tell her. "Break time, then. I have to go to hockey practice."

She lifts her head. "You do? Really?"

"Yeah. I got the text just as we were heading into the restaurant. I don't know what it all means. Maybe they won't need me this weekend, but I'm happy to show up and work out with them."

Lianne is practically bouncing on the seat now. "That's awesome. Should I buy tickets to the finals at Lake Placid?" She whips out her phone.

"Don't jinx me," I say quickly. "Can you wait?"

She looks up. "Wow, really? You're superstitious? You told me you weren't. On that first night we walked back from the rink."

I hesitate. "Not *often*."

Lianne explodes with laughter. "Omigod, seriously? How is that different from not saying the name of the Scottish play?"

Busted. "Okay, fine. It's the same thing. I'm a hypocrite."

"You're the best one, though." She crawls in my lap and kisses me.

And I realize I don't need to play in any more games. I already won the only one that matters.

The Fifteenth Minute has ended.
And yet...
Soon you'll have Leo's story: ROOKIE MOVE!

Sarina's next series The Brooklyn Bruisers picks up with Leo Trevi's story! Turn the page for a preview of ROOKIE MOVE (Brooklyn Bruisers #1.)

Also By Sarina Bowen

TRUE NORTH
Bittersweet (True North #1)
Steadfast (True North #2)
Keepsake (True North #3)

The Gravity Series:

Coming In From the Cold
Falling From the Sky
Shooting for the Stars

And:

HIM by Sarina Bowen and Elle Kennedy
US by Sarina Bowen and Elle Kennedy

The Ivy Years:
The Year We Fell Down #1
The Year We Hid Away #2
Blonde Date #2.5
The Understatement of the Year #3
The Shameless Hour #4
The Fifteenth Minute #5